D0511365

Proposing to the PLANNER

Wedding Party Collection

Wedding Party Collection

April 2017

May 2017

June 2017

July 2017

August 2017

September 2017

Proposing to the PLANNER

Wedding Party Collection

Susan STEPHENS
Aimee CARSON
Teresa CARPENTER

All rights reserved including the right of reproduction in whole or in part in any form. This edition is published by arrangement with Harlequin Books S.A.

This is a work of fiction. Names, characters, places, locations and incidents are purely fictional and bear no relationship to any real life individuals, living or dead, or to any actual places, business establishments, locations, events or incidents. Any resemblance is entirely coincidental.

This book is sold subject to the condition that it shall not, by way of trade or otherwise, be lent, resold, hired out or otherwise circulated without the prior consent of the publisher in any form of binding or cover other than that in which it is published and without a similar condition including this condition being imposed on the subsequent purchaser.

® and TM are trademarks owned and used by the trademark owner and/or its licensee. Trademarks marked with ® are registered with the United Kingdom Patent Office and/or the Office for Harmonisation in the Internal Market and in other countries.

Published in Great Britain 2017
By Mills & Boon, an imprint of HarperCollins*Publishers*
1 London Bridge Street, London, SE1 9GF

WEDDING PARTY COLLECTION: PROPOSING TO THE PLANNER © 2017 Harlequin Books S.A.

The Argentinian's Solace © 2012 Susan Stephens
Don't Tell the Wedding Planner © 2014 Aimee Carson
The Best Man & The Wedding Planner © 2015 Teresa Carpenter

ISBN: 9780263931129

09-0917

Our policy is to use papers that are natural, renewable and recyclable products and made from wood grown in sustainable forests.
The logging and manufacturing processes conform to the legal environmental regulations of the country of origin.

Printed and bound in Spain
by CPI, Barcelona

THE ARGENTINIAN'S SOLACE

SUSAN STEPHENS

For Carly.
Intuition tells me to be excited
about my new editor.

Susan Stephens was a professional singer before meeting her husband on the Mediterranean island of Malta. In true Mills & Boon Modern style they met on Monday, became engaged on Friday and married three months later.

Susan enjoys entertaining, travel and going to the theatre. To relax she reads, cooks and plays the piano, and when she's had enough of relaxing she throws herself off mountains on skis, or gallops through the countryside singing loudly.

CHAPTER ONE

SHE had to close her mind to the man on the shore. Getting the old boat safely into its berth was more important. But he was like an elemental force, his gaze fixed and unswerving, with the most magnificent physique Maxie had ever seen. Tall, ripped and tanned, with wild black hair and dangerous eyes. A gold earring glinted in what light there was. Low-slung jeans over a flat, muscular belly were enough to throw anyone off course…

So think of the snarling face that would stop a rhino in its track and your concentration will come flooding back.

She had sailed the boat this far and she wasn't turning back now.

Bringing the trawler through mountainous waves single-handed had been nothing short of a miracle. They had barely made it out of the harbour when the skipper had declared himself out of action after consuming the greater part of a bottle of Scotland's finest. Maxie would be the first to admit her qualifications for sailing a boat this size were slim. She had once helped to crew a sixty-eight footer, but this old rust-bucket was proving rather more cantankerous. And she was more than a bit rusty, Maxie accepted as the deck lurched beneath her feet.

Glancing at the man on the dock, she guessed he was

waiting for her to fail. His massive forearms were crossed over his formidable chest, and his black eyes blazed with mockery and scorn.

'Welcome to Isla del Fuego,' Maxie muttered beneath her breath. But, however unfriendly the welcoming committee, she was going to berth this bucketing monster if it killed her!

Which it probably would, Maxie registered with panic as the ancient fishing craft crashed into the dock.

With relief she saw the elderly skipper had made it out of his bunk in time to take the wheel. Boiling black storm clouds suggested the weather wasn't about to change any time soon, which for a wedding planner on a scouting trip for an excited bride was somewhere south of perfect. And if the man onshore worked for the Acostas, who owned the island, he would need some serious retraining in the art of welcoming guests before the wedding, Maxie concluded, trying not to look at his glowering face.

She could always tell Holly the island was unsuitable...

The idea flitted across her mind, but it wasn't an option. She'd seen Scottish castles in worse settings transformed into fairytale palaces on a warm spring day, and damp French *châteaux* revealed in all their ancient glory when the sun shone. Plus, she trusted Holly. The bride was a smart girl, and June was a famously fabulous month in which to get married. Bottom line? If Holly wanted to get married on Isla del Fuego then it was up to Maxie to make it happen and the man on shore would just have to suck it up.

Dios! What had the storm washed in? Some pin-thin, drooping violet with—

With a very accurate and surprisingly powerful throw,

Diego conceded as he caught the rope the girl tossed him. But she had no business sailing Fernando's fishing boat—let alone slamming into the dock, thanks to her poor reading of the weather. She was lucky to be alive after sailing to the island in a storm.

'Are you ready?' she called, preparing to toss a second rope.

With his stiff leg he could only move at half her speed. The second she turned her back he limped as fast as he could to get into position before she could see him lurching like a drunk.

'Here it comes,' she warned him, in a voice that was both light and musical, yet which somehow crested the howl of the wind.

Catching the rope, he secured it. It appeared fate had a sense of humour, sending an attractive girl to the island when he could least handle the action. Resentment swept over him as he watched her darting nimbly about the deck. When his brother's fiancée had called to warn him the wedding planner was on her way he had accepted his self-imposed exile was over, but to have some lithe young girl call time was insulting. He had come down to the dock to meet the principal of the events company—someone older and sophisticated, with a keen sense of style—not some kid in jeans and a hooded top with long dark hair hanging in sodden straggles down her back. Was his brother's wedding of so little importance they'd sent some underling?

'Well caught!' she yelled, having fired another rope at him.

Well caught? There had been a time when nothing physical had been beyond him, but then his horse had rolled on him during a polo match, shattering the bones in his leg. It had been pinned in half a dozen places. He had been back on a horse and training rigorously, but it was more than a year since the accident and he had yet to regain the subtleties of sensation required for the top class game, leaving his future in polo uncertain.

'No harm done,' the girl yelled as she leaned over the rail to check the hull for damage.

'It could have been a costly mistake,' he roared back. 'You've been lucky this time.'

'Lucky?' She laughed.

He felt a surge of interest, but in his current state that was soon snuffed out. She could take a look around the island and report back to Holly, but the moment the wind dropped she was history.

No one had said planning a wedding on a remote island would be easy, Maxie reasoned, dashing spray out of her eyes. And time was of the essence, the bride had insisted. No wonder, Maxie had thought when she'd seen a photo of the groom. She had always known organising a high-profile event on a tiny island would be fraught with difficulties, but she hadn't bargained on being met by a man who made her heart beat nineteen to the dozen. She had always loved a challenge, but as a scholarship girl at an upscale school, with a home life that could best be described as chaotic, she'd made a choice early in life to remain safe on the outside looking in while other people enjoyed the arrangements she made for them.

Safe? Pulling back from the rail, she took a few steadying breaths before preparing to disembark. Nothing was safe here—especially the hard-eyed man on shore.

'Watch your step,' he barked as she started her perilous crossing of the narrow plank.

'I will,' she called back tensely, wondering why he didn't come to help her if he was so concerned.

Oh, stop fussing. She could manage. She was fine. This commission was every wedding planner's dream, and she had no intention of starting out by falling in the sea. A big society wedding between Ruiz Acosta, a fabulously wealthy Argentinian polo player, and Holly Valiant, a celebrity agony aunt who had made her name by writing a column based on living with Ruiz, would have readers hanging on Holly's every word. Having tamed the playboy, Holly was about to marry him—and the world was waiting with bated breath to see the wedding. A wedding Maxie was going to arrange. It was a commission that would take her business to the next level, and as her income supported everything she cared about this trip *was* going to be a success.

The man onshore had turned his attention to the skipper. Maxie had the basics of Spanish, but she fell short where colloquialisms were concerned. 'Is he offering to help us?' she called out.

'Something like that,' the elderly skipper admitted sheepishly.

I bet, she thought, hoping Señor Acosta would have more charm. She stared at him again and quickly looked away. There was something in the man's eyes that said he had the sort of experience no woman with any sense would choose to get close to. And Maxie had plenty of sense. Though she was lousy at relationships, Maxie conceded with a shrug. Her ideal date was a civilised chat in a civilised restaurant with a civilised man—not a walk on the wild side with a barbarian with an earring and tattoos. She couldn't deny the man's edgy good looks had stirred something inside her, but he was food for her fantasies and nothing more.

'Are you from the bridal agency?' he demanded in a deep, husky voice.

'That's right,' she confirmed, halfway across the sloping plank. 'Could you give me a hand?' She had stopped in the middle of the plank, uncomfortably aware of the turbulent water churning greedily beneath her feet. If he'd grab her suitcase she could hold the guide ropes with both hands.

'Try walking tall,' he suggested. 'Look where you're going instead of looking down…'

Thanks very much. She'd take her chances with the fishes. But when he turned his irritation on the skipper she'd had enough. 'If you have anything to say, you can say it to me,' she insisted in Spanish. 'I chartered the boat, and I made the decision to sail to the island.'

His gaze darkened. 'You speak our language?'

'I would have recognised your tone of voice if you'd been speaking in Ket…a language spoken only in Central Siberia,' she muttered to herself—but he heard her.

'If you're so clever you should have more sense than to persuade an old man to bring you out to the island in a storm.'

Addressing his next words to Fernando, he spoke in a very different tone. 'You look chilled to the bone, Fernando. You will stay in the guesthouse until the wind drops. I'll have Maria come over with hot food and clean linen for you.'

'Si, Señor Acosta, y muchas gracias.'

Señor Acosta? Maxie groaned inwardly. 'So you're Diego Acosta?'

'Correct,' he confirmed.

The ironic twist to the firm mouth might make her senses roar but this wasn't the best of starts. Acosta might look more like a dangerous pirate than an international polo player, but his co-operation was crucial as he part-owned the island. 'I'm very pleased to meet you, Señor Acosta,' she said as she stepped with relief onto the shore.

Ignoring the hand she had extended in greeting, he turned away.

Diego Acosta wasn't sophisticated and he wasn't charming. He certainly wasn't her usual type of wedding contact, who looked to Maxie for guidance. The idea of this man looking to anyone for direction was a joke.

'Give me your bags, Fernando,' he called out in Spanish, staring out to the boat over her head.

Diplomacy was an essential part of her skill set, Maxie reminded herself. She had dealt with plenty of difficult characters in the past—starting her training on her father, who had been a Class One bully when she was younger, before illness had reduced him to a shell. She had learned how to handle him and she would learn how to manage Diego Acosta—though she would have to be subtle. She couldn't risk offending him. The Acosta family was so powerful they could destroy her hard-won reputation at a stroke. 'I'm Maxie Parrish,' she said, stepping in front of him so he couldn't ignore her. 'Holly's wedding planner?'

The dark gaze blackened. What the hell had she said now?

Parrish? Memories festered inside him, though common sense told him Parrish was not an unusual name.

'I spoke with Holly before I left the mainland—' the girl was explaining.

'Parrish?' he interrupted, powerless to stem the tide of memories.

'Yes, Maxie Parrish,' the girl repeated. 'From a company called Dream Weddings. Holly said she'd call to warn you I was arriving today.'

'She did,' he agreed, 'but she forgot to tell me your name.'

'Is there a problem with it?' she demanded, smiling faintly.

'Not at all,' he assured her in the same detached tone. 'I suppose I was expecting someone older.'

'I wouldn't send anyone else to scout a job,' she assured him in the same courteous tone. 'I always make the first visit and the last, Señor Acosta, as well as every other visit in between.'

She said this as if it were a gauntlet she was throwing down, but pleasantly. He wasn't fooled. He could sense the steel beneath the accommodating manner, and his hackles rose even as more basic needs surged in response to this intriguing combination of feminine fragility and rock-solid resolve. Either way, with his brother on a polo tour and his bride-to-be at his side, Diego was stuck with their wedding planner—like it or not.

Diego Acosta was staring at her and frowning as if he thought they might have met before, which was impossible. She never forgot a face—and would never forget a face like his. 'I can only apologise if this is a bad time for you—'

And then she saw the cane.

She should cut him some slack, Maxie resolved. A man like Diego Acosta, stripped of his full physical powers, would not be having a *bad* time—he would be having the worst time imaginable. She had researched the family to get a sense of who they were, and knew one of the brothers had been injured in a riding accident, but she hadn't realised he was still suffering or that he would be her host on the island.

'I'll take your suitcase,' he offered brusquely.

Disaster struck as he lifted it. His cane skidded on a

stone and he stumbled. She reached out to save him, but it was the worst thing she could have done. Cursing viciously, he snatched his arm away and made off in the direction of the car park with one leg dragging badly. In the faint hope of building bridges, she chased after him.

'I hope the weather's better than this in June,' she yelled against the wind. Even limping with a cane he had opened up quite a gap. 'This might not look like a great venue at first sight, but I'm not easily put off.' She wasn't even sure if he'd heard her. They were heading down a stony path in the direction of a car park, where the only vehicle was a powerful off-roader. 'Holly assures me the island is beautiful in June…'

He wheeled around so suddenly she almost cannoned into him. 'And what do *you* think, Ms Parrish?'

With Diego Acosta towering over her it was hard to think at all. 'I haven't seen enough to make a judgement yet,' she said honestly, wondering if her heart would slow down long enough for her to breathe. She had never experienced this sort of reaction to a man before, but Diego Acosta exuded a powerful sexual energy, which for someone with below average experience of men was quite something to take in.

'Do you expect me to show you around?' he asked, wincing as he eased his leg.

'How kind of you to offer,' she said mildly. She could feel the resentment crackling round him, but she wouldn't want anyone to see *her* in pain, either—and at least he wasn't bundling her back on the next boat. 'I look forward to hearing everything you can tell me about the island.'

'I can see this is going to be an interesting trip, Ms Parrish.'

Her composure was shattered by a single, burning glance. 'My thoughts exactly,' she agreed, wafting the hair out of her face with a suddenly shaking hand. 'Shall I put my suitcase in the back?'

Her intention had been to save him the risk of stumbling again, but she'd only managed to create more offence.

'I'll take it,' he snapped, his expression darkening as he swung her heavy bag from the ground as if it weighed nothing.

'That's very kind of you. And please don't worry, Señor Acosta. I won't be hanging around. This isn't a pleasure trip for me—it's purely business.'

'What else would it be?' Folding his arms, he leaned his tight hips against the side of the vehicle.

Her heart juddered uncontrollably. Diego Acosta might be the most arrogant man on the face of the earth, but her body liked him—far too much. 'All I need while I'm here is a map and a bike,' she explained, doubting any woman could remain immune to quite so much man.

'A bicycle? On these mountains?' Resting his stubble-blackened chin on one shoulder, Acosta shot an ironic glance at the jagged peaks surrounding them.

'A motorbike,' Maxie explained. 'Your brother, Ruiz, said you have one on the island?'

'Did he?' Diego Acosta replied coolly. Dark eyes narrowed in suspicion as he stared at her. 'I trust you're not suggesting I lend you my bike?'

Her stomach tightened as he straightened up to his full, imposing height. 'I ride a bike at home.' She had the satisfaction of seeing surprise colour his arrogant gaze, but in the interest of good business she decided not to push too hard on this yet. 'I quite understand if you'd rather not lend your bike to a stranger—'

'You haven't seen my bike,' he said, with all the confidence of a man who hadn't met too many women like Maxie before. 'I think you'd be safer taking the Jeep.'

She recoiled at the put-down, but all she said was thank you. Who liked being patronised? But this wasn't about Maxie's pride. She was here for the bride, and to earn the money that kept her father safe and well looked after in a nursing home. Glancing inside the vehicle, she hoped Diego Acosta would take the hint. He might be impervious to the elements, but she was freezing cold and wet. She was glad when he swung the door wide, and launched herself into the welcoming warmth of the luxurious interior.

'Now we wait for Fernando,' he announced, bringing the gale from hell with him as he entered the vehicle. Tossing his cane in the back, he swung into the driver's seat using just the formidable power in his arms.

She hoped they wouldn't have to wait long. Every part of her was prickling with awareness in the confined space. They were seated so close—too close. To distract herself she reached inside her bag to find her business card. 'You can check me out on this website.' She held it out to him. 'There are plenty of reviews from satisfied clients. I'm sure you won't be disappointed with the services I offer.'

'I should hope not.'

Something in Diego Acosta's voice made heat curl low in her belly in a way that was both inconvenient and inappropriate. Silence was her safest bet, Maxie concluded, noticing he barely glanced at her card before stowing it in a pocket on the door, where it would probably stay until it yellowed.

Fernando joined them soon after, much to her relief. She gripped the seat as they drove off, but she needn't have worried as Diego Acosta drove with the same arrant confidence with which he appeared to do everything else.

'How long do you plan to stay, Ms Parrish?'

'That's hard to say…' Her senses sharpened when he met her glance. 'Except I'll be as time-efficient as I can be.' She guessed this was to reassure them both. She had a real sense of invading the dark space of a man who had retreated to this remote island after his accident and who wanted to be alone—and she was in no hurry to stay a moment longer than she had to.

'How do you normally proceed?' he demanded.

'I spend a few days researching the bride's preferred venue, deciding if it's viable or not, and then I make suggestions, with photographs to illustrate my thinking.'

'And when the weather's like this?' he said abruptly, making a gesture that encompassed the storm ravaged landscape outside the windscreen. 'How do you tempt the bride then?'

'The sky seems to be brightening,' she pointed out, determined not to be put off at such an early stage. 'The bride is already in love with Isla del Fuego, Señor Acosta, and please believe me when I say I won't get in your way.'

'I can't see how we can avoid each other on such a small island.'

She tried reasoning that he'd been injured and craved solitude, and yet had been thrown into the path of a wedding—the most social of occasions. No wonder he was climbing the walls. But did he have to kick her on the way?

'You're very quiet,' he observed.

Staring at impossibly strong forearms and powerful yet sensitive hands could do that to a girl. She quickly dragged her gaze away.

'Are you regretting your decision to arrange a wedding here, Señorita Parrish?'

'On the contrary, my mind is buzzing with ideas.' He needn't know the details.

'Your name?' he queried thoughtfully as they slowed to take a bend. 'It seems familiar to me. Are you sure we haven't met before?'

'It's quite a common name.' She said this to a soundtrack of Fernando snoring. 'I'm sure we haven't met before. I would remember. And I doubt we move in the same circles.'

'What do you mean by that?' he said, frowning.

'Just that I have never been to a polo match and I doubt you crash weddings.'

'I'm surprised you haven't added polo to your list of things to do,' he said sharply. 'You have been hired to arrange the marriage of a high-profile polo player.'

His concerns on behalf of his brother were understandable. 'I've read a lot about the game, and I've watched a lot of films regarding the sport, documentaries—you know.'

'Which is hardly the same thing as attending a match.'

'That's something I intend to put right as soon as I can. I'm looking forward to it,' she added keenly. 'It looks such a thrilling game!'

'It is.'

She could have bitten off her tongue when he shifted position to ease his leg.

'How long have you been in the wedding business, Señorita Parrish?'

'Please—call me Maxie. Everyone does.'

'Are you going to answer the question?' he said, ignoring the olive branch.

'Both Holly and your brother have my references,' she said, rattled by this inquisition.

'It's a simple question.' Diego Acosta swung the wheel

so abruptly she was thrown into the side of the vehicle as the off-roader lurched onto a minor road. 'Why should I read your references when you're sitting next to me and can give me the answers yourself?' he added, with a certain amount of justification and a whole heap of ire.

Because she had edited her CV so carefully, maybe? 'I'm happy to answer any question you care to put to me.' Within reason, Maxie amended silently.

There was a lot of information about herself that she didn't share—like the fact she had been in business since the onset of her father's illness and the cost of his nursing care meant she couldn't earn enough working for anyone else on a fixed salary. She had struck out on her own, determined and desperate, with one goal in mind: her father's dignity and privacy had to be preserved. And it had been. And would continue to be, whatever provocation Diego Acosta tossed her way.

CHAPTER TWO

'I'VE been arranging weddings for friends for as long as I can remember.' Maxie had decided that if she was going to be forced to explain herself she might as well take the lead.

'And why would they ask *you?*' Diego Acosta demanded.

'I guess because I was always the one who put on events at school. Arranging weddings turned out to be a natural progression of that.' She only now realised that that was exactly what had happened.

'How long is it since you left school?'

'I'm twenty-six.' And enough was enough. 'I've been a successful wedding planner with my own company for over five years now, Señor Acosta.'

'My brother led me to believe that his wedding planner would be someone older with a great deal of experience. And excuse me for saying so,' he added, not sounding in the least bit sorry, 'but you seem far too young to handle a job of this size and importance.'

'All weddings are important to me,' Maxie said, bridling. 'And though I realise you are unlikely to have heard of me, please don't judge a book by its cover, Señor Acosta. I may not wear a business suit while I'm traveling, any more than you wear one when you're down on the dock, but I'm serious about what I do. And excuse *me* for saying so,' she added, thinking it better to get things straight from the off, 'I'm not your brother's wedding planner. I was hired to do this job by Holly Valiant.'

'I'm sure you'll agree with me that Holly has a somewhat rose-tinted view of the island?'

'As I said earlier, I haven't had a chance to make any assessment yet. I'm completely impartial at the moment.'

And not about to roll over, Diego realised, fighting off the interest this provoked. If Maxie Parrish had anything to do with it this wedding would happen—and he was on notice. He couldn't remember the last time anyone had decided his agenda.

'I do wonder,' she said, distracting him, 'if the island falls short in so many ways, why you chose to come here to recuperate?'

'I beg your pardon?' He couldn't believe she had voiced those thoughts. No one mentioned his injury in front of him. No one even risked glancing at his leg. His brothers might—his sister Lucia definitely would. *But strangers?*

'Sorry if I'm being nosy,' she said. 'I'm just curious as to what drew you here.'

'Childhood memories,' he said sarcastically, hoping that would shut her up. Everyone had tiptoed round him since the accident. No woman had ever challenged him. Yet this kid had jumped right in!

'Whoa—slow down,' she said, grabbing his arm as he stamped down on the gas.

He glanced at the tiny hand on his arm. She looked too, and quickly withdrew it. 'I thought you liked speed?' he mocked her, in a pointed reminder of her claim to ride a motorbike at home.

'I ride my bike responsibly,' she said mildly.

She wasn't scared to take him on.

Seducing the wedding planner had never been part of his plan. It still wasn't. He must have too much time on his hands even to let thoughts like that occur to him. The type of woman he favoured was older and knew the score. She knew how to dress and what to say. More importantly, she knew when to remain quiet. She did not look like a fresh-faced tomboy, who dressed like a boy and insisted on speaking to him like a man.

'Are you all right, Fernando?' She had turned to check on the elderly skipper.

'My apologies if I woke you, Fernando,' he said, glancing in the rearview mirror.

The old man was more interested in hearing what Maxie had to say. *'Soy muy bien... Gracias,* Maxie,' he was saying, in a fonder tone than Diego had heard him use before.

When the girl had settled back in her seat she shot a glance at him. Was she reassuring him that Fernando was okay? Or was she playing it her way and to hell with him? She might look like a kid, but there was a lot going on behind that shrewd grey gaze, and he couldn't help wondering what other surprises Ms Parrish had in store for him.

'And when exactly did you learn to skipper a boat?'

'I helped to crew a yacht once—a friend at school. Her father was mad for sailing.'

He shot her a look that suggested *she* was mad. He couldn't believe she had thought it safe to transfer such tenuous experience to the open ocean in a barely seaworthy tub, but it told him something about her. She wasn't afraid of a challenge. Her cheeks pinked up when she caught his cold, assessing stare. Those pink cheeks told him everything he needed to know. Maxie Parrish might think she had all the answers, but she had none where he was concerned.

A client was always right. A client's brother-in-law-to-be had rights also—just so long as Diego Acosta didn't mistake her for a doormat. He had begun questioning her again about how she had grown the business so quickly. His lack of confidence in her was no big deal. It took time to win a client over. And, in his favour, the fact that this wedding was so important to him showed a strong family bond between Diego and his brother Ruiz.

'I had arranged quite a few weddings already when I was asked to plan one for a friend who works in television. She was so thrilled by the results that when she returned from honeymoon she asked if I could present a wedding feature for Valentine's Day—the perfect wedding, that sort of thing. Everything took off from there and I haven't looked back since.'

'But you haven't organised a wedding on a small island, where deliveries are uncertain and the electricity supply is erratic at best,' he pointed out.

'That's true. But generators can be hired, and I would have any supplies we need shipped over well in advance. I'm happy to take on the challenge.'

'I'm sure you are. And you're nothing if not prepared.' He shot a glance at her wet clothes.

'Had I known I would be sailing a boat today, I would have worn something more appropriate.'

'Why *were* you in charge of the boat?' He glanced at Fernando through the rearview mirror.

Maxie checked too, only to find Fernando was snoring again. 'Fernando was feeling a little unwell and I was glad to help out.' She left it there. Maybe Diego Acosta was trying to catch her out or embarrass her, but whatever his motive she wasn't going to land Fernando in trouble. 'I enjoyed the experience,' she said, brushing it off as if the terrifying voyage through raging seas had been nothing to her, 'and I never make the same mistake twice.'

'I should hope not,' Diego Acosta replied.

For some reason she was staring at his lips. She quickly looked away. She might be soaking wet and freezing, but her body was distinctly warm. 'If Holly decides to hold her wedding here and we encounter any problems, rest assured. I will deal with them.'

'That's what you're being paid for, isn't it?'

Diego Acosta grimaced and eased his leg as he spoke. She'd already worked out his mood was largely affected by pain or lack of it. 'It *is* what I'm being paid for,' she confirmed. And now she was wondering why, with all the money in the world to buy the best treatment available, the injury was still troubling him. And if it hurt so much why didn't he just take something for the pain, like everyone else?

'If this job is going to be too much for you, I'd rather you said so now,' he said, throwing her a lifeline she was supposed to grab eagerly and with gratitude, Maxie suspected.

'I always make a full evaluation before I come to any decision,' she explained calmly.

Her work as a wedding planner gave her such an intimate window into people's lives it wouldn't be the first time she had been invited in only for a client to draw back and ask themselves if this stranger would be sensitive to their needs, or if their most intimate secrets were about to be raked over and exposed to public scrutiny. Just because Diego Acosta was a testosterone-packed hunk it didn't mean she would treat him any differently from the rest.

'I think I've already explained that I won't need to trouble you for most of my time here.'

'*If* you stay on the island,' he said, as if this was by no means certain.

'Why wouldn't I?' she countered, careful to keep her tone bland and friendly. 'Judging by your earlier remarks, I assume you wouldn't want Fernando risking his fishing boat a second time in a storm.'

The elderly skipper chose that moment to stop snoring, and lost no time endorsing her words with heartfelt agreement. Maxie guessed Fernando was in no hurry to leave Isla del Fuego until he had received some coddling from Diego Acosta's staff.

'If there's a hotel here,' she added, 'I don't even need to trouble you for a room.'

'This is a small private island, with a small resident community,' Diego Acosta pointed out. 'There are no hotels, as such.'

'Perhaps bed and breakfast in a private house?' Maxie suggested hopefully.

'You will find no fairy godmothers on Isla del Fuego with rooms to spare, Señorita Parrish,' Acosta informed her.

No wonder. If there *had* been a fairy godmother her wand would have withered to a twig by now.

'You will stay with me,' he said, with zero enthusiasm.

Maxie's throat dried. Stay with him? Yes, it made sense, but—

When in doubt, smile and say thank you. That was the advice she always gave to anxious brides. 'Thank you,' she said politely, and as that seemed to be the end of Diego Acosta's welcome speech she directed her attention out of the window, to where the stubborn sea mist was lifting away like the curtains in a theatre, drawing back to reveal a scene that would make any audience gasp. Dramatic black peaks soared directly out of the raging sea, while at the side of the road luminous green foliage, made brilliant by the rain, competed for attention with striking banks of magenta blossom. 'How wonderful,' she murmured, forgetting the thunderstorm at her side for the moment.

'I wouldn't get your hopes up,' Diego Acosta commented, with a particularly male brand of humour. 'I live a rough, spare bachelor's life on the island, with very few home comforts.'

'I was referring to the view,' Maxi explained, chalking one up to the wedding planner. 'It's absolutely stunning.' And absolutely perfect for the wedding of a passionate couple like Holly and Ruiz, she thought.

Diego said nothing, but she noticed his fist tightening on the wheel. She guessed he would have preferred her to be a walk-over who would have given up on Isla del Fuego long before now, leaving him to brood alone. Hard luck, mister!

Did he read minds too? Maxie wondered when Diego Acosta shot her a glance. She was out of her depth here and they both knew it. She wasn't exactly a vestal virgin. She knew enough about sex to hope that one day she'd meet someone who knew what they were doing. Diego Acosta knew. She could feel it. While he, like the hunter he most assuredly was, must have felt her heat as she responded to him.

'There's just one thing,' he said.

Only one? 'Yes?' she enquired politely.

'While you're here you'd better call me Diego.'

She trialled the unfamiliar syllables beneath her breath. And shot bolt upright when she saw the look on his face. 'Diego it is,' she agreed, wondering if this might be just another ploy by Señor Acosta to make her feel uncomfortable.

'While you stay on the island there are conditions,' he said, adding to this suspicion.

She listened carefully as he listed the risks she might encounter on a volcanic island. She appreciated the heads-up, but it didn't change her mind. Diego Acosta was by far the biggest danger she was likely to encounter.

'Stray into caves and get lost—' his tone of voice brought her back to full attention '—or climb peaks that are unstable and I won't be able to help you.'

'Bottom line: it would be unwise for me to go adventuring on my own,' she said briskly.

'Correct,' he said. Relaxing back, he fell silent.

Maybe it was the hypnotic swish of the windscreen wipers, or maybe she had been too long out at sea, but the words just shot out of her mouth without the slightest intervention from her brain. 'Perhaps it would be safer if you showed me round?' she suggested.

'Me?' The black stare was incredulous.

She back-pedalled furiously, not wanting Diego Acosta to think she couldn't handle this on her own. 'Or I'm sure there's someone else who can show me round—Fernando, for instance?'

'Shouldn't we let Fernando enjoy his break?'

She could hardly argue with that.

'I'll take you,' Diego Acosta offered grudgingly.

Touring a mysterious island with Diego Acosta was not something a sensible woman would choose to do, but then he added, 'Who knows the island better than me?'

Maxie could only respond with, 'Thank you. I welcome any help you can give me. For Holly and your brother's sake, I think we should both do our utmost to make this visit a success.'

A cynical smile greeted this, though Diego Acosta's gaze remained fixed on the road. 'It appears my brother's fiancée has the most determined of champions.'

'She does,' Maxie confirmed, wondering if it would ever be possible to relax while Diego Acosta was around.

'Is something troubling you?' he prompted.

'No. Nothing.' She was staring at his thighs, Maxie realised, quickly looking away. They both looked equally impressive to her, but as that clearly wasn't the case she couldn't help wondering if he might benefit from the same massage therapy she had used to ease her mother's pain. 'I was just starting to plan,' she said, arranging her face in a thoughtful expression.

'Plans based on what?'

'Plans based on what I've seen so far.'

'They must be flimsy plans,' Diego observed, slowing the vehicle. 'Fernando,' he said, glancing in the mirror, 'this is where you'll be staying until the weather settles.'

'*Gracias,* Señor Acosta,' the old man enthused.

Maxie stared out of the window at a picturesque dwelling painted blinding white. Lovingly restored, it had a flower-festooned entrance and brilliant green shutters either side of tall, arched windows. A cactus garden framed the villa in vivid spikes of green, while the glittering black lava in which it was planted provided a dramatic contrast. Beyond the unusual garden the ocean was slowly turning from sullen grey to crystalline blue beneath a rapidly brightening sky.

'Do I get out here too?' She was keen to investigate further.

'No, you stay in the vehicle,' Diego ordered as he opened the door to get out. 'Unless you want to share the single bedroom with your skipper?'

'No, thank you.' Maxie firmed her lips. Each time she

thought she was getting the hang of dealing with Diego he had some new taunt up his sleeve. And that slack she had thought she should cut him? She was all out of rope.

Maxie sat in the vehicle, tapping her fingers on her bag as she watched the two men stroll up the path. They appeared perfectly happy to leave her to her own devices…

He might have known Maxie wouldn't stay where he'd left her. He had barely walked through the door when her heart-shaped face appeared at the window. Fernando beat a hasty retreat upstairs. He couldn't blame the old man. It was time someone informed Señorita Parrish that while she was on the island she did as she was told. He gave her a black look when she smiled at him—his body responded also.

'This is nice,' she said when she walked through the door, ignoring his hostile manner as she stared around. 'Do you mind?' she said, lifting her camera.

'You're here. You might as well.'

She was already snapping away, while he was trying not to acknowledge the pleasing scent of rain-washed air she had brought with her into the house.

'Perhaps some of the wedding guests could be housed here,' she mused out loud.

'I'll have to see if the cottage is available.'

'I'm sure you can make it so,' she countered, with a smile he guessed she used on all her clients. 'This place is beautiful,' she enthused. 'Did you design it?'

'What do you think?'

She cocked her head to look him straight in the eyes. 'I'm guessing no.'

'You'd be right.' He thumbed his stubble as he watched her at work, cursing the ruined leg that forced him to prop himself up against the wall.

'Everything's so well put together,' she observed as she clicked away.

'Blame my sister Lucia.'

'Oh, I think she's a marvellous designer.'

'I'll be sure to tell her you said so.' He vaguely remembered Lucia saying that her hard-nosed brothers must understand that mellow furnishings and comfortable sofas were essential if they didn't expect their guests to live like horses in a barn.

'I love this!' Maxie exclaimed, touching one of the hand-painted vases reverently.

He hummed and shrugged, refusing to admit that seeing what Lucia had done through Maxie's eyes was a surprise to him too. Her final camera shot was one of him. 'Holly will adore this,' she assured him confidently. Having checked the image first, she brought it over to show him.

Her scent, her warmth, her physical presence after he'd been so long alone almost overwhelmed him. 'Let's draw a line under this,' he said brusquely, barely glancing at the image. 'I have things to do.'

'Of course,' she said, putting her camera away. 'I'm sorry if I've delayed you, but I was just thinking we could use this room in some of the backgrounds for the album.'

'Really?' he said, wanting this over with. But in spite of his impatience his gaze found time to stray to her lips.

'Settings like these,' she was explaining, 'will give such personality and uniqueness to the photographs. And these stone walls are lovely,' she added, stroking them thoughtfully.

He was more interested in watching those small hands trace the centuries-old stone, until his leg chose to throb a warning that he wasn't match-fit—for polo or for women.

'I'm sorry,' she said, mistaking his grimace for a look

of disapproval. 'I must be keeping you.' Another few moments passed. 'Are you all right?' she asked.

'Yes,' he bit out, but his damaged leg called him a liar and dragged as he moved past her to the door. Anger erupted inside him. The fact that Maxie's breathing had speeded up when he brushed past her only heaped more humiliation on top of him.

'Don't worry—I'll shut the door for you,' she offered.

Catching hold of the door before she could reach it, he slammed it shut behind them, consoling himself with the thought that he had dealt with more wilful ponies than he could count, and the harder they were to handle at the start the better they pleased him when he finally broke them in.

He seethed all the way to the Jeep. Tossing his cane in the back, he swung in and Maxie jumped in beside him. Her lithe, agile form was another unintentional smack in the face for him, but as she turned to close her door her hair, which had dried into an inky cloud, brushed across his naked arm. He inhaled deeply, dragging in the scent of vanilla and lavender—a delicate and ultra-feminine combination he would never have expected the business-like Maxie Parrish to choose.

'Hurry up,' he blazed as she fumbled with her seat belt. 'I don't have all day.'

'You've really been very patient,' she agreed. 'I can't thank you enough for showing me the cottage, and I promise not to take up so much of your time in future.'

He hummed sceptically in reply. She was good at pretty apologies. It remained to be seen how she behaved when he piled on the pressure. It hadn't escaped him that the faster Maxie worked the sooner she would be out of here—and he could get back to licking his wounds in private.

CHAPTER THREE

HOLLY hadn't warned Maxie what to expect when she arrived at the Acosta family's holiday home, so when Diego drove over the brow of the hill she gasped. The elegant stone building looked more like a palace than someone's occasional home.

Reaching for her camera, she asked, 'Could you stop here for a moment?'

Diego Acosta drove on.

He had said he was in a hurry, Maxie remembered as the viewpoint disappeared behind them, and she could always come back alone.

She couldn't have been more surprised when he drew to a halt on the cliff edge and with a nod of the head indicated she should get out here. Not very gallant, but she'd take what she could get.

She had to concede he was right. This was a much better view, Maxie realised as she climbed down from the vehicle. The palatial old house sat on the top of a black lava cliff. At the foot of this a ruffled silver ocean stretched to the brightening horizon. The rain had stopped and the wind had dropped. She hoped the fresh air would clear her head, and made a play of fiddling with her lens to buy some time away from him.

'If you angle your camera like this...'

She started at the sound of Diego's voice. She hadn't even heard him coming. Lightning bolts shot down her spine when he reached across to tilt her camera.

'You can capture the house framed by the mountains on one side and the ocean on the other,' he explained. 'It's a famous view.'

Thankfully, he backed off while she worked, swiftly and efficiently, remembering he'd said he had other things to do.

'That was a great camera opportunity. Thanks for stopping,' she said when she joined him in the Jeep.

The massive shoulders eased in a *so what?* shrug. 'Research is what you're here for, isn't it?'

'That's right,' she agreed, putting her camera away neatly in spite of the fact that Diego Acosta's darkly glittering glamour was distracting to the point where her fingers were co-operating like sausages. She was used to men who came in uniformly drab design and were all the safer for it.

They drove into the Acosta holiday home compound through some impressive wrought-iron gates and turned into a cobbled courtyard framed by lushly planted flowerbeds. The planting was in stronger colours than Maxie was used to, but it worked here—the scale, the colour, everything was bold. In the centre of the courtyard there was a fountain, spurting plumes of water into the air, while shrubs and trees softened the edges of the old stone house. And the house, far from being the gloomy lair she had half expected Diego might inhabit, appeared to be a beautifully restored piece of history that had been loved and cherished over the years.

He parked at the foot of a wide sweep of stone steps at the top of which stood an older woman in front of some solid-looking double doors. The doors were open wide in welcome, and were flanked by twinkling windows that gave an impression as warm as the woman's smile.

'Welcome to Palacio Acosta,' Diego said. 'Or as some have dubbed it,' he added with a cynical curve of his lips, 'Palacio Too-antiquated-for-words.'

'Well, I think it's lovely!' Maxie exclaimed, wondering who on earth could have said such a thing. The thought that it might have been one of Diego's ex-girlfriends made the hair stand up on the back of her neck. Not that it was any of her business.

'May I introduce our wonderful housekeeper, Maria?' Diego said politely, standing back at the top of the steps so the two women could meet.

'I'm very pleased to meet you—' The words were barely out of Maxie's mouth when Maria gathered her close for a bear hug. If Maria worked for a monster she was certainly resilient, Maxie reflected when the housekeeper finally released her.

'I'm going to check the horses,' Diego said, swinging away. 'Maria will show you where everything is.'

'Thank you. And thank you for collecting me at the dock.' She hadn't expected him to stick around, but it would have been nice. *Nice?* It would have been challenging, electrifying, and all the other words associated with extreme sport. 'See you later.'

Business came first, and bearing in mind Diego's warnings about the terrain she thought it wise to arrange an agenda with him so they could discuss safety issues further.

Turning, he gave her a look that made Maxie wonder if she had sounded desperate. 'I imagine our paths will cross again as we're living in the same house,' he observed coolly.

'Whenever suits you.' She didn't need to turn her back

to hide her red cheeks. He'd already gone. Unaccountably she felt the loss of him already, Maxie realised as Diego limped away.

The moment he was out of earshot, he rang his brother. 'What the hell are you trying to do to me, Ruiz?' Diego demanded furiously, grimacing as he leaned back against a fence post to ease the pressure on his leg.

'If I knew what you were talking about,' Ruiz replied, 'maybe I could help. Your temper certainly hasn't improved,' he observed. 'My advice to you is to get back on the polo circuit as fast as you can.'

'Don't you think I want to?' Diego roared over the crackling line to Argentina, where Ruiz was currently playing the game they both loved, with Holly cheering him on from the sidelines. Shouldn't Holly be here to deal with her pain-in-the-ass wedding planner? 'Don't you think I'm obsessed with getting back into the game?' he flashed on the heels of this thought.

'I've never heard you so angry before,' Ruiz commented laconically.

'We might be brothers, Ruiz, but there are limits to what I'm prepared to do for you. I came here to recover in private—not to play host to some confetti addict.' He stopped at the sound of a muffled protest, and then sighed as his soon to be sister-in-law, the well-named Holly Valiant, seized the phone from his recently reformed playboy brother.

'You won't have to do a thing, Diego,' Holly promised him breathlessly from the other side of the world. 'Maxie is the most fantastic wedding planner. She will do everything. You *have* met her?' Holly prompted when he said nothing. 'She *has* arrived, hasn't she?' Holly asked with growing concern.

'She's here,' he confirmed flatly.

'Brilliant,' Holly enthused, completely missing the warning note in his voice. 'There's nowhere else on earth I would rather be married than Isla del Fuego.'

'You will have to excuse me, Holly,' he broke in politely. 'I have things to do. We can talk about your wedding some other time.'

'Oh…' All the air left her sails. 'Of course,' she said quickly. 'I imagine you're busy with the horses.'

Another long silence followed, and he could imagine Holly wondering if she'd said the wrong thing again. 'Yes, I'm busy with the horses,' he confirmed, to put her out of her misery. His attention switched to the ponies in the paddock, and to the one in particular that had fallen on top of him during the match. Months had passed since then, and the horse looked well and was moving easily—which was more than could be said for his owner, Diego reflected grimly.

'Is there something wrong?' Holly asked, forcing him to refocus on the call.

'Not really… There is one thing. The name of your wedding planner.'

'Maxie Parrish?' Holly supplied with her usual enthusiasm. 'She's great, isn't she?'

'Could you put my brother on the phone?' he said, keeping his voice carefully neutral.

'Of course…'

He could hear the strand of anxiety in Holly's tone, and then she covered the handset and said something to his brother.

'Diego?' Ruiz drawled, in a voice that suggested there were plenty of things he would rather be doing than talking to his brother.

'Parrish?' Diego drove on. 'Holly's wedding planner is called Maxie *Parrish*.'

'So?' Ruiz queried.

'Parrish,' he repeated.

'Dream Events is the name of the company, isn't it?' Ruiz remarked vaguely, clearly far more interested in his bride-to-be than anything else. 'Her references checked out. Even I was impressed. There must be thousands of girls with the surname Parrish, Diego. And, anyway, you should be over that.'

Maybe he should be, but he wasn't.

'It can't be the same family,' Ruiz said confidently.

'And you know this for a fact?'

But Holly had seized the phone again. 'Have I done something wrong?' she said. 'Please tell me if I've done something wrong, Diego.'

'You have done nothing wrong,' he soothed.

Where could he begin? And why rake up the past and ruin Holly's romantic moment? She wasn't to blame for a tragedy Diego had set in motion all those years ago.

'Would it be better if we rang you some other time?' Holly was asking with growing concern.

'No,' he said, making a conscious effort to gentle his tone. 'Tell me about the plans you'd like for your wedding, Holly.'

He felt bad when he realised all the fizz had left her voice, but she soon recovered, and as Holly started telling him her exciting news he drifted back to a black time in his life when he had taken one too many risks with tragic consequences. His time out now, with his injury from the polo field, could only be a relief for his opponents—for when Diego played he remembered what he'd done, and when he remembered he cared for nothing. Which made him a danger not only to himself but to everyone around him.

'You should get back to the game,' Holly told him softly, as if she could read some of these thoughts. 'You're needed, Diego. Your brothers need you. The team isn't the same without you.'

He hummed. 'I'm trying, Holly.'

'I know you're training every day. Things will get easier, Diego—trust me. And if it's my wedding that's bothering you—'

'There *are* other places you could get married,' he pointed out as Maxie's face flashed into his mind.

'But none as beautiful as Isla del Fuego,' Holly argued.

He gazed in silence across the paddock towards the sea, seeing the view as if through Maxie's camera lens. It was a scene of almost theatrical grandeur, he conceded. The pewter sea, in perfect accord with his mood, thundered against the black lava cliffs, casting diamond spray into the air. *And when the sun shone...*

'Are you still there, Diego?' his brother demanded, having taken the phone from Holly.

'I'm still here,' he confirmed. In body that was true, but his mind had strayed back to the past.

'How many people in the world have the surname Parrish?' his brother demanded. 'I know that's what's worrying you. Come on, Diego,' Ruiz insisted impatiently. 'You're the numbers guy in the family. You should know.'

This was true, and was thanks mainly to their elder brother Nacho, whose foresight and love had saved Diego from the blackest despair. Back in his arrogant youth Diego had lost money in a deal gone unimaginably bad, and it was Nacho who had told him that if Diego wanted to handle money he should learn how. Diego had gone on to train as an accountant, and now controlled all the family finances.

'Are you still there, Diego?' Ruiz pressed.

'I'm still here,' he confirmed.

'You're far too tense,' Ruiz commented dryly. 'And I think we both know the reason for that. According to Holly, Maxie Parrish is a good-looking woman, and you are on the island together—practically alone. Have you lost your edge, Diego?'

He stared down at the receiver as if this was news to him, and then said, 'Maybe I'm not that interested?'

'And maybe you're kidding yourself!'

'And maybe you're in danger of sharing the same rose-tinted spectacles as your bride.'

'Leave Holly out of this,' Ruiz warned.

'All I need is a sound leg, a good mount and a chance to get back to the game I love,' he thundered.

'We'll talk again when you've come to your senses,' Ruiz said, leaving him staring in frustration at the phone.

'What a wonderful home!' Maxie exclaimed, turning full circle to soak up the atmosphere in the elegant and welcoming hallway as Maria bustled round with pride.

'This house has been in the Acosta family for generations,' Maria explained.

'What a marvellous heritage,' Maxie said, thinking back to her own, very different family home. The father who had been so unkind to her mother when she was young had been broken by her mother's illness. It had been a struggle for him to keep up with all the extras her mother had needed, so, understandably, home comforts had been low on his list. When a hole had appeared in the sofa Maxie had thrown a rug over it, and on one famous occasion she had deconstructed a carpet sample book to patch the stairs. 'My mother would have loved this,' she said wistfully, turning slowly to take everything in. She hardly realised she'd been speaking out loud until she felt Maria's compassionate touch on her arm.

'Come,' Maria insisted, shepherding her towards a magnificent mahogany staircase.

There was no patching here. An impeccable runner in mellow earth tones climbed the polished stairs and was held in place by gleaming brass stair rods. The effect was both impressive and cosy.

It was too late to help her mother now, or to wish that her parents' lives could have been easier, but at least her work allowed her to earn enough to make her father's last years comfortable.

'Please,' Maria encouraged, pointing to Maxie's camera.

The Acosta home was so much more than a sum of its parts, Maxie realised as she looked at everything through her lens. The rugs were a little faded, and had been worn thin by the passage of many feet, but they were all the more attractive for that. Everything was a little rough around the edges, she noticed now, but that only added to the ambience of a much-loved home. It was a warm, happy home, and she could feel the influence of previous generations all around her.

'I love this house!' she exclaimed impulsively. She loved the grand piano sitting discreetly beneath the sweeping staircase, with a stack of music to one side as if the pianist had just stepped out for a moment. She loved the family photographs clustered on top of it, and the scent of beeswax in the air. 'There couldn't be a better setting for a family wedding,' she said to Maria.

'Perfecto,' Maria agreed, nodding and smiling as if she and Maxie were as one.

'I'm going to call Holly right away and confirm her choice of venue,' Maxie enthused, remembering that first there was another call she had to make…

Her first evening with Diego loomed. Oh, good, Maxie thought wryly, wondering how that would turn out as she brushed her waist-length hair for the umpteenth time. Blue-black and gleaming now she'd washed the salt out of it, her hair lifted and floated around her shoulders in most un-Maxie-like abandon. She usually tied it back for business. She had intended to tie it back tonight, but for some reason she wanted Diego to see her looking relaxed, for him to know that he didn't scare her.

Though goodness knows what they'd talk about, Maxie mused as she studied her perplexed reflection in the mirror. What she knew about polo could be safely inscribed on the top of a pin, while Diego was hardly the typical wedding cake fanatic. But this was work, and she'd get on with it. Replacing the silver-backed hairbrush on top of the lovingly polished French antique dressing table, she stood and frowned, remembering the news from the nursing home hadn't been good. Every day she hoped for improvement, knowing deep down it would never come.

She must remain focused on her work, Maxie reflected, firming her jaw. Work kept her grounded. Work paid the bills. Work kept her father safe.

Walking across the faded Aubusson rug to the beautiful old armoire, she picked out one of her 'all occasions' dresses. In pale cream silk it was equally suitable for an up-town business meeting or supper with friends. It was the dress she chose when she didn't want to look as if she was trying too hard. She teamed it with a pair of discreet nude-coloured sandals, then applied some shadow to her eyes, and some lipgloss. Now she was ready to face the tiger in his lair.

It was hard to remain tense in such a beautiful setting, Maxie realised as she walked across the room. Mellow evening light was streaming through the French doors dressed with filmy white muslin, while the open windows brought the scent of the beautifully tended gardens into the room. The bedroom was incredibly feminine, with several flower arrangements she had no doubt Maria had arranged, while a grand old four-poster bed took centre stage. Draped with floating ivory fabric, it had a beautiful hand-stitched quilt that picked up all the various pastel shades. She would never choose to decorate a room so prettily herself, but she loved it so much it made her wonder if she'd grown up practical because she'd had to be, or if practical was her nature. The only certainty was that tonight she was having supper with an unpredictable man, Maxie concluded. And he was probably counting down the seconds until she left.

'Diego!' It took her a moment to gather herself when she found him standing outside her room. 'Are you waiting for me?'

He was leaning against the wall, and the look he gave her suggested Maxie was in serious danger of flattering herself. 'I was on my way down to supper,' he said, giving her a lazy once-over. 'I presume that's where you're heading too?'

She was burning from his scrutiny while *he* looked amazing. How was it that some people only had to throw on a pair of jeans and any old top to look good? She could smell the soap from his shower, and his thick black hair was still a little damp and curling wildly round his swarthy face, catching on his stubble. But when he straightened up and she saw the cane propped against the wall she knew he had probably stopped outside her room because his leg was hurting him, and as they walked towards the head of the stairs she tried to measure her step to his without making it seem too obvious. His leg seemed stiffer than ever tonight, and she wondered if the damp weather had affected it. Hanging back, she could see how heavily he was relying on his cane.

He was glad Maxie was behind him and couldn't see the surprise on his face. Discovering the young tomboy transformed into a poised and confident woman had been a revelation to him. But why was he surprised? She was a successful businesswoman. He just hadn't had it thrust in his face before. She looked stunning in the simple dress, and he could imagine her walking into a meeting and getting any terms she wanted out of her suppliers—an image that irritated him when he thought of the men she would meet in the course of her work. Perhaps Ruiz was right about the route to rehabilitation and relaxation.

Right on cue the muscles in his leg stabbed a warning that he was more likely to grind his jaw in pain than soften his lips to seduce Maxie.

'I love your house,' she commented as they walked downstairs.

'It isn't strictly mine,' he said, putting her straight. 'The family shares it.'

'Don't you think that's why it's so lovely?' she said, pausing to examine an old oil painting of some disreputable-looking ancestor.

The Acosta men hadn't changed that much, he reflected, then, realising Maxie was waiting for him, wondered if she was taking it slowly on purpose—making allowances for him?

'I think it's a real family home,' she said, oblivious to his blackening mood.

'Yes, it is,' he said, waiting for her to go first before he tackled the last flight of stairs.

'Don't you love this hallway?' she said, trailing her slender fingers down the mahogany banister as she reached the hall ahead of him.

He concentrated on her naked shoulders and the cascade of silky black hair tumbling in luxuriant waves to her waist. This led him on the shortest of journeys to the neat curve of her buttocks, clearly visible beneath the clinging fabric of her dress.

'Well, I think it's perfect!' she said, turning to look at him.

'I can't see much wrong with it,' he agreed.

'How wonderful to have holidayed here when you were children. I love visiting houses like this.'

The last girl he had brought to the *palacio* had asked for the 'powder room' in order to touch up her make-up. Then she'd told him she hated the house. It was so dated, she said, proceeding to give him a list of requirements for her next visit. Fortunately the sea had been calm that day. He'd shipped her out on the next boat.

Maria was in the kitchen with an array of dishes that would have fed an army of gourmands. He ate in silence, while Maxie and Maria chatted away like old friends. Maxie handed him an agenda of things she wanted to cover, and he might have been surprised by her approach if he hadn't seen her dressed for business as she was tonight. He accepted the paper from her, glanced at it, and got on with his meal, wondering again about the tomboy who could transform herself so convincingly into a sophisticated businesswoman in no time flat. Did she have a boyfriend—a lover? Maybe she had children? He didn't know anything about her. Maybe she was married? That thought made him tense.

When they had finished the meal and the dishes were being cleared away—a duty Maxie had insisted on sharing with Maria—she tossed him a cloth. 'Wipe the table down, will you?' she asked him casually. 'While I load the dishwasher?'

He stared at the cloth in his hands while Maria, clearly in shock, bustled across the room to take it from him. His grip on the cloth tightened. 'Take the rest of the evening off,' he told Maria. 'You deserve it. And thank you for a delicious supper.'

'Gracias, Señor...' Maria said, backing out of the kitchen as if she never wanted to forget the sight of him holding a cleaning cloth.

Maxie had her back turned to him as she continued clearing up. When she'd switched the dishwasher on, she straightened up and turned round. 'Would you like to see the shots I've taken so far?'

Remembering the quicker Maxie got what she'd come for, the quicker he could be alone again, he said, 'Why not?'

He had to admit Maxie surprised him yet again. She might be an excellent wedding planner, but her photographs were also out of the ordinary. She had shown the island in a way he'd never seen it before, highlighting aspects which transformed it from a forbidding prison into a treasure trove of possibilities. Seeing Isla del Fuego through Maxie's eyes was a revelation to him.

'Is something wrong?' she asked when he grimaced.

'No. Everything's good.' Except his leg, which was cramping again. 'Your photographs are very good.'

'Thank you.' She turned to go. 'An early night for me, I think,' she advised him as she headed for the door.

Animal instincts battled with his common sense, while his leg screamed in protest. *'Buenas noches, señorita,'* he ground out as she left the room.

CHAPTER FOUR

SHE had had the worst night's sleep ever. Was it wrong to want a man who looked like a pirate to behave like one? Was it crazy to lie in bed wondering what would happen if she crept to the door and left it temptingly ajar? As if she'd be so stupid. She wouldn't have the first idea of what to do if she *had* done something so ridiculous and Diego had walked in. She had heard him coming upstairs and remained absolutely still as she'd listened to the water run while he took his shower. She had imagined him standing beneath the spray naked. No wonder she'd had a sleepless night.

Leaping out of bed, she drew the curtains on a brand-new day. The sun was shining and it was hard to believe she had been greeted yesterday by stormy skies and a glowering man. Opening the window and leaning out, she dragged in the scent of blossom and grass, intensified by the refreshing rain and now the warmth of the sun. So where was Diego? She glanced round the empty gardens, guessing he'd be with his horses. She'd take a shower, make her calls, and then she'd check the agenda she'd given him. She had no time to waste on fantasies involving dangerous men sweeping sensible girls off their feet and carrying them away to make passionate love to them until they couldn't stand.

But she was only human, and Diego Acosta was one heck of a man.

He had been up before dawn, after a restless night spent tossing and turning at the thought of a woman he wanted in his bed sleeping in a room just down the landing.

So what had held him back?

Slamming his cane against the wall with a vicious curse, he took a shower and changed into clean jeans, desert boots and the first top that came to hand. Opening his bedroom door, he found her walking down the landing towards the stairs.

'Good morning, Diego,' she called to him, oblivious to his black mood. 'I hope you slept well?'

'Maxie,' he said briefly.

'Are you coming down to breakfast?' she asked as she ran down the stairs.

Was he supposed to follow at a snail's pace?

'Maria has promised to make pancakes today,' she called back to him as she hurried across the hall towards the kitchen.

She looked so fresh-faced and innocent in her simple top, blue jeans and sneakers. 'I'm going to check on the horses,' he said, craving fresh air and the empty pampas.

'No problems, I hope?' she asked, pausing with her hand on the kitchen door.

Problems? What? More than she could see as he moved stiff-legged down the stairs? 'One of the ponies kicked my best horse last night,' he ground out.

'Oh, no!' she exclaimed with concern. 'I'm so sorry. No lasting harm done, I hope?'

'I don't know yet,' he snapped, frowning. Socialising was good for recovering horses, but there was always the risk they might get hurt, and he felt responsible for what had happened. It was another black mark on the day.

'Perhaps I can see your horses later?' she suggested.

Before he had a chance to refuse this request she had disappeared inside the kitchen. His black mood thickened when he heard her laughing with Maria. She was really making herself at home.

Thanking Diego's housekeeper for the delicious breakfast, Maxie reflected on the many amusing tales Maria had told her about Diego growing up. It was probably just as well he hadn't joined them in the kitchen, or Maria almost certainly wouldn't have opened up the way she had. Maxie had been her usual guarded self. She never talked about her childhood, and preferred to look to the future and build rather than waste time thinking about what couldn't be changed. She had spent too many nights barricaded in a room with her mother when her father had returned home drunk after yet another failed business deal to want to look back. Her own relationships with men had scarcely fared any better. She seemed to have the knack of finding younger versions of her father. No wonder creating events for other people suited her so well. She had long preferred to view the world from a safe distance.

She was scarcely back in her bedroom when her father called her on her mobile. 'What a great surprise,' she said, her face wreathed in smiles.

'Don't ring me now,' he howled. 'It isn't convenient!'

'But you called me,' Maxie pointed out, all her elation evaporating.

'Can't you remember the simplest thing, Maxine?' her

father bellowed, as if she hadn't spoken. 'I have a board meeting at nine. I've got no time for your jabbering now!'

'Dad, I'm sorry—' But the line had already been disconnected. He was as confused as ever, she realised. Her father hadn't attended a board meeting in his life, as far as Maxie knew, and he wasn't about to start now.

She took a moment to compose herself, and then sniffed and straightened up. Checking her reflection in the mirror before she left the room, she remembered her father's nursing staff telling her to get on with her life. They were probably right, but it had been so long since she had pleased herself, without making her responsibilities top of the list, she had almost forgotten how.

Or maybe not, Maxie thought. A faint smile touched her lips when she spotted something interesting in the courtyard. It wouldn't hurt to take a closer look.

Diego had checked the horse and was satisfied the wound was superficial. Having returned to his room to take a shower, he was rubbing his hair dry when the messaging service on his phone trilled. It was a text from an anxious Holly, wanting to know what he thought of Maxie. Were his feelings supposed to have changed towards Maxie since Holly's last call?

He texted back: *She's here. She's fine. Doing her job, as far as I can tell.*

Holly texted back immediately: *Is that it?*

That's it, he confirmed, stowing the phone. What else should there be?

He was just easing his leg when he heard something that made him lurch across the room as fast as he could to stare out of the window. With a violent curse he left his bedroom in such a rush he forgot his cane. With his stiff leg lagging behind, he used the brute strength of his upper body to swing down the stairs, and, limping across the seemingly endless stretch of hallway, he launched himself at the front door and flung it wide. 'What the hell do you think you're doing?'

'Oh, hello,' Maxie replied, turning on the seat of his prized custom-built Harley. 'I hope you don't mind. I saw your bike and I couldn't resist!'

She looked pretty hot on his bike...

And she was making no move to dismount.

She caressed the controls.

'I hope you weren't thinking of taking my bike for a ride?' he derided, making what, without his cane, was embarrassingly slow progress down the steps.

'I have ridden a bike before.'

'Not like this, you haven't,' he fired back at her, cursing beneath his breath as he closed the distance between them at a limp.

'I'm not a child, Diego…'

That much he could see for himself. And there wasn't so much as a trace of guilt in her eyes. 'Do you normally take things that don't belong to you?'

'I wasn't taking it. I was sitting on it,' she protested.

A flashback to his past fuelled his anger. He had first started riding bikes with a friend who was dead now. That thought led to the name Parrish banging in his head. 'Don't you dare,' he warned as Maxie's fingertips strayed dangerously close to the controls.

She had never done anything like this before. She had never rebelled or taken anything that didn't belong to her without asking permission first. She had been all business, all correctness and restraint for so long she couldn't imagine what she was doing.

'Off,' Diego commanded, in the coldest voice she had ever heard.

She could accept she was doing something wrong, but was it that bad? Something inside her flipped. 'Okay, so you don't want this wedding here. I get that. You don't want me here. I get that too. But as your brother part-owns this island, and his fiancée has hired me to give an opinion, I'm going to stay until I'm in a position to do that.'

'Then get back to work and get the hell off my bike!'

'I've done my work,' Maxie raged back. Springing off the bike, she took a stand. 'For your information, I stayed up half the night to finish my work. Holly will have my report the second she wakes up. What have *you* done apart from feel sorry for yourself?'

Diego paled. 'What did you say?'

'Isn't that what this is about?' Maxie demanded as all the pent-up feelings she had suppressed for years burst out of her. 'So you can't play top-class polo? You can still ride a horse, can't you? You're still breathing!'

'I should stop there, if I were you,' Diego warned her quietly.

'Why? Does the truth hurt, Diego? How long have you been on the island, exactly? Are you *never* going home? And if the pain's so bad why don't you take painkillers like everyone else?'

'You're really pushing it, lady…'

'Am I?' she said, standing her ground when he took a step towards her. 'Perhaps it's time someone did. Maybe I shouldn't have sat on your bike—but for God's sake, Diego, it's only a bike. I was hardly going to roar away on it. Where would I go?' she demanded angrily, staring around. 'This was an island the last time I looked!'

'Are you finished?' he demanded, looking more ferocious than she'd ever seen him with his ruggedly beautiful head thrown back, earring glinting, black eyes blazing.

Absolutely, devastatingly, gorgeous...

As they glared at each other Maxie slowly began to realise that the attraction between them was mutual. She drew a sharp breath in as Diego came towards her. Incredulity mixed with excitement and sheer blind terror at what she had stirred up churned inside her. He backed her towards the bike. She could feel the cool metal against her overheated skin and the leather seat pressing into her back. Passion boiled in Diego's stare—in hers too, she had no doubt.

'Next time ask me first,' he ground out.

She gasped as he seized her arm. 'Get off me!'

What was more terrifying? The cold, blind fury in Diego's eyes, or the cruel twist of his smile? Just his grip on her arm was alarming. But as they stared it out it was as if they were joined in some deeper, primal way. Almost as if they were meant to be like this—close, passionate, exclusive and intense.

'I said, get off me!' she raged.

Diego merely angled his chin to stare down at her, as if she were a particularly interesting wild creature of a type he had never encountered before.

'Don't you hear me?' She tried and failed to shake herself free. 'Don't you dare look at me like that—don't you dare smile!'

Diego's answer was simple. She dragged in a shocked breath as he swung her off her feet and dumped her back on the saddle. Swinging in front of her before she had chance to protest, he started the engine and kicked the stand away. 'You want a ride?' he snarled over his shoulder. 'Then I suggest you hold on.'

A red mist clouded his vision as he powered up the

bike. Maxie hadn't just breached his privacy, she had opened Pandora's Box on the past. She had insulted him. She had—

No. He refused to contemplate, even for one second, that she might have held up a mirror to his face. He wanted her, but he also wanted her gone. He couldn't inflict himself on anyone—his leg, his mood, the danger that lurked inside him, all of it poison. She wanted to know why he was here on the island? For everyone's safety. That was why. She had chosen to ignore the warnings. Her bad luck. She hadn't seen him like this. She hadn't seen him with the devil on his back.

They shot away so fast she almost fell off the bike. She clung to Diego as he accelerated, taking the bike at such speed round the first corner that his jean-clad leg brushed the road. Yes, she had ridden a bike before—it was the easiest way to cut through the London traffic—but there was a world of difference between her 125cc commuter bike and Diego's white-hot Harley.

At first all she could think of was not falling off, but gradually she realised that Diego could ride a bike at speed as well as it could possibly be ridden. She still clung to him like a limpet. Forget prudent, sensible behaviour—this was a matter of staying alive. Resting her cheek against his hard, warm back, she felt his muscles flexing, and against all that was sensible she felt safe. The grey top he was wearing held the scent of soap and warm, clean man. And at least she didn't have to look into those mocking eyes, Maxie consoled herself—though she did have to be careful where she put hands that badly wanted to explore Diego's muscle-banded torso. Of course she wouldn't let them—any more than she would acknowledge the effect of sustained vibration on a body that had been too long without sex.

When he finally stopped the bike she dismounted shakily.

'Well?' he demanded.

'Awesome!' she exclaimed, before realising Diego expected her to be broken by the experience. But it had been amazing. And if he didn't like it… 'I can't believe I waited so long to do that,' she said, finger-combing the tangles out of her hair. 'You're an amazing rider.'

Easing onto one hip, he stared at her long and hard. 'You must be a sucker for speed.'

'Maybe I am,' she agreed.

Ruffling his hair, he turned away. He couldn't pretend she hadn't surprised him. Maxie Parrish was fearless. Was he in such a hurry to get rid of her now? Maybe having company wasn't all bad. At least Maxie had something about her. Behind that cool exterior was a leather-clad biker-girl with a ferocious temper—which made him wonder what other passions lurked beneath the surface of Maxie's carefully manufactured veneer. He'd have to be unconscious not to want to find out.

Did they actually have something in common? Maxie wondered, exhilarated by the bike ride. Had the same jolt of electricity joined them briefly?

'What now?' she pressed, feeling she could cope with anything. Her lips pressed down with disappointment as she gazed around at the uninspiring shrub and rock. Nothing could compete with that bike ride, and this was the dullest part of the island she'd seen so far.

He only now realised that the passion driving him had brought them to a very interesting part of the island. 'The Green Caves,' he informed Maxie.

'I don't see anything,' she said, staring around an apparently empty stretch of ground.

'That's because you're not looking in the right place.'

He took in her flushed face and windswept hair. She looked great.

'Where am I supposed to be looking?' she said. 'There's nothing but scrub here.' She gestured around. 'This definitely wasn't on my agenda.'

'Neither was my bike,' he reminded her. 'Do you always play by the rules, Maxie?'

'It's the safest way,' she said with a shrug, but she didn't hold his gaze.

She followed Diego out of curiosity. She wasn't sure if this was a joke or not. There was nothing to look at of any interest—apart from Diego. He was still limping, but not too badly today. She guessed that was due to the adrenalin coursing through his veins after the ride.

'Welcome to the Green Caves,' he said, stopping dead in his tracks.

She followed his stare down to some stone steps cut into the ground.

'As we're here,' he said with matching cool, 'I might as well show you the underground caves so you can share the info with Holly.'

'Thanks,' she said briefly, relieved Diego had got used to the idea of his brother's wedding being held on the island.

'Once we're underground in the Green Caves you must stay close to me.'

No hardship so far. 'Okay,' she agreed.

'Did you put sightseeing on your list for the guests?'

'Yes,' she confirmed, ignoring his offer of a steadying hand.

'Hey!' he exclaimed, saving her from falling when she stumbled on the steps. 'I'm supposed to be the one who's compromised here.'

There was no humour in his voice, or on Diego's face

as he set her back on her feet, but it was the first time he had mentioned his injury, and as steps forward went that wasn't a bad one. 'Thanks,' she said casually as they carried on down the steps in what was almost comfortable silence.

The staircase ended in an underground passageway, dimly lit by some low-voltage lighting. 'We're under the sea,' Diego explained when she paused to listen.

'And the lights?'

'Solar panels. Quite a recent addition.'

As he moved on she wondered if Diego felt more relaxed too. More importantly, she wondered if he registered her as a woman at all, or if she was merely someone he felt he had to show round for the sake of his brother? He had never looked more the pirate, with his harsh, chiselled face, but that firm, sensual mouth belonged to a more sophisticated sensualist altogether. And now erotic possibilities were flooding her mind—which was hardly helpful when she needed to be concentrating.

'The excavation of these caves goes back centuries,' Diego was explaining. 'And as each new generation takes ownership more improvements are made.'

'That sounds impressive,' she agreed, and her gaze followed Diego's strong, tanned hand as it moved lightly over the stone wall.

'I like to think so,' he said, shooting a keen glance at her.

'After you,' she said lightly. There wasn't enough space in the tunnel to pass him without touching.

He moved away.

They now entered a cavern the size of an aircraft hangar. Stalactites hung like weathered spears above their heads, while dripping stalagmites lined the path. She spotted a sheer drop on one side of the cave, but when she went to take a closer look Diego held her back. He was by far the bigger danger, she thought, glancing at his hand on her arm.

'How deep is this chasm?' she asked him on a dry throat.

'Shall we find out?' he suggested.

Reaching into the back pocket of his jeans, he pulled out a coin. As it spun and flashed in front of her she wondered what it would be like to have Diego on-side, to have someone special to confide in, but then the coin landed in glassy water just inches from her feet and the illusion shattered into numberless ripples.

'The surface is so clear and still it acts like a mirror,' Diego explained.

Creating a false impression as misleading as her own far-fetched hopes and dreams, Maxie thought wryly. But it was a great place to bring wedding guests, and she told him so. 'Though I won't tell anyone about the coin toss,' she explained. 'I think we should keep that a secret between us so it has maximum impact for the guests when they discover the secret of the caves.'

'Do you like keeping secrets, Maxie?'

She balked at that. 'Sometimes,' she admitted. The caves suddenly felt oppressive. 'Is that it?' she prompted.

'There's just one more thing I think you should see.'

Her gaze lingered on his back as Diego led the way. He was such a powerful man, with only the limp to remind her that all was not well with him. If the leg had been attached to anyone else it might have been a good time to suggest trying out the massage technique that had worked so well for her mother—but not while it was attached to Diego Acosta.

The next cave contained an underground lake. A natural chimney allowed light to flood in, giving the water an unearthly glow. Diego was hunkered down at the water's edge, where tiny albino crabs were scuttling in the shallows at his feet.

'They are unique and vulnerable,' he explained.

Diego's hard face had softened. This was a side of him she hadn't seen before. It made her even more certain that she wasn't the only one who had allowed the past to colour her life. As she stared at the broad sweep of his shoulders and his strong, tanned neck she wanted to ask so many questions, but she was here for a fact-finding trip of the island, not him, and so she settled for, 'I didn't take you for a nature-lover.'

'Oh, I love nature,' he said, standing up to fix her with an assessing stare. 'It's people I have a problem with.'

Okay. She turned her attention to gathering more shots for Holly.

They held concerts in the underground theatre here, Diego explained as he led the way into the incredible facility buried deep in the bowels of the earth. 'We invite people over from neighbouring islands.'

As you do, Maxie thought wryly. 'How many people can the theatre seat?' She had immediately reverted back to business mode and was taking notes.

'Three hundred or so—more if we take the seats out.'

'It would be perfect for a party after the wedding breakfast,' she mused out loud, though of course it would be up to Holly to make the final decision.

She was standing too close to Diego, Maxie realised as her body thrilled a warning. Moving away, she stared down the steeply raked aisle to the unusual stone stage, with its backdrop of rough-hewn rock glowing amber beneath the lights. She took some shots, made a few more notes, and then turned to go—almost colliding with him.

As she skirted past she could hear his steady breathing above the thundering of her heart and something made her ask impulsively, 'Do you mind if I stop by to watch you training your horses?'

'You'd find it boring, surely?'

'No. But if I'd be in the way—'

'You wouldn't be in the way.'

If her heart had been thundering before, it was out of control now. 'Are you sure?'

'I'm sure.'

They climbed back up the steps and emerged into the light. 'Do you still think you can ride my bike?' Diego asked.

She stared at the big black monster, sensing there was a bigger decision to be made here than whether she could ride his bike. 'Yes, I do,' she said.

Diego needed someone to stand up to him. She needed to test herself. Bring it on.

CHAPTER FIVE

THE bike seemed to have grown bigger, while Maxie seemed to have shrunk. Drawing in a steadying breath, she tried not to register anything when Diego swung onto the saddle behind her—and failed miserably. Her back lit up like the Fourth of July. At least he couldn't know how she was feeling—and at least he couldn't see the tension on her face.

'Just thumb the starter button, Maxie.'

There was another moment when he reached around her to guide her hands and his hard, muscular torso pressed into her back. The temptation just to close her eyes and lean against him…

'Did you get that, Maxie?'

Diego's tone was enough to eject her from that day-dream. 'Got it,' she confirmed.

'Good. You may have ridden a bike before, but I promise you you never rode a bike like *this* before.'

'Like everything else on the island, I'm sure it's extraordinary,' she said dryly, smiling as she turned on the engine. It purred like a kitten.

'Squeeze, don't grab at the controls,' Diego warned as she upped the revs. 'You have to make love to them.'

'I will,' she said briskly, not wanting to think about making love in any context right now.

'If you do exactly as I tell you,' Diego added, 'you'll find the bike will respond like a—'

Like a lover? 'Like a bike?' she suggested.

'Like the most responsive of bikes,' Diego amended coolly.

Blowing out one last steadying breath, she released the brake and hit the throttle.

'You're doing ninety,' Diego yelled above the wind. 'Slow down or I'm taking over!'

She laughed as exhilaration took her over, and only slowed at the next bend. She took the corner well and didn't speed up again. She'd had her moment. She wasn't trying to provoke Diego. She just wanted to push the boundaries for once in her life.

That was Maxie Parrish, Maxie concluded wryly as the countryside turned from a dun-coloured blur into a crystal-clear image of scrubland punctuated by the occasional tree, she always knew when to pull back.

'You ride well,' Diego commented now he could be heard over the engine.

She could only blame the island for freeing something crazy inside sensible Maxie. 'Thanks for letting me ride!' she yelled back.

As Diego eased back in the saddle, she felt the loss of him instantly.

'Do you ride a bike every day?' he said.

'Every day to work—and sometimes when I'm at home.'

'Home?' Diego queried, frightening her with the speed of his pick-up. 'Do you live alone?'

'I do now,' she said lightly.

'No boyfriend.'

'No…' She drew the word out as if she had no time for one, which was true.

'You don't live with your parents, then?'

'No.' She took a moment. 'My mother's dead.'

'I'm sorry for your loss,' Diego said, leaning forward to speak in her ear. 'My parents too—both of them.'

'I'm sorry.'

'It's been quite some time now.'

'But it never gets any easier, does it? I think about my mother every day. I still miss her. I always will. I suppose you just learn coping strategies.'

'I suppose you do,' Diego agreed, and then after a moment he added, 'What about your father, Maxie?'

Every part of her was instantly on red alert. 'He's retired,' she said, reverting to the one-liner that always got her through. 'He lives quietly now.' She waited tensely, and was relieved when Diego let the subject drop.

'Take a left here,' he instructed. They were almost back at the *palacio,* and were entering a fenced lane beyond which lay endless paddocks where countless horses were grazing.

She stopped the bike and Diego got off. With the immense power of his upper body he barely used his legs as he vaulted lightly over a gate. A sleek bay pony, instantly recognising its master, came trotting over. Nuzzling Diego's pockets imperiously, it consented to consume a packet of mints.

'Are you going to ride him?' Maxie asked almost simultaneously with Diego springing lightly onto the horse's back. His injury counted for nothing now. Nudging the horse into a relaxed canter, he was at one with it immediately—but she guessed that when it came to playing polo at a professional level the stiffness in Diego's leg would hold him back. Climbing the fence to watch, she rested her chin on her arm.

'I come here every day to train,' he explained as he cantered past.

She could understand why. The steady rattle of hooves was so soothing.

At least it was until another horse, wanting to join in the fun, bucked its way across Diego's path, causing his horse to shy and then to rear. Diego only just managed to stay on, and the effort wrenched his leg. Dismounting, he bent double in pain. Maxie felt sick and wished she hadn't been there to see it.

The one thing she knew she mustn't do was turn away and have him think she was disappointed in him. 'Can I help?' she called out when he didn't move.

He didn't look up as he waved her away, but she saw the grimace of pain on his face. She couldn't imagine what it must be like to have been at the top of his game only to stare failure in the face now, day after relentless day.

The first thing he did when the pain had passed was to check his horse, and then with a kind word he slapped its rump to urge him back into the field. When he limped towards her she said nothing. There was no need for words. Their eyes met briefly and that was it. In some ways it was the closest they'd come.

The hot red sun was sinking slowly behind the mountains as Diego rode the bike home. They had been out for hours and she'd hardly noticed time passing. The black peaks were framed in a shimmering gold, and even the sea had calmed into a smooth lilac disc. It was an incredible sight, but the day had gone flat. Diego took the bike at a modest speed, as if he didn't want to invite any more disasters. When they reached the house and she dismounted, he rode away without another word.

This feeling, like a lump of lead in her stomach, was

due to her getting too involved, Maxie concluded as she walked across the silent hallway. Did she really think she could ease Diego's pain? What if she tried and it didn't work?

What if, what if, what if...?

She was a doer, not a dreamer—wasn't she? How could she make things right for Diego?

Back in his bedroom, Diego raked his hair impatiently and swore as if that could blank out what had happened. What had possessed him to ride a horse in front of Maxie? Why had he let her watch? Why had he questioned her about her father and simply let it go? Was he afraid to hear the truth? Was he afraid to face the truth about his leg—his future—his place in the Band of Brothers polo team? Was he afraid to face the truth about Maxie?

The chances of one Parrish being connected to another in a world of individuals with the surname Parrish was practically non-existent. And if he asked her and there *was* a connection he doubted she would answer him honestly anyway. She would just strengthen her defences, making the elusive Peter Parrish even harder to find. It would save a lot of grief if he just hired a private investigator and waited until he had some answers.

He gazed out of the window at the pool house. There was still a very good chance he could make a full recovery. He had to believe that one day full feeling would return to his leg. One thing was sure—the enemy of his progress was inactivity. He'd take a shower and have a swim. If he could do nothing more than religiously practise the exercises he'd been given in the hospital then that was what he'd do.

* * *

Back in her room, Maxie picked up the phone to call Holly with the good news about the caves. 'Yes, I'm fine,' she confirmed when Holly spoke without breath or break about her concerns for Maxie. 'This isn't about me,' Maxie reminded Holly good-humouredly when she could finally get a word in. 'It's your wedding—though the next time you might warn me what to expect on the unreconstructed man front!'

'There won't be a next time,' Holly said, laughing down the phone. 'And I doubt anyone could warn you about the Acosta brothers. They're unique!'

'They certainly are,' Maxie agreed, laughing too. She went on to explain what she had seen and how she thought they could use the caves as part of the entertainment for the guests. They chatted some more and Holly thanked her for the photographs.

Maxie had crossed to the window by this time, only to see Diego crossing the garden. On his way to bed down the horses, she presumed. She pulled back just in time as he looked up, making her heart thunder and her body yearn.

This was madness, Maxie told herself firmly, finding she had to wait until even his shadow had disappeared before she could concentrate enough to finish what she'd been saying to Holly.

'Are you still there?' Holly demanded.

'I'm still here,' Maxie confirmed. 'I was just distracted for a moment.'

'By Diego?'

'How did you know?' she said, smiling.

'Maxie, please. Relationships are my business, remember? Agony aunt?' Holly prompted. 'My whole job revolves around sniffing out sparks.'

'There are no sparks.'

'Right,' Holly agreed without conviction. 'So, what do you really think of him?'

'I don't know what you mean. I'm here to arrange your wedding. I hadn't even noticed Diego, to be honest…'

'Oh, he *has* made an impression on you,' Holly interrupted with amusement. 'Remember, I have seen him—so nothing you can say will ever persuade me that you haven't *noticed* Diego. Did you even say that, by the way?'

'Could we concentrate on business and your wedding plans, please?'

'For now,' Holly agreed. 'So what do you think of the island so far?'

'Fabulous. Perfect for your wedding,' Maxie said honestly. She gave Holly some more back-up information to flesh out what she'd already told her. 'So if you're sure you're happy to leave everything to me—'

'That's why I hired you.'

'I'll send some more notes through later today.'

'Put some juicy bits in this time,' Holly insisted with a laugh.

'Not a chance,' Maxie exclaimed, pressing her back against the cool of the wall in the hope that it might soothe her overheated body. 'Sorry to disappoint, but this is strictly business, Holly.'

'Now you've upset me,' Holly protested, forcing a sob into her voice. 'I was planning on us being sisters-in-law one day, so I'll always have someone around to organise my life.'

'Well, as that's never going to happen—'

'All right—so concentrate on my wedding for now. Just think of it as a rehearsal for your own.'

'Holly,' Maxie warned in a mock-stern tone. 'Seriously.

Stop this.' And that was as far as she got before Holly laughed again and cut the line.

Did Holly even know Diego? Did she think for one moment he would look at someone like Maxie? Diego had been right about Holly—she did look at the world through rose-tinted spectacles. Getting to know Diego any better than Maxie already had would be the most insanely dangerous thing she could do.

And what if she wanted to?

She just had to get a hold of herself, Maxie told her inner voice impatiently, wishing she didn't feel quite so mixed up. After all the excitement on the bike what she needed was to cool down, Maxie concluded, searching for her swimming costume. She couldn't do any more work on Holly's wedding plans today so she might as well take some time to chill out—if that was possible while she and Diego lived under the same roof.

Grabbing her things, she was just about to leave the room when she decided to make a quick call first. 'Dad?'

'Maxie? Is that you?'

The fact that her father seemed to be totally switched on now, despite his earlier confusion, was incredible. 'How do you feel?' she asked eagerly, thrilling at the sound of his voice.

'Wonderful,' he assured her.

'That's the best news I've heard all day. And don't you worry. I'll be back before you know it to take you out, and we'll have a great time—'

'Take me out? Take me out where? Who is this?' her father quavered in a voice that chilled her. 'Why do you want to take me out?' he demanded suspiciously. 'What have I done? You can't blame *me*,' he exclaimed on a rising note.

And then he started yelling and swearing just like the

old days, only almost worse, Maxie realised, because now he didn't know what he was saying. She knew she should be relieved when a nurse took over the phone, but instead she just felt beaten. It took a good few steadying breaths this time before she could accept that it was her father's illness that had beaten them both.

'Everything's fine this end,' the nurse assured her. 'Are you okay?'

'I'm fine,' Maxie confirmed. *Fine. Fine. Fine. She was fine.*

Emotion filled the room, leaving no air to breathe. Ending the call, she gave herself a moment, waiting for the tide of emotion to pull back, as it did every time, only to regain its strength for the next onslaught. Drawing in a shaking breath, she checked she had everything she would need at the pool house. The thought of a brief spell of solitude and mindless exercise had never seemed more appealing.

Swimming was one thing Diego could still do really well. After years of training he had plenty of muscle power in his upper body, and if one leg worked less smoothly than the other the water supported it and he could still maintain a credible speed. And swimming was one of the very best exercises for his injury, the physios had told him. The cool of the water after the heated bike ride was certainly welcome. His regular stroke allowed him to focus his mind and plan his next move. With Maxie around the name Parrish was constantly in front of him, so it made sense to him to get to the bottom of the Peter Parrish mystery once and for all.

All he wanted was the chance to confront the man with what he'd done—what they'd both done. He hoped then he could start looking forward—maybe one day he might even forgive himself. Performing a powerful tumble turn using just one leg, he cruised to the side just as Maxie walked through the door. He huffed a humourless laugh, guessing she'd take one look at his scars and probably faint. Even his brothers had flinched when they had first seen them. Like the painkillers he refused to take, nothing could change the past, but to have her see him stumbling and scarred felt like some sort of penance. His guilt for what had happened all those years ago required constant feeding.

'Hello, Diego,' she said, seeming surprised to see him. 'You don't mind if I take a swim, do you?'

'Do you want to wait until I get out?'

'I can, if that's what you'd prefer?'

'No problem for me—help yourself.' He swung out of the pool on his arms and then, predictably, after his ease of movement in the water where he was weightless, he stumbled. It took him a moment to regain his balance and straighten up. As the pool water streamed from him he waited for the inevitable gasp.

'Is your leg troubling you again?' she asked, staring at it intently. 'I expect the adrenalin from the bike ride has worn off.' She laughed. 'Or maybe you've overdone it in the pool,' she said with more concern, glancing at the settling water.

Brushing past her, he reached for a towel. He saw her wince when he staggered, and the next moment she had reached out to grab it for him. 'I can pick up a towel without your help, thank you.'

'Oh, for goodness' sake, Diego!' Picking the towel up, she threw it at him.

Catching the towel knocked him off balance again, and he had to hop a couple of times before he could regain it. 'Well?' he demanded when she stood staring at him.

She could see that Diego was trying to keep the pressure off his injured leg, but what else had rattled his cage? The scars, Maxie guessed. They were bad. And she could imagine he didn't want anyone seeing them. Well, it was too late now. She could see a lot of scar tissue she was sure would loosen if treated with the proper emollients, which suggested to her that Diego had performed his exercises regularly to build back muscle power, but that he had neglected to treat the recovering skin.

And she wasn't here to offer a diagnosis, Maxie reminded herself firmly. She was here to swim. It was important to remain detached and businesslike, she thought to herself as she removed her sarong. *So that was why her hands were trembling.*

Thankfully her swimming costume was respectable in the extreme. She went swimming to exercise, not to flaunt her body, though Diego's lazy appraisal made her wonder why she'd bothered putting a costume on at all.

'This is a fabulous pool,' she said, giving herself an excuse to turn away. 'Would the wedding guests be allowed to use it?'

'Of course they would.'

Hearing the same tension in his voice, she decided to have it out with him. 'Have I done something to upset you? I apologise if I have. Or is it your scars?' she asked bluntly, unable to ignore the elephant in the room any longer. 'Do you think I can't bear to look at them? Do you think I'm revolted by them? Is that how shallow you think I am?'

'I have no thoughts on the subject at all.'

'Really?' she said in a challenging tone. 'Then please stop staring at me like that. If you don't want me to use the pool, I'll go.'

A cynical smile tugged at Diego's lips. 'Brave talk, Maxie.'

'Brave?' she said. 'You'd know all about that, wouldn't you, Diego?'

'What do you mean by that?' He wasn't smiling now.

'You're brave,' she said bluntly, holding his cold gaze without blinking. 'Everyone knows how brave you are. Don't you prove it each day you exercise to get your strength back? When we all know how monotonous that must be for you, especially with so little to show for it, and just the hope that some time in the future you'll be fully mobile again. Wasn't it a brave decision to let your horse live when everyone said his leg was beyond repair and he should be shot? Holly tells me a lot of things about you,' she said before he could get a word in. 'So if you're so brave you won't mind me touching your scars. You won't mind me massaging them—easing them—helping you…'

When he threw his fierce dark head back and laughed in her face, she added, 'Or are you just too damn proud to accept anyone's help, Diego?'

'You've got some nerve,' he grated.

'Yes, I have,' she agreed in the same calm voice, 'so you can stop with the menacing act. I'm here. I'm alone. And I'm not afraid of you. What are you afraid of, Diego? Failure? Are you afraid you'll never play top-class polo again? If that's the case you'll let me try to help you. If that's not the case, then you're just the most unpleasant man I've ever met!'

Diego was staring at her as if he couldn't believe what she'd said. But someone had to say it. She knew how hideous it must be for him to have her see him in pain, but she was here and there was no avoiding it. Better to tell him what she was thinking, rather than hide behind awkward politeness for the rest of her stay.

'I believe I can help you,' she said with conviction. 'I learned some massage techniques from a physio in the hospital and they helped my mother.'

'And do you really think I'm going to let you try them out on me?'

'Why not?' She held the hostile stare unflinching. 'What do you have to lose, Diego?'

'So where my physios have failed you think you can help me?'

'I can try,' she said quietly.

'One of these days you're going to meet yourself coming back,' he exclaimed with an angry gesture.

She could see where Diego was coming from. Yes, she was pushy, and, yes, she was taking a risk in offering to try, but she had always tried to help and she couldn't shake that off just because Diego hated her seeing him like this.

Everyone felt vulnerable sometimes. 'Please let me try, Diego. It can't do any harm, can it?'

His expression suggested she had better not get this wrong.

CHAPTER SIX

MAXIE was already regretting her reckless offer—maybe because her natural impulse to help had never been challenged by such rampant maleness before. Diego was relaxing on one arrogant hip and staring down at her, as if daring her to touch him—and the truth was she wasn't so sure she dared.

'There's oil on the table,' he said, with the mocking smile firmly fixed on his lips.

'What is this?' She turned the bottle in her hands.

It was a potion he had bartered for with some quack in return for a lead rope and a packet of mints. 'I don't know. It's massage oil. Does it matter what it is?'

As she turned to look at him he wondered if this was the moment when she'd make some last-minute excuse and pull out. But, no—removing the cork, she sniffed the liquid inside the bottle.

'It certainly smells like muscle relaxant.' Upending the bottle, she rubbed some between her thumb and fingers. 'And I think there are emollients in here too. I don't think it matters where it comes from, just so long as it works…' Her grey gaze held his steadily.

'Then you'd better get started,' he said.

She was right. He had nothing to lose. Let Maxie try her hocus-pocus on his leg. The risk of embarrassment to him was hugely outweighed by the thought of her dark head bent over him as she worked diligently with those tiny hands in an attempt to ease his pain—an attempt that would fail, but still…

'Well?' he prompted. 'It's time for you to put your technique to the test.'

Putting a towel on the lounger, to protect it, she indicated that he must stretch out on top of it. 'I'm going to warm the oil first,' she explained.

He had to admit that after so long a drought the sight of Maxie warming massage oil in her tiny hands was a provocation too far. Grabbing a towel, he covered himself with it. 'Do your worst,' he said, and then he closed his eyes to blot out the sight of both Maxie and his scarred leg.

What madness had brought her to this point? Maxie wondered as her oiled hands hovered above Diego's spectacular form. Telling Diego to relax was a joke when she was the one most in need of stress relief. The thought of touching him as intimately and as firmly as she must was a daunting prospect. But exciting too.

'I'm ready,' he prompted.

'Good.' And now she must ignore him and concentrate on what she had to do. She had helped her mother, but could she help Diego? *She had to help him.* Tugging a cushion off one of the other loungers, she put it on the floor at his side and knelt down.

'The injury is here,' Diego said, pointing to a place just below his knee. 'But it seems to affect all my leg right up to—'

She cut him off. 'I'll find it.' Closing her eyes, she inhaled deeply and began to work.

'Don't you need to see what you're doing?'

'Please be quiet.' She said this calmly, then explained

in the same soothing tone, 'If I close my eyes and concentrate it allows my senses to come into play. If you talk, I'm distracted.'

She heard him shift position restlessly. Diego didn't like to be told what to do. She was certain no one had ever told him to be quiet, other than perhaps his siblings, but as he relaxed and the stillness of the room enveloped them both she began to feel the resistance of damaged flesh and muscle beneath her fingers and worked with more confidence.

He couldn't believe he was allowing Maxie to do this. Struggling to relax, he knew that if she proved even one iota less than good he would shrug her off and never forget this intrusion into his private world. Dissatisfaction at being so slow to heal was steadily eating away at him without this interference from her.

'I'm not hurting you, am I?' she asked him as he flinched with self-loathing.

'No,' he snapped as she hit a tender spot.

Maxie's small hands were surprisingly strong, but then he remembered the heavy ropes she'd tossed to shore. She might be small, but in determination Maxie was not to be underestimated. Against the odds, he began to relax. He stared down at her dark, silky head as she worked. There was something about her touch, her scent, her calming approach, her very presence when he had spent so much time alone, that made her intriguingly different—and incredibly, beneath her skilful fingers, he felt his damaged muscles begin to yield and loosen. Having lived with pain since the accident, his relief was indescribable. Closing his eyes, he rested back against the cushioned headrest…

'Does that feel better?'

He couldn't believe he'd been asleep, or that her voice had wakened him.

'Well?' she prompted. 'Has it helped?'

He flexed his leg and could hardly believe there was just a low, throbbing ache where so recently there had been acute, stabbing pain. And the dull throb was probably due to the force of Maxie's fingers. 'It's a lot better,' he admitted.

'Well, don't look so surprised. If you patronise me I won't do it again.'

His mouth tugged in the first real smile. 'I shall consider myself chastened, Señorita Parrish.'

'You do that,' she advised. 'I'm going to wash my hands now.'

He caught hold of her wrist as she moved away and had the satisfaction of hearing her suck in a sharp breath. She stood trembling and aware as he held her, reminding him of one of his wild ponies. When they were first captured and brought to him they averted their gaze just as she was doing now, as if to look at him would be an admission that they wanted to stay. He felt how vulnerable she was beneath his huge fist, and how delicate her bones were. He could feel her pulse fluttering beneath the skin and felt some primal urge to protect her. For Maxie's sake he let her go.

She felt light-headed as she walked the length of the swimming pool on her way to the changing rooms. And that wasn't just the Diego effect—which was disturbing enough in itself. Her mother had always said Maxie had healing hands, and though Maxie had laughed at this suggestion sessions did take a lot out of her. She could only describe it as her own strength pouring into someone else. How did Diego feel about it? Why had he caught hold of her wrist? He had let her go again, she remembered wryly.

She took her time washing her hands. Closing her

eyes, she prepared herself for a return to a world with Diego Acosta in it and a wedding planner with an increasingly bad habit of straying from her brief. But at least she'd had good news to give Holly. Palacio Acosta had the best facilities for a wedding that Maxie had ever seen.

By the time she returned to the side of the pool Diego was standing on his good leg, flexing the other. 'Does your leg still feel better?' she said, hoping there hadn't been some unexpected reversal.

The dark gaze reached deep inside her. 'There is some improvement,' Diego admitted. A faint, attractive smile played around his lips, making a crease in his cheek. 'Same time tomorrow?' he suggested, pulling on his jeans.

She quickly averted her gaze and stared over his head. 'I'll see if I can fit you in,' she said.

'You do that.' Diego's dark eyes were amused as he fastened his belt. 'Or we could run a barter system,' he suggested, tugging a polo shirt over his head. 'I teach you to ride. You work on my leg?'

'Why not?' she said, still dwelling on his naked torso, covered now—unfortunately. 'That sounds fair.' And totally insane.

'I'd better find you a good ride,' he said, with the attractive crease back in his cheek.

'You better had,' she agreed.

And there it would have ended, with a good bargain made, had she not been trying so hard not to look at Diego when she walked past him. If she had been paying any attention to where she was going instead of avoiding his glance she wouldn't have tripped over the leg of the lounger and he wouldn't have been forced to catch her.

'Careful.' His face was only a breath away.

'Thank you,' she said, pulling away as if he had burned her.

'My pleasure,' Diego murmured, with a great deal too much insight in his voice and in his eyes for Maxie's liking.

This was like trying to take on the forces of nature single-handed, she concluded. Her heart was pounding a tattoo, and if she couldn't trust herself to behave what hope was there? But instead of taking things further as Diego so easily could have done, he let go of her arm and stood back to let her pass.

He wanted her. His hunting instinct was in full flood, but his instinct also told him to keep her safe. From him. He wanted to thank her for bringing him relief from pain, but he knew where that would lead. And he could sense that Maxie was vulnerable. In business she had all the confidence you would expect, together with the skills necessary to succeed, but in her personal life… He knew nothing about her personal life, except that she was innocence personified compared to him. What was she hiding? he wondered as he stared into her cool grey eyes.

Damn it. She hated being on the back foot. Diego had almost certainly guessed how much she had wanted him to kiss her.

'Are you coming?' he said, holding the door.

To buy time, she grabbed a couple of towels and waved them at him. She needed a moment. But she couldn't keep him waiting all day… 'Excuse me,' she said politely when she reached the door. The open space with Diego in it was far too small to pass without brushing against him.

'Excuse *me,*' he replied, but instead of moving away he moved in.

Catching her close, he smiled into her eyes, and with such exquisite confidence she could only gasp as he brushed her lips with his. And then he proceeded to tease her mercilessly with kisses to her neck, before pulling back as if to study the effect. He must have known she was lost. Closing her eyes, she pressed her palms flat against Diego's chest. Two could play at this game. She slowly traced the map of muscle to his neck and then linked her hands behind his head. Opening her eyes she found him smiling down at her.

'Maxie,' he murmured in a faintly chastening tone.

'Yes?' she whispered.

Taking hold of her hands, he gently drew them down again.

'Don't tease me,' she warned, ready to push all her past failures aside in the hope of achieving one perfect moment.

'Is that a challenge?' Diego asked, drawing her attention to his lips.

A dam burst inside her. Pressing against him, she reached up. Locking her hands behind his neck she exclaimed with relief when Diego's grip tightened. Dipping his head, he brushed her lips with his. Parting them with his tongue, he searched deep. It was a fiery exchange, as if she filled some empty part of him. He certainly fulfilled every one of her wishes. A wild sound escaped her throat when his hands first touched her breasts, and she shivered with desire when he caressed them with a tenderness that amazed her. He chafed her erect nipples until she could hardly breathe and every part of her was on fire for him. Her lips were bruised and swollen from his kisses—she loved his taste, his warm, clean-man scent. The urge to battle Diego's strength and share his passion consumed her, and uttering his name in a half-sob of desperation she thrust her hips greedily against the brutal thrust of his erection.

'Maxie—' It took her a good few moments to realise that everything had changed and that Diego was gently disentangling himself. She was lost in a world of sensation until he held her at arm's length to whisper, 'Enough…'

What had she done wrong? Why had he kissed her in the first place? Why respond to her at all if only to draw back now? And then, in the most humiliating and provocative of gestures, he reached out to stroke her hair, as if he could tame her like one of his ponies, or pacify her like a child. 'Don't,' she warned, pulling back.

'Don't you think I know?' he said, holding her firmly in front of him. 'Don't you think I can read you like a book?'

'What do you know?' she asked, outraged.

'You can't use me to practise on.'

'Of all the arrogant—'

'You haven't enjoyed sex in the past,' Diego said, ignoring her, 'and you want to know what it would be like. So what am I supposed to do about it? Throw you to the ground and ravish you? Is that really what you want?'

She had to wait until her breathing steadied before she could trust herself to speak. By then she was ready to accept that Diego had only responded to the signals she'd sent him and that she couldn't blame him for that any more than she could blame herself for wanting him.

She had to calm down and pull this back. How else could she continue working with Diego to make Holly's wedding day the best it could be?

'I'll see you at the house.' Diego said this in an impressively normal voice and he stood well clear of the doorway.

'Sure.' She knew she should be relieved he could turn it off so easily and knew she must do the same. 'I expect

I'll see you at supper,' she managed in her usual businesslike voice, as if she *hadn't* just flung herself at him. 'You go ahead. I'll gather up the rest of the things here.' Along with her senses, she hoped.

Diego walked off in the direction of the stables while Maxie clung to the fact that he had seemed to take their encounter very much in his stride. Not so good was discovering she was the type of woman he found so easy to resist. She couldn't pretend that didn't hurt—especially when every part of her had just woken up to the most amazing possibilities.

Diego was seething with anger, all directed at himself. He had ignored every one of his self-imposed warnings and paid for that with the discovery that just being close to Maxie was enough to rock his self-control. He was in the barn now, walking down the line of stalls, searching for the soothing effect the horses always had on him. Today it eluded him. He and Maxie lived different lives. Making love to her would be the easiest thing in the world, but a brief period of elation would be followed by regret. And what form would that regret take for Maxie? Hadn't he done enough damage in his life? For him, regret would only involve more self-loathing, knowing he had taken something pure and good, just because he could, and trashed it. He was bad news and Maxie deserved better. The animal inside him might be clamouring to be fed, but the man he was said no.

Maxie spent the next week working as hard as she could on Holly's behalf. She worked pretty hard at avoiding Diego too. When she had to meet up with him to work on his leg she made sure it was always under Maria's watchful eye. Diego wanted her to continue the treatment, and Maxie had to prove to herself that she could. What had happened in the pool house couldn't be allowed to interfere with his treatment when they could both see signs of improvement.

Maxie had decided that the answer in the long term was to train Maria, and ask Maria to pass on the knowledge to whoever could help Diego at his next port of call.

One evening, when she arrived in the kitchen, she found him pacing up and down impatiently. 'You're here at last,' he said, throwing her one of his black looks.

'Yes, sir,' she murmured dryly.

'I want you to come outside,' he said.

She looked at Maria for clues, but Maria just smiled at her and shrugged, as if to say Maxie would have to wait and see. The first thing she noticed when she stepped outside was the huge bonfire. 'What are you burning?'

'Can't you guess?' Diego demanded as he matched his stride to hers.

'Your cane!' One of the stable lads was stoking the fire with it. But as she tried to grab it Diego stopped her. '*Gracias,* Maxie,' he said, staring into her eyes.

She went blank for a moment, seeing nothing but him, and then Maria was hugging her and the groom was laughing as he fed the fire with more branches. 'You don't need your cane!' she exclaimed as the penny dropped.

'I knew you'd catch on eventually.' Diego's eyes were dark and amused.

'But what a massive turning point. This is wonderful!'

'You have no idea,' he agreed, turning serious.

'I do have some,' Maxie argued quietly.

'But I still get my treatment,' Diego threw back at her as he turned for the house.

'So what about my riding lessons?' she called after him.

Diego stopped dead in his tracks. That was a very nice

back view, she thought, wondering if Maxie Parrish and danger were joined at the hip these days.

'We start tomorrow,' he said, slowly turning to face her.

'Suits me,' she agreed, playing it as cool as he had.

Diego's recovery was all she cared about, but with that embarrassing encounter at the pool house still fresh in her mind she was going to have a word with Maria. Linking arms with the housekeeper, she outlined her plan.

'I'm ready for my treatment,' Diego announced, the moment Maxie walked through the door.

He was sprawled back on the chair where he usually sat when she massaged his leg, with his powerful arms stretched across the back of it as he regarded her through half-closed eyes. The slight smile on his face only proved how right she was to make some changes.

'There's been a change of plan,' she announced.

'Oh?' Diego demanded, instantly suspicious.

'Sí, Señor!' Maria exclaimed enthusiastically, bounding forward. 'Today I am to perform your massage!'

'What?' Diego's eyes were points of steel, but Maria quickly came between them and lost no time getting to work.

'I won't always be with you,' Maxie explained, as Maria pummelled and rubbed with all the fierce efficiency of a champion bread-maker. 'And I'm sure you'll agree that in Maria I couldn't have a better deputy. She'll pass on everything I've taught her to the next person, and so on…'

Diego's gritted teeth suggested Maxie would pay for this.

CHAPTER SEVEN

'SO, YOU'RE frightened of me?' Diego observed—a little smugly, Maxie thought—when Maria had left them.

'Rubbish,' Maxie protested, concentrating on loading the dishwasher. She had offered to clear up, knowing how busy Maria was. She had taken up enough of the good-hearted housekeeper's time already.

'You can't trust yourself to touch me,' Diego mocked as he reclined in his chair.

'You wish,' she murmured under her breath.

'Why else would you deputise Maria?' Diego challenged.

'You're going to trip over that ego of yours one day,' Maxie observed coolly, stretching up on tiptoe to put some bowls on the top shelf. 'The only reason I asked Maria to help is so you won't be left stranded when I leave.'

'When are you planning to leave?'

Diego's sharp tone surprised her. 'My work here is almost done,' she pointed out, turning to face him. 'All the suppliers I need are in place for the wedding, and I've got a full programme of events planned. I'm only waiting for Holly's go-ahead.'

'Great,' Diego said, without enthusiasm.

Springing out of the chair, he stalked to the window

to stare out. She couldn't leave. There was too much unfinished business between them. He wanted to know more about Maxie—who she was, and why she was so reticent about talking about her family. He wanted to unearth Peter Parrish, and there was always that faint chance that Maxie might be able to lead Diego to him. Either way, he wasn't ready to let her go.

'Good,' he said, changing his plans as he swung round. 'It's time for me to go too. I've been here long enough, and thanks to you my leg is almost better. I'm match-fit and my horse has recovered. What point is there in staying?' He shrugged, a little pleased to see the surprise in Maxie's eyes.

She had put her challenge out there, hoping, she supposed, that Diego would talk her out of it, only to learn that he wasn't going to. So this extraordinary adventure was over.

Moving things round at the sink so he couldn't see the disappointment on her face, she resigned herself to a life of fantasy. She had seized life briefly, but then had taken fright and let it go again. 'It will be good to get back,' she said brightly.

'You're a terrible liar, Maxie.'

'I always tell the truth,' she argued as Diego's lips tugged in a smile.

'Do you?' he said.

'Yes,' she said hotly.

'I like that,' he commented, angling his stubble-blackened chin to stare at her.

'What?' she said, still churning inside.

'I like the way you've changed since you first arrived on the island. I like the way the buttoned-up business-woman has lost her bit and bridle on the island.'

Yes, but *he* didn't want to take advantage of it. 'It's

just a shame you haven't changed from the charmer who met me on the dock,' she countered.

'I think we've both changed,' Diego argued thoughtfully. 'But don't change the subject, Maxie. We're talking about you—not me. I want to know more about you.'

'Like what?' she said defensively.

'I'd like to know why you shrink back into that same defensive shell every time you take a call from England.'

'I don't!'

'Don't you?'

She exclaimed with shock when Diego dragged her close. 'So who is the real Maxie Parrish?' he demanded. 'Is it the buttoned-up businesswoman with the weight of the world on her shoulders? Or is it the firebrand who tore up the road on my bike?'

She tried to fight him as he kissed her, savagely and without break. Balling up her fists, she thrust them against his chest, only to encounter solid rock, but Diego broke away as quickly as he had claimed her.

'When are you going to be honest with yourself, Maxie?'

She was still shaking, her hand across her mouth as if that could hide the proof her arousal. How could she have allowed this to happen again? She stared at Diego with furious eyes, wanting to throw a punch at his arrogant mouth. She wanted to spit in his black, piratical eyes. She was panting and furious and—and inconveniently aroused, Maxie admitted silently as she fought for control. And while the urge to pummel the living daylights out of Diego was certainly one option, he had lit something inside her that refused to be extinguished.

Grabbing hold of him, she yanked him close and took what she wanted, and as much as *she* wanted, for as long as she wanted, until with a fierce, angry sound she let him go.

'Dios!' Diego murmured, wiping his mouth with the back of his hand as he stared at her in amazement. 'I knew I was right—but not that right!'

'Don't flatter yourself,' she flashed.

Turning abruptly, she left the room.

What now? Maxie asked herself, furious at her loss of self-control as she stalked across the courtyard on her way to who knew where. By the time she reached the fence surrounding the paddock where the horses were grazing she was ready to admit she had actually followed her inclinations for once.

Climbing up a rung of the fence, she leaned her chin on her arms. Actually *living* life wasn't half bad, she reflected, tentatively examining her lips with the tip of her tongue, though perhaps in future she should spend a little more time thinking about the consequences of her actions before putting them into practice. Diego had turned the tables on her pretty comprehensively, leaving her lips with a swollen and throbbing reminder of how thoroughly she'd been kissed. Plus, he was right again, Maxie conceded with a rueful sigh. There was definitely passion lurking inside her somewhere.

'Now you've got that out of your system, are you ready for your first riding lesson?'

A lightning strike couldn't have shocked her more. Wheeling round, she took in Diego's dark, amused gaze at a glance. 'Riding lesson?'

'Unless you don't feel up to it?' he said, lips pressing down in a mocking reminder of her exhaustive assault on him.

She held the stare with a cool one of her own. 'I'm up to it,' she said, wishing the imprint of Diego's hands on her body hadn't left quite such a searing brand.

'I have just the horse for you,' he said, smiling pleasantly, which in itself was enough to make her suspicious.

'Would that be a stamping stallion to cart me off? Or a donkey?'

'You'll just have to rely on my judgement,' he said, and with one last amused look he vaulted the fence into the field.

Maxie studied Diego's powerful, athletic body as his easy stride ate up the distance across the field. Riding lessons had never been like this before. He returned with a mild grey pony and, tacking up, showed her how to hold the reins. Cupping his hands, he offered her a leg up. She was careful not to touch any part of him she didn't have to as she lowered herself gently onto the saddle.

'Are you listening, Maxie?' Diego demanded after they had been walking for a while.

'Of course I am.' She dragged her gaze from his wild, thick hair.

'Then loosen the reins,' he said impatiently.

She did so as she took in the wide sweep of his shoulders. Diego was such a big man. If a man that size made love to her would she enjoy it, or would he prove too big for her?

'Put your heels down,' Diego rapped in a voice that definitely suggested she had missed something. 'Aren't you listening to a word I say?' he demanded.

'I'm hanging on your every word,' she said solemnly, and for the pony's sake she would try. She was enjoying the gentle rocking movement of the horse—enjoying the chance to be close to Diego too, without the need for combat or conversation.

'You're a good pupil,' he remarked when he drew the pony to a halt.

'With an excellent teacher—even if he is a little impatient.'

Diego's glance sent heat streaking through her. She should know better than to challenge him. 'Well,' she said, turning in the saddle to gaze back at the house, 'I should be getting back.'

'I thought you said you had finished your work?'

'I have, but—'

'You have calls to take?' Diego suggested.

Warning signals flattened her enjoyment of the last hour. 'I'm due to ring Holly with a report,' she said quickly.

Diego released the pony into the field, and they were walking back to the house when he started to ask her more questions about her family. She didn't want to lie, but she wasn't going to betray her father's trust, either. 'There's just me and my father.'

'And that's it?' Diego pressed, frowning. 'No husband? No partner? No special boyfriend?'

She laughed. 'No one. Don't look so surprised. It works for me.'

'I think what you mean is it's all work for you,' Diego remarked dryly.

Just when she had relaxed into a laugh, he went on, 'So, no brothers or sisters, Maxie?'

'That's it,' she confirmed. 'You only think it's odd because you grew up in a crowd. What was that like, by the way?' she added, determined to steer the conversation away from herself.

'Noisy and chaotic.' Diego shrugged. 'Nacho brought us up. We gave him a hard time. No privacy—'

'No wonder you like it here,' she said. 'And it must have been fun when your friends came round—all this space?'

'Yes, it was,' Diego agreed gruffly. 'So what about your father, Maxie? Do you see a lot of him?'

'No,' she said quickly. Too fast. Alarm bells were ringing loud and clear now. Why the sudden interest in her father? She had done everything she could think of to protect his anonymity—booking him into a private nursing home under a different name where the staff was both loyal and discreet. 'Why are you so interested in my father?'

'Just curious.'

Her father's bungled business interests had never stretched to South America, of that much she was sure. He'd been ill for years, so he could never have met Diego—unless Diego had been just out of school.

'His name isn't Peter, is it?' Diego prompted lightly.

Maxie's heart stopped, and then began racing uncontrollably. 'No. Why?' That was not the name her father went under at the nursing home. She hated lying to Diego, but tell one person a secret and they told the next one, who told the next one, and in no time the whole world knew.

'I knew someone once with the surname Parrish,' he said with a dismissive shrug. 'That's all.'

'Common name,' she confirmed. She didn't know a lot about her father's business interests, other than to say he'd used to run a small and not very successful investment outfit. She couldn't imagine a wealthy South American from a polo playing family having anything to do with such a small-time broker, and it was a relief when Diego started to talk about a swimming machine for horses that strengthened their legs.

But just when she was relaxing into that topic he threw another curve ball. 'So you don't like talking about your home life, Maxie?'

'Only because there's nothing to tell…' Diego was way too perceptive, and she only now realised that her hands were clenched so tightly she was in danger of drawing blood from her palms.

When they got back to the house he made some excuse to put some space between them. He wanted to call his investigator. He had lots of gaps to fill in now.

'Thanks for the riding lesson,' Maxie said when they parted in the courtyard.

The blush in her cheeks suggested Maxie was remembering more than riding his horse. It made him keener than ever to find out the truth, and for his investigator to confirm that Maxie had nothing to do with Peter Parrish. She stood up to him like no other woman apart from his sister, and he liked that. He liked it a lot. In fact, Maxie Parrish was turning out to be the most intriguing and complex woman he had ever met.

If only he could bury the past once and for all…

He was confident Ruiz was right. There were countless people with the surname Parrish—and he hated the dark, twisted part of him that said nothing in life was ever that easy.

Diego's mouth firmed even as his heart lifted when Maxie walked into the kitchen that evening. He stared at her, hunting for something dark beneath those clear grey eyes, but there was nothing outwardly to suggest that Maxie might have any connection with Peter Parrish. He had still had no answers from his PI yet, but despite Ruiz's belief that the two were unrelated Diego still held a niggling doubt he could not explain.

'Good evening, Diego.'

'Good evening, Maxie…'

Putting down his newspaper, he registered the smell of

soap and some light scent she was wearing. Fresh jeans and a long-sleeved white top made her look young, casual and relaxed. Her hair was still a little damp from the shower, and the thought of burying his face in the silky flesh above her shoulder was intoxicating. There were so many ways he could put his dark thoughts behind him…

He settled for leaning back in his chair and putting the first part of his plan into action. 'I imagine you have plenty of work waiting for you in London?'

'Yes,' she said.

Actually, there was quite a gap in her schedule, Maxie silently acknowledged. Not knowing what she would find when she reached the island, she had built in some extra time to allow for a change of venue had that proved necessary.

'Good.' Diego's lips pressed down with approval. 'I'm very pleased to hear it.'

Was he? Something in Diego's voice wasn't quite right. This thought was followed by a shiver of foreboding for which she had no explanation.

'Supper,' he announced as Maria came bustling between them with steaming plates of hot food.

'Yes,' Maxie murmured, accepting everything was indeed normal as she shook herself round.

He spent another restless night making plans. Keeping Maxie close was number one on his agenda. He wanted to know more about her, but he also acknowledged that he wanted her in his bed.

Fortunately, Holly provided him with the perfect excuse when she rang him first thing. 'The charity event?' he murmured, his mind racing as a plan began to take shape in his head. 'Of course I haven't forgotten about it.' Ideas were coming thick and fast now. 'Of course I'll be home. I can't organise it from a distance, can I?' he said, dangling some tasty bait.

'But you know someone who can?' Holly prompted with a smile, supplying him with exactly the right cue.

'Do you mean Maxie?' he said, injecting surprise in his voice.

'Who else but Maxie?' Holly demanded, laughing at his apparent slowness to catch on.

'I suppose I could approach her…' He said this thoughtfully. 'We'll just have to hope she can work our charity event into her schedule.'

'If you ask her she will. I know she will. Please ask her, Diego!'

'All right,' he agreed indulgently. 'For you, I will.'

Maxie woke slowly and cautiously, and then groaned when she remembered everything that had happened the day before. Touching her lips before she had even opened her eyes, she hummed in rueful confirmation that they were still swollen, and that the area round them was still abraded where Diego's sharp black stubble had raked her skin. She reached for the pot of moisturiser by the side of her bed. She couldn't possibly afford an affair with Diego. She'd have to start buying face cream in bucketloads.

There was no chance she was going to have an affair with Diego, Maxie told herself firmly as she got out of bed. She was a realist, who was going to pack and get ready to go home.

Showering and dressing as fast as she could in T-shirt and jeans, she raced downstairs. A couple more photographs and one more report to the bride and she was done—out of here with her reputation more or less intact. By some miracle, Maxie concluded, as her body warmed just at the thought that Diego might be around.

Maria greeted her gaily with, *'Buenos dias, señorita.'*

'Buenos dias, Maria.'

'Señor Diego is waiting for you outside.'

'He is?' Maxie's heart began to thunder as she glanced out of the kitchen window.

'Your riding lesson,' Maria trilled.

'I thought I had one yesterday?'

'Practice makes perfect,' Maria assured her with a twinkling smile.

Maxie wasn't so sure about that. Grabbing a piece of toast and an apple, she paused to give Maria a hug. 'You're the best,' she said, giving the smiling housekeeper a squeeze before taking her concerns outside. Taking a deep breath, she steadied herself as she stared up at the man on the back of the impossibly fired-up stallion. 'Good morning, Diego.'

'Good morning, Maxie.'

Hmm. Something wasn't right here. Diego was holding the mild grey pony on a lead rope at his side, while his mighty stallion pawed the ground and snorted imperiously. All right so far. It was just that look on his face—confident and…sexy. She laughed when the grey gelding turned a patient face towards her as if to say, *These guys are a pain, aren't they?*

'Yes, they are,' she said, stroking the grey pony's velvet muzzle.

'Who is what?" Diego demanded suspiciously as his stallion's bridle chinked an impatient warning.

'You don't need to know,' Maxie murmured, resting her cheek against the pony's warm, firm neck for a soothing moment.

'Are you ready for your second lesson?'

'As I'll ever be,' Maxie agreed, wondering where this one would lead.

'Good. And I've got something else for you to consider.' Springing down, he looped the stallion's reins over his arm and helped her to mount up.

'Tell me?' she prompted once she was settled in the saddle.

'I've got another job for you—if you want it?'

She couldn't afford to turn work down. And she'd do almost anything to spend some more time with Diego, Maxie realised. Which was both dangerous and absurd.

'We hold a big charity event in Argentina every year at the *estancia,*' Diego explained as they started off down the path.

Maxie's mind automatically switched to business, and was soon filled with plans to ship things out to South America, along with the additional complication of sourcing dependable operatives without actually meeting them. *Argentina...*

'I take it you're pleased with my work?' She had to bat away seductive images of the wild pampas, and everything that went with it.

'Holly's very pleased with the work you've done here,' Diego explained. 'She's passed on that enthusiasm to the family. They want you to run things for us—as I do.'

'How can I help?' she said, desperately hanging on to a hank of mane as Diego urged their horses into a trot.

'Think Mardi Gras—parades, floats, stalls, fireworks and music...lots of music,' he called back over his shoulder, encouraging their horses to go faster.

'Mardi Gras is a little out of my range,' Maxie admitted hanging on for dear life.

'That's something that can be addressed, surely?' Diego countered.

'Can we slow down if we're going to discuss this? It's hard to talk when my teeth are clattering like castanets.'

'Of course,' Diego agreed with an amused look. 'Though all I need to know at this point is do you want the job or not, Maxie?'

'I'd love to pitch for it,' she admitted. With most of the loose ends tied up here, there *was* that gap in her schedule.

'I think you can take it you're the preferred supplier.'

'That's great.' She could hardly refuse another big job. 'I've just got one reservation.'

'Name it.'

'Will it include a polo match?'

'Of course.' Diego laughed. 'But we'll handle that. You just have to do everything else.'

'So, let me get this straight. You want me to arrange a charity event in Argentina the same way I've handled Holly's wedding—that is to say by e-mail and by phone?' She was already setting up the building blocks in her mind, Maxie realised. Apart from her personal concerns she would never refuse to help a worthy cause unless it was absolutely unavoidable.

'I was thinking of something rather more hands-on than that,' Diego admitted, slanting a look at her.

'Like what?' Maxie's antennae were already pinging warnings.

'You'd have to come to Argentina so you can see for yourself what has to be done.'

Her heart was banging in her chest, and it took her a jolting bounce or two before she was ready to speak. 'I'm afraid I can't,' she said then.

'Why not?' Diego demanded.

'Because my responsibilities keep me at home—I have a business to run.'

'Which you have proved you can run from anywhere in the world. Argentina is hardly as isolated as this island.'

And it *was* a great opportunity. So why did she feel that same shiver of apprehension, as if invisible walls were closing round her?

'You won't even have to sail a boat to get there,' Diego was telling her. 'I'll fly you there in the jet.'

'How exciting.' Under other circumstances she might have been overwhelmed by Diego's offer—but right now? She would be on his territory, and a long way from home.

But then he hit her with the clincher. 'Holly will be in Argentina at the same time as you, and as she travels the world with my brother this might be the only chance you two get to meet face to face before the wedding. My family needs you in Argentina, Maxie. And don't forget I need my therapist,' he added with a grin. 'Come on,' he pressed. 'Why the hesitation? Is it really so hard to visit Buenos Aires and the pampas *and* earn lots of money? You can't let us down,' he added, baiting her with his dark, intense stare. 'I've told my brothers all about your magic hands and they can't wait to meet you.'

Oh, great. The thought of meeting the Acostas *en masse* was daunting enough without that. Yes, but how many years of fees at the nursing home would a commission like this pay? Could she afford to refuse Diego's offer if it secured her father's future?

'You're making good progress with your riding,' Diego observed, forcing her back to full attention. 'I think you're safe to go a little faster.'

'No,' she exclaimed.

'Do you mean the riding or the event?' Diego called over his shoulder.

'I'm happy to accept the job,' she called back tensely.

'Excellent. I'm sure you won't disappoint us, Maxie.'

'I never accept a commission unless I'm sure I can exceed a client's expectations.'

But this time she might have bitten off more than she could chew, Maxie conceded when she saw the expression on Diego's face.

CHAPTER EIGHT

MAXIE felt as if the common sense she had lived by all her life was being jangled out of every one of her bones as her pony picked up speed to keep up with Diego's stallion.

'You'll find it easier if you move up and down like this,' Diego said as he demonstrated a rising trot. 'Keep it easy and relaxed, Maxie. Roll your hips like me.'

That settled it. 'I don't need to come to Argentina to do this job for you.'

'Of course you do,' Diego argued firmly.

'But I can organise everything from a distance,' Maxie protested. Accepting Diego's invitation would be madness, she realised, trying not to watch his muscular hips effortlessly thrusting back and forth.

'How can you possibly imagine the scale of the celebrations we're planning unless you come over?' he said.

True, Maxie conceded worriedly. So it would have to be a short visit—just long enough to take a look-see and get out with her heart intact. 'It shouldn't take me too long,' she mused out loud.

'Good. I'm glad that's settled,' Diego agreed.

'Can we slow down now?'

'I thought you liked speed?' Diego shouted back.

'I like control better,' she countered. And right now she was in danger of losing control of both the horse and her life. And that wasn't a situation she could allow to continue.

'Relax and it will all be fine,' Diego assured her, reining in alongside.

Was he talking about the horse or the charity event? But wasn't she a co-ordinator of fabulous events for other people to enjoy? This job in Argentina would take her business global, providing security for both Maxie and her father. She couldn't afford to turn it down. She'd call the nursing home as soon as they got back. Depending on the news on that front, she'd make a final decision. Caring for her father always posed a dilemma. If she didn't travel for her work she couldn't afford his fees at the nursing home, but when she travelled away from home she felt guilty.

'Stop dreaming, Maxie, and catch up.'

Diego had stopped beneath the sheltering canopy of a jacaranda tree. The frowzy purple blossom, dislodged by the wind, was drifting round him, creating a deceptively soft and dreamlike scene—but this was *business*, Maxie reminded herself as Diego explained that she would have the considerable weight of the Acosta name behind her in Argentina.

'I've done very well so far,' she said wryly, 'but I'd appreciate any help you can give me. A charity event on the scale you're proposing will need quite a bit of thinking about, and I want to check a few things before I give you my final answer.'

'Don't take too long,' Diego warned.

'Hey!' she protested, when he turned his horse and nudged it from a standstill into a canter and her horse followed.

'Have some confidence,' he called back. Maxie was a natural horsewoman. It was something in the hips. His lips tugged in a smile. He was enjoying this uncomplicated time together, but something told him it wouldn't last long.

The trip to Argentina went without a hitch. Maxie's contacts had been able to put her in touch with people in Buenos Aires, and the nursing home had given her the nod, so she was good to go. Diego had promised to introduce her to people who might be able to help her business further and was full of practical advice. There was no danger to her heart at all—which should have reassured her, but which left her with a niggling sense of regret.

The jet landed in brilliant sunshine, and her head was soon spinning with all the new sights and sounds. The thought of visiting not just Buenos Aires, the Paris of South America, but the pampas, with the most exciting man she had ever known, was exciting. She would soon grow accustomed to the seductive samba rhythms and the intoxicating scent of spice and heat and passion, Maxie reassured herself as Diego strolled towards a sleek black limousine.

So why the sense of doom approaching?

'Please excuse me, Maxie,' he said, fielding a call as they settled into the limousine with what seemed like acres of kidskin between them.

'No problem,' she murmured, knowing she would probably have to take quite a few business calls herself before they arrived at their destination.

One of the first things she noticed as they drove out of the airport was the colossal billboards lining the road. It was the first inkling she had of Diego's place in Argentina. The billboards featured the impossibly good-looking Acosta brothers. She recognised the groom, Ruiz, right away—smiling down with confidence. Diego's older brother, Nacho, appeared aloof. Kruz looked so laid back it was hard to imagine him in polo-warrior mode. And then there was Diego.

The same apprehension she'd felt when she got off the plane was back again, because Diego radiated danger. It was something in his eyes, Maxie concluded, glancing sideways at him. There were ghosts in Diego's life she couldn't begin to understand, and as theirs was a business relationship she could hardly ask him. He was still very much a mystery man, dangerously attractive and maybe dangerous to know. She wouldn't like to be his opponent on the polo field, or anywhere else for that matter, that was for sure.

'We'll be staying in Buenos Aires for a couple of nights,' he explained, stowing his phone. 'You'll get a chance to familiarise yourself with the city and with our usual suppliers. Then we'll travel to the *estancia* and you'll get the chance to see your first polo match. A friendly with Nero.'

Maxie laughed. 'Is there such a thing as a friendly polo match?'

Diego's mouth tugged fractionally. 'You'll soon find out.'

'Nero must be a good friend?'

'One of my closest. I trust him to tell me—'

Diego stopped and stared away, but she knew what he had been about to say. Nero would tell Diego if he was up to playing at international level. 'Either way it will be an important match,' she said.

'The most important,' Diego confirmed.

He didn't need to tell her that the chance to play at international level again meant everything to him. She knew as soon as he could after the accident Diego had been back on a horse, and he'd been training relentlessly ever since. His leg was so much better now she was sure he had nothing to worry about.

After they had been driving for a while he asked the driver to pull over. *'Empanadas,'* he said, pointing to a street stall. 'Delicious little savoury pastries,' he explained. 'You'll love them, Maxie. I'm starving. You must be too.'

'I'm always ready to eat,' she agreed with a smile. Diego was like a different man in Argentina. She should stop with the niggling doubts and make the most of this opportunity to do business with a man like no other. It would be something to hold on to when she went home to men with office pallor and perpetual sniffles, though she couldn't help wishing that Diego had shown some inclination to kiss her again.

She laughed when he bought up half the stall. 'This is crazy,' she said as he shrugged, but the tiny pastries were delicious, and it was fun being together and relaxed for a change. She was amazed by how quickly people recognised Diego, and autograph-hunters were soon clustering round. 'How do you cope?' she asked him when they got back in the car.

'I owe my success to these people,' he said, dipping his head to wave out of the window. 'I play to win for them.'

But when they drove off again, and a shadow crossed his face, she knew Diego was worrying that he might not live up to everyone's expectations. He was returning to polo after a long time out through injury.

'I'll work on your leg right up to the match,' she promised impulsively.

'I'm counting on it,' he said.

His dark, amused gaze made her heart thump like a jack-hammer. She was only doing a friend a favour, she reasoned, smoothing her jeans as an excuse to break eye contact. She had never risked getting too close to anyone, and she wasn't getting close now. None of her relationships had lasted—partly because she'd chosen the wrong men, but mostly because she had never forgotten the way her father had treated her mother. Yes, her father had changed when her mother had become ill, but it would have been nice for her mother to have had some happiness before that.

When Diego glanced at her, as if suspecting she was visiting some past regret, she only wished she could explain what she was thinking. But they weren't close enough for that—plus theirs was now a business relationship, and Diego had as many secrets as she did, Maxie suspected.

'We'll be staying at my apartment in the city,' he explained, providing a welcome distraction. 'You'll have your own suite of rooms, and can come and go as you like while you're in Buenos Aires.'

She had rather hoped Diego would show her round.

She pulled back when he suddenly wiped one firm thumb pad across the full swell of her bottom lip. 'Crumbs,' he explained.

The pastries, Maxie realised with embarrassment. 'Is that it? Or am I covered in crumbs?'

'I wouldn't know,' Diego murmured, his firm mouth tugging with amusement. 'I can only see those on your mouth.'

And now her face was burning. Diego had definitely relaxed since they'd landed. Was he intentionally turning up the heat?

Whatever was happening, she had to keep her feet on the ground. She had a job to do, and for all she knew Diego had a squad of girlfriends waiting in Buenos Aires with another team on standby at the *estancia.* A man like Diego Acosta would hardly be without a significant other.

An idea she should waste no time getting used to, Maxie concluded when their limousine stopped at a junction and a group of young girls, spotting Diego, started making remarks and frowning as they tried to work out who he was with. Maxie couldn't blame them for dismissing her. In his blue jeans, dark jacket and crisp white shirt, Diego looked like a film star—while if she was really lucky she might get a job sweeping the set. It was a relief when they drove off again.

'Tell me how I can help you while you're here?' Diego suggested, seemingly oblivious to all the attention.

Maxie thought for a moment before speaking. 'I'd like you to give me a taste of Buenos Aires.'

'I'll try to give you more than you expect.'

That was what she was afraid of. 'Like what?' she asked.

'I think you should wait and see. We'll drop our things off at the apartment and then I'll take you into town and you can pick up something special to wear tonight.'

'For what occasion?'

'Business, of course!' Diego laughed: a flash of white teeth against his tan.

This sounded like business of a type she was unfamiliar with, Maxie concluded.

Diego's apartment in the best part of town was off-the-scale fabulous. His penthouse occupied the entire top floor of an elegant historic building. When they'd reached it, in a private elevator with an ornate wrought-iron door, they stepped out into an airy lobby with a domed ceiling that wouldn't have looked out of place in the Vatican. Grand double doors at one end of this spacious hallway had just been swung wide by a smiling middle-aged woman.

'My housekeeper, Adriana,' Diego explained.

Adriana ushered Maxie into a light-filled world, packed with sleek modern furniture and the latest high-tech gizmos. Very Diego, Maxie thought as she took in the striking décor of stark white walls punctuated by vivid flourishes of modern art. Floor-to-ceiling windows in the living room took in both the new and the venerably old buildings that comprised the exciting cityscape of Buenos Aires.

'This is stunning,' Maxie exclaimed, looking around.

'I call it home.'

'Lucky you.' Diego was so confident and overwhelming, while she was…overwhelmed. She took in the pale leather sofas, smoky glass tables, and the stainless steel conversation pieces at a glance. There was everything here a wealthy man might need. She was relieved to hear that Adriana lived on site, as she had no intention of becoming another of the home comforts Diego so obviously took for granted.

'Adriana will show you to your room,' Diego explained. 'Please make yourself at home, Maxie.'

It might take more than a single visit to feel at home in a place like this, Maxie concluded as the smiling housekeeper led her down a stylish corridor lined with discreetly framed pen and ink drawings of polo ponies.

The suite of rooms would easily have gobbled up Maxie's small house in London with room to spare. There was a large bedroom with a walk-in wardrobe, as well as a sitting room and a fantastic cream marble bathroom. She'd take a quick shower and then go shopping, Maxie decided. She had to make a start on filling those wardrobes—not to mention the shoe rack. Well, if she tried really hard she might actually manage to fill one small corner…

'Do you have everything you need?'

She whirled around to find Diego at the door. 'Are you kidding?'

'Good. I'll leave you to settle in and then I'll take you into town. See you in the hall in half an hour?'

'Thank you.'

She couldn't pretend the thought of going out with Diego didn't make her pulse race. She took a long, hot shower and then changed into casual clothes.

When Diego turned the corner into the hall and walked towards her she had to accept that seeing him never got any easier. Diego had also taken a shower, and his thick black hair was still damp and curled attractively around his face and neck.

'I hope I'm all right dressed like this,' she said, indicating her jeans and flat shoes. 'I wasn't sure what to expect, but I thought if I'd be walking—'

'You look great,' he said, barely glancing at her as he walked to the door.

Diego had a sister so he probably blanked out fashion questions as a matter of course, but Maxie wondered if she had underplayed it. Diego was wearing jeans and a crisp white shirt again, but he always looked outstanding, while she felt like a little grey mouse standing next to a tiger.

She might have known Diego would drive a bright red Ferrari. She might have known the moment he stepped out of the building he would be mobbed. She took refuge in the car, not wanting to be subjected to another trial of brief and dismissive scrutiny.

'You should stay with me,' he said when he joined her moments later. 'Why did you run off like that?' Closing the door, he gunned the engine. 'I could have used some support.'

It took her a moment before she realised he was serious. It had never occurred to her that someone like Diego might need anything in the way of a boost. 'I'll be there for you next time,' she promised wryly.

'Make sure you are,' he said, slanting a glance at her before lowering his sunglasses. 'That's why I love the pampas. It's such a contrast to the city. I can be anonymous there—unless we have a match, of course.'

'Tell me more,' she encouraged. This was such a contrast to the dark, brooding man who had met her off the boat, and she was curious about Diego's life before the accident.

'We never appreciated the space on the pampas when we were young. My sister Lucia, in particular, positively loathed it. She always felt she was missing out on everything that was happening in Buenos Aires. But now?' He shrugged. 'I guess Lucia feels as we all do that the *estancia* is both our sanctuary and a playground where we all relax. We have one of the best polo pitches in the country,' he confided, as if this might come as a surprise to her.

'I can't wait to see it,' Maxie said, thinking how frighteningly close she felt to him suddenly. How was she supposed to remain safely on the outside looking in now?

She didn't *have* to risk her heart, Maxie told herself sensibly. There was such a thing as friendship. They could just be friends.

CHAPTER NINE

WHEN Diego dropped her off, he explained to Maxie that she was on the most exclusive shopping street in Buenos Aires. She would be spoiled for choice, Maxie realised, wondering where to begin. How incredible was this? Maxie Parrish, a girl who arranged things for other people, was suddenly at the centre of all things up-scale and fabulous. And better still—thanks to the success of her business—she could afford it.

But Maxie soon discovered that money wasn't the problem. Being treated as if girls who wore jeans and sneakers couldn't afford to breathe the air on this exclusive street was. After trudging round every shop to no avail, she gave up. Spotting a market, she thought, why not? Buenos Aires wasn't known as the Paris of South America for nothing. The relaxed sprawl of colourful stalls reminded Maxie of the Left Bank markets in Paris. You never know...she thought, crossing the road to explore.

Fortune favours the brave, Maxie mused as she picked out a flirty dress and some sandals to go with it. She had wanted to buy a pair of simple flip-flops, but the young stallholder had wagged a finger at her and picked out a pair of sexy heels. Maxie felt like a baby stork when she tried them on, but the stallholder insisted she must have them.

'You'll be dancing on the street tonight,' she assured Maxie.

Maxie couldn't picture Diego dancing on the street—though she would like to, Maxie mused as she added a shawl to her purchases in case it grew chilly that evening. With her shopping expedition over, she rang Diego, who had promised to pick her up as soon as she called.

'Where are you?' he said, answering at the first ring. 'Alto Palermo? Avenida Santa Fe?'

'No—close to the market,' she explained, giving general directions.

'What?' he exploded.

'Don't fuss—I can have a coffee until you get here.'

'Don't fuss?' Diego roared. 'Like anywhere else in the world, some parts of the city are safer than others.'

'And this part is perfectly safe,' Maxie insisted. 'For goodness' sake, Diego, I'm not a child. I run a company—'

'And you are a visitor in a foreign land,' he flashed.

'Are you mistaking me for a woman who has lost her way, as all the assistants in those posh boutiques seemed to think I had?' Before directing her to what those shop assistants had explained would be a more affordable part of town, Maxie remembered angrily.

'What are you talking about?' Diego demanded.

'The assistants who refused to serve me just because I'm wearing jeans and sneakers?' she blazed back, wondering where all this passion had been hiding. 'I've told you where I am,' she flashed as anger and humiliation battled inside her, 'and I've told you I'm going to have a coffee.'

'*Dios,* Maxie!' Diego rapped down the phone. 'You'd better tell me which café. And where it is.'

She hadn't found one yet. She gazed around, searching for inspiration. 'Tortoni's?'

'Don't move a step. I'm coming for you!' Diego roared, nearly shattering her eardrum.

'See you in the café—' Maxie stared at the silent receiver in her hand. Diego hadn't even given her a chance to cut the line. But as she prepared to cross the road it occurred to her that it *was* rather nice to have someone to care about what she did. She hadn't had that since her mother had died. She could look after herself, of course, having done so for most of her life, but that didn't stop Diego's protective streak being a nice thing about him. But he was only concerned to hear she had strayed from the safety of the main shopping area, Maxie reasoned as she stared up at the façade of what appeared to be a popular café. Diego would feel that same sense of responsibility for all his employees. She only had to think about Maria and Adriana to know that.

As the door of the café opened she was greeted by a gust of warm air and the pungent smell of coffee. The noisy interior was full of men hunched over coffee cups as if the inky brew was the elixir of life, and families noisily sharing platters of food with all age groups represented, their happy faces reminding Maxie of so many mixed bouquets as they nodded their heads in time to the music.

And what music! The insistent throb of tango instantly invaded her veins. Couples were dancing between the tables, their gazes fixed on each other as they moved in a way she had never imagined could be so earthy and yet so sophisticated. She could hardly bear to blink in case she missed anything as the waitress showed her to a table.

Maxie was so enthralled by the dancing she allowed her coffee to go cold, and only snapped to at the sound of screeching brakes. This was swiftly followed by the slam of a car door, and she wasn't the only one staring at the entrance as Diego stormed in. Her breath caught in her throat as his glance swept the room.

'Maxie,' he growled, heading straight for her.

Diego nodded to a waiter, who quickly pulled out a chair.

'Hello, Diego.' Maxie tried to remain cool as her heart thundered nineteen to the dozen. How could anyone look so gorgeous? How could anyone carry such an air of command? It was enough to transfix every man and woman in the place, she noticed—but then Diego wasn't just a famous polo player, he was a frighteningly charismatic man, whom she guessed every woman wanted to go to bed with, and every man longed to call friend.

But he was hers.

Well, sort of, Maxie reasoned, trying not to give way to the waves of longing washing over her. She stared down in bewilderment at the crumbly little pastries on the plate in front of her, which the waiter had just put down without her ordering them.

'Eat,' Diego instructed. 'I'll watch your mouth.'

Trying to read Diego's thoughts was always a non-starter. Was he teasing her, or was that a threat?

'Eat,' he repeated while she was still trying to work this out. And with that he turned away as if she was of no further interest to him.

'Excuse me, *señorita*?'

She glanced up to find one of the men who had been dancing the tango leaning over the table, trying to attract her attention. 'Yes?'

'You are not dancing?'

'No,' she agreed, wiping her mouth on her napkin.

'I would like to dance with you.'

Diego swung round so fast the table rocked. 'The *señorita* is with me,' he barked.

'Pardon, señor,' the man said with a bow, giving way.

Diego was interested now. He was so interested she couldn't say, 'I was going to refuse…' fast enough before he moved his chair back and stood up.

'You should have told me you wanted to dance, Maxie.'

'But I don't. In fact, I can't dance,' she explained.

'Why not?' Diego frowned.

Conscious that everyone in the café was staring at them now, she reduced her voice to an urgent whisper. 'I'm hardly dressed for it.'

Resting one strong hand on his tight hips, Diego scanned the room. All the couples dancing were dressed in everyday clothes, she noticed.

'Are you all out of excuses?' he demanded.

Not quite. 'I have two left feet.'

'Lucky for you I have one of each.'

Staring at Diego's outstretched hand, she pulled back in her chair. 'Seriously—I can't dance.'

'But I can.'

Which was how she found herself in the arms of a man she couldn't even look at without remembering how his kisses felt, or wondering what else he might be expert in.

'I find dancing is much improved if you move your feet,' he said, drawing her close. 'Just a suggestion, Maxie.'

'Of course.'

She would dance one dance with Diego and then sit down. There were so many people dancing between the tables that with any luck he would give up and she could start breathing evenly again. But somehow the dancers managed to avoid each other, and Diego was more intuitive than most. Of course he was, Maxie reasoned, fighting her body's best attempt to melt against him. Diego was an international sportsman whose life revolved around second-guessing the competition. Now, if she could just concentrate instead of being distracted by erotic images bombarding her brain she might even be able to move her feet in time to the music…

When the dance ended she was reluctant to leave Diego's embrace. All the more reason to pull herself together, she concluded, heading back to the table. 'This has been excellent research,' she informed him as he sat down. 'I think we should have dancing at the charity event.'

'Really?' Diego murmured. 'What an original idea. Somehow I expected better of you, Maxie.' After a moment, he added, 'So, what did you buy to wear tonight?'

'I bought a dress in the market.'

He seemed surprised.

'It was pretty and I liked it. What's wrong with that?'

'Nothing,' he said. 'I'm just surprised you didn't find anything in the shops where I dropped you off.'

She had no intention of reliving how embarrassing her experience in the upscale part of town had been.

'Maxie?' Diego prompted.

'If you must know, I wasn't joking when I told you they wouldn't serve me.'

'Honestly?' Diego sat back. 'I can't believe it.'

'Only because it would never happen to you.'

He frowned. 'But *why* wouldn't they serve you?'

'I'm not sure,' Maxie admitted. 'I can't think of anything other than the way I'm dressed.'

'Or maybe it's the slogan on your T-shirt?' Diego suggested, his dark eyes glittering. '"Drama Queen"? That's hardly you, is it, Maxie?'

'It's supposed to be ironic.' She lasted a moment and then began to laugh.

Diego wasn't smiling. 'The people in those shops need a wake-up call,' he said, standing up.

'Where are you going now?'

'To put a few people straight.'

'There are worse things in life than assistants who don't want to assist.'

'They are being paid to help customers find what they are looking for,' Diego argued, 'Even if that customer *is* a drama queen,' he added dryly. 'Come on,' he insisted, holding out his hand. 'I'm taking you shopping.'

Diego's approach to shopping was masculine and methodical, and while the usually meticulous Maxie would accept she was better known for her bemused dawdle when it came to choosing clothes, she was content to let Diego take the lead on this occasion. He was stopped every five minutes and asked for his autograph, which he always gave with a smile, good grace and a few kind words, and when they entered one of the high-class stores where Maxie had been ignored, far from seeing a shortage of assistants, they were mobbed.

'Just have everything sent over,' Diego stated on each occasion. 'My friend needs time to make her selection.'

Maxie's eyes widened. She did? Everything Diego had picked out looked fabulous to her, and there were mountains of clothes awaiting her perusal. He didn't even need to pay, because everyone knew him and said she could have the clothes on sale or return.

'The items the *señorita* has selected will be despatched

immediately by special courier,' they were assured in every shop.

And the clothes just kept on coming—shoes, bags, the most outrageous lingerie—and all of it would be waiting for them when they returned to the apartment.

'How can they be back before we are?' Maxie reasoned out loud when she remembered the speed at which Diego drove.

'If we beat them back we won't buy,' he said, and with such charm that the shop assistants were still swooning when they walked out of the shop.

'So that's how it's done,' Maxie remarked when they were back in the Ferrari. 'I should have taken you shopping with me in the first place.'

'I'm always available.'

Really? Somehow she doubted that. Maxie exhaled shakily as Diego removed the sunglasses from the top of his head and settled them in place. How far had she strayed from her businesslike brief now? 'You must tell me how much I owe you.'

'Nothing as yet.'

'But I have to pay my debts.'

'And I wouldn't have it any other way, *señorita,*' Diego assured her with a grin.

As he released the brake and eased into the evening traffic he couldn't remember enjoying himself so much for a long time. He couldn't bear injustice. Especially where Maxie was concerned, Diego realised, resting his chin on his arm when they got snarled up in traffic. He flexed his leg, which now felt better than ever. Who deserved spoiling more than Maxie? If it hadn't been for that Parrish shadow hanging over them…

'Problem?' she said when he frowned.

He relaxed back in his seat. 'Traffic.'

He was a simple man. All he asked was to be match-fit and for people to be honest with him. Trust was paramount to him. After the investment disaster trust mattered to him even more. Thinking back to the trust Nacho had placed in him, he realised he only associated with people he could rely on these days.

And Maxie?

He grimaced as he shifted position. Could he trust her? Who *was* Maxie Parrish? Who did he know who didn't talk about their family? What was she hiding? Maxie's explanation that he'd grown up in a crowd didn't wash. Surely everyone was proud of their family, even if they had one parent and no siblings. What was the difference? Family was family.

'You are preoccupied,' she remarked.

They had stopped in more traffic, which had given the old guilt plenty of time to wash over him. The more he enjoyed himself with Maxie, the more he remembered the friend who was dead—the friend who should be out with a girl now, having fun. The friend who should be laughing and loving instead of rotting in his grave—a grave Diego had helped to put him in. Peter Parrish had also played a part in it. No wonder he was preoccupied.

They drew to a halt outside his apartment, where men were already unloading their shopping parcels from a van.

'The driver must have broken every speed restriction in the book,' Maxie commented as they watched the stack of boxes wobbling their way to the entrance.

Lighten up, he told himself fiercely, realising he was grinding his jaw. 'Do you want me to report them for speeding?'

She laughed. When they had first met Maxie hadn't smiled, and neither had he. Her head had seemed to be occupied solely by business, while he had shut himself away like a dangerous animal. They'd both changed quite a lot since then. Wasn't this better?

'What?' she said.

He was staring at her, Diego realised. He wasn't about to tell Maxie where his thoughts had been. Whatever had happened in the past, maybe it was time to live a little. He gave an easy shrug. 'I was just thinking I'm looking forward to tonight.'

'Me too,' she said lightly.

But he couldn't remember ever wanting to spend an evening with a woman quite so much.

She had only opened a fraction of the packages stacked neatly in the dressing room of her suite. It looked as if Christmas and her birthday had come together times ten. 'I've got an idea,' she said later, when they were sipping coffee in Diego's office where she had made a start on her work.

'Tell me,' he prompted.

The coffee cup hovering a hair's breadth from Diego's sexy lips held her up for a moment. 'We tell the stores we've visited today about your charity and choose a few of the things from the selection of clothes delivered we think might sell well. It's such a high-profile charity, and with the Acosta name attached...'

'It would be excellent publicity for all involved? I hope you're right.'

'I am,' Maxie said confidently.

'Then go with it. How do you propose to sell the items? An auction?'

'A Dutch auction,' Maxie explained, growing in enthusiasm. 'I've run one before and it was a huge success. The donated goods are displayed and people put sealed bids on anything that takes their fancy. I think we could raise a lot of money—'

'You're full of good ideas,' Diego interrupted, 'but when are you going to fit this one in?'

'I'll get everything sorted out before we leave for the *estancia*. That's what phones are for—and the internet,' she mocked as she glanced at his desk.

Having made a point of telling her she could work from anywhere, he could hardly disagree. 'Good to know you won't be slacking while you're here.'

'Oh, don't worry. I won't be.'

'I was joking, Maxie. There's only one other person I know who's as dedicated to their work as you.' It was his turn to glance at the desk, where six monitor screens were winking.

'We make a good pair—I mean…'

'I know what you mean,' he assured her as her cheeks fired up. 'Well,' he said, standing up and stretching, 'I'm going to get ready.'

'You haven't said where we're going yet.'

'Just wear that dress from the market—it's the prettiest, isn't it?'

'I'm surprised you noticed.'

'I notice everything.'

Was he joking now? she wondered as Diego's smile made more than her cheeks heat up.

She waited for him in the kitchen. This was just another research opportunity, right? Perhaps if she told herself that enough she would believe it…

Nope. That didn't work. Her heart didn't believe it and neither did her body. And when Diego walked into the kitchen her bedazzled eyes didn't believe it either. Just for a change he looked amazing. Close-fitting jeans and a tight-fitting top with desert boots was all it took to do that. It was the way the clothes clung to Diego's powerful frame, Maxie decided, that made him so sexy.

'Are you ready?' he prompted, dipping his head to stare into her eyes.

'Absolutely,' she confirmed, hoping she sounded more businesslike than she felt.

And then her phone rang.

'England?' Diego murmured as she covered the mouthpiece.

'Work,' she said. Of course it wasn't work. She hated lying to Diego as much as she hated staring into her father's heart-wrenchingly blank eyes, but no one was going to find Peter Parrish through *her*.

Her father was ranting again. Moving out of earshot, she tried to soothe him. 'I'm sure it will be all right. Have you taken your medicine today?' She was whispering and trying to act as if this was a business call. 'I see,' she said, practically swooning with relief when a nurse rescued the phone and was able to assure her that everything was in hand.

'Are you ready to go now?' Diego asked as she ended the call.

'Yes.'

'Come on, then.'

She glanced up to find Diego smiling faintly, but his eyes betrayed the calculation behind them. That shadow crossed her path again, and she had to reassure herself quickly that this evening was just research for work—and, anyway, what could she possibly do to upset Diego?

She heard the music first—or rather the drum beat. Rhythmical and deep, it was unashamedly primal and had drawn people from all quarters of the city. There was no point taking the car, Diego had explained, as most of the roads were blocked off for the carnival procession. Maxie didn't mind at all. It was fun walking with the high-spirited *portenos,* as the city-dwellers were known, pretending she was one of them. Take that fantasy to the next level and she could imagine they were a couple—or she might have done had there not been a yawning gap of a couple of yards between herself and Diego.

'Hey,' he said, pulling her close when they were briefly separated by a group of people.

The fantasy was back on track, but it would have been better if Diego's sexy vibes were heading her way, instead of him just having to grab hold of her to stop her getting lost in the crowd.

He enjoyed holding Maxie's hand. But he wanted more than that. He wanted to make love to her. He wanted to find out if those calm grey eyes would fire with passion as they had when she'd kissed him…

'Carnival?' she said, distracting him. 'That's the theme you want for the charity event?'

'Hardly original,' Diego agreed. 'But there's something for everyone and it works every time.' He should be glad Maxie had pulled him back to business, but after that phone call—after *all* those mysterious phone calls—he wanted to drill everything out of her. Although if he pushed too hard he knew she would retreat back into her shell.

They were entering a large square where competing groups of musicians were trying to make as much noise as they could.

'Carnival can be dangerously overheated,' he yelled in her ear, 'so stay close to me.'

Oh, no. She should be concentrating on how to adapt this city-sized carnival to something on a suitable scale for the Acosta event—not thinking about Diego's minty breath on her ear.

'What do you think so far, Maxie?' he shouted above the noise.

'Like I've only ever worked in monochrome before,' she admitted, making a grateful return to business mode. 'If I can capture all this—' She gestured around.

'You will,' Diego yelled confidently, locking his strong arm even more tightly around her shoulders as they got jostled. 'But no more business tonight—tonight is fiesta. Once a year we can forget about everything and just let go.'

That was what she was afraid of. There was danger behind Diego's laughing eyes, and she had too many secrets to let herself go, as he suggested. In fact it was time to move away from the danger zone. The crowd was so dense now they were locked together like lovers. Diego glanced down. Their stares met and held and it was the most natural thing on earth when he kissed her.

There was nothing *natural* about it. Diego was her employer and she was here on business. Purely business, she told herself, slowly melting.

'Have you seen enough?' he murmured, nuzzling his mouth against her lips. 'Is there some more research you feel you should do?'

'No.'

'Do you think we'll make it back to the apartment?' he murmured, smiling against her mouth.

'We can only try.'

Locking his arm around her shoulders, Diego led her swiftly away.

CHAPTER TEN

THEY ran laughing into the apartment. Slamming the door behind them, Diego leaned back against it and dragged her into his arms. 'I've wanted this since the first moment we met…'

'Liar.' Locking her hands behind Diego's neck, she threw up a challenging stare. 'I haven't forgotten your face when you stood on the dock watching me berth that boat.'

'Will I ever forget?'

'Brute!'

'Sloppy sailor.'

'Savage.'

Diego stopped her talking with a kiss. 'I should have done that a long time ago,' he said, swinging her into his arms.

Carrying her into the bedroom, he kicked the door shut behind them and lowered her to the ground in front of him. She held her breath as he slowly slid the shoestring straps of her dress from her shoulders, never once taking his eyes from her. The sliver of silk fell to the floor, revealing the racy lingerie Diego had chosen for her in all its insubstantial glory.

'Very nice,' he murmured approvingly.

'I'm glad you like it,' she said, realising that Diego

gave her confidence as he dropped kisses on her shoulders and on her neck, and made her shiver with desire when he whispered outrageous things in her ear. He made her laugh until she cried and begged him for more. 'You'd better not stop this time,' she warned, teasing his bottom lip with her teeth.

'You're very forward, Señorita Parrish…'

Yes, she was—incredibly. Maybe because something deep deep down told her this was going to be different. Because Diego was different. She had waited a long time for this and she wasn't about to play the shrinking violet.

'You're overdressed,' she said, shivering with nerves and anticipation.

Diego had no inhibitions, and tugged off his top without a word.

'Shameless,' she whispered, filling her eyes with his incredible form as she trembled with sexual excitement. He was so big. And those sexy tattoos… 'Your belt?' she prompted.

'Whatever you say…' Releasing it, he let it hang. Undoing his jeans, he dropped them and kicked them away. 'Boots?' he suggested.

'Not a bad idea,' she agreed, loving the fact they shared the same humour.

'We made it to the apartment,' he commented. 'What are our chances of making it to the bed?'

That was clearly not a serious question as Diego didn't wait for her to answer. Swinging her into his arms, he carried her over to the bed and set her down gently on top of it. Stretching out beside her, he made her pulse rage out of control. His earring flashed in a beam of light stolen from the hallway, and as she stared into his sleepy black tiger eyes he seemed more a creature of the night than ever. The width of his shoulders was deliciously intimidating. The power and promise in his muscular, deeply tanned body stormed her brain with erotic thoughts. By the time he took hold of her in a grip so light she could have broken free at any time she was on fire for him, but Diego made no move to drag her close. He was waiting for her to come to him, she realised when she read his eyes. That was the deal. That was Diego's deal.

He had never wanted a woman more, and had to smile when Maxie, in her typical up-front way, felt she had to explain to him that her experience in the bedroom was below average, but not non-existent.

'Thank you for being so frank with me,' he said, adopting the same serious tone, though he couldn't quite keep the smile from tugging at his lips.

'Are you disappointed with me?' she said, moving restlessly in his arms.

'Disappointed about what?' he asked, brushing his lips across her mouth when he wasn't teasing her lips with his tongue.

'That I'm not a virgin and I'm not an expert either?'

'Let me think,' he replied. 'Hmm. No. I just want to kiss you again.'

'This isn't fair,' she complained when he released her. 'I know nothing about your experience. Okay,' she said quickly, 'I don't want to know.'

He kissed her again. Over and over. He was hungry, but he held back, knowing Maxie had been disappointed in the past and probably expected the worst now. Everything was by the book for Maxie, and she had been reading too conservatively. It made him more determined than ever that she was going to remember tonight for all the right reasons.

She had never imagined Diego could be so gentle, so

caring, or so controlled, or that his murmured promises could both reassure and excite her. They had run into the apartment like two storm fronts meeting, but this was better, she realised as he slowly undressed her.

'Patience,' he murmured, working some magic with his hands when she angled her body to show how much she wanted him.

'Don't make me wait too long,' she warned shakily as Diego kissed a leisurely path across her neck and on over her chest. His hands knew just where to touch, and promised more pleasure than she had ever known. Closing her eyes, she indulged herself by exploring Diego's extraordinary physique, but when she felt the size of his erection pressing against her she sucked in a nervous breath.

'Relax' he murmured, adding some more suggestions to excite her.

'Is that even possible?'

'Why don't we find out?' he said with a kiss.

She parted her lips under the pressure of his tongue, and as Diego's kisses grew more heated so her own hungry demands grew. He suckled her nipples through the cobweb-fine lace of her bra then, opening the catch, he pulled it off and tossed it aside. Breath shivered out of her as he made a light pass with his stubble-blackened chin across the sensitive peaks, and he drew another soft moan of need when he moved his attentions to her belly. She was trembling uncontrollably now, but Diego continued teasing and stroking as she writhed helplessly beneath him.

It wasn't until his fingers found the most needy part of her that she went still. She wasn't going to move a muscle to distract her mind from the most amazing sensation she had ever known, and as if knowing this Diego held her firmly in place, forcing her to enjoy everything he wanted to do to her. It was a relief when he stripped her flimsy thong away, and when he pressed her thighs wide she doubted she would survive the pleasure. But she was going to have the best time ever struggling for survival, she realised when Diego buried his face deep.

She hadn't expected such a big man to be capable of such finesse, or to be so intuitive, Maxie realised. Had she really thought Diego would be too strong for her—too big, too quick, too passionate, too frighteningly intense? He was the most skilful lover. He didn't make her feel as if she was in a race, but gave her all the time in the world to lie back and drown in pleasure. He was wholly…rhythmically…dependably…focussed on satisfying her most outrageous desires.

Too much so, she realised suddenly with alarm, realising she couldn't hold on.

When Maxie fell she fell *big,* Diego realised as her hips worked furiously beneath his hands. He made sure she enjoyed every moment, and when she quietened he held her in his arms until she was calm again, kissing and stroking her as he soothed her. When she could focus on his face she laughed—softly, sexily. It was the most intimate moment he could remember sharing with anyone, and he couldn't have anticipated the rush of emotion he felt when he gathered her in his arms. Just for once he was going to let the name Parrish mean something *good* to him. How could he not, when Maxie had done so much for him? This woman hadn't just healed his leg she had given him his life back. He laughed softly when she wanted more, and whispered some more suggestions to make her gasp.

'Please,' she whispered urgently.

He had never experienced this level of feeling before, he realised as he protected them both. Maxie was swollen and moist and ready for him, but still he took her gently, testing and teasing by withdrawing completely after giving her just the tip. Predictably, she told him off for that. She couldn't know it was taking all he'd got to hold back. And she *wouldn't* know, he determined as he pressed her knees back. Sinking into her silky, welcoming warmth, he knew he was stretching her, and so he caressed her delicately and rhythmically, both to reassure and to please her all the more.

'Yes?' he murmured.

'Yes,' she groaned, pressing her thighs open for him.

The only reward he wanted was to see pleasure in her eyes. She didn't disappoint. He kept her suspended on a plateau with only one way down, and a single word was all it took. *'Now,'* he murmured against her mouth. Exclaiming with relief, she stabbed her fingers into his buttocks and drove him on, until violent spasms claimed her and left her gasping in their wake.

She slept in his arms, and when she stirred he couldn't have been more surprised as she reached for him. 'You've been having things far too much your own way,' she complained groggily, with barely enough strength to open her eyes.

'Explain,' he whispered, dropping kisses on her face as he stroked her hair.

'I think you need putting in your place, *señor.*'

'Please,' he said wryly, resting back when she moved over him. And now it was his turn to suck in a ragged breath as Maxie began to kiss her way down his chest and on across the banded muscles of his belly. It wasn't often his muscles trembled like this, but when her sharp teeth nipped at him and her hot tongue worked with such purpose he realised Maxie had taken to lovemaking with the same enthusiasm she showed in every other area of her life.

'Why are you laughing?' she demanded, lifting her head.

'I'm enjoying myself.'

'The feeling's mutual,' she assured him. 'What?' she said when his expression changed.

'You,' he admitted. Reaching up, he swung her beneath him. 'I like being with you.'

'I like being with you too.'

He laughed. They were both so guarded they deserved each other. He kissed her again, and that kiss deepened into something that bound them. Moving over her, he took her slowly and with more care than ever. He was so much bigger than she was, brutish after years of training, while Maxie was small, and for all her bravado vulnerable, and the last thing he wanted to do was to hurt or frighten her in any way.

She felt so safe with Diego, even when their hunger for each other burned white-hot. It pleased her to pleasure him, and when he groaned and threw his head back she teased him with feather touches that made him exclaim with pleasure. When she mounted him and eased herself steadily down it was the most natural thing in the world to move her hips languorously back and forth.

You don't need lessons for this, she thought wryly when Diego suggested, 'More?'

'Oh, yes, I think so,' she agreed, as his strong hands took control of her buttocks.

Neither of them could hold on, and the ending left them both exclaiming with surprise.

When she was calm again Diego drew her into his arms. Cupping her face in his hands, he kissed her in a way that made her eyes sting. The passion between them couldn't have been hotter, or his kisses more cherishing as she fell asleep.

He watched over her as she slept. Her dark hair was spread like a smoky cloud across his pillows, while her eyelashes created crescent shadows on the flawless bloom of her cheeks. He wanted to kiss her slightly parted lips, but he didn't want to wake her. She was breathing steadily and sighing from time to time, as if she had never been more content. He could stare at her all night. It was hard to believe he could fall so completely for a woman about whom he knew practically nothing!

What if...?

He moved his head from side to side on the pillow, as if that could dislodge the doubts. Maxie couldn't be part of that terrible time. It was unthinkable that he could be lying here with the daughter of the man who had caused the death of his closest friend...

Yes, Oresto was dead—and Diego was responsible. His closest friend—a man he had known from childhood—and nothing would bring him back. Not this self-flagellation, that was for sure. His guilt wouldn't soften the grief for Oresto's family, and Diego must accept what couldn't be changed or he would damage even more people, he realised, gazing at Maxie.

She sat up in bed, instantly awake the moment the light of a new day hit the window. She could hear Diego in the bathroom, shaving and cursing. He sounded in an extremely good mood, Maxie thought as he came back into the bedroom, wiping his face on a towel.

'You're awake,' he said. Dropping the towel, he launched himself onto the bed. She screamed with laughter and embraced him.

'You're crazy—do you know that?' she demanded, covering him in kisses.

'Good morning, Señorita Parrish,' Diego said, returning her kisses with interest. 'I trust you slept well?'

'I would have done, but this man kept me awake all night,' she said, frowning.

'No. Really? Where is he?' Diego demanded, glancing fiercely round the room. 'Let me kill him so my honour is satisfied.'

'I think your honour is very satisfied,' she observed, happily stretching.

And then her phone rang.

In the space of one strident peal, that carefree mood—her sense of completeness, togetherness, of sharing everything they were and had between them—shattered into tiny, ugly pieces.

'You'd better answer it,' Diego said, moving away to give her some privacy.

'Sorry,' she said, holding the phone to her chest until he was out of earshot. Winding the sheet round her body she rushed across the room to the window, where the reception was good and there was no chance Diego could hear her. She glanced at him with more apologies ready on her lips.

'Go ahead,' he said without expression. 'I'll get dressed.'

'Your father has a small infection,' the nurse was saying while Maxie stared at the empty space left by Diego. 'But you should be fine to continue your business trip,' the nurse added, 'so enjoy it while you can.'

Maxie's heart sank at the implied warning, and sank again when she thought what it meant for her tender new relationship with Diego. 'You'll let me know if anything changes?' she urged, already feeling the ice of loss creeping through her veins.

'Of course,' the nurse assured her briskly.

Maxie stood still for a moment when she had ended the call. She'd seen the expression on Diego's face. Goodness knew who he thought was ringing her at this time in the morning. How was she going to answer his questions? She couldn't lie to him. She couldn't pretend it was a business call. Since sleeping together something had changed between them. They had placed their trust in each other. Was she going to break that trust now?

She didn't have to say anything unless Diego brought it up, Maxie reasoned. This was her problem and she would sort it out. She just had to hope there would be time to finalise everything for the charity event before her father's condition worsened.

'Problem?' Diego asked, towelling his hair.

'Nothing I can't handle.' Did her voice sound as false to him as it did to her?

'Are you sure?'

'I'm certain.'

'That's good,' he said, tossing his towel onto a chair, 'because I've got news for you. While you were on the phone I took a call from my brother. We're leaving for the *estancia* today.'

'Today?'

'Do you have a problem with that?'

'No, of course not.' She would be moving further away from her father, but one step closer to finishing the job. Which meant she would be leaving Argentina and Diego for good. 'Great,' she said, forcing a smile.

No man was in for the long haul, Maxie reminded herself, not unless guilt held him close, she realised, with her mother's experience clear in her mind. And she wanted more than that. Perhaps it was as well she would be leaving soon.

Diego explained their travel plans and seemed more concerned about her meeting his family than the mysterious phone calls she'd been taking. 'I can't wait to meet them,' she said, thinking he had become a little reserved on the subject.

'You may not see too much of me,' he explained in a way that chilled her, 'as I will be preparing for the match when we reach the *estancia.*'

'I wouldn't expect anything else,' she assured him. Walking across the room, she rested her face against his chest. 'I know how much this first match means to you.'

'I wouldn't be playing at all if it wasn't for you.'

But there was chill in his voice, as if mentally he was pulling back. Even the arms that had held her so securely felt mechanical, somehow. 'I'll do anything I can to help you,' she said, 'and please don't worry about me when we arrive at the *estancia,*' she added, hoping that by teasing Diego she would restore his former good mood. 'I'll be so busy there's no chance I'll get in your way. So you'd better not get in mine.'

There was a pause, and then he responded as she had hoped he would. 'I'll still need my therapist,' he said, in the warm tone that could sometimes be frighteningly elusive.

'As I will need mine,' she assured him.

Diego's kiss was long and deep, and when he pulled his head back to look at her there was something in his eyes that should have filled her with all the reassurance in the world. But it vanished quickly. 'Well, we'd better get on,' he said briskly. 'I imagine you have packing to do?'

'Yes, I have,' she said, knowing that nothing this good ever lasted.

She should also remember that Diego had shadows too, Maxie reminded herself. Let him get this first match out of the way, and then she would tell him about her father and there would be no more secrets between them.

CHAPTER ELEVEN

THE flight from Buenos Aires to the airstrip at Estancia Acosta took no time at all with Diego at the controls, but the intimate look they'd shared when Diego secured her seat belt before returning to the cockpit made any separation far too long. It would be so easy to get used to having him around, Maxie reflected, and that was foolish.

The jet landed lightly on a bleached strip of sand set like a golden ribbon on a plain of richly coloured flatlands. The airstrip was empty other than their jet and a solitary truck, beside which stood a traditionally dressed Argentinian cowboy. A *gaucho,* she realised, breaking free of her concerns. She had finally arrived on the pampas.

Their jolting journey to the *estancia* was a great introduction to the local scenery. Diego sat up front while Maxie leaned out of the open window, letting the warm breeze mess with her hair and her senses fill with the scent of ripe corn and lush green grass. Everything was on such a vast scale—from the huge skies to the seemingly endless grasslands that stretched away to the misty purple horizon. The flat land was punctuated by paddocks populated with herds of wild horses, and there were more ponies clustering by the fence as they approached the towering gates of the Acosta family home, which loomed out of the ocean of grass like the entrance to some Wild West ranch.

The moment they drove up to the front door people poured out, and when she climbed down from the truck Maxie was engulfed in a whirlwind of warm-hearted greetings. Diego was at her side throughout, though to her disappointment he insisted it was too soon for lengthy introductions as Maxie was tired from their journey. It was almost as if he didn't want her to meet his family properly, she thought as everyone said they understood, and agreed that Maxie must retire to her suite of rooms and that a dinner tray should be sent up.

'What a wonderful family you have,' she exclaimed as Diego escorted her into the house.

'I'm pleased you think so,' he said, with that same chill note. 'They certainly took to you.'

Was that a criticism? she wondered, trying to read him.

'I'll see you in the morning,' he said as the housekeeper loomed. 'I'll be in my old room, if you need me.' Her heart shrank a little more when Diego added in the same cordial tone, 'Don't set an alarm—sleep in for as long as you like.'

It was almost as if he didn't want her to spend time with his family, when she wanted to be up with the lark so she could get to know everyone. And she hadn't planned on sleeping alone.

She should stop being unreasonable and realise that now Diego was home he probably didn't want everyone knowing they were having such a passionate affair. What did she think this was? Meet the family prior to an announcement? She was here on business—or had she forgotten that?

* * *

Diego ground his jaw as he walked to the stables. The suspicions were back. There was still no news from his PI, so he had no way of knowing if Maxie was involved with Peter Parrish. Yet he had brought her to his family home—to the house where he had used to play with Oresto when they were children—a house that held so many treasured memories. His family had welcomed her with open arms—no suspicions. There was only Diego wondering why Maxie looked so very pleased to be here. Why so pleased? Was she on a scouting mission so she could report back to Peter Parrish?

Now he was being ridiculous, Diego accepted. Maxie was a welcome guest who had been employed to do a very important job for the Acosta family. She would not be reporting back to some unseen enemy. It was he who was out of step.

She took a bath in the comfortable old-fashioned bathroom, trying not to feel too disappointed. But she hadn't expected the break with Diego to be so sudden, nor that he would usher her away from his family as if he was ashamed of her. She would handle it the only way she could, Maxie concluded—she'd do her job and she'd do it well. She had to meet Holly, the bride-to-be, tomorrow. So however Diego wanted to play it there was only one game plan for Maxie, and that was to be the best guest she could be as she finalised all the arrangements with which she had been entrusted.

It had been such a confusing day, with such a multitude of new things to take in, that Maxie had expected to stay awake worrying half the night, but once she slipped beneath the starched white linen sheets she was asleep within minutes.

Everything looked better in the morning. Far from

sleeping in, as Diego had suggested, she threw back the curtains at dawn. The ranch had come alive at first light. She could hear people banging around in the kitchen, and she couldn't wait to get down there and see everyone.

She showered and dressed, and then booted up her laptop to check her mail. The stores were on board with her idea for an auction, which was great. It was all systems go for the charity event, at least. Closing the computer down, she left the room and ran downstairs to find Lucia and Holly waiting for her in the hall. Within minutes it was as if they had known each other all their lives.

'Well, we do have rather a lot in common,' Maxie pointed out when Lucia commented on this.

'Yes,' Lucia agreed wryly. 'Wild men of the pampas.'

'I wouldn't put it quite like that,' Maxie argued, laughing even as she wished this was true.

'Well, I would!' Holly said, hugging Maxie impulsively. 'I couldn't be more pleased to meet my wedding planner at last.'

Lucia smiled. 'And those wild men haven't been accountable to anyone in their lives. It's about time we brought them into line. We will welcome your input, Maxie.'

'Me?' Maxie exclaimed, knowing she'd better get a few things straight. 'When I said we have a lot in common, I was thinking about the work I'm doing here for the charity event and for your wedding, Holly.'

But the two girls refused to go along with this. 'And I suppose Diego has nothing to do with it at all?' Lucia said, exchanging an amused glance with Holly.

This was how close friendships started, Maxie thought. She didn't have the heart to tell the girls that where Diego was concerned their excitement was completely misplaced.

* * *

The next week flew by, with Maxie constantly working on her phone or on her laptop, contacting suppliers and putting things in place for the charity event as well as tying up the last few loose ends for Holly's forthcoming wedding. Diego was busy too, both with his training and with the many business meetings he held each day with his brothers. More importantly, he seemed to have relaxed into the idea of Maxie being part of the family, for however short a time, and though there was still something there she couldn't put her finger on they hadn't been able to stay apart for very long.

She felt at home, Maxie realised, gazing out across the paddock from her bedroom window. Shadows were lengthening as the bleaching light of day gave way to a soft lilac dusk, but the brothers were still training tirelessly for the forthcoming match. Diego glanced up, as if he sensed her staring at him. She knew that look, and her body responded along with her heart.

Springing down from his horse, Diego handed the reins to one of his brothers and, vaulting the fence, came towards the house. Hugging herself, she pulled back from the window.

She stood with her back to the door, trembling with anticipation, when Diego walked in. Walking up behind her, he kissed her neck as he pushed the robe she had flung on after her shower from her shoulders. She was naked beneath it. No words were spoken. None were needed. Diego lifted her so she could lock her legs around his waist. Throwing her head back as he entered her, she let the pleasure come. Diego was so strong and sure, and she was always so hungry for him. There was no finesse today. This was a storm of passion as they rode towards a horizon they had never failed to reach. Holding her firmly in place, as he thrust steadily at the tempo he knew she liked, he took her strong and deep, with the type of stroke that always brought her quickly to the edge. She didn't even think of holding back and tumbled gratefully, bucking furiously until the storm had passed and she rested spent in his arms, while her muscles throbbed a powerful reminder in the aftermath of pleasure.

'Do you think we should take this to bed?' Diego suggested wryly.

'Only if you allowed me to undress you,' she whispered.

Rolling back his handsome head, Diego smiled. 'I'm already undressed,' he pointed out.

'That's where you're wrong,' she said, lifting his top out of his tight-fitting breeches. Standing on tiptoe, she tugged it over his head, revealing the magnificent torso that always excited her—especially now, when his muscles were pumped and defined after exercise. The breeches were next. They clung to him like a second skin, outlining the evidence of both Diego's stamina and his size. 'Are you never at rest?' she said, cupping her hands around him.

He shrugged, which made her smile.

'Why are you smiling?' Diego murmured speculatively.

'I have no intention of stroking your ego when it clearly doesn't need any more attention,' she said.

'You're right. Please don't waste time stroking my ego,' he said as he kicked his breeches away. 'Bed?' he suggested. 'I think that's a much better option, don't you?'

Before she could answer this Diego had lifted her and put her down on the bed. Turning her, he took her gently, rocking her back and forth, while she sighed with pleasure. She was so receptive, so incredibly sensitive;

it seemed the more they made love the more she wanted Diego, and the more responsive she became. He was such an unselfish lover. There wasn't a part of her he hadn't pleasured or a request he hadn't fulfilled.

'Now,' she murmured in the way he had taught her, angling herself shamelessly and gasping with excitement as his grip tightened on her buttocks. He was so good at this. Clutching the pillow as sensation grew beyond the point of bearing, she cried out, 'I can't—it's too big—too strong—' Thankfully, Diego ignored her and, screaming wildly, she had the satisfaction of feeling him fall with her in a frenzy of explosive pleasure and release.

Could anything be more perfect than this? Maxie wondered as she pulled on some clothes after her shower. Even if she must go home soon, at least she had tasted life to the full.

Diego had returned to his training. His brothers had accepted him back in the floodlit arena as if a bedroom break in the middle of training was a perfectly natural thing.

Everything about this visit had exceeded her expectations, Maxie realised. Diego was…Diego. While the job was going even better than she had anticipated. Her career was thriving, thanks to the associated publicity, and a huge bonus to all this was the relationships she had formed with Lucia and Holly. She had particularly enjoyed hearing Lucia's stories about Diego.

'He needs someone like you to take him out of himself,' Lucia had confided. 'Diego can become very insular at times. He shuts us out—like the time he went to Isla del Fuego to recover from his injuries, allowing none of us to help him.'

Maxie had wondered about this, and had asked, 'Has he done that sort of thing before?'

Lucia's face had creased with concern and, not wanting to pry, Maxie had quickly changed the subject. Spotting Lucia in the courtyard now, she waved out of the window to attract her friend's attention, yelling that she would be right down.

Lucia greeted her with a hug. 'It's so good to have female company,' she said, glancing at the paddock. 'Come on—let's go and see what they're doing.' Linking arms with Maxie, she drew her towards the training field, where the men were shouting at each other as they wheeled their horses at impossible angles and galloped back and forth. 'I love them all dearly,' Lucia confided, 'but they can be a little overpowering.'

'I can imagine,' Maxie agreed wryly. 'I can't think what it must have been like for you growing up in a household of such strong-minded men.'

'Hell,' Lucia assured her. 'They wouldn't let me tie my own shoelaces in case I tripped over them. But now there's Holly—and you.'

'But I won't be staying,' Maxie pointed out.

'You must,' Lucia insisted.

'I can't. I'm afraid I have to return to reality some time.'

'Don't be silly. Diego will never let you go.'

'He can't keep me here,' Maxie said gently.

'Don't you want to stay?'

Lucia looked so crushed that Maxie gave her a hug. 'Of course I do, but life doesn't always work out the way we want it to. That doesn't mean that you and I can't be friends.'

Lucia's warmth was something she couldn't bear to think of losing, any more than she could bear to think about leaving the only man she would ever feel she belonged with and this wild and beautiful land Diego called home.

'I think we should all do our best to change your mind,' Lucia said stubbornly, making a signal to her brothers that it was time for them to come in and eat supper. 'After all, you can work anywhere in the world, can't you?'

'Well, yes, as long as I'm free to travel. But—'

'No buts,' Lucia insisted. 'Don't you love Diego?'

Maxie paused. How could she possibly express her feelings for Diego? 'If only life could be more straightforward,' she said.

'It can be if you want it to be,' Lucia insisted. 'You have to fight for what you want, Maxie.'

Everything was black and white for Lucia, Maxie realised as the men cantered past and she exchanged a quick glance with Diego. She only wished she could share Lucia's innocent belief in the rightness of love and natural justice in life, but unlike her whimsical friend she was just too much the realist.

'With you at the helm, Holly's wedding is going to be a fabulous success,' Lucia enthused as they walked back to the house. 'I can't tell you how much we're all looking forward to it.'

'With your family in attendance, how can it be anything but a success?'

'Isla del Fuego *is* one of the most romantic places on earth,' Lucia said thoughtfully, 'but I would never get married anywhere but here on the *estancia* in Argentina.' Squeezing Maxie's arm again, she whispered in her ear, 'So I hope you're taking notes, my friend. Because I don't want anyone but you to arrange my wedding.'

Maxie laughed, glad at the change of subject. 'Do you have anyone in mind?'

'No, of course not,' Lucia protested.

But something in Lucia's eyes said yes, so Maxie

probed a little deeper. 'Tell me about the opposing polo team...'

'What do you want to know?' Lucia said defensively. 'Nero Caracas and his team are called The Assassins,' Lucia explained, but then her eyes narrowed and she drifted off into her own thoughts.

'Do you know the team well?' Maxie asked innocently.

Lucia's lips pressed down as she thought about it. 'Nero's gorgeous, of course, but he's off the market. He only got married recently, and he has a beautiful wife called Bella, as well as the most adorable baby girl called Natalia—Tally for short. I only know the rest of the team through my brothers—' Lucia stopped.

'And?' Maxie prompted, suspecting Lucia was holding something back.

'And they're all gorgeous, as well as the most amazing fun—except for one,' Lucia said frowning.

'And he is...?'

'Luke Forster—he flew over especially from America to play for Nero's Assassins. Don't know why they've asked *him* when there are so many perfectly good home-grown players here in Argentina.'

'Perhaps this Luke is better?' Maxie suggested tactfully.

Lucia huffed. 'He's supposed to be the best there is outside Argentina.'

'Well, there you are,' Maxie said soothingly. 'And I expect you'll tolerate his company somehow?'

'I suppose I'll have to,' Lucia agreed. 'But right now I'm more interested in you and Diego. You've done so much for him, Maxie. You can't walk out on him now.'

'I've no intention of walking out on him. Your brother has done more for me than you'll ever know.' He had allowed her to shake off the past and look forward to the future with confidence, Maxie mused as she stared at Diego, who was checking his pony's legs. Her heart rolled over when he glanced up. She had always known this affair must end, and that she and Diego led very different lives, but that didn't make it any easier.

So enjoy it while you can...

'I can't tell you what it means to Diego, having you here,' Lucia said, giving Maxie's arm a shake to bring her back from the daydream. 'And what you've done for our charity—what you've achieved in so short a time—is incredible. Especially when you've been finishing up Holly's wedding arrangements too.' Lucia shook her head as she waved her arm around to encompass all the colourful stalls decorated with bunting and flags, as well as the various groups of entertainers Maxie had imported from Buenos Aires in readiness for the great day. 'You're a marvel, Maxie.'

'As long as you and the family are happy with what I've arranged.'

'Happy?' Lucia squeezed Maxie's arm. 'I think you must know that's an understatement.'

It was one of those golden moments when she should feel nothing but happiness, Maxie realised, but instead she found herself wondering if she had ever been more on the outside looking in. For this world of staunch family loyalties and unshakeable togetherness was one she could never truly be part of.

CHAPTER TWELVE

LIFE was a game of snakes and ladders, Diego reflected as he showered after training. Even in his blackest and most despairing mood he had clung to that. When the doctors had told him he might never regain full use of his leg he had dared to believe he would play again. Then fate had brought him Maxie Parrish—a girl he'd be tempted to share everything with had it not been for all her secrets.

What about his?

He had never told anyone outside the family about Oresto. The shame he felt at having introduced his best friend to a low-life swindler had never left him. The consequences for Oresto had been catastrophic, and even now Diego realised, when he heard the three girls laughing uproariously in the kitchen, the shadow of Oresto's death could still fill him with niggling unease.

'Is everything ready for the match?' Maxie asked him brightly when he walked into the kitchen, her eyes sparkling as she came up to him.

Ruffling his hair, he dragged her into his arms and kissed her. That was his answer. It was the only answer that made any sense to him.

His impulse garnered lovestruck glances from both Holly and his sister, who quickly looked away. He saw them exchange knowing glances when he and Maxie pulled apart.

Would he ever get enough of her? Probably not, he thought as two of his brothers barged noisily into the kitchen. Maxie flashed an intimate glance at him before going over to them to discuss the arrangements she'd made for accommodating the stable lads who were flying to London with ponies they were exchanging with another breeder. He watched as she chatted easily with men whom most found intimidating. There was no denying she fitted right in.

The Acostas were a strong team, who supported each other through thick and thin. The fighter in him said that whatever secrets Maxie was hiding they could sort them out together. He had grown to care about her, and all that mattered to him was Maxie's happiness. She was unique. She was loyal. She got on with everyone. She made things run smoothly for the family. He could tell his brothers were as pleasantly surprised as he had been that on top of all her other responsibilities Maxie had managed to schedule the transportation of the ponies with the minimum of fuss and disruption on the day of the match.

'You're a fantastic organiser, Maxie,' observed his brother Kruz, who wasn't noted for giving out praise lightly.

'The addition of women into our wolves' den is a big plus, don't you think?' his brother Ruiz demanded, clapping Diego on the shoulder.

'At least I have some support, now Holly and Maxie are on my team,' Lucia put in.

'And at least we don't have to suffer Nacho's cooking,' Kruz added wryly.

'*You* cook if you don't like it,' his sister Lucia taunted, tossing a pack of steaks at Kruz, which he caught with a grin before heading outdoors to start the barbecue.

'What's all this?' Nacho growled, kicking his boots off at the door.

'We were just saying how much we love your cooking,' Lucia told him, with a wink in Maxie's direction.

Diego was content to soak all this in. He didn't know when he had ever seen the family so happy, or the dynamics of the group working so well. And a lot of that was due to Maxie, he realised as he pulled her into his arms. Maxie brought everyone together.

'This woman is very special to me,' he announced, never taking his gaze from Maxie's face.

'Like we don't know that,' Lucia exclaimed, hugging them both.

Did she dare to hope that this could last? Closing her eyes, Maxie wished she could stop time right here, right now. But time marched inexorably on.

The day of the match dawned bright and clear. The sense of excitement at the *estancia* was electric. Maxie had really pulled the stops out with the carnival, and the big house with its massive courtyard and formal gardens provided a perfect backdrop for the funfair in the field, the colourful stalls lined up in the home paddock, and the musicians warming up. The various bands were trying to outdo each other, but no one cared because this was fiesta, this was carnival. Everyone had made the effort to travel deep into the pampas—by jet, by helicopter, or by battered truck and motorbike. Some of the families arrived in horse-drawn carts piled high with their belongings for several nights' stay, and Maxie had organised the best of facilities for all of them to ensure that nothing could go wrong today.

* * *

He thought of Oresto a lot on the morning of a match. He always did. He wanted to tell Maxie how he thought about his friend each time he played, and how he felt guilty for enjoying the youth and life Oresto had lost. He wanted to tell her all of it before he cantered onto the field, because playing polo at this level was dangerous and he never knew what might happen—horses could suffer serious injury and riders had been killed. Did he want Maxie to find out about Oresto from anyone but him? What sort of a coward would that make him?

He brooded darkly on this as he went to make one last check on the ponies, but when Maxie waved to him on her way to the stands, arm in arm with his sister and Holly, he knew he couldn't mar her happiness with his memories. It was enough that she was here for him, on this the most important playing day of his life—his first day back after injury—the day when he must prove himself or withdraw from the game completely, for he would never let his brothers down.

He would speak to Maxie after the match, Diego determined. There were a lot of things he needed to straighten out with her. Working out a way for them to be together was top of his list. Maxie could continue her career anywhere in the world, so there was no reason why they couldn't be together. Smiling, he caught sight of her huddled in a giggling group with his sister and Holly, and it only confirmed his decision to can the last of his doubts and brush aside the black cloud of grief that always lodged over him before fire flashed through his veins when the match began. He couldn't interrupt the girls when he'd never seen Maxie so happy and relaxed.

Dios! The opposing team was on fire. Diego urged his mount into an even faster gallop. Nero Caracas in particular, along with his wing man, the American number one Luke Forster, were burning up the field. Their horses might as well have wings—they could turn a one-eighty in a heartbeat.

And Nero had his new wife to impress, Diego remembered, checking out Maxie in the stands as he galloped back to change his horse at the end of the second chukka. Just seeing her face reassured him that he had something important to fight for too.

I can't, Maxie had been about to say. But how could she say that? How could she even think it?

'Of course I'll leave immediately,' she confirmed, remembering the jet was fuelled and ready on the airstrip, waiting to take the exchange ponies to England. Fate could be kind sometimes, and at other times incredibly cruel. It was playing some hideous trick on her today by offering to be both.

'What's wrong?' Lucia demanded, sensing trouble.

'I have to leave immediately,' Maxie explained, texting furiously to make sure the flight didn't leave without her.

'You can't leave now!' Lucia exclaimed, grabbing her arm. 'Diego needs you here. They're losing the match, which means his chance to play again at international level is at risk. You can't walk out on him…'

Maxie saw her new friend's incredulity slowly turn to anger.

'I can't believe you'd do this to Diego,' Lucia said coldly.

She had to go. Maxie's father had suddenly taken a turn for the worst. And, as if that wasn't bad enough, a private investigator had been snooping round. Nothing else on earth could make her leave.

'Lucia, I must.'

'Must you?' Lucia said flatly, turning away.

All the warmth Maxie had felt at being welcomed into the heart of such a wonderful family turned to cold that invaded every part of her. So much so that when she stood to leave the stands—to leave Diego and the *estancia.* Argentina and the Acostas, without so much as a word of explanation to any of them—she was shivering violently beneath the fierce sun.

'Please tell Diego I love him…'

'Shouldn't you tell him that yourself?' Lucia demanded coldly.

'Please, Lucia.'

'Maxie, I'm struggling to understand this.'

'I wouldn't go if I didn't have to.' Sinking down in her seat again, conscious of precious seconds ticking by, she gripped Lucia's arm. 'Please don't think I'd do this if there was any other way.'

At first Lucia wouldn't look at her, but finally she relented. 'Can I do anything to help?'

Closing her eyes, Maxie tried not let emotion get the better of her. Lucia's big-hearted gesture was so typical of the whole Acosta family. 'I only wish you could, but this is something I have to do myself.' Embracing Diego's sister fiercely, she dashed away her tears and left the stand.

The first half had ended miserably for the Acostas. The team was down ten two. Diego was pacing impatiently, waiting for the grooms to bring up his next pony, when the call came through. It was his PI. For a moment he couldn't speak, he couldn't think.

Maxie was Peter Parrish's daughter?

The PI was at pains to explain that Maxie couldn't have been involved in the scam as she'd been too young.

His head was still reeling when he grabbed hold of

a groom. 'Tell them to hold the second half.' The man looked at him as if he'd gone mad. 'Tell them to wait for me,' he repeated as he sprinted for the stands.

Why hadn't she told him?

Fury coiled in his stomach like a venomous snake. He had brought Maxie into his family. He had trusted her. His could see the similarities now in the curve of her mouth and in a certain cadence in her voice. Peter Parrish had been a mesmerising charmer.

'Diego!'

He almost ran her over as she ran from the stands. He blocked her path so she had nowhere to go. He didn't speak. He didn't need to. She could see everything on his face.

'Diego, what is it? Did Lucia call you? Did she tell you I was leaving?'

'Leaving?' His phone buzzed imperatively. He ignored it. 'No one told me you were leaving. I had no idea.' He said this in the same chilling tone as his world disintegrated in front of his eyes. 'I came to see you—to speak to you—but now I find you're leaving in the middle of the match. Where are you going, Maxie?'

'To England. I have to—'

She was agitated and glanced at her watch, reminding him there was a flight to the UK waiting on the airstrip.

'I didn't want it to be like this, Diego.'

'How should it be?' he asked her in the same quiet voice. 'Were you just going to sneak away?'

'I need time to explain, Diego, and there is no time.' She glanced round, as if seeking the freedom he was denying her.

'This is one last chance for you to be honest with me.' His voice had hardened.

'What do you mean?' she said defensively. Her normally steady grey gaze was restless and distracted.

'Why are you leaving?' he demanded. 'What is so important it can't even wait until the end of the match? Who are you going to see, Maxie?'

Each second she remained silent marked a year since he had introduced his friend Oresto Fernandez to an unscrupulous crook named Peter Parrish. They had been young bloods in London, trying to prove themselves independently of their families. Diego's stake in what had turned out to be a scam had been small, just a trial to see how things worked out. He hadn't realised Oresto was gambling with family money. They had lost everything, and the friend he had grown up with and loved like a brother had hung himself in despair.

'Why are you looking at me like that, Diego?' she asked him fearfully.

As if he hated her? As if he hated everything surrounding Peter Parrish and anyone connected to him?

When tears of panic and bewilderment clouded Maxie's eyes he felt nothing. The crowd was already seated, waiting for the second half. A posse of grooms had just rounded the corner, searching for him.

'You have a decision to make,' he told Maxie coldly, turning away.

Diego's face was dark with fury. Maxie had chosen her father. The pilot of the jet had just called to confirm that she was safely on board. His brothers, seeing his expression, had begged him not to play.

'The match is going badly and the Acostas don't lose,' he told them. 'We do not play our greatest rivals at a charity match and canter off in front of our home crowd defeated and disgraced. That doesn't happen. It has never happened. And it won't happen today.'

'There are substitutes who can take your place,' his brother Nacho pointed out, pulling him away to clap a reassuring hand on Diego's shoulder.

'And risk my place in the national team?' Diego shook his head. 'You can rely on me, Nacho.' And for once even his formidable brother didn't argue with him.

He played like a man possessed. He took on the great Nero Caracas and nearly unseated him. It was said that when Diego Acosta played at his fiercest and most intimidating best the devil rode on his shoulder. Today he *was* the devil.

CHAPTER THIRTEEN

SHE was leaving her heart in Argentina, while duty and a very different type of love was taking her to England. It was too late to wish she had told Diego about her father. He couldn't have come with her anyway. And why would he want to? How could she be so selfish as to even think of asking him in the middle of a match that would decide Diego's future?

Even now she might arrive too late to find her father alive. With no one to see her she let the tears come as the powerful jet engines carried her swiftly above the cloud line and everything she had longed to be part of. She had to find the old, organised Maxie, who would immediately know what to do, but she was gone.

So she'd get her back, Maxie determined fiercely. First she had to prioritise. There would be other matches, but this visit with her father couldn't wait. She couldn't live with herself if she didn't go to him and he died alone.

And Diego?

She would call Diego the moment she arrived in London. She would tell him and he would understand. She *hoped* he would understand, Maxie amended as her heart contracted into a tiny, defensive ball.

* * *

Nacho's helicopter took Diego to Ezeiza International. From there the flight to London would take the same time as the jet. He was a mere six hours behind her. The trail was still hot.

His investigator was waiting for him at Heathrow with a fast, unobtrusive car. 'Move over, I'll drive,' he told the man. 'Just give me directions.'

And that was the extent of their conversation until he pulled in through the gates of the Nuttingford Nursing Home.

'What's this?' he said, peering out of the windscreen at the imposing Victorian façade. 'Has Peter Parrish taken to swindling old ladies these days?'

'It's a retirement home, for those who can afford it,' his investigator explained.

'Thank you.' He cut the man short. He could see for himself that there was everything here to make a con-man's twilight years extravagantly comfortable. Anger exploded inside him.

Peter Parrish was evidently prospering in this over-blown honeypot while Diego's friend Oresto was rotting in his grave. Spinning the car across the gravel, he screeched to a halt in front of the steps. Springing out, he slammed the door and took the steps in a couple of bounds. The front door was open and the PI followed him in. He was ready to do murder by the time he reached the reception desk, so perhaps it was as well that the investigator supplied the name under which Maxie had registered her father.

'You can leave me now,' he told the man, dismissing him without a glance.

He would confront Peter Parrish first, and then he would tell the world about a man without scruples so no one else would ever fall victim to his scams. If Maxie was with him… He steeled his heart. If Maxie was with her father she would have to admit her role in covering up his whereabouts and lying about his name. She must accept the full extent of her father's fraudulent dealings, together with their tragic consequences.

Guilt and anger vied inside him as he mounted the stairs, dragging on stale air at least five degrees warmer than it should have been. The thought of redemption and penance within his grasp drove him on. The upcoming confrontation wouldn't raise Oresto from the grave, but it would be the end of a journey he had once feared would never be over.

Stalking along a richly furnished corridor that boasted a faint scent of overcooked cabbage and beeswax, he found the room on the second floor. One of the better rooms, the receptionist had told him. As if he cared. As if he was interested in anything other than the fact that Peter Parrish had feathered his nest at the expense of who knew how many others apart from Oresto. He grasped the handle and threw the door open without the courtesy of a warning knock.

'Diego!'

'What the hell?' He whirled in turmoil before he had a chance to see inside the room, to find Maxie standing right behind him. His angry mind threw him back to the past even as he tried to absorb this new information.

She had just been coming out of the restroom when she spotted Diego. So he knew. He'd come. He was here for her. This was right. In that instant all the lonely sorrow banked up inside her changed to relief. He understood, she registered numbly as Diego steered her towards the empty visitors' lounge. When they were both inside he shut the door and leaned with his back against it so no one could disturb them.

'Well?' he said.

Oh, thank God to be with someone who understood

without the need for words. Diego's voice penetrated the mud in her head, just as the sight of him filled her heart with soothing balm. 'Oh, Diego…' She stopped. There was so much she wanted to say to him. 'Thank you for coming.' He made a sound, as if to say anything else was unthinkable. She could see the passion in his eyes—the fierce, fierce passion. 'I wish I could have waited for you. I wish I could have stayed to see the end of the match, but this…' Her hands lifted and fell again. There were no words.

'The match?' he said without inflection.

'I know how much it meant to you…' She lifted her gaze then, and stared him in the eyes.

'You had to be here,' he said in the same calm voice, his burning eyes the only reflection of the deepest of passions swirling inside him.

'Yes, I did. Thank you for understanding.'

The sound he made now was both primal and terrifying. *'Understanding?'* he spat out, grabbing hold of her. She cried out like a frightened animal when he yanked her close. Staring furiously into her eyes, he said, 'I only understand that you're here with *him*.'

'Yes, I know—I should have been with you.'

'Me?' he said, staring down at her as if she were his most loathsome enemy. 'You were *never* with me.'

'What are you saying?' Shock coursed through her even as bewilderment sapped the strength from her legs. 'Diego, I don't understand…'

'You don't understand?' he raged. 'You were always with *him*—calling him—speaking to him—thinking only of him.'

'Diego, please!'

He let her go as suddenly as he had grabbed hold of her and stood back, breathing heavily, lost in some place where she couldn't reach him. The world was going crazy. This wasn't her tender lover or the friend she had trusted above all others.

'Diego, what is it? Are you talking about my father? Are you jealous of my father? Diego?'

A discreet tap on the door made them both go still. Maxie's heart contracted. She knew what this meant.

'Diego,' she said softly. 'I have to go now.'

When she left him his fury subsided, leaving only the knowledge that he loved Maxie with all his heart, and that life without her was unthinkable. If she wanted to be with her father in private he would understand. He would be here for her, whatever happened. If Peter Parrish chose to ridicule and belittle him, then he would take that on board too. Love had no boundaries, no restrictions. Love was unconditional.

Walking over to the window, he stared out, remembering Oresto as the rain fell bleakly down.

The door to her father's room was partly open, and she heard the nurse outside explaining to Diego in an undertone, 'He doesn't have long. Please don't stay for more than a few minutes…'

The nurse's voice seemed to come from a long way away, while Maxie was in a bubble that excluded the rest of the world, apart from her father and now Diego. When the door swung wide to allow him in and she saw Diego framed in light calm fell over her, as if Diego being here at this particular time was part of the natural order of things. All the petty concerns and fears that jabbed away, making small problems seem huge, had been collected up in a holding pen to be dealt with at some later time. It was the only way individuals could cope with great grief, she supposed.

She heard Diego murmur something in reply to the nurse and then they were alone. Still holding her father's hand in both of hers, as if she could will some of her own strength into him, she turned to look at Diego.

Why hadn't she told him? He had remained in the visitors' lounge until he had begun to wonder if Maxie had left him again. He'd gone looking for her and a nurse had explained. And here she was, seated on an upright chair, holding the gnarled hand of the old man on the bed. His heart pounded with concern for her even as incredulity swept over him. Was *this* his enemy? Was *this* the man he had wasted so much of his life hating?

It took him a few moments to accept there could be any connection between the confident, robust individual he remembered and the frail old man who lay dying on the bed. The shades were drawn and there was no sound other than the ticking of an antique mantel clock and the old man's involuntary breathing. Peter Parrish had passed to the last struggles of a body ready to surrender, and while Maxie appeared resigned to this, he could feel her anguish and her deep sense of impending loss.

'Diego,' she whispered, reaching for him.

Taking hold of Maxie's hand in a firm grip, he raised it to his lips and pressed a long kiss against her palm. Only then did he straighten up to stare down at Peter Parrish. So this was the devil on his back. This was the man who had haunted him. How sweet were those thoughts of revenge now?

'I'm so glad you're here,' Maxie whispered.

He stared down into her eyes and saw only goodness in them. Maxie had never been to blame for her father's actions. She hadn't been hiding wickedness from him—she had been hiding love. Peter Parrish might be undeserving of that love but he was Maxie's father. And if there was one thing Diego understood it was family. There was only one thing he could do now, and that was to forgive Peter Parrish as Oresto's family had forgiven him.

Diego reflected as he watched her moisten her father's lips with a sponge left for that purpose. This was life. This was Maxie's life. A great shame washed over him when he thought how badly he had misjudged her. He hadn't really let her in. If he had he would have told her about Oresto and she would have been able to confide in him about her father.

'I would have left the match to be with you,' he whispered.

'I couldn't have asked you to do that,' she protested in an undertone. 'Your first match back, Diego? Don't you think I know how important that was for you?'

He shrugged this off with a rueful breath. 'I'm just another player. There are always substitutes standing ready, longing for the chance to prove what they can do. You should have told me what was happening, Maxie. I would have brought you here.'

'I never thought you'd want that level of commitment.'

'What are you talking about?' he demanded incredulously, drawing her away from the bed to an alcove, where they could talk without disturbing her father.

'I've seen what love can do, Diego. I know how destructive it can be.'

She glanced at her father as she spoke, and it killed him to see her wringing her hands. Capturing them in his he held them safe as Maxie told him how her father had mistreated her mother and how he'd later been eaten up with guilt when her mother had become ill.

'But the guilt was too late,' she said. 'Just as it's too late for me to tell my father that I love him.'

'It's never too late,' he argued fiercely, dragging her close. 'You're here now, and I think your father knows that. I think he knows you've always been here for him, and that your forgiveness for whatever he's done in the past is limitless and was never in doubt.'

'Do you really think so?' she said, searching his face.

'I know it,' he ground out fiercely, holding her tight. 'I know it just as surely as I know that love can last. I know it in the same way that I know I can't live without you. Can you ever forgive me for not being here for you—for not telling you how I feel about you before this?'

'For not expressing your emotions?' She smiled sadly. 'Diego, we're both lousy at that.'

'So if I tell you I love you?'

The tension in her face softened. 'I never thought of you as a romantic, Diego.'

'And I never took you for a coward, Maxie Parrish. I still don't. So if I ask you to marry me, will you risk it?'

'Just hold me,' she begged him, nestling close. 'For now, just hold me.'

They stood for a long time without speaking, and when he released her she turned back to her vigil. He caught her before she reached the bed. 'I'll take over,' he said quietly. 'Please… Let me do this for you, Maxie.'

She looked at him in bewilderment.

'You need a break,' he said, appealing to her common sense. 'Sit down for a moment outside and gather your strength. I'll call you right away if you're needed.'

'I can't believe you'd do this for me.'

'I'd do anything for you,' he said simply. When she rested against him he felt how exhausted she was, and he knew he wouldn't tell her the history he shared with her father now. He wouldn't tell her for a long time, and only then if he thought she was ready to hear it—so maybe never. The only thing that mattered to him was caring for Maxie and supporting her when she needed him, and he thanked God for giving him this opportunity.

When they left the nursing home he realised Peter Parrish had taught him a valuable lesson. While he had been sitting with Maxie's father, doing all he could to make the man comfortable in the last hours of his life, he had taken the opportunity to review his own life, and had realised that the only thing that mattered was love.

'I should have told you about my father long before this,' Maxie said, worrying her lip as she frowned.

'No, you shouldn't.'

He was holding her in his arms on the bed at the *palacio* on the Isla del Fuego, where they were staying for Holly's wedding. They hadn't talked about Maxie's father since the funeral, when Diego had said a few words over the grave about forgiveness and redemption and moving on. Maxie was still tender after her father's death and needed constant reassurance. She had been holding it together for so long she hardly knew how to let go. He understood how vulnerable a strong person could be, and his heart had gathered her in.

'Why are you telling me all this now?' he said, kissing her brow.

'Because I want to share everything with you,' she said, turning her clear gaze on him. 'I don't want there to be any secrets between us.'

'And there won't be,' he pledged, dropping a tender kiss on her lips.

This return to Isla del Fuego, where they had first met,

first kissed, first argued, first loved, had been a poignant homecoming for both of them. He would always remember what Maxie had done for him here, as well as what she had created for Holly's wedding—scenes of such celebration and love that the old house and the island on which it stood had been reinstated in his memory as a happy place rather than a prison.

'Have I thought of everything?' she murmured, worrying because today was the long-awaited day of Holly's wedding.

'You know you have,' he reassured her, drawing Maxie into his arms.

The guests had been brought in by ferries which had been met on the dock by fleets of horse-drawn carriages, specially decorated with ribbons and flowers for the occasion. The weather, unlike on Maxie's first sighting of the island, couldn't have been more perfect, and everyone had enthused that this was going to be a wedding like no other. Even his hard to please brother Ruiz was in a perpetual state of ecstasy at the sight of the joy and anticipation on Holly's face.

And now he and Maxie were resting on the bed after the final dress rehearsal. The sex was always phenomenal between them, but just lying together quietly was good too. 'So, come on,' he coaxed, 'tell me what's on your mind.'

'I want to tell you everything,' she murmured against his mouth. 'Then we needn't speak of it again. But there is something I want you to know.'

'If it's worrying you, and it will make you feel better if you tell me, then do so,' he said. He would do anything to make Maxie happy.

'My father didn't always tread a straight line.'

His impulse was to tense. He caught it in time.

'But there was a reason for it,' she continued. 'When

my mother became sick we had no money for her care. That was when I learned how to massage her leg, because it saved paying for extra sessions from the therapist. I soon became good at it.'

'Because it mattered to you?' he guessed.

She smiled sadly. 'Because it helped my mother.'

He gave an encouraging nod.

'My father couldn't afford the treatment my mother needed,' she went on, 'and so he started to borrow money—more and more money.'

A downward spiral that had ended with Peter Parrish trying to swindle two cocky Argentinian youths out of a fortune, Diego realised.

'He wasn't a bad man, Diego. He was a desperate man. The money wasn't for him, but for my mother.'

He hushed her and drew her close to kiss the top of her head, thinking this hardly mattered now. But Maxie tensed and pulled away, her eyes full of some unspoken horror.

'What is it?' he said.

'It went wrong, Diego,' she said, staring at him with that same look in her eyes. 'My father's plan went horribly wrong. Someone died because of him. I was too young to know the details, but I heard my mother crying one day as she confided in a friend that a young man had lost all his family money and killed himself because of my father's actions. There were more rows, and my father was never the same after that. His intention, foolish though it was, had been to save life—not to destroy it. I think he went mad with grief, and then dementia took over. My mother died shortly afterwards, so he felt it had all been for nothing.'

'But none of it was your fault, Maxie,' Diego insisted gently. 'You can't go on blaming yourself for something your father did so long ago. And you mustn't,' he insisted. 'Your father was trying in every way he knew to care for your mother, as you later cared for him. He could see no further than that any more than you could see further than your duty towards him. Don't you think I understand that now?'

Her eyes slowly cleared. 'You do, don't you?'

Maxie had taught him that love came at a cost, and that sometimes that cost was high. She had been right to defend her father. It was not right that Diego had allowed thoughts of revenge and rage to rampage through him for so many wasted years, or that he had allowed that fury onto the polo field, where it had nearly killed him and his horse, and had made him a danger to every other player in the game. He kissed her again to confirm in his own mind that all that was behind him now. She tasted so good, so sweet and fresh…so different, somehow.

What was different?

Some primal memory stirred inside him. 'Why are you telling me this now?' he repeated gently, moving his head on the pillow so she had to look at him.

'Because it's more important than ever that you and I don't have any secrets between us,' she said, holding his gaze trustingly.

He looked at her, frowning slightly. 'Why more important than ever?'

'Because we're going to have a baby, Diego.' She stopped and bit down on her lip, as if she wasn't sure if he'd be pleased.

He shot up in bed. 'Are you sure?'

'I'm positive,' she said quietly.

He exclaimed with pleasure—anticipation—excitement—a world of emotion flashing behind his eyes. 'Can we tell everyone?' he exulted.

'No, it's too soon. And the timing could be better.'

'How could it be better?' he demanded. 'The timing is perfect,' he argued fiercely.

'Beating the bride to getting pregnant isn't so great—especially when you're a wedding planner who is supposed to be so organised.'

'Nonsense!' he exclaimed. 'You got it exactly right—for us.' Dragging her into his arms, he gazed into Maxie's eyes intently, as if he would see some change there too. 'All right. I won't tell anyone,' he promised. 'At least not today. You're going to be a mother!' he exclaimed softly in wonder.

'And you're going to be a father,' Maxie agreed wryly. 'How do you feel about that, Diego?'

'How do I feel?' he demanded incredulously. 'As if the world and everything in it is mine.'

'Diego,' she murmured when they finally found the willpower to break apart, 'we've got a wedding to go to.'

Picking his watch up from the bedside table and glancing at it, he raised a brow.

'You are impossible,' she breathed as he pressed her down on the bed.

'And you are the wholly irresistible mother of my child,' he said, starting to unfasten the buttons on her blouse.

He had made love to Maxie in the way he intended to live his life from now on, Diego reflected as he examined his unusually smooth, freshly shaved face just before the wedding. Taking her gently and with reverence, he had experienced a deep calm and certainty inside him as she sighed with pleasure in his arms. She was the mother of his child, and they had a lifetime ahead of them in which he intended to demonstrate his love for Maxie in so many ways—not all of them calm and with reverence, he amended, smiling to himself as he racked his brain for ways they hadn't made love yet.

'You look fantastic, Diego.'

He turned to find her standing in the doorway. Tousled and sexily sated, she looked fantastic too, wearing nothing more than a sheet. 'You'd better get a move on,' he told her.

'Don't I know it?' she agreed. 'But it won't take me long to shower and dress.'

She looked him over again. Diego was Ruiz's best man, and Holly had requested he wear a pale, lightweight linen suit with a white open-necked shirt and a vibrant orchid in his buttonhole to pick up the colour of the bridesmaids' dresses. Maxie adjusted his collar at the back, and then passed him some cologne which he slapped on reluctantly.

'Are you sure you like this?' he demanded, grimacing.

Maxie grinned. 'I like everything about you.'

'Later,' he murmured, teasing her as he comforted himself that they had all the time in the world now and that nothing could ever part them again. 'You'd better get ready,' he urged, dropping a kiss on the top of her head. 'You're the one person who can't afford to be late today. And I don't want Holly coming after me for distracting her wedding planner.'

'She'd be jealous if she knew the reason,' Maxie teased him.

'Not after tonight, I'm guessing,' Diego told her dryly, on his way out of the room.

Maxie would be in the background today, making sure

all her arrangements ran like clockwork. Her outfit would consist of a businesslike white shirt tucked into cream linen trousers, her only adornment the radio earpiece with attached microphone which she used to co-ordinate the various stages of the celebration.

'Quick shower, and then I'll see you downstairs,' she shouted after him.

'See you down there,' he confirmed from the door. He was heading for Ruiz and patted his pocket to make sure he had the ring. 'I love you,' he murmured, holding Maxie's gaze for one long, lingering moment.

CHAPTER FOURTEEN

EVEN Maxie was blown away by the scene she had helped to design. The vast courtyard was dressed with a profusion of colourful blossom, while the wedding arbour where the couple would exchange their vows was a fragrant mass of lush white flowers and soft green foliage. Gilt chairs with the palest gold seat pads were lined up either side of the pastel primrose carpet down which the bride would glide.

Having checked with her assistants that there was nothing more she could do for now, she ran up to the terrace at the top of the steps and watched the remaining guests taking their seats. The air of anticipation was electric. An orchestra was setting the scene with an elegant Bach concerto while people chatted easily to each other. This was the moment she always enjoyed. She had done everything possible to make a perfect day for the bride, and now it only remained for the main players to take the stage.

A fanfare announced the arrival of Ruiz, accompanied by his equally striking brother Diego. A rustle of excitement swept the crowd as they walked down the bridal carpet, stopping from time to time to greet friends. It looked like a scene from a fairytale, she thought as Diego turned to look at her. She shared a brief look, and then got back on her radio to let everyone know the groom and best man were in position. It was only when she had finished the call that she spotted trouble brewing.

All the guests were looking forward, towards the arbour where Ruiz and Diego were standing, but one elderly woman was staring back at Maxie. She didn't look like the usual troublemaker—someone who might have had too much to drink—this was a small, inoffensive-looking woman with neat grey hair. But the man seated at her side *did* look like trouble, and as he turned to stare Maxie was shocked to see the look he gave her. She couldn't imagine what she'd done to deserve it. It was obviously a case of mistaken identity. But the man was on his feet now, with the older woman hanging on to his wrist.

'Hold the bride,' Maxie rapped into her radio mike. 'I need a good ten to fifteen minutes here.'

A second call to the leader of the orchestra had them breaking into a jolly piece and playing much louder than they had before. The chattering guests were none the wiser, Maxie confirmed with relief. If words were to be exchanged this could be done discreetly now. She also warned Diego of a slight delay, taking care to make nothing of it. A last call to Lucia worked in her favour.

'I'm not ready yet,' Holly yelled in the background, and, seizing the receiver from Lucia, added, 'Haven't you heard of the bride's right to keep the groom waiting?'

'No, I never heard that before,' Maxie said, forcing a wry note into her voice. Cutting the line, she hurried down the steps to what was looking more like trouble with every passing second.

She spoke to the man first. 'Can I help you?'

She backed away as he came after her, with the older woman, Maxie presumed his mother, hot on his heels.

She wasn't running away from either of them. She was drawing them out of earshot of the other guests. Leading them behind a screen that divided the wedding congregation from the linen-draped tables where the drinks for the champagne reception were sitting. She asked politely once again what was wrong.

'You don't know me,' the man rapped with an ugly expression. 'But I know you.'

He came towards her, with his mother hanging on to his arm.

'My name is Maxie Parrish,' Maxie said evenly. 'I'm Holly's wedding planner. If I can help you in any way…?' Her voice might sound calm, but her heart was thundering at the sight of so much barely contained anger.

'My name is Alessandro Fernandez,' the man snarled, as if this should mean something to her. 'And this is my mother, Señora Fernandez.'

'I'm very pleased to meet you, Señora Fernandez,' Maxie said politely, extending her hand. Instead of shaking it, the old lady started to cry. 'Your mother's upset,' she exclaimed, when Alessandro took another menacing step towards her. Walking between him and his mother, she ushered Señora Fernandez towards one of the chairs set out for the older guests—and gasped with fright when Alessandro tried to grapple it from her.

'Alesssandro!' Señora Fernandez exclaimed, equally shocked.

Diego erupted round the screen, flinging himself between Maxie and Alessandro. It took all three of his brothers to hold him back. Flinging the chair aside with a roar of fury, Alessandro squared up to Diego, at which point Señora Fernandez entered the fray.

Maxie's first impulse was to shield the older woman. 'Can't you see you're upsetting your mother?'

'*I'm* upsetting her?' Alessandro ground out. 'I think

you will find it is you, Señorita Parrish, who insults my mother with your very presence at this wedding!'

'I'm the wedding planner,' Maxie pointed out. 'Why would I not be here? And how have I upset you?' Something made her look at Diego for the answer.

Before anyone had a chance to speak Alessandro's mother stepped in. 'This behaviour does you no credit, Alessandro. It will not bring your brother back.' Turning to Maxie, she added, 'Why is it only women who understand?'

The older woman's voice was tinged with such sadness that Maxie shot another look at Diego, but he was pinning Alessandro to the spot with a warning stare. She didn't know anyone in Argentina, Maxie reasoned. What could she possibly have done to have caused such distress?

'Alessandro.' Diego's voice was low and menacing. 'Your mother is right. This does no good.'

'And what do *you* know?' Alessandro sneered. 'You have no heart. You have no feelings. You're not capable of feeling anything, Diego. Does this woman know that?' he said, sparing a withering glance for Maxie.

'Alessandro!' Señora Fernandez exclaimed, her voice pure steel. 'Have you forgotten yourself entirely? Apologise to Señorita Parrish this instant, and keep your rough house behaviour for the polo field where your aggression can be safely channelled.'

If all these fierce-looking men were encouraged by their mothers to work off their aggression on the polo field no wonder they couldn't be beaten, Maxie reflected as Diego stepped forward.

'Señora,' he said with a courteous bow to Alessandro's mother, 'may I offer you a refreshing drink before we return to our seats?'

But Alessandro wasn't finished yet. 'How could you allow this woman to come here?' he hissed, staring at Maxie as his mother graciously accepted Diego's offer.

'Not now, Alessandro,' Diego warned, conscious of Maxie standing behind him in a state of bewilderment. Alessandro's expression of fury was nothing to the hurt he could see on Maxie's face, which seemed to say, *What haven't you told me?*

'Will everyone please take their places?' she said in a calm voice. 'Ruiz?' she prompted, escorting the groom towards the screen behind which his guests sat waiting. 'You wouldn't want Holly to be upset by any further delay, would you?'

Ruiz was instantly in the moment. 'Of course not,' he said, heading off.

'Diego, Nacho, Kruz,' she added firmly. 'Please go with your brother.'

'And leave you here?' Diego demanded, as his brothers peeled away.

Holly was issuing instructions over her radio, and it was Señora Fernandez who took the floor. 'Please remember this is a public occasion,' she told her son. 'If you care anything about family pride, as you say you do, then this is your chance to prove it.'

'Gracias, señora,' Maxie said gratefully as the men finally left the two women together. 'I don't understand what provoked this, but perhaps you and I can talk after the wedding?'

'I would like that,' Señora Fernandez agreed.

Having restarted the programme for the day, Maxie thanked Señora Fernandez again for her intervention.

'You were doing very well on your own,' Señora Fernandez insisted. 'You seem to have a talent for handling hotheads,' she added wryly.

There was iron in that voice, but also sadness, Maxie thought as the older woman reached out to touch her face. 'Let's go,' Señora Fernandez announced, heading for the screen. 'We have a wedding to celebrate, don't we, Maxie?'

'Yes, we do,' Maxie agreed, hoping she'd stop shaking soon as she gave the go-ahead to the bride.

He had thought he'd lost everything after the accident, but that had been nothing compared to this, Diego realised. Getting through the wedding with good grace was the hardest thing he had ever had to do. He hadn't had a chance to explain what had happened to Maxie, and now he wondered if he was about to lose everything he cared about. He had tried to draw Maxie's attention during the long day, but she was always busy and there had been no chance for a private word. But every second he left her bewildered about what had happened was too long, and he had his speech to make yet.

Was it only she who was in the dark? The wedding ran as if on oiled wheels, but there was no chance to ask Diego about the heated exchange as Maxie would be on duty until the last guest went to bed.

She insisted on staying until everything had been cleared away, and Diego came looking for her to remind her that she had a baby to think of now.

'I wanted to speak to Señora Fernandez before I turned in.' She snatched a glance at her watch and grimaced when she saw the time.

'Señora Fernandez will be fast asleep by now,' Diego confirmed. 'You should be too.'

'What was that about, Diego?'

'I'll answer questions tomorrow.'

'No. Tonight,' Maxie insisted as all the hurt and bewilderment welled up inside her. 'We promised we'd share everything,' she reminded him.

'And I will.'

'Now, Diego.'

He took her to the stables, and they walked down the line of stalls where horses were breathing softly. 'You never did tell me who won the polo match,' she said.

'Does it matter?'

'You scored the winning goal.'

'Lucia told you? All I could think of was getting back to you. I just wanted the match over with. The only irony was winning my place back on the team when I thought I'd lost everything.'

'And today at the wedding?' she prompted. 'Why does Alessandro hate me so much, Diego? I don't even know him.'

Opening a door onto the hay barn, he took her inside. 'This is where I come when I have something on my mind,' he said. 'The horses are good company.'

'You mean they don't answer back?' Maxie suggested wryly.

Diego huffed a laugh. Shrugging off his jacket, he tossed it on a bale of hay and brought her down with him. 'Señora Fernandez and Alessandro are my best friend Oresto's mother and brother. Many years ago Oresto met a man who promised him he could change his life. That man was your father…'

Maxie drew in a sharp breath. 'Diego…?'

'I introduced them, and together we thought we could make lots of money. But sadly this story does not have a happy ending. I think you know how it ends…'

'The boy who killed himself?' Maxie exclaimed softly.

'Now it all makes sense. That lovely woman—Diego, I can't bear it. No wonder Alessandro was so angry when he realised who I was.'

'We can't change the past, but we can learn from it. I've laid my ghosts, Maxie. It's time for you to do the same.'

'I can't believe you were so closely associated with my father all those years ago. It's incredible to imagine it.'

'Our lives were intertwined before we even knew it,' he murmured, kissing her brow.

'What a tragedy,' she whispered, shifting restlessly in his arms. 'I can understand why Alessandro hates me.'

'Alessandro doesn't hate you. He will see sense and calm down. He always does.'

'But Señora Fernandez—'

'—is a very special woman. She forgave me many years ago. She told me that no more young lives should be wasted because of money. And I think she likes you.'

'I hope so,' Maxie murmured, relaxing.

'I repaid all the money Oresto lost—with interest.'

'And my father?'

Diego would never speak ill of the dead, let alone remind Maxie of a bad time in her life. 'I learned a lot from your father,' he said honestly.

'About what not to do?' she suggested.

His answer was to kiss her, and when he released her he said, 'I'll do everything in my power to keep you safe and prove that love can last, that it can become stronger with each passing year.'

Reassured, she snuggled close—and was so exhausted she slept until dawn.

'So, what shall we do now?' he said, turning to look at her as she stirred sleepily.

'I don't know,' she admitted. 'Have you got any ideas?'

'I've got a few,' he said.

It was three months later when Diego led Maxie through the doors of a prominent London store. They were staying with Ruiz and Holly in their London home, and making the most of all the wonderful shopping opportunities.

'What are we doing here?' Maxie demanded. 'The store is closing, Diego.'

'Not for you,' he said, steering her towards the elevator.

Not for Diego Acosta, Maxie amended wryly as a uniformed security guard personally escorted them in the opposite direction to the crowds heading home. She was touched to find Diego was taking her to the floor that specialised in nursery equipment.

'This is where you get to pick what you want and I get to pick what I want,' he explained.

'So, what do *you* want?' she said, frowning as she gazed down the aisles packed with baby equipment. 'I don't even know where to start—there's so much to choose from!'

'True,' Diego agreed. 'But I've already made my choice. If you'll have me, Maxie…?'

'Are you serious?'

'I'm down on one knee in front of witnesses. Will you marry me, Señorita Parrish? I should warn you before you answer there is one condition.'

'Which is?'

'You find another wedding planner to arrange our big day.'

After choosing the equipment for their first child's nursery, he took Maxie to a fairground. He wanted her to have something frivolous and fun to remember the day by, and he locked that memory in with a rather serious diamond ring. Maxie could run a business for as long as she wanted, but when they were together he wanted both of them to make time to have fun together—fun was something that had been conspicuous by its absence in Maxie's life before they met, as far as he could gather. 'I love you, Señora Acosta-to-be,' he told her as the big wheel soared into the sky.

'And I love you too, *señor,*' she told him, snuggling close. 'More than you will ever know.'

'Show me that ring,' he teased her.

She held up her hand to admire it.

It would take many years of persuasion before Maxie would believe that he *hadn't* arranged fireworks to choose that precise moment to light up the sky.

EPILOGUE

MAXIE's wedding dress was the most feminine thing she had ever worn. A simple column of ivory silk, overlaid with the most exquisite cobweb-fine Swiss lace, skimmed her body to her hips before flaring into a fuller skirt with a filmy lace train. She held a modest trailing bouquet of blush pink peonies and fragrant white freesia, interspersed with the palest green feathery foliage. Lucia and Holly were her attendants, and there was one very special page boy—a six-month-old baby boy. Though Jaime Acosta slept peacefully throughout the ceremony in Señora Fernandez's arms.

Needless to say Jaime already had his first pony. Diego had picked out a small grey for his son within an hour of his birth. Diego might be a little crazy, and Maxie was definitely the person people came to when they wanted something sorted out, but Maxie thought that was why it worked so well between them: they were like two pieces of a jigsaw that fitted perfectly together.

'Ready?' Lucia demanded in a voice full of suppressed excitement as she carefully handed Maxie down from the horse-drawn carriage outside the tiny chapel at the *estancia*.

'For anything,' Maxie agreed, squeezing Lucia's hand.

'That's just as well,' Holly agreed wryly.

'You look beautiful,' Señora Fernandez exclaimed—sentiments that were echoed by the housekeepers, Maria and Adriana.

'Thank you,' Maxie whispered, kissing each of the older women on the cheek in turn, before dropping a kiss on her son's downy brow.

'I'm so happy for you,' Holly exclaimed, tweaking Maxie's veil. 'Wait until Diego sees you!'

Maxie had to admit it was quite a transformation from the bedraggled girl who had arrived on a tiny island in the middle of a storm with only business on her mind.

Had she really thought she was ready for this?

When Diego turned to look at her as she entered the chapel the breath left Maxie's chest in a rush. She hardly remembered the ceremony, but when they came out to the cheers of their guests as man and wife she did remember the look she had shared with Diego throughout, the silent pledge that bound them for life. And with the blessings and goodwill of everyone around them there was only one duty left for the bride…

'Oh, *no!*' Lucia exclaimed as she caught Maxie's bouquet.

As if Lucia hadn't batted every other woman out of the way in order to leap up and snatch it for herself, Maxie thought, laughing as she turned around. 'You can always give it back to me and I'll throw it again,' she suggested.

'No way,' Lucia replied, to groans of complaint from the other women. 'These flowers need water,' she explained briskly, as a certain American polo player hoved into view.

Then Diego was at Maxie's side, with their son in his arms. 'The jet is waiting,' he murmured discreetly. 'Can we leave now? I can't wait to have you on my own.'

'I love you,' Maxie whispered, staring deep into her husband's eyes. 'I love you both so much.'

'You've given me more than you know,' Diego said, putting a protective arm around her shoulders, 'and my love for you grows stronger every day.'

* * * * *

DON'T TELL THE WEDDING PLANNER

AIMEE CARSON

For dearest Claire,
whose hard work, exuberance
and sheer talent are an inspiration.
With love.

The summer she turned eleven, **Aimee Carson** left the children's section of the library and entered an aisle full of Mills & Boon novels. She promptly pulled out a book, sat on the floor, and read the entire story. It has been a love affair that has lasted for over thirty years.

Despite a fantastic job working part-time as a physician in the Alaskan Bush (think Northern Exposure and ER, minus the beautiful mountains and George Clooney), she also enjoys being at home in the gorgeous Black Hills of South Dakota, riding her dirt bike with her three wonderful kids and beyond patient husband. But, whether at home or at work, every morning is spent creating the stories she loves so much. Her motto? Life is too short to do anything less than what you absolutely love. She counts herself lucky to have two jobs she adores, and incredibly blessed to be a part of the Mills & Boon's family of talented authors.

PROLOGUE

Dear *Ex Factor,*
I'm in desperate need of help. My best friend is marrying my former boyfriend and now she's asked me to be her maid of honor. My ex and I dated for over three years and everyone thought we'd eventually marry. The breakup was messy, but when he started dating my BF we all managed to reach an understanding. I'm really happy for my girlfriend and I want to be there for her on her big day, but I dread all the comments from friends and family. What should I do?

Callie: First off, congratulations to all three of you for working through your differences so that everyone remains friends. Secondly, I've been in your shoes, having recently arranged the Ex-Man's wedding—*my* ex-boyfriend—which he ruined with a zombie invasion. :) If *you* are happy for the bride and groom then most of the guests will see this. Unfortunately, there will be those with thoughtless comments and questions. I found it best to be prepared. So formulate a few vague, generic responses beforehand so you won't get caught unprepared.

Ex-Man: I think you only need one response: "I'm mainly here for the free food and beer." And if you're planning a zombie invasion to liven up the reception, don't tell the wedding planner.

CHAPTER ONE

MAN, WHAT A lot of work just to get hitched.

Matt weaved his way through the sightseers enjoying the ballroom of the historic Riverway mansion, a plantation that had once taken part in producing 75 percent of the world's cotton, but was now reduced to group tours and a venue for weekend events. He knew he was headed for the outdoor, private wedding reception when he spotted two Southern belles in authentic dress.

Choosing a Civil *War* theme to celebrate a marriage seemed wrong. But who knows, maybe the couple enjoyed the irony? Regardless, given the authentic mansion worthy of Scarlett O'Hara and the costumes of the guests, the wedding planner was either a genius…or insane. Matt was pulling for the latter, because he absolutely needed Callie LaBeau to be insane. If she were a reasonable, rational individual, she'd refuse Matt's request. Which meant his plans to fly in, fix his problem and fly back home would be over. And he'd be screwed.

Catching up with the two ladies in 1800s dresses, petticoats rustling beneath, wasn't hard. Their hoopskirts caught as they tried to open one of the French doors leading to the backyard, and their attempt to cross the threshold side by side didn't work out so well.

Matt bit back the grin and the fatigue of thirty-six hours on two hours of sleep, pulling open the other door.

The one in an ugly yellow-colored dress tossed him an inviting smile. "Thanks."

"Bathroom breaks must be a real bitch," Matt said.

The lady in lavender laughed. "You have no idea."

"Do either of you know where I can find Callie La-Beau?" he asked.

Lavender lady jerked her thumb toward one end of the outdoor reception. "Last time I saw her, she was over by the bar."

Matt took that as good news. Alcohol would definitely be a requirement in a crazy setting such as this, hopefully softening the wedding planner toward Matt's cause.

"I think she's the only one in royal-blue." Yellow dress sounded a little jealous.

Matt took the exit leading out to the twenty-acre grounds that smelled of freshly cut grass and held the crowd of wedding guests in Civil War costumes. Kerosene lamps sat on tables covered in white and dangled alongside Spanish moss in the giant oaks. The trees provided a canopy for the reception, the soft lamps casting a glow against the twilight sky.

He hoped the lamps were fake or the theme would soon be overrun by the yellow of firemen suits.

Fortunately, the lighting was low enough that Matt's dark pants and white, button-down shirt blended with the attire of the staff posing as servants. As for the male guests, half wore blue Union uniforms while the others sported gray Confederate uniforms—given the choice of a Southern theme, most likely the bride's side of the family. Matt scanned the brightly colored Southern belle dresses dotting the scene and spied one of royal-blue in front of an old-fashioned buggy being used as a bar.

Relief relaxed his shoulders. Today's four-hour flight to New Orleans had been turbulent and hot, hopeless for snagging a few minutes of shut-eye. A cold beer would go down good about now.

He approached the makeshift bar and leaned a hip against the wagon. "Callie LaBeau?"

The woman turned, and Matt was hit with a vision of hair the color of dark honey, wide, brown eyes and a slim but clearly female body filling out the bust of her gown. Appreciation thrummed through his veins, but he ignored the distracting sensation.

"Matt Paulson." He stuck out his hand.

"Colin called and said he was sending you my way."

A palm briefly pressed against his. The soft skin and the drawl, as honey-soaked as her hair, brought to mind hot, Southern nights filled with heated skin and sweat-soaked sheets.

Stick to the plan, Paulson. Get in, take care of the problem and get out.

She released his hand and her lips quirked. "Though Colin didn't mention he was sending you *now*."

There was no irritation in her voice, only the calm tone of one who dealt with life's surprises and upsets with grace and dignity. He liked her already.

She'd need that skill set for what he had in mind.

"Colin told me I could find you here." He scanned the guests milling about. "I assumed you were scoping out a venue for an event. He didn't mention I was walking into the middle of an actual wedding reception."

"Colin's a good friend, and I owe him a lot. But he's

an obsessed gamer," she responded with a shrug that said it all.

Matt understood. Over the course of the past two years, he'd learned that the geekdom world was built on the backs of those whose lives revolved around the game. Outside social conventions often didn't compute. His brother's life currently consisted of work and spending hours immersed in the world of *Dungeons of Zhorg,* having traded one obsession for another. Matt just hoped Tommy's current fixation lasted.

Because dungeons and dragons and trolls beat the hell out of crystal meth.

As always, the years-old ache in his chest hurt as he remembered a time when his brother was gaunt, paranoid and delusional. Sick and wasting away right in front of Matt's eyes.

His stomach roiled, and he pushed the memories aside. "Should we meet up tomorrow or do you have a minute?"

"I'll be out of town all day on Saturday. How long are you in New Orleans?"

"Until Sunday morning."

She let out a huff of humor. "Now it is, then."

Callie reached into the bodice of her gown. The sight of those graceful fingers dipping into her cleavage hiked his brow and tightened his groin. Fortunately, he kept his expression one of amused sarcasm rather than the truth: a sleep-deprived guy who found the sight a total turn-on. A grin curled her mouth as she pulled out a tiny pocket watch.

"I try to keep things as authentic as possible. As the one in charge, that makes things difficult. Working without my tablet has been a real pain." She glanced at the time and blew an escaped strand of honey-colored hair from her cheek. “My assistant can keep an eye on things for a bit. But you only have twenty minutes until I need to prepare for the cutting of the cake.”

Twenty minutes wasn’t a lot of time to convince someone to do the impossible.

He ordered a beer and Callie requested a club soda. After she spoke with her assistant, who wore a similar gown in red, and looked a lot more harried than the wedding planner herself, they headed to a small bar along the back of the house that wasn’t in use.

“What I wouldn’t give to lean back in that seat right now.” Callie looked longingly at a chair at one of the few empty tables, like a student eyeing an espresso after an all-nighter. “But this dress makes relaxing impossible. And I’m tired of sitting up straight.”

“That getup doesn’t look comfortable, either.”

“The petticoat is stiff and the corset makes breathing impossible.” She leaned against the counter, her brown eyes intrigued. “So tell me about your wedding-day fantasies, Mr. Paulson.”

A bark of shocked laughter shot from his mouth. Hell, before he could think about tying the knot he’d have to be in one place long enough to successfully date someone. And that wouldn’t happen anytime soon. If ever.

How many times had he tried, and miserably failed, to be the long-distance boyfriend? How many times had he tried, and failed, to keep a relationship going? An occasional round of great sex was one thing, but that held a woman for only so long. And there weren’t many willing to play second chair to his responsibilities to Tommy. Eventually, they all left, the resentment toward his priorities too much to overcome.

Matt cleared his throat. "I'm not here to discuss my fantasies."

Fantasies.

Another stab of awareness hit, stronger than the one before. Damn, why were they even using the word? Currently *his* fantasies consisted of a brown-eyed beauty wearing an old-fashioned dress with a ridiculous hoop beneath. But the thought of unlacing a corset was surprisingly…hot.

He settled next to her at the counter. "I'm here about my brother's wedding."

Was that a hint of interest that flickered through her eyes?

Before he could decide, she glanced down at her drink and took a sip before carefully setting down her glass. "So why isn't he here?"

"Can't get the time off work."

More accurately, with Tommy's track record, he couldn't risk losing another job.

"And the bride to be?" she drawled.

A history as bad as the groom's. Perhaps worse.

"They had prior commitments," Matt said instead, sending her a smile that didn't encourage further questioning. "I had a few days off, so I volunteered to come down and get the ball rolling."

She eyed him steadily. "Dedicated of you."

Matt's lips quirked dryly. She had no idea.

"What can I say?" he said with an easy shrug. "I'm a hell of a brother."

Matt glanced down at the woman who stood a good six inches shorter than him. A height which was just high enough for a great view down the front of that ridiculous outfit that displayed her breasts as though they were a commodity. Perhaps during the time period of the dress, they had been.

Man. He rubbed his eyes. The fatigue was clearly getting to him. He'd worked four twelve-hour shifts in a row, the E.R. packed with patients every night—just how he liked it. The last night he'd encountered a trauma case that left him flying high on adrenaline, unable to sleep. He loved the challenge, and he was damned good at emergency medicine, too. He'd finished up a satisfying two weeks of work in one of the busiest E.R.s in Los Angeles and had been set to climb on a flight back to Michigan to check on Tommy. Until his brother had called and shared his and Penny's plans for the wedding. So, instead, Matt had headed to LAX and climbed onto a plane bound for New Orleans.

"Don't be too impressed, Mr. Paulson."

Matt blinked, forcing himself back to the present and the lovely set of boobs. "Come again?"

"The corset pushes everything up. They're not as big as the dress makes them look."

He quirked an eyebrow, amused by her admission. "Who said I was looking?"

Even the laugh that escaped held a hint of the South. "No one had to say anything, Mr. Paulson. I can see your eyes with my own."

Matt scrubbed a hand down his face. "Sorry. I haven't had much sleep in the past thirty-six hours and I got a little distracted. And I think you should call me Matt." A hint of a grin finally crept up his face. "I'm guessing the formalities aren't necessary once you get caught leering down a woman's dress. How much time do I have left?"

Her lips quirked as she reached in to her bodice "It's now seven forty-five. You have ten minutes left." She tipped her head curiously. "Don't you wear a watch?"

"I do," he said. "I just enjoy the sight of you pulling that watch out of your dress."

Her warm laugh encouraged him to settle more comfortably against the counter.

"So tell me about your *brother's* wedding fantasy," she said.

She turned and leaned her elbows back on the counter, and he wondered if she knew the position put her on even better display. From the focused look on her face, he'd say no. The woman had slipped fully into themed-wedding-planner mode. He forced his eyes away from the expanse of skin of her bared shoulders and the line between the curve of her breasts.

"Simple," Matt said. "His fantasy involves a video game."

Callie groaned. "That's why Colin sent you to me."

"Tommy and Penny want their wedding to be a *Dungeons of Zhorg* weekend set here in New Orleans," he said. "And since I volunteered to come and hire someone to organize the wedding, I wanted to check and make sure there wouldn't be any legal problems with the plan. So I hunted Colin down to clear up any copyright hassles."

"Which would only be a problem if you were selling tickets to the public. I assume this is a private party."

"More or less."

Her eyebrows drifted higher. "So which is it, more or less?"

Here was where things were about to get tricky.

Matt shifted on his feet, trying to get comfortable against the counter. "They want to combine their wedding with a LARP event for their fellow gaming friends. You know, a live-action—"

"Live-action role-playing. Yes, I know. I dated Colin long enough to be well versed in geek speak."

Matt felt his brow crinkle in surprise.

So Colin was her ex. When Matt had searched the creator of *Dungeons of Zhorg* out at Rainstorm Games and found him in his office late on a Friday afternoon, Matt's opinion of the geeked-out gamer had been complete. Fortunately, the man had no problem with Tommy and Penny's plans. In fact, Colin thought a newspaper article about the event would be good publicity for his game. Matt had told him he'd check with Tommy before agreeing, but figured his brother and the equally geeked-out fiancée would be thrilled. Matt could just see the headline now.

Ex-Drug Addicts Saved by Finding True Love Through the *Dungeons of Zhorg.*

Everyone would love the story. Hell, *Matt* loved the story.

He just wished he could believe the current state of affairs would last.

The familiar surge of unease filled his stomach like a concrete truck unloading its contents. Damn. If he'd learned anything over the years of Tommy's addiction, it was that taking care of today was the best Matt could do. Sometime it was *more* than Matt could do.

And often, his best just hadn't been good enough.

Matt pushed the thought aside and returned to the more interesting topic of Callie. "You and your ex must have remained pretty good friends if he's sending you my business."

Her eyes crinkled at the corners. "You'd have to pry the game controller from his cold, dead fingers before the man would admit the truth, but he owes me. I helped him track Jamie down after they first met. Now they're married." Callie let out a chuckle. "That and he wants to ensure the wedding gets done right. You know, with the proper attention to Zhorg detail." He heard, rather than saw, the roll of her eyes in her tone. "But a ceremony shouldn't be too hard to pull off."

"Actually, the entire weekend needs to be planned."

"Wait," she said, straightening up from the counter to face him. "I thought you just needed me for the wedding part. You want me to be in charge of the entire LARPing *event?*"

After several years of experience as the locums doctor in various E.R.s located in big cities across the country, Matt had learned how to handle addicts flying higher than a kite, as dangerous as a violent criminal.

Much like a cornered wild animal, the key was to never let 'em see you flinch.

He maintained her gaze and adopted his best soothing tone. "Yes. But the weekend doesn't need to be that elaborate. Throw up a few tents, offer a little food, and the guests bring their own costumes. And we can call it a day."

He knew he'd totally downplayed Tommy and Penny's vision for the weekend, but Matt thought they were dreaming too big anyway. He'd told them both pulling off exactly what they wanted would be impossible, short of crawling into the video game itself.

Her brow scrunched and several seconds ticked by.

"How much time do I have?" she asked.

"Two months."

"You're kidding, right?"

"I'm completely serious."

"Impossible. Sorry, Mr. Paulson, you'll have to find someone else." She reached out and took his wrist, pushing up his sleeve to peek at his watch. And then gave him a pretty smile. "Time's up."

Momentarily stunned, he watched her head toward the cake table.

Until he remembered his goal, and took off, following her through the crowd. "I love what you did with *The Wizard of Oz* wedding," he said, keeping stride with Callie. "And having the Mad Hatter as the wedding officiant in the *Alice in Wonderland* theme was inspired."

Did he sound as stupid as he felt?

"How did you learn about that?" she asked.

"Colin gave me one of your brochures. He said you're the best in the business."

Callie cast him an amused glance but kept on walking. "Are you trying to use flattery to change my mind?"

"You bet," he said. "Is it working?"

"Not yet, but feel free to keep trying."

"The Elizabethan venue was spectacular—" he dodged two Southern belle dresses and a Confederate soldier "—and *The Three Musketeers* theme was cool, as well."

She shot him a wry look. "Pirates," she said. "It was a pirates theme."

"Whatever," he said. "Who else is better qualified for a *Dungeons of Zhorg* themed wedding?"

Callie stared out across the crowd of guests milling about as they enjoyed appetizers. A furrow of concentration between her brows, she appeared to be running through the idea in her head. She chewed on her cheek before swiping her lower lip with her tongue. The sight of the now damp, full mouth was putting a whammy on his libido.

Huh, if he was this easily distracted, it was well past time he sought out some female companionship. To take the edge off, so to speak. Or maybe he simply needed sleep.

"Okay. It might be doable. Crazy, mind you. But doable," she drawled, and then looked around the current scene. "After all, crazy *is* my specialty."

Matt smiled his first real smile since Tommy had shared his engagement news and Matt couldn't decide if the marriage would make conditions better…or worse.

The potential for an epic screwup was great.

Callie sent him a wide smile back. The gesture wasn't sexual, but the genuine nature lit her eyes in a way that left them sparkling, sending another bolt of heat and awareness up his spine.

Too bad his flight out was Sunday. And there was no way he could delay the trip. He'd already gone two weeks without flying back home, to the childhood house Matt had moved back into, sharing the residence with Tommy since the very first round of rehab had failed, all those years ago.

He cleared his throat. "Fantastic," he said.

Mission accomplished. Problem addressed, solution found and past time to move on. Or, as the motto went in the E.R., treat 'em and street 'em. Everything was turning out better than he'd planned. He'd even get a full night's sleep tonight.

"Let me know how much to put down as a deposit.

I'll get you my email so you can send me the invoices as we go." He slipped his wallet from his pocket and pulled out his card, filling in the contacts. "And here are Tommy and my cell phone numbers too, just in case you have any questions—"

"Wait." Her brown eyes grew even wider as she took his card. "You're not leaving, are you?"

Concern edged up his back, making his shoulders feel stiff. "I have a hot date with the king-size bed in my hotel room—a rendezvous I'm really looking forward to. And Sunday I *have* to head back home."

Callie leaned closer, bringing that lovely view in a more direct line of vision. "Listen, Mr. Paulson."

How was he supposed to listen, much less concentrate, with a view like that? And clearly the stress of the upcoming event had knocked them back to a last-name basis instead of first.

"You're lucky I have a light enough schedule and an assistant to help me," Callie said. "But I can't do this alone. There are too many decisions that need to be made, and made quickly, too. I won't take responsibility for making the wrong ones. Someone needs to be around to help."

"Both me and my brother will be available by phone and internet."

"Not good enough. We can't afford to play phone tag. Not with so little time and so many big choices to be made."

"What choices?"

"Venue, for one. This won't be your average setting. We'll need a large outdoor park with adequate parking. Food, for another. A menu based on medieval times? Complicated. And from what I remember about LARP, there are games revolving around the video. And they'll need to be authentic."

"Tommy and Penny won't care about the details," he lied.

They would care. In fact, they'd care too much. That's what made a fan crazy enough to base their entire wedding around a video game. An obsession about even the minutest of details.

"I once had a client who said she didn't care. But she did," Callie said. "Despite the fact the bride and groom were thrilled with my work, the one paying the bills wasn't." She tipped her head. "Who's paying for all of this?"

"Me."

Something flashed in her eyes that he didn't recognize. Probably questions and comments and opinions about a wedding being paid for by the brother of the groom. Not your traditional arrangement. But then again, who else was there? No one.

And there hadn't been for a long time.

Callie, to her credit, didn't pry. "Then, officially, you'd be my boss. If you want me to agree to plan this event, you're going to have to at least stick around long enough to make a few of the major decisions."

"How long?"

"Depends on how our hunt for a venue goes. Can't say for sure. Maybe a week?"

Damn. That would mean he'd go almost a month without physically checking in on Tommy. The last time Matt had done that, he'd missed some early clues, and Tommy had wound up in rehab again.

But that was two years ago and he'd promised Tommy he'd take care of this.

Matt turned his options over in his head. As far as he could see, he didn't have any. He'd only just convinced the woman to take this project on. Refusing her now would be counterproductive. And finding someone else to participate in this harebrained idea would be absolutely impossible.

"All right," he said, raking a frustrated hand through his hair. "I'll give you until Tuesday and then we can reassess from there."

"Fine. But we need to get started right away, beginning with a meeting to list exactly what y'all want. I have to go out of town tomorrow, family stuff I have to take care of. But I'll put together a list of potential park sites and Sunday we can make the rounds to check them out. We can use the drive to put together our ideas for the wedding weekend."

Sticking around to help nail down the details for this crazy event? Not exactly what he'd had in mind when he'd climbed on the plane today. Matt could afford two more days in New Orleans before heading home. And Callie's brilliant smile helped ease the frustrating turn of events.

"Sunday morning it is," he said.

"Forecast calls for a heat wave the next few days or so." Callie's grin grew bigger. "Hope you like the weather hot, Mr. Paulson."

The playful grin brought about one of his own.

"Ms. LaBeau," Matt said, leaning close. "I like everything hot."

Matt entered his hotel room and toed off his shoes, unbuttoning his shirt as he headed toward the bathroom. Fatigue made his movement clumsy as he flicked open the front of his pants. After tossing his clothes aside, he flipped on the water and stepped inside the marble shower, groaning as hot water coursed over his hair and down his skin.

The ache in his muscles had started during the cramped four-hour flight, and now finally eased. Matt leaned his hand against the wall and bowed his head, letting the wet heat wash away the remainder of the stress of the past thirty-six hours.

It looked like his plans to get in and out of New Orleans quickly so he could check on Tommy had just bitten the dust. As a consolation, he now had a little more time to spend with Callie LaBeau. And the next time they saw each other, he will have had a full night's sleep.

As far as screwed-up plans went, this one could have been worse.

But the time had come to rethink his approach.

First up, place a call to Tommy. A phone check never gave as much information as a face-to-face interaction, but it beat no contact at all. Unfortunately, no one could assess weight loss and skin color over the phone. Of course, the first sign Tommy was slipping was the way he refused to look Matt in the eyes.

Second, the trip around town to locate an available park. Matt ignored the tightening in his groin as he considered a day in the car. With Callie. Alone. Awareness definitely hung in the air around them, though he sensed a hint of reluctance on her part. A reluctance that could have meant anything.

Because they were working together.

Because she had a boyfriend, though Matt doubted that to be the case.

Because she still carried a torch for Colin…

Matt soaped himself clean, picturing the golden skin and the honey-colored hair and big brown eyes. The little dip in her upper lip. The way she nibbled on the inside of her cheek while lost in thought. The pink tongue that licked the corner of her wide mouth.

He pictured that mouth on his skin. The teeth. The *tongue* traveling down his chest. Past his abdomen. The lips closing around his—

He slammed his eyes shut.

Fifteen minutes later, clean and refreshed and a whole lot more relaxed, Matt padded from the bathroom and into his bedroom. He dried his hair and wrapped the towel around his waist, heading to the window and pulling back the curtain. The lights of New Orleans spread out before him. As much as he dreaded the conversation, he picked up his cell phone and punched speed dial.

He hated the way his stomach tightened before every contact. After two years of a sober Tommy, Matt should have stopped bracing for the worst every time. Only problem was, Tommy had achieved sobriety before. Six times total. Every relapse had gotten harder than the one before. And had broken Matt's heart a little more.

"Hello?"

Despite everything, as always his brother's voice made Matt smile.

"Tommy. Fought any good dragons lately?"

The laugh on the other end sounded robust, easing a little of Matt's nerves.

"Dude, you should have seen the troll that Penny took down the other day," Tommy said.

"Big?"

"Massive."

"Hope her cooking isn't going to your waist. Your chain mail still fit?"

When Tommy's chuckle finally died down, he said, "That headhunter called again today."

The news formed a knot in Matt's chest and expanded, the pressure creating a wound that would never fully heal. The first time the recruiter from Jaris Hawking Healthcare had called about a job, Matt had been thrilled. At the time he'd been too busy cleaning up the last of his brother's latest mess to search for a job, but things with Tommy had seemed to be settled and Matt was ready to finally make the longed-for career move. Matt had spent hours researching the busy hospital in Miami, looking forward to the excitement he craved. But just when he'd been set to sign the papers, Tommy had relapsed again, requiring another round of rehab. And a family member to be there to ensure it happened. Matt had finally realized that he'd never be able to move.

Giving up that dream had hurt like hell, but there was no sense rehashing old disappointments.

Tommy went on, "They said they were desperate for someone with your talents."

"I hope you told him I'm still not interested." If he repeated the lie enough, he just might begin to believe it. Besides, he had more important things to ask. "How's work?" He aimed for a nonchalant tone, but he knew Tommy saw straight through the question.

"You don't need to check up on me, Matt." Tommy didn't sound annoyed, just resigned. "Work is fine. Penny is fine. *I'm* fine."

"You sure you two geeked-out lovebirds want to get

hitched during a lame-ass reenactment of a video game? Not too late to go for the Elvis wedding in Vegas. Or better yet, a pirate-themed adventure wedding in Hawaii. Think of it. A week's vacation in Maui with all expenses paid by yours truly. What better wedding gift could a brother ask for, huh? I could do with a base tan myself."

"The wedding absolutely has to be in New Orleans. We want trolls. And dragons. And Matt…?"

Matt dropped onto the bed, leaning back against the headboard and propping up his feet. "Yeah, sport?"

"I'll pay you back."

Matt's lips twisted wryly as affection kicked him the chest. Every goddamned time. The kid had spent the past twenty-five years worming his way into Matt's heart, until Tommy was so firmly entrenched, there was nothing Matt could do. He could picture his brother's wavy brown hair, earnest face and appreciative gaze. Beneath those ribs beat a heart of gold.

Amazing what havoc an addiction could inflict.

"You bet you'll pay me back," Matt said with a teasing tone. "With twenty percent interest. Wait, I forgot about inflation. Make that thirty percent. Didn't I tell you? You're my retirement fund."

"Which means you're screwed, bro."

Matt let out a scoff. "Better odds than on Wall Street."

Tommy laughed. When his brother finally grew silent, Matt went on.

"Seriously, though?" Matt said. "Don't worry about the money. That's what brothers are for. Just…"

Keep it together.

Stay clean.

Don't break my heart again.

"Just make sure that future wife of yours doesn't kick your ass on level ten like last month or I'll have to disown you," Matt said.

Matt could hear the smile in Tommy's voice. "You got it."

CHAPTER TWO

TWO DAYS LATER Callie studied Matt as he drove her Toyota out of New Orleans. It had been a long time since Callie had been so curious about a guy. Matt was friendly, charming, and sexy enough to eat with her fingers. There'd been no sign of embarrassment at being caught staring at her cleavage.

Even now the memory left her body vibrating with energy.

But a lingering hint of hesitation clung to him, a reserve that was fascinating. Intriguing. He'd shown up at the reception two nights ago with *goal* written all over his face.

They'd been traveling for about an hour now, but hadn't had a chance to talk much about business. Callie had been too busy directing him around town to potential parks to use as the site for the *Dungeons of Zhorg* weekend. The first two were mostly a bust. But she had high hopes for the one they were heading to now.

She'd asked Matt to drive, explaining she needed to take notes while they discussed the plans for the event, listing out the pros and cons of the two sites they'd just checked out. But the excuse sounded lame, even to her. Especially considering she spent half her time giving

Matt directions. But she didn't care. Because with his attention on the traffic, and her vantage point from the passenger seat, she was free to enjoy the view.

And she wasn't talking about the city she loved.

Matt's lean, muscular frame filled the driver's seat of her car. Given the heat wave that had settled in yesterday, he'd wisely chosen to wear shorts. Shorts that allowed a view of hard thighs. Muscular calves.

He'd had to push the seat all the way back to allow room for his long legs. His olive-colored T-shirt clung to a broad set of shoulders and biceps that flexed with every turn of the steering wheel. Not grossly big. More like well-defined and…just right. Enticing. Callie preferred the casual clothes to Friday night's slacks and button-down. Because today he looked more relaxed. He also looked as though he'd gotten some sleep.

A large truck ahead of them whipped into their lane, and Matt reacted instantly to avoid the hit. No cursing. No frazzled look. Not even an indrawn breath or a frown for the dangerous driver.

Just like Friday night, when he'd shown up so focused, he employed a plan-and-attack mantra while driving. *Goal* written all over his face. Focused. Decisive. He never hesitated. And he had lightning-fast reflexes, if the maneuver he just pulled was anything to go by. They turned into the parking lot of their next potential venue, a grassy park on the outskirts of town.

Matt turned off the car and glanced at Callie, and she realized he'd just caught her studying him. Very closely. And thoroughly.

"Is this the equivalent of me staring down your cleavage?" he asked.

She ignored the heat thrumming through her veins

and exited the car, missing the air-conditioning already and waiting for him to follow suit to respond. "Just admiring your quick reflexes."

From across the roof of her Toyota, his lips quirked. "So you were checking out my…skills."

She bit back a smile. "We have a lot of planning to do, Mr. Paulson."

"Matt."

"Matt," she said without missing a beat. "I'm just trying to figure you out. And decide whether you're gonna be the guy who makes my job easier or harder."

Normally she meant the words in the sense of a client being difficult. Hard to please. And far too demanding in their wedding-day wishes. Or incapable of making up their mind.

With Matt she knew the decisions would come quickly and decisively. Yep, with Matt the easier or harder delineation was based on Callie's ability, or inability, to stay focused with such a fine specimen of male anatomy on display.

"What have you decided?" he asked.

"I'm not sure yet," she said with a tiny grin. "I'll let you know when I figure it out."

After a few beats filled with a scorching temperature courtesy of New Orleans's latest heat wave and Matt's assessing gaze, he gave a sharp nod and headed up the brick walkway.

Fortunately the path was lined with oaks providing shade from the relentless sun. The playground to their left hummed with the activity of a few families crazy enough to brave the temperatures. An ice-cream truck was parked along the curb. The beautifully maintained park was clearly well run, the amenities nice. Even the current weather had been addressed. Misting machines with large fans had been set up along the path in front, providing blessed relief from the heat.

A drop of sweat trickled between her breasts and she ignored the long, lean legs of Matt as he walked beside her. The view wasn't helping her struggles with heat stroke.

"So there's a large private area of the park that is available for rent on the dates we need," she said. "This place is a little farther out of town than I wanted, but there's ample parking." She could feel his eyes on her, but she kept her focus forward as she came to a stop at the field.

She pointed at the outdoor building sitting in the middle of the field. "The pavilion can be used as the main structure and where the food will be served. We're going to want the restrooms close by, even if it does ruin the medieval feel."

"Better to ruin the Middle Ages feel than contract cholera."

Callie smiled but continued on, "There's more than enough space to set up the tents and the sites for the various games." She studied the grassy field, a natural border provided by oak trees. "We can set up the gaming tent over here."

He shot her another appreciative glance, and this time she couldn't resist.

"What?" she said.

"You've already given this a lot of thought."

"We don't have much time."

Matt leaned back against the oak. "Why did you agree to arrange this event?"

"It's my job. This is what I do."

He hesitated and crossed his arms as if settling in to wait for a better reason. Callie longed for a cool breeze, or heck, just a breeze would do. Anything to lower the temperature brought about by the Southern climate and Matt's disturbing eyes.

"Because I owe Colin," she said. "Our breakup was… complicated."

Translation: I screwed up big-time.

"But we've managed to remain friends," she went on. "And he's a regular contributor to my blog, *The Ex Factor.*"

At his look of confusion, a grin slid up her face. "It's a he-said, she-said column where readers can pose questions and we offer opinions from our unique perspectives."

"Is that the only reason you agreed to take this on? Because your ex helps you out?"

"Isn't that enough?"

He squinted across the field. "I'm sure you have better ways to spend your time than arranging a weekend LARP event."

Was he speaking for her or for himself?

Callie nibbled on her lower lip and looked across the field. How to explain? Because if her business became successful enough, everyone would forget about her mistake in college? Because maybe, just maybe, if she landed a big enough event with the proper publicity, her parents would stop waiting for her to muck up again?

She liked her life, damn it. And while she hadn't left for college with the plan of losing her scholarship and getting kicked out, she was delighted with what she'd built. She was happy, *proud* of all she'd accomplished despite her initial flub.

Now if she could only convince her family to be proud, too….

She pushed the thought away and shrugged. "Every little bit of publicity is good for business."

Matt studied her with those observant brown eyes that always set her on edge, mostly in a good way. Making her aware of what she wore. Making her aware of what she said. Normally she focused on business or was totally relaxed. Then again, her clients usually consisted of happy couples or middle-aged parents. Dreamy *eligible* men didn't knock on her doors wanting her services. And it was a little disturbing to be second-guessing every little thing as she went.

And if he thought her answer to his question was bull, he didn't say.

When she couldn't take those eyes studying her anymore, she turned her attention back to the field before them. "It's more than we need, but I think this works perfectly. You agree?"

"You're the expert."

"I'm sure I'll have to remind you of that sometime in the future." She lifted her hair from her neck, longing for a cool breeze. "Let's head back before you're treating me for heat stroke."

The walk back toward the car was even more uncomfortable, the sun now higher in the sky. Matt's silence and his occasional glances left her thinking he planned to quiz her further. And with the hot temperature, and the hotter gaze—not to mention the zillion questions she saw in his eyes—didn't make for a comfortable walk. Perhaps she should do a little quizzing of her own.

"So, tell me why you got elected to travel to New Orleans to arrange a wedding," she said.

His lips twisted wryly, but he didn't answer right away, so she went on.

"Over the years, I've worked with mothers, fathers, sisters and friends of the bride," she said. "But I've never worked with the brother of the groom before."

An amused light appeared in his eyes. "It's an honor to be your first."

She kept her gaze on his profile as they headed up the walk, the sound of the misting fans droning ahead. "Which doesn't answer my question."

"I told you, Tommy and Penny are up in Michigan. They both have jobs they can't afford to lose. And I happen to have the time."

"Where are your parents?"

"Dead."

A pang of sympathy hit, and she studied his expression, looking for clues to his thoughts. There weren't any.

"I'm sorry," she said. "How old were you?"

"Twenty-one. The year Tommy turned sixteen."

Leaving you in charge, she didn't say. Raising a teenager when Matt was barely past the stage himself had to have been a massive struggle.

Turning the news over in her head, Callie headed for one of the few massive fans that didn't have kids hopping up and down in front of it. A large oak provided shade and when she stepped closer to the machine, the cool mist hit her skin, and Callie almost groaned in relief. A fine spray of water coated her face, her neck, and her T-shirt and shorts. But she didn't care.

With the way Matt looked at her, a hosing off wouldn't be out of order.

"Where are Penny's parents?" she asked.

"They disowned her four years ago."

Disowned? Her eyebrows shot higher, but Callie held her tongue, despite the curiosity. What kind of parent abandoned their kid?

When she didn't respond, the buzz of the huge fan filled the air, and Matt shot her a look. "She's a recovering drug addict."

No wonder. The news explained the edge she sensed churning just beneath the surface of one Mr. Matt Paulson.

"That must be hard on your brother," she said.

Matt turned and faced the fan, closing his eyes and letting the mist hit his face. "He's a recovering addict, too."

She lingered on his profile as the words and everything he *hadn't* said settled deep. So much tension. So much emotion. She couldn't read the thoughts in his expression but they were present in the taut shoulders, the flat line of his mouth. His short, sandy hair grew damp and curled at the edges, just above his ears. His bangs, thicker than the rest of his hair, developed a wave as water accumulated. The drops left a sheen to his skin, his throat and those lovely, lovely arms.

Matt definitely had the sexy shtick down pat. A wet Matt? Even more so.

"Sad that Penny's parents won't forgive her," she said.

"They have their reasons." Matt didn't open his eyes, just continued to enjoy the cooling mist. Or pretended, anyway. "She put them through a lot. Lying. Stealing. Disappearing for weeks on end until they weren't sure if she was alive or dead from an overdose. I'm sure they just couldn't take it anymore. They're just trying to protect themselves."

Had Matt tried to protect himself?

"But still..." she said. She knew what it was like to screw up. Not in as grand a fashion as a drug addiction. Her screwup was tiny in comparison. But she knew how it felt to work hard to overcome your mistakes, only to have nobody let you forget.

"Now she's clean," she said.

"She's been clean before."

Callie let out a scoff. "'My good opinion once lost is lost forever.'"

He opened his eyes, and that brown gaze landed on hers, sending a self-conscious flush up her face. She could read the question and surprise in his expression. She hadn't meant to wear her own struggles quite so clearly, or to sound quite so personally invested.

She shrugged, trying to ease her discomfort. "Just a quote from Mr. Darcy, from *Pride and Prejudice.*" When he didn't comment, she went on, "My favorite book."

On her thirteenth birthday her mother had taken her to the library and she'd checked out the paperback. She'd spent the next two days glued to the book, her mother practically dragging her from her room to come eat dinner. Growing up poor meant Callie could relate to the Bennet sisters. She'd admired Lizzy's courage and her determination to marry for love only, despite the very real risk of poverty, causing Callie's transformation from a total tomboy into a romantic. The book had had such an impact, she'd spent the weeks after imaging Lizzy and Darcy's wedding, and she'd developed a passion for bridal magazines and picturing the perfect ceremony.

Starting Fantasy Weddings had been a natural extension of that passion.

"I've never read *Pride and Prejudice,*" Matt said.

"I'm not surprised."

A lull in the conversation followed, and she wanted to ask about Matt's experiences with his brother, to learn the details about the current state of the relationship between the two. However, Callie sensed asking anything more would go over like a hot toddy during a heat wave.

"How did Tommy and Penny meet?" she asked.

"As total geekster gamers and pros at your ex's zombie apocalypse game, they were selected as beta testers for *Dungeons of Zhorg.* That was how they met online. And then they discovered they'd fought the same addiction, and eventually fell in love. I think—" He pursed his lips. "I think the game helped keep them from slipping. Gave them something to focus on."

Which would explain Matt's willingness to take on this crazy task.

"I have to admit," she said softly, "I'm a sucker for a romantic story." And this one really struck a chord. Two people who'd lost themselves in a dark world and managed to pull out with the help of each other and a video game. Slaying dragons online as they fought their personal demons.

Callie smiled at the ridiculously fanciful thought. But no wonder Colin agreed to the weekend wedding/festival named after his latest game.

When Matt didn't comment, Callie went on, "Who's going to give Penny away?"

"She asked me, but I told her to get one of her *Dungeon of Zhorg* buddies. I can't do it because I'm Tommy's best man."

She let out an amused huff. "It's not like this is a traditional wedding. No reason why you can't be both."

"I'm not her family."

"You will be."

Two seconds ticked by before he hiked a brow. Mist had accumulated on his neck and trickled down to gather in the hollow at his throat. She had the sudden urge to lick the spot, and heat shot up her limbs and settled between her legs.

Shoot. Admiring the man was one thing. Wanting to treat him like her favorite brand of ice-cream cone was another.

And while he looked slightly put out by her pushing, the light in his eyes held a hint of amusement. "Does the family counseling come with the cost of your services or will that be extra?"

Callie grinned. "Just the cost of a trip to the ice-cream truck."

If she couldn't lick the real thing, she could at least enjoy the substitute. The lopsided smile he sent her did nothing to quell her appreciation of his form.

"So I'm buying?" he asked.

"You're buying."

In the end Callie chose a lemon-lime Popsicle, while Matt went with his favorite, chocolate. Cooler now that they were damp from head to toe, they wandered beneath the oaks back to Callie's car, in no particular hurry. Not only because of the relief they'd accomplished the most pressing task, selecting a site for the

DoZ weekend. But also because Matt felt no sense of urgency to leave.

Especially when Callie looked as if she'd just entered a wet T-shirt contest. It had been a while since his college buddies had dragged him to such an event during his relatively carefree undergraduate days. At the time he'd thought the rigors of academics and obtaining the grades for medical school had been stressful.

But then his parents had died, leaving him solely responsible for Tommy.

And the sight of Callie's lovely chest beneath the wet garments did more than just bring back great memories of happier times, it also turned him the hell on.

Not exactly conducive to his get-in and get-out goals.

Her damp shirt clung to her skin, and he could make out the lace of the bra beneath. White, if he wasn't mistaken. And if he tried hard enough, he could imagine the darker circle of skin beneath the center of each breast. He could definitely make out the rounder buds.

"I told you they weren't as big as the slutty Scarlett O'Hara dress suggested."

Busted.

The relaxed look on her face eased the tension in his shoulders. Though she certainly had good reason, she didn't appear overly annoyed by his tendency to check out her form. In fact, she seemed more…amused. As though he was just a stupid kid who couldn't help himself.

Which wasn't too far from the truth, aside from the *kid* part. The *stupid* description fit just fine.

"I promise," he said. "I'm not a total pervert."

"Does that mean you're a partial one?"

He threw back his head and laughed. When the

amusement finally passed, he shot her a grin. “I guess it’s up to you to let me know.”

They reached her car and Matt opened the door for her before rounding and climbing into the driver’s seat.

He closed the door and faced Callie, who was still licking the Popsicle.

Why hadn’t he noticed how hot the image was until now? The tip of her tongue catching the drips. The way she nibbled at the side. How much the vision reminded him of his fantasies during the jerk-off session in the shower that first night. Probably because he’d been too distracted by the sight of her breasts beneath that wet shirt.

Maybe he really was a perv.

He gripped the steering wheel. “Where to now?”

“Home,” she said.

A completely inappropriate surge of adrenaline shot through his body, only to be doused by her next statement.

“I have some things I need to do today for another event coming up in two weeks,” she said. “And I really want to take a shower and wash off all of this sweat. Where do you want to meet tonight to discuss the rest of our plans?”

She twisted in the seat to face him, one long *bare* calf curling beneath her. The tanned leg looked smooth and he wondered if the skin was as silky as it looked. Heat gathered at the nape of his neck, and the relentless sun through the window lit Callie’s form, making ignoring her impossible.

He cleared his throat. “Preferably somewhere cool.”

Her eyes lit, and that wide grin returned to her pretty face. “I have just the place.”

CHAPTER THREE

CHRIST, THIS WASN'T really what he'd had in mind.

The chill seemed to hang in the air of The Frozen South, an ice bar taking up the top floor of The River's Edge Resort and Casino overlooking downtown New Orleans. The crowd fairly thick, the noise seemed even thicker. Most likely everyone else had the same idea: escape the heat wave outside. And the establishment was the perfect choice.

Ice blocks holding tiny neon lights made up the bar. Ice sofas, ice chairs and ice sculptures were the mainstay of the furniture and the décor. Fortunately, fur rugs lined the seats. Good thing, too. Anyone bold enough to drink too much in this environment might forget to protect their skin and wind up stuck to their chair. Some of the patrons chose to have their drinks served in ice cups. And because the management clearly had a sense of humor, costumers could even keep their cups. Of course, with the hot weather still chugging along outside with a relative heat index nearing one hundred degrees, by the time the club goer arrived home all they'd have is a wet hand that smelled of vodka.

But Matt's beef with the choice wasn't the crowd. Nor was it the cool temperature, a relief after the blistering day outside. Callie's frozen margarita looked inviting and his beer was the perfect temperature.

No, Matt hated the need for Callie to be covered in so many clothes.

Matt had sprung for the best cover package, which included a parka best suited for exploring the Arctic and a hat that framed her face, limiting his view of the honey hair he enjoyed. The only thing he had going for him was that she hadn't zipped the jacket closed.

He leaned in to speak at her ear. "You sure you don't want to go somewhere quieter?"

She turned to look at him. A maneuver that brought them face-to-face, her lips close to his.

Huh. The impulse to lean in and kiss Callie smacked him across the face like a pheromone-soaked glove, but he squelched the urge. How the hell could he plan this crazy wedding and get home to check up on Tommy if he was constantly looking at Callie, wondering what she'd taste like? With that honey hair and that honey accent, would her mouth have the same flavor?

A stupid, fanciful thought that was getting him nowhere closer to his goals.

He cleared his throat. "We might accomplish more without the noise."

Two beats passed, but Matt couldn't read the look in Callie's eyes.

"It feels good in here," she said. "Besides, the view is awesome."

Matt mentally shook his head and forced his gaze out the large window.

True, the lights of downtown New Orleans at night were definitely awesome. Unfortunately, he hadn't traveled to New Orleans to enjoy the view. But Callie in a blouse, wearing a sweater zipped up to her throat, paled in comparison to her breasts on display in a slutty Scarlett O'Hara dress. Or a wet T-shirt.

Though the gently curved hips and the shapely butt in formfitting jeans almost made up for the lack of cleavage.

Almost.

"So..." Callie stared down at her notebook, obviously completely unaware of the distracting thoughts mucking up Matt's concentration. "The games we've got listed so far are an ax-throwing competition, an archery competition and sword fighting. Though having all three feels redundant. Today I made a few calls and found a magician available those two days."

Magicians. Great. But Matt was too caught up by the play of beautiful lips and teeth and tongue as Callie spoke to pay much attention.

"A local group can provide something resembling strolling minstrels," Callie went on. "Though they won't be quite as authentic as we'd like. I checked with the park this afternoon, and horses are allowed. Which is good because apparently Penny would love to have jousters, so I contacted a branch of the Society for Creative Anachronism and—"

"Wait. *What?*"

Matt's mind stuck, spinning on all the information. Though only one piece of news stuck out.

Callie set her list down and looked at him. "The society is a living history group that's devoted to re-creating the Middle Ages. There's a branch just outside of—"

"No." Matt shook his head. "You spoke to Penny?"

For some reason the news felt odd. Strange.

She tipped her head curiously. "You gave me the

contact numbers, remember? So I called and spoke to both Tommy and Penny today." She hiked an eyebrow. "After all, I *am* arranging their wedding."

Matt couldn't speak, and Callie went on.

"Anyway, Tommy is gathering volunteers among their DoZ friends attending to run the sign-up for the competitions and then the competitions themselves during the event. And Penny is going to coordinate any of the Society of Anachronism volunteers who can attend on such short notice."

"Damn." Matt plowed a hand through his hair. "This thing is growing out of control."

At this rate he'd never get back home to check on Tommy. Matt's stomach tensed. It had been *how* many days since he'd last laid eyes on Tommy?

Regardless, if the explosion of the wedding weekend kept up, Matt would be stuck in New Orleans figuring out how to clean up horse dung from a park and how to find swords and— *Jesus,* why did Callie have to smell so good?

"I suppose now wouldn't be the time to tell you about the dragon Colin is donating to the cause?"

Matt rubbed his forehead. "Dragon?"

Callie's lips twisted wryly. "Not a real one, of course. One they used at the launch party of *Dungeons of Zhorg.*" She eyed him closely, like he looked as if his head bordered on exploding.

Matt wasn't sure but it might have been true.

"At least all of Tommy and Penny's guests are DoZ friends who are bringing their own costumes. Looks like you and I are the only ones who need to rent something."

Matt blinked, biting back the urge to call the whole damn thing off. "I am not dressing up as a troll."

Callie laughed. "I pictured you dressed more as a crusader. You know, chain mail and the whole nine yards. Anyway, because of Mardi Gras, New Orleans has great costume shops. I have several we can visit tomorrow."

Chain mail?

A crusader?

Christ, he'd almost rather go as a troll. The only thing he had left to hope for was finding Callie a slutty medieval gown.

"How does the dress fit?" Matt called through the dressing-room door.

"Give me a minute. I have to find my way inside the stupid thing before I can tell you. If you don't hear from me in ten minutes, send help." Callie stared down at the mound of fabric big enough to hide a nest of baby gators and their mama in. "Make that fifteen."

In truth, she needed a few minutes alone to recover.

Last night's graphic dream involving Matt made looking him in the eye this morning pretty gosh darn difficult. Colin's plans for publicity were growing and, as the publicity plan grew, so did the importance of this event. Now there was the potential of the story getting picked up by a local channel, so she did *not* need to be getting sidetracked by the killer hot looks of the brother of the groom. Still, looking hardly hurt anything…

Until the looking did indecent things to her dreams.

Callie pushed the thought aside and searched for the bottom of the dress. Actually, the outfit consisted of two pieces, the first part white satinlike material with a beautiful gold brocade pattern on the skirt. The second part was an overdress of robin's-egg-blue with a solid gold band at the bodice and split in front, forming an inverted V to showcase the design of the skirt beneath.

She slipped the first part over her head, wondering how Matt was faring with the costume-shop owner, an eccentric elderly man Callie had instantly adored.

Callie hadn't had an occasion to use this establishment before, but the moment she entered she'd known she'd found a gem of a resource. Not only did the owner carry a wide variety of quality costumes, he had a serious collection of props. And the stuff wasn't cheap and flimsy, either, but high-quality.

The huge crucifix on the shelf would be perfect for the *Interview with the Vampire* wedding she was organizing. Callie longed to come back and comb through the assortment of odds and ends, though the process would take some time. The owner was sweet, eccentric and carried a wide assortment of interesting items. Unfortunately, his organizational skills sucked. Searching through the racks and racks of costumes would have been easier if the shop was organized better. But their high-quality costumes made up for the inconvenience.

Matt probably would argue no.

A sharp knock on the door pulled her out of her thoughts. "Need help?"

She bit her lip and stared in the mirror. Handling the complicated fastening system in the back would be impossible on her own. Then again, having Matt in here, alone with her. Her back so exposed…

Say no. Tell him to go away.

"Sure," she said instead, opening the door.

In a medieval costume that would do a knight proud,

Matt stepped inside. And there wasn't a woman alive that wouldn't have been satisfied by the way his gaze landed on her figure and his eyebrows shot higher.

He let out a low whistle. "That gown is something. You look gorgeous."

A flush of heat left her feeling stupid.

Come on, Callie. Get your act together.

"Thank you," she said. "You, uh, look good, too."

Matt's pants looked appropriately made of unrefined material. Over the crudely cut, long-sleeved shirt, he wore a chain-mail shirt. A huge sword hung on the scabbard at his waist.

Matt let out a scoff. "Maybe, but this stuff is heavy."

"Most authentic costumes in New Orleans."

"I think I'd rather go with the cheap stuff that doesn't weigh a thousand pounds." He rolled those broad shoulders. "Man, how did men fight in this getup anyway?"

"I have no idea. But at least you don't have to wear a dress that pinches your waist to nothing and flattens your boobs," she said dryly.

Matt was clearly biting back a grin. "I definitely prefer the slutty Scarlett O'Hara over the prim and proper medieval princess. Allow me?" He nodded down at the laces hanging open in the back.

She hesitated a second. Was that amusement flickering through his eyes? Gritting her teeth with determination, she then turned to face the mirror. Matt stepped closer, bringing a scent of spicy soap. When she briefly met his gaze in the reflection, a shock of awareness jolted her limbs and burned her belly.

The intimacy of the room, the muted lighting and the strange costumes made the whole situation surreal and, God save her from her overactive imagination, a little romantic.

Given this was Matt in chain mail with a sword at his side, a whole lot of sexy was on display, as well. Her heart did a crazy twist when Matt reached for the laces at her back.

Crap, don't picture him undoing the dress. Just... don't.

Dying to cover her nerves, she eyed him speculatively in the mirror. "Does this make you my lady-in-waiting?"

One side of his mouth curled up in amusement. "No," he said. "And before you get any other crazy ideas in your head, I'm nobody's knight in shining armor, either."

Matt's fingers whispered against her as he fixed the corset-inspired lace-up fastening in the back. Careful not to move, Callie concentrated on the warm brushes of skin on skin that sent currents of electric heat skittering up her spine. As touches went, this one bordered on being an incredible tease.

His gaze on the task at hand, lips set as if in concentration, Matt said, "You sure are going all out on this. I mean—" his eyes crashed into hers "—Tommy's *my* brother."

Callie blinked and mentally shoved her libido in a box. The most truthful explanation wouldn't go over so well, for sure.

Especially with Matt.

She held his gaze in the mirror. "They deserve the wedding of their dreams."

She'd never meant the words more, but she also knew reciting the slogan from her website didn't cover everything she'd poured into this event so far. And everything left yet to do. After talking with Tommy and Penny yesterday afternoon—they'd both sounded so sweet and sincere on the phone—Callie's heart had melted more.

In a way, her screwup had torn her and Colin apart. Years later, and she was *still* alone. Tommy's and Penny's screwups had led them to one another and now they were getting married. Their heartwarming story was one of the most inspiring Callie had ever heard. And she'd heard some doozies, stories of lost loves reunited and second chances and those who'd survived devastating illnesses to go and achieve their happily-ever-after.

But Tommy and Penny's tale of overcoming the effects of the bad choices they'd made struck a chord in Callie. After talking to the two, Callie's ideas for the weekend had exploded. So now there was more work than originally planned. Not that she feared hard work. In fact, she'd grown quite used to it.

But Matt clearly couldn't figure out why she'd brought more work on herself.

"I guess because I know what it's like to mess up your life," Callie said. "In college, I made some seriously stupid decisions."

The fingers on her back grew still, and Matt's eyes met hers in the mirror again. His gaze didn't budge as he remained silent, most likely waiting for her to go on. Callie's throat suddenly felt twice baked and lacking in all moisture.

"I let a lot of people down," she said. "Including my parents. And Colin."

"Tell me."

With those words, her immediate thought was *no* because the story was too personal, cut too close to the bone. But maybe if she shared the ugly truth about her past this would help Matt. She'd sensed there was tension between him and his brother. Maybe he'd find a way to move on, as well. The idea of her story helping others was kind of appealing.

Time to put your big-girl panties on, Callie.

Matt's focus dropped back to her dress and he resumed his task. Maybe he sensed that telling the story would be easier without his eyes studying her so closely. Despite his focus being elsewhere, she could tell by the tension in his shoulders and the set of his mouth that Matt's attention was solely on her.

She cleared her throat to loosen the muscles. "I grew up poor, in a little town north of here. My parents sacrificed a lot to move us to the city so I could go to a better high school. They wanted me to attend a university and be the first LaBeau to get a college degree."

"Did you have trouble in high school?"

"Nope. I did well," she said. "Straight-A student. I wound up with several acceptances to excellent schools. My parents wanted me to accept the scholarship at a smaller college closer to home, but I..."

Callie stared at her reflection in the mirror. She'd been so dumb, thinking her ability to adjust to a new high school translated into an easy adjustment to a new town and a large university.

"I wanted to get out and see the world," she said. "I mean, high school seemed fairly easy. How hard could an out-of-state larger university be? So I accepted the Wimbly Southern deal."

His gaze ticked back to hers in the mirror. "Scholarship?"

"A full ride," she said with a nod. "Tuition. Room and

board. Books. The works. Even some spending money so I didn't have to get a job. I only had to concentrate on my studies. For a girl with parents who could barely afford the rent, it was a big deal."

He cocked his head, the fingers at her back now motionless. "Let me guess. You flunked out and lost the scholarship."

Callie hesitated. She could say yes and let that be the end. His short sentence summed up the events accurately. But she knew leaving out the most important bits would be taking the coward's way out, and certainly wouldn't explain about her commitment to Matt's brother and his fiancée—a couple she'd only spoken to once on the phone.

"Yes, but there's a little more to the story," she said.

"How much more?"

"My grades slipped because I fell in with the wrong crowd. I was lonely, and the party kids were the only ones who would have anything to do with me."

In hindsight, she realized how lucky she'd been in high school. Moving just before the tenth grade should have meant she'd been the odd one out, friendless and alone. Instead, things had come together easily. She'd had plenty of friends and was well liked by her classmates. Some of that might have had to do with her dating Colin, his popularity rubbing off on her. Either way, things had fallen into place and she'd never missed a beat.

College, on the other hand, had been a disaster.

Callie cleared her throat. "But the party crowd comes with certain expectations, and I went out too much." She rolled her eyes. "That alone would have been enough for the Moron of the Year Award, but one night I went to a party at a house."

Matt's going to hate what comes next.

She gripped the skirt of her dress, wishing the silken folds could sooth her nerves, and she gathered her courage before she went on. "The police raided the place because the man was a drug dealer."

Matt sucked in a breath and his lips went white, and she knew the news had hit him viscerally. He looked as if he'd received a solid punch to the solar plexus. She whirled around to face him, laying a hand on his arm. Her heart pumped hard in her chest.

The rest tumbled out of her mouth. "I didn't know who he was or what he did to make money, Matt." She stared up at him, emphasizing every word and trying hard to convince him of the truth with her gaze. "He was a friend of a friend of a friend. It sounds like a stupid cliché, I know, but I honestly had no idea who the man was. But—"

She bit her cheek and held her tongue, staring at Matt. Callie shoved her hair back from her face, disturbed by the slight tremor in her fingers.

"We all got taken down to the station and…and they found marijuana in my purse."

"Jesus, Callie."

And then Matt just seemed to stop breathing, as if this final piece of the sordid story was just one insult too many. There was no way out but the truth. And the faster she got this over with, the sooner her heart would start beating again.

Callie drew in a shaky breath and pushed on. "I know. I *know.* I was stupid and depressed and I just wanted something to make it all go away. It was the only time, I swear."

The stupid move would follow her around the rest of her life. She briefly pressed her eyes closed. The shock of her arrest had been difficult enough for her, but it had been horrible for her parents. Years of being the perfect kid, the perfect student, had made her fall from grace all that much more painful. Especially given their car had been plastered with so many Student of the Week bumper stickers the chrome on the bumper had all but disappeared.

"I called my parents, who couldn't come to help me out, so they sent Colin." She winced at the memories of the complete and utter humiliation when Colin had strode into the police headquarters, clearly furious. "He drove up to Wimbly, even though I didn't ask him to," she said, realizing she was rambling again. "And then, of course, things between the two of us started to fall apart and I—"

The look on Matt's face gave no indication as to what he was thinking. The knot in her stomach tangled a little tighter, so she hurried on, beyond ready to push on to the next subject.

"I just think, after everything they've been through, Penny and Tommy deserve the wedding of the century," she said.

The tension in his body had eased a bit, and he leaned back against the wall, arms folded across the chain mail on his chest. For one bizarre moment, she realized she missed his hands on her skin. Callie smoothed her hand down the satiny skirt of the underdress.

"And if I can help Colin out with a fantastic publicity opportunity *and* prove to my parents my business is a success, all at the same time, so much the better."

Parked against the wall, Matt continued to study her.

She still couldn't tell what he was thinking. That she was an idiot? That she deserved to return to New Orleans, the stink of shame following on her heels? True.

But jeez, the whole mess had taken place ten years ago.

"Aren't you going to say anything?" she asked.

There was a two beat pause before he answered. "You're right." She held her breath as he went on. "The dress does flatten your breasts too much."

A bark of surprised laughter escaped Callie, one part humor and a hundred parts absolute relief. "Oh, my God, you really *are* a perv."

He smiled, crinkles appearing around his eyes, the tension of the moment finally broken. "Are we done with the confession now?"

Callie released her death grip on her skirt, muscles finally relaxing.

"Beyond done," she said.

"Good. Now could you please help me get this son of a bitch off?" He pulled at the chain-mail shirt a bit, letting it drop back to his chest with a *ching*. "I'm about to die of heat stroke here. And no way in hell do I want to pass out and be carted off to the nearest emergency room in this getup."

"Sure, turn around."

She spent a minute wrestling with the clasp at the nape of his neck, her fingers fumbling a bit as she tried to ignore the soft tickle of hair against her fingers. Against her will, awareness washed over her again, and her gaze slid past his broad shoulders down to his trim waist and lean hips. The body looked solid and rugged and was impossible to ignore, especially in the kind of getup that hinted at strong heroes, epic battles and undying devotion to a lady.

Ridiculous, Callie. You're absolutely ridiculous.

"Now face me and lean in," she said.

Matt turned and bent forward at the waist, and Callie pulled the hem up his trunk and over his head. The chain mail was heavier than it looked, pulling the shirt beneath along, as well. The whole ensemble dropped to the floor with a *clank* and Matt straightened up.

Holy hell. What had she done?

Now she had to hold herself together in the presence of a shirtless Matt with sexily mussed hair. While her heart thudded, Callie tried to drag her gaze from Matt's chest, but failed. The well-honed muscles had a dusting of hair that tapered at his waist, passing over the flat abdomen and disappearing beneath his pants.

A small smirk quirked his lips. "Are you checking out my cleavage?"

Several seconds passed before her brain could arrange the words in the right order. "You don't have man boobs."

"Good thing, too."

Time seemed to grind to a halt as they both studied each other. And then Matt stepped closer, with *goal* written all over his face, and the tension returned, ten times worse than before. But this time the air was filled with a sexual charge. Electric currents prickled just beneath her skin and spread, producing goose bumps as they went.

And her briefly returned ability to speak fled even faster than before.

"Only problem I see with this scenario?" He grabbed a fistful of fabric just beneath her fitted waist and slowly drew her closer, her pulse picking up speed with every step. "You are way overdressed."

Callie tried to protest. "The owner is—"

"Currently engrossed in a conversation with a customer about the history of Mardi Gras."

She blinked, trying to process all the input threatening to blow a fuse in her brain. Too many sparking impulses firing at once. Just the bare torso alone was enough to shove her senses into complete meltdown. But toss in the sight of all that lovely, lovely skin covering muscles and sinew and bone? The rudimentary pants clinging low on lean hips? She could just make out the top of his briefs. Blue.

Matt continued to slowly pull her forward, until her body finally met his—naked chest to, unfortunately, *not* naked chest. His eyes zeroed in on her lips, and several thoughts flashed through her brain at once.

This isn't why you're here, Callie. You need to stay focused on the job.

His mouth covered hers. And just like the focused man who'd hunted her down at the wedding reception, this man was all about the goal, as well. He tipped her head back and his lips pressed in firmly, opening Callie's mouth wide and taking his time with each retreat. Several deep, wet kisses followed. Forceful, yet unhurried. Heat and moisture and hard lips registered just before his tongue rasped against hers.

For a brief moment her mind splintered, and she moaned.

Matt gripped the fabric on the outside of her thighs, settling her legs on either side of his thighs. Unfortunately, the mounds of fabric between them prevented the satisfaction of feeling his hard body pressed against hers.

"Jesus," he muttered, arching his hip. "How the hell did people wear these bloody clothes?"

She gripped his arms, hoping to keep from melting into the floor. The fingers twisted tight in her dress hauled her that last little bit, and she had to adjust her stance to allow his leg to settle between her thighs. Then there was a skitter of pleasure up her spine from the pressure, the fabulously delicious *friction*...

My God.

She closed her eyes.

"Too bad my brother wasn't into *Space Vixens from the Planet Venus,*" Matt said, nibbling his way from one side of her mouth to the other.

"Why would you say that?"

Geez, she sounded so breathless.

He dove in for another openmouthed kiss, and several mind-spinning seconds later he said, "Because their costumes were smaller. Much smaller."

Another drugging kiss consumed her, his tongue hot and demanding and doing unspeakable things to her body. His hand drifted to the small of her back to keep her pressed close. That leg pressed firmly against the part of her anatomy that desired the contact the most.

And those little rudimentary pants and thin briefs did nothing to hide the hard shaft pressed along her hip.

The sensation too fabulous to lose, she pulled herself a little higher up his leg, and the slow drag of fabric settled more firmly against the sensitive area between her thighs. Callie let out a whimper.

Good Lord. She needed to… She had to…

Matt's hands landed along her shoulder blades and began to undo those laces he'd worked so long and hard to fasten. As the back of the dress slowly fell open, cool air slid down her skin. The contact sent an illicit thrill skittering up her spine.

Surely she should be letting out some sort of protest? Where was her vow to keep her hands to herself? Where was her focus? Even more important, where was her sense of decency?

A loud laugh from somewhere in the store broke through Callie's lust-muddled brain, and they both went still. Callie silently counted to five and listened to Matt's harsh breaths before she gathered the strength to open her eyes.

Lips brushing against hers, he said, "I'm thinking we should fix our clothes."

Which totally was in contrast to the palm pressed flat against her back, holding her firmly against his chest.

"Um…yeah," she muttered against his lips, embarrassed by her less than brilliant response.

"What's on the agenda for tomorrow?" he said. "Searching out a pack of traveling circus performers to juggle flaming torches?"

Her lips smiled against his. Something about his teasing tone and his easygoing manner made the moment less awkward.

She stole a quick kiss before answering. "No," she said. "Though we do need to find someone who can transport a dragon from Colin's storage house to the park."

He pulled his head back and hiked a brow dryly. "Well, that shouldn't be hard at all."

"We're in New Orleans," Callie said. "This town

plans, produces and pulls off the Mardi Gras parade every year. There are plenty of people who can properly transport a dragon."

"So tomorrow will be about securing dragon transport?"

Callie opened her mouth to say yes and then bit her lip, remembering that her aunt had called this morning and asked for her help sorting through the stuff at the dock house. Callie had promised to drive up to Aunt Billie's place despite her suspicions the favor wasn't the real reason her aunt wanted Callie to visit.

While she was always pleased to see her favorite relative, the visit never came without a risk. But there was definitely a way to cut down on said risk. Bring backup. Provide a distraction, so to speak. Matt was the perfect person to help in that regard.

Callie eyed Matt. His hair was adorably tousled and his lips looked ruddy from their kisses. And something about his manner always put her at ease, even while revving up her body…

Talk about distractions.

"Actually," she said, "I have to head up to Clemence tomorrow. I was hoping you could ride along. I have to see my aunt Billie, and I think you should get out for an authentic taste of our cuisine and experience the bayou."

"Sightseeing wasn't really in my plans."

"But there's so much to see and this is your first trip to town. You can't come to New Orleans without sampling a little of rural Louisiana."

He tipped his head and looked down at her. Why was she holding her breath, hoping he'd say yes?

"Will there be mosquitos?" he asked.

"Big ones."

"Gators?"

"Most definitely."

"Dirt roads?"

"With potholes the size of Texas."

His lips twitched, as if fighting a smile. "Sounds enticing," he said dryly.

"On the bright side, my aunt makes the best shrimp étouffée in three counties. And she has a successful restaurant to show for it."

"Now that sounds good."

The response encouraging, Callie had to smile. "Hope you like it hot."

"Ms. LaBeau," Matt said, leaning close, his lips whispering across hers, "I like everything hot."

CHAPTER FOUR

THE TWO-HOUR drive up to Clemence, located north of Baton Rouge, passed pleasantly enough. At least, as pleasant as possible given Callie remained distracted, both by Matt's presence in her car and the destination.

As usual, the closer Callie drew to her old hometown the more her stomach filled with knots. Visiting Aunt Billie always managed to be fun and painful at the same time. Hopefully, with Matt along, Callie could avoid the painful part. From the first moment her family had learned of her mistake, her aunt had been her staunchest supporter, which always made Callie feel even worse for letting her down.

Once they'd finally left Baton Rouge behind, the roads grew narrower, quieter and lined with oaks. More important, now that they were getting close to Po Boy's, her aunt's restaurant, the roads were filled with the occasional pothole.

"Man," Matt said as he steered around one. "You weren't kidding about the condition of the roads." He glanced into his rearview mirror. "That one should be named Grand Canyon, the junior."

The conversation was as good a lead-in as she'd ever get. "So what's it like where you're from?" Callie asked.

She twisted in the passenger seat of her car and leaned back against the door to better study Matt as he steered her car down the road. "Where do you live again?"

"Manford, Michigan."

Which hardly answered the question burning in her brain. She hiked a brow, encouraging him to go on.

Two beats passed before he answered. "Midsize town. We have a mall, a couple of movie theatres and the hospital is decent enough. Though the emergency room isn't as big as I'd like."

Something in his tone told her that last statement represented a massive understatement.

"I thought you worked as a traveling doc," she said.

He cleared his throat. "I have a part-time job at Manford Memorial. That allows me enough free time to travel as a locums, picking up shifts in bigger cities."

"If you prefer living in a larger city, why are you living there?"

Several seconds ticked by. "It's home." He gave a shrug, the act as vague as his words.

But his voice gave him away, the lack of excitement almost palpable. Callie loved New Orleans, loved everything about the town that managed to merge quirky and a unique cultural heritage with its own brand of Southern charm, all at the same time. The city merged the concepts with a kind of easy grace that amazed her, every single time, and provided the perfect backdrop for her business. Despite the strained relationships, her family was here, too. She'd grown up in the area and couldn't imagine living anywhere else.

Matt, apparently, had little affection for his own town.

"Promise me something," she said, and he looked

at her curiously. "No matter what happens, don't go to work for the Manford Chamber of Commerce doing tourist promotion, because you would really suck at the job."

Matt laughed, and she admired the strong throat, the even, white teeth. His sandy, tousled hair that begged to be ruffled, and Callie flexed her fingers against the urge to reach over and run her fingers through his hair.

In an attempt to dodge a pothole on the left, Matt steered the Toyota to the right, and the front tire hit a second pothole. He shot her a look, and Callie lifted a shoulder. "You get used to it."

He glanced at her from the corner of his eye. "You grew up out here?"

"Yep," she said. "Born right here in Clemence Parish. Spent my childhood playing in the water, fishing and catching crawfish."

"A tomboy?"

"And proud of it."

She pointed out the turns, the roads growing narrower, until finally they hit the dirt road that dead-ended into Po Boy's. There were a half dozen or so cars in the gravel parking lot, shaded by huge oaks, and Matt pulled into a spot in the front.

They exited and rounded the car. Matt came to a stop to stare up at the wooden building.

"Aunt Billie's restaurant looks…interesting."

Callie grinned at the expression on his face. The paint on the siding was peeling and cracked, the wood beneath faded to gray where exposed to the sun. The front porch held several tables and chairs, but Callie knew the customers preferred the back and the view of the river.

"Authentic," she said.

He hiked a brow. "Safe?"

She bit back a smile. "Absolutely."

They made their way up the wooden front steps. Matt's hand settled into the dip in her spine, and the heat seeped through her shirt and warmed her skin. Unfortunately, the temperature change didn't stop there. The feeling settled deeper, curling low in her stomach and spreading between her legs. Good Lord. Yesterday's dressing-room incident had clearly left an indelible impression.

They stepped into the restaurant filled with wooden tables and chairs and a few customers. As usual, Aunt Billie sensed her arrival before Callie had taken ten steps inside.

Her aunt appeared from the doorway leading into the kitchen. "Callie, hon. It's been way too long." She enveloped her in a hug before gripping Callie's arms and pulling back to give her the once-over.

Billie LaBeau loved to cook, loved to eat and she had the well-padded frame of one who did. But her generous nature dwarfed everything else in comparison. Despite the distance in the lineage, Aunt Billie took her Creole roots to heart. More important, she'd been the only relative to accept Callie's choices, without treating her life as if she'd settled for a seriously lower second best.

Not once had she looked at Callie with disappointment or thrown out little asides that alluded to how much Callie had screwed up. And while she constantly harped at Callie to visit more often, there was never any judgment in her tone.

"This is Matt Paulson," Callie said.

"'Bout time you brought a man around here again."

Billie shot her a grin. "Haven't done so since Colin. And you were eighteen years old then."

The implied *ten years ago* went unsaid and Callie fought the urge to close her eyes. Perhaps Matt's presence wouldn't be quite the protection that she'd hoped.

"Matt is a *client,*" Callie said.

Hopefully the emphasis on the word would clear up any misconceptions. Aunt Billie's only response was a raised eyebrow at Matt's hand on Callie's back, sending heat shooting up Callie's neck and flaring across her cheeks. Who needed to say anything with a facial expression like her aunt's? Matt was studying Callie, clearly amused by the conversation and the nonverbal communication.

"Welcome, Matt," Aunt Billie said. "I hope you brought your appetite."

"I never leave home without it."

Aunt Billie let out an amused snort. "That's good to hear. And Callie?" Aunt Billie returned her focus to Callie. "The family reunion is in two weeks. It's not too late to change your mind and attend."

Crap, the reunion. She'd forgotten about the annual event that she had no intention of attending, *ever.* She couldn't imagine anything worse than all the family members—those who'd been so proud she'd been accepted to Wimbly—talking about her behind her back. Mentioning her mistake again to her face. Callie had lost count of how many times she'd been told how lucky she was to be afforded the opportunity.

Many of whom now never missed an opportunity to remind her of how much she'd lost when she'd mucked it all up.

Her aunt propped a hand on her ample hip. "I'd love to have all of my family back in the same place again."

"Maybe," Callie said vaguely. "My schedule is pretty busy. I'll have to check the dates."

The look her aunt sent made her message clear. She didn't believe Callie would show up, and Billie sure as heck wouldn't pass up the opportunity to hound her more. Her suspicions about her aunt's recent call to sort through her stuff from the dock house suddenly didn't seem so paranoid. Billie hadn't suddenly been bitten by a late-summer spring-cleaning urge to clean out an old building that seldom got used anymore. She'd planned on slowly eroding away Callie's excuses.

But the thought of all her relatives looking at her as if she'd failed…

Damn it.

"Well, check them dates and try a little harder to squeeze your family into that busy schedule of yours, ya' hear?" Billie said.

"Work has been busy."

"All the more reason you need to come back for a visit," Billie said. "Let your people know how you're doing."

Callie murmured something polite and vague. Billie shot her a sharp look and then seemed to give up, letting the subject go. They spent some time catching up as Billie gave Matt a tour of the kitchen, showing him around and dolling out her blunt brand of humor as they went. Callie liked the laid-back way Matt dodged her aunt's repeated attempts to nail down the details about their relationship. Finally, her aunt seemed to realize that there would be nothing more forthcoming.

"I finally decided to send someone out to do the repairs on the dock house. The stuff inside needs to be sorted, too," Aunt Billie said. "And since you're the only one that goes out there anymore, I need to know what you want me to keep and what I can toss."

A wave of affection hit Callie, and she reached out to gently squeeze her aunt's hand. "Thanks."

She knew her aunt would have torn the thing down by now if not for her. And losing the dock house would be like losing a piece of herself.

"But first, y'all take a seat out on the deck and I'll bring you some lunch," Billie said.

Callie couldn't resist and she sent her aunt a smile. "Make sure you make Matt's shrimp étouffée extra special."

They settled at a table out back, the edge of the deck lined by the Mississippi River. Despite the rustic surroundings, Matt appeared totally at ease. She liked that he seemed comfortable no matter where he was, whether at a classy ice bar or a backwoods restaurant. They settled into easy conversation, which ended when Aunt Billie brought sweet tea and two bowls of shrimp étouffée. Callie watched with satisfaction as Matt took his first bite, eyelids stretching wide. To his credit he swallowed and appeared completely unflustered as he reached for his iced tea before taking a sip.

For some reason, she couldn't resist. Matt Paulson brought out the flirt in her.

"I thought you liked it hot," she said.

The deep, throaty chuckle sent a shocking shiver up her spine. When was the last time a man's laugh made her this...*aware?* Because that was the only word to describe the feeling vibrating just beneath the surface of her skin. Like a potential lightning bolt loomed close and the hairs on her arms lifted in anticipation, expecting the strike at any moment.

To cover, she pulled out her notebook. She still liked to handwrite her initial to-do list before entering information into her laptop later. There was something about the physical act of writing that always got her creative side going. While they ate, Callie went over where things stood for the LARP weekend.

Matt never said a word outside of answering her questions, finishing his bowl of étouffée without a complaint. By the end, sweat dotted his temple, and he reached for his iced tea regularly, but, after that first look of shock…nothing.

When he shoved his bowl back, he sent her a smile. "Did I pass the LaBeau initiation right?"

Callie propped her elbows on the table. "You did," she said. "With flying colors, too."

A waitress refilled their iced-tea glasses and cleared their lunch dishes away. Matt took a sip of his tea, eyeing her over his glass, and an uncomfortable feeling prickled the back of her neck.

He set his glass down. "How come you refuse to come back to your family reunion?"

"I didn't refuse. I…" She pressed her lips together and slid her gaze out over the river. "I just don't have time."

"Bull," he said softly.

She ticked her gaze back to his. "It is always easy to question the judgment of others in matters of which we may be imperfectly informed.'"

Matt lifted a brow. "Mr. Darcy again?"

"No. His love interest, Elizabeth Bennet. You should read the book."

"Maybe someday," he said with a chuckle. But clearly he wasn't about to be derailed from the topic at hand. "Some people aren't lucky enough to have any family, Callie," he said, and guilt stabbed her in the gut. "Seems a waste for you to avoid yours."

She opened her mouth to defend herself, feeling uncomfortable. She couldn't formulate an intelligent response so she tried another diversionary tactic instead.

"You ready to go for a ride in my boat?" she said.

The raise of his eyebrow let her know he was on to her, but then his grin turned positively sinful. "Is that what they're calling it these days?"

The suggestion slid through her and stirred her blood, but she remained outwardly calm as she played dumb. "I don't know what you're talking about."

"I was hoping there was a hidden meaning in that question," he asked.

He leaned forward and crossed his arms on the tiny table, his face mere inches from her face. A jolt of awareness shot through her body. The proximity sent a skitter of nerves just beneath her skin.

Hazel. His eyes were hazel.

For a moment, intrigued by the discovery, she couldn't respond.

She'd thought his eyes were brown. Of course their first meeting had taken place outside at dusk, with the only lights offered those of fake kerosene lamps. At the park she hadn't gotten close enough to tell, and during the brain-meltingly hot moment in the dim fitting room she'd been distracted by that hard chest on display. But now, in the full light of day, and with them so close, she could make out the yellow and green specks mixed in with the brown.

"Nope. No hidden messages," she said. "I thought I'd show you where I used to go fishing as a kid. But I *really* want to see how the guy who prefers the city deals with a boat ride in backcountry Louisiana."

"Is this another initiation rite?"

A grin slid up her face. "Maybe," she said. "Think you can handle it?"

"I can handle anything you've got."

Fighting words if she'd ever heard them.

Her brow hiked higher. "Cocky, aren't you?"

He tipped back his head and laughed. And once again she was presented with a vision of a strong throat and even, white teeth. The laugh lines around his eyes weren't as deep as his thirty years would suggest. And Callie wondered if that meant his smile rarely made it all the way to his eyes.

"Because I'm that kind of guy, I'll let the obvious comeback for that question slide buy."

"A sign of intelligence."

"Well—" he stood up "—let's get the rest of this family hazing over with."

When they went back inside the restaurant, Aunt Billie wouldn't let him pay, of course. Callie smothered the smile as Matt wasted ten minutes trying to change her mind, without success. Callie's grin finally appeared as she watched Matt wait for Aunt Billie to return to the kitchen before he passed by their table and left enough to cover the bill plus a very generous tip. The man never came up against a problem he couldn't solve.

And what would she do if he finally turned that determination on her?

* * *

Fighting the doubt, Matt hooked his hands on his hips and stared down at the old fiberglass boat tied to the wooden dock. "You sure this thing is safe?"

"Of course it is."

Callie, loose-limbed and agile, ignored the tiny ladder fixed to the side of the deck and hopped inside the boat with the grace of a cat. Beneath her cutoffs, toned, tanned legs ended in delicate sandals. Her beautiful shoulders now on display beneath a feminine T-shirt. Opposed to Friday night's arrangement, her hair hung loose.

And, as promised, a heat wave had settled on top of the delta. The muggy temperature was stifling. Although her T-shirt was damp, her face slightly flushed, she didn't appear bothered.

Man, how did the woman handle the weather and still look so cool?

She turned and looked up at him, a smile on her lips and a challenge in her eyes. "Don't you trust me?"

His lips twitched. "Only to a certain extent."

Eyes twinkling, Callie remained silent and sent him an I-dare-you hike of her brow. After a moment's hesitation, Matt let out a light scoff and climbed down into the boat.

"Feel free to drive," she said. "I get the feeling you like to be the one steering the boat."

"Was that a metaphor?" Matt said as he sat in the driver's seat.

"Definitely."

Surprisingly, the outboard motor of the flat-bottomed boat started easily, and Matt realized that, despite being old, the boat had been carefully maintained. Given the earlier conversation with her aunt, he got the distinct feeling Callie used it more than anyone else.

Curious about why, he steered up the canal while studying the woman up front. Callie had stretched out on the bench on the bow, eyes closed and face tilted into the breeze, obviously enjoying the wind in her hair. In the bright light he could make out streaks of gold mixed with the honey-colored strands.

The towering cypress trees lining the canal blocked most of the direct light, but the lazy heat sat on them relentlessly, the air smelling of damp earth. Spanish moss hung like tinsel in a Christmas tree, adding more of an eerie mood than a festive one.

Matt settled back in his seat, surprised at the stillness of their surroundings. Other than the ripples from their boat, and the quiet purr of the small motor, nothing moved or made a sound. Several minutes passed with the boat following the serpentine path. They rounded a curve and a lake opened out before them. Ten minutes later Callie pointed Matt in the direction of a small boathouse on stilts, blending with the trees.

"Here we are."

Matt hopped up onto the porch that also served as a high dock. Beside the wooden structure a large rope hammock—looking brand-new and out of place next to the ancient building—stretched invitingly between two oak trees. After securing the boat, he reached down and pulled Callie up onto the dock.

"I hadn't planned on taking the time to sightsee while in New Orleans." And yet, here he stood in the middle of friggin' nowhere, all because he hadn't had the willpower to resist a day with Callie. "But if I had made plans, I certainly would have chosen something a little less…" He stared across the cypress-tree-lined lake and the lapping water. The endless stretch of nothing but water and trees. "Wild."

"I promise," she said, grinning up at him, "when we get back I'll take you out on the town and show you the best New Orleans has to offer, like a nice dinner out. A little dancing. And if you're really lucky, maybe even a tour of my condo. But until then—" She backed up slowly toward the edge of the dock, flipping off her sandals and slipping her watch from her wrist, leaving Matt uneasy. The light in her eyes set him on edge in ways that weren't safe to consider.

"Where are you going?" Matt asked. A thrum of anxiety curled in Matt's stomach, and he looked out at the water. "I don't think—"

"Holler when you see a gator." And with that, Callie pivoted and dove into the water.

The splash came, raining cool drops on Matt's face and shirt, and he nearly groaned at the brief relief from the heat. In her T-shirt and shorts, Callie swam toward the center of a clearing beneath the low-hanging branches of several cypress trees and turned to tread water, smiling up at him.

"You coming in?" she said. "It's the final LaBeau initiation rite."

"What the hell do I get in return for passing all these tests?"

A smile crept up her face. "A permanent spot at the family table at Po Boy's."

"If you're not going to be there, then what's the point?"

She shot him a you're-not-funny look, and he decided to let the issue slide.

"Besides," he said, "I'm not sure that's an honor the lining of my esophagus would survive."

"I told Aunt Billie to make yours extra hot."

He tipped his head as the realization hit him. "Yours wasn't as hot as mine?"

"Nope. Can't stand it spicy. I always order it mild." The playful light in her eyes was almost worth suffering through étouffée that could be used to strip paint from wood.

Almost.

"Coming in?" she asked.

He stared down at her, hands on his hips, and a smile tugged at his lips. "Promise this is the last of the LaBeau family torture?"

"Last one, I swear."

"Okay," he said.

The woman clearly felt in her element. And while he might be a bit of a fish out of water in the backwoods of Louisiana, there were still some things that he controlled. Showing the lovely Ms. LaBeau a thing or two suddenly seemed incredibly important.

And too much fun to pass up.

After the years of worry and fear and sacrifice, he suddenly felt the urge to indulge in something just for himself. A moment to be something more than just a doctor, a brother and a stand-in parent. It had been far too long since he'd had sex, and today he was going to leave his many roles behind, save one: that of a red-blooded man in the company of a beautiful woman.

He flipped open his snap. To her credit, she didn't react except for a slight flaring of her eyelids as she continued to tread water. As Callie stared up at him, he struggled to keep the amusement from his face as he slid the zipper down. He waited for her to say something. A protest. A sound of encouragement. A mocking comment. Or, at the very least, a flicker of her gaze away from him.

Nothing.

Instead, Callie kept treading water, eyes on Matt as he hooked his hands in his shorts and shoved them down, kicking them aside. His briefs clung to his hips and, for a nanosecond, he considered shucking them, too. But he wasn't prepared for the likely ending to a bout of skinny-dipping. For one split second he mentally kicked himself for not considering the need for condoms. But right now the sun beat down on his back and sweat trickled between his shoulder blades and the water looked cool. Even better, the expression on Callie's face was inviting.

He executed a shallow dive, slicing through the water, and broke the surface just two feet from where Callie continued to tread water.

Her cheeks were flushed, whether from the heat or the sight of him in nothing but briefs, he wasn't sure.

"You know," she said dryly, "I wasn't kidding before. There are gators in these waters. So you best keep all your dangly bits inside your underwear."

He laughed, secretly pleased with the first words out of her mouth. "Thanks for the warning."

Matt fought the urge to cup her neck and drag her close for another kiss. Memories of their time in the fitting room that first night flooded his mind. The taste of her mouth, the feel of her hip.

Good thing the water was fairly cool because spontaneous combustion felt like a possibility. Unfortunately, despite being a strong swimmer he couldn't figure out how to follow through on the impulse to take that mouth in the way he wanted without drowning them both. Instead, he stretched out on his back to float, biding his time until she climbed out of the water and onto the dock. In wet clothes.

Just thinking about the sight made his groin grow tight.

Pushing the thought from his mind, he stared up at the canopy of cypress trees and the sunlight peeking through the leaves, letting the peaceful scene wash over him. For the ten years since his parents had died and he'd assumed responsibility of Tommy, he'd been living life on edge. The roller-coaster ride of Tommy's addiction had worn him out, leaving him constantly braced for the next bad happening. Taking a moment to just relax was a revelation.

"This is nice," he said.

He turned his head and met Callie's face just a few feet from his, also floating.

"I love Louisiana." Her smile wrinkled her nose in a way that could only be described as cute. "Never want to live anywhere else."

What would that be like? To live where you wanted, instead of where you had to?

He'd been stuck with Manford as his home base for so long, looking after Tommy, that he couldn't imagine a life anywhere else. But nothing about his hometown appealed to him. Never had. Never would. He'd grown up there dying to get out. But when his parents had died during his third year of college, he'd had no choice but to transfer back home before his senior year. To attend medical school and complete his E.R. residency in Detroit. Commuting as much as he could.

Sleeping in the on-call room when too tired to make the drive back home.

Sometimes he wondered if his brother's life would have turned out differently had Matt been around more during Tommy's early years of college.

He hated those self-defeating thoughts.

"But as much as I love New Orleans—" Callie's hand brushed his "—every once in a while I have to get out of town and come back here. It's so…peaceful."

They continued to float for a few more minutes, and every muscle in Matt's body slowly relaxed, until he truly felt like a floater, washed up on the beach. No tension. No worries about what tomorrow would bring.

A distant rumble of thunder broke the peace and sent them swimming for shore. Matt reached the dock first, hauling himself up. He turned and leaned down to take Callie's hand, pulling her up onto the dock… and straight into his arms.

He made no pretense that his actions were an accident. He dragged her dripping body up against his, until the wet T-shirt pressed so enticingly against her breasts was plastered against his chest. His body let out a sigh of relief.

"I've been thinking about this since the dressing room," he said.

She leaned back and eyed him. "I'm guessing your thoughts didn't include a dock house and a battered deck."

"The setting is irrelevant."

Since their kisses in the costume-shop dressing room, Matt hadn't been able to think of much else besides getting Callie back in his arms. And now that he had her here, he was going to take full advantage.

He swooped in for a kiss, gathering those soft lips against his, and a tiny moan escaped Callie. The sound shot straight to his groin.

Matt pressed his hand to the back of her head and molded himself more firmly against her. Water dripped from Callie's hair, landing on his arms, and Matt was surprised the drops didn't hit his overheated skin and fizzle into vapor. The taste and the feel of Callie in his arms were just as good as he remembered. He touched his tongue to her lower lip, and she opened her mouth wide, letting him inside. But, good God, this time it wasn't enough.

Ignoring the warning voices in his head, he lifted Callie into his arms. When she wrapped her legs around his waist, her body just brushed the top of his hard shaft. This time the groan came from him.

"Callie—"

He eyed the scene and then, decision made, headed for the hammock. Callie pressed herself more firmly against Matt.

"Callie."

She wasn't helping his self-control here.

He tumbled her back onto the hammock, the action creating a gentle rocking motion, and caught his weight with his hand. He stared down into brown eyes framed with thick lashes, wet from their swim.

"I'm not prepared for this." Even as he said the words, he stretched out beside her, covering that soft body with his own. The smell of shampoo—magnolia scented, maybe?—came from her hair.

Stupid, really, to torture himself this way. He pressed his forehead to hers. "I just want to enjoy holding you for a moment." His lips tipped up at the edges. "Minus the audience on the other side of a dressing-room door."

"I figured the perv finally wanted to cop a feel."

The image of doing exactly that left Matt's chuckle sounding strained. When Callie shifted slightly beneath him, pressing more of that soft body against his, the amusement died on his lips.

"Whatever we do," he said, "we leave the clothes *on.* I don't have a condom, but I know I'd have a devil of a time focusing on the technicalities if you were naked."

Matt swiped his hand down her side, cupping her thigh, and she closed her eyes. "So the clothes stay on," she said. "Got it."

The verbal agreement spiked his pulse higher, and he pressed her mouth open again with his, finally realizing the honey-colored hair and the honey drawl matched her honey taste.

Jesus, he needed to touch her.

He unsnapped her cutoffs and flattened his palm low against her slender belly.

"Matt." She arched her back in invitation, pressing closer, her eyes still closed. "I thought we'd agreed about the clothes—"

"We did. I'm not taking them off," he said. "I just want to touch you."

He fumbled briefly at the edge of her panties, cursing softly along the way. Why the hell was he so clumsy? But the need rushing through his veins made his fingers feel too hot and too eager and too greedy to go slow.

Matt shifted and tilted his head to take more of Callie's mouth as he finally succeeded in slipping his hand beneath the elastic band, seeking out the sweet spot that would bring about the response he craved. If he couldn't take exactly what he was dying for, then he wanted to hear Callie calling his name. He knew the flush staining her cheeks now had nothing to do with the heat wave. Goose bumps peppered her skin as he slid his palm lower with a purpose.

When he reached his goal, the soft folds beneath his fingers, Callie arched against him.

"Matt." She reached for his arms, her eyes wide. "I need—"

"I know what you need."

Callie gripped his forearm and he paused, refusing to give up his position, before stroking her between her legs.

With a groan, Callie closed her eyes. "That's mighty presumptuous of you."

"At this point," he said dryly. "I don't think either of us is thinking much beyond the big O."

She sounded out of breath. "You're too goal-oriented."

"Isn't that the point of all this?"

"The point is," she said, shifting a little lower down his chest, "to enjoy the journey en route."

And then Callie's hand landed on his hard-on, and Matt sucked in a breath and froze. The images ricocheting around his head included one of him shucking her pants and sliding between her thighs. But the one that wreaked the most havoc was of Callie's face, eyes dreamy and jaw slack as he thrust hard and brought them both to a rousing finale.

"Callie. I'm not sure—"

She tunneled her hand beneath his underwear.

"You're not sure of what?" she said, and she began

to stroke him through the cotton briefs, sending a stab of pleasure down his groin and searing his skin.

The urge to roll over and pin Callie beneath him sent a small shudder down his spine.

Matt let out an undignified curse. "I'm not sure this is wise."

She smiled against his mouth and then gave his lower lip a little nip. "If you get to touch me, then I get to touch you."

Well, hell, who could argue with logic like that?

Matt had just about adjusted to the fingers stroking him through the cotton when she ran her finger across the sensitive head, pulling an embarrassing groan from his mouth.

"Hmm," she murmured. "That was fun. Let's see if I get the same response again."

Matt left her lips and ran his mouth down the curve of her breast toward the center. The wet layer of cotton and the lace beneath were frustrating, but he continued to nip, placing sucking kisses along the path from one side to the other. He flicked his tongue across the tip, the partial bud growing fuller in response, and he grinned. Her fingers on his erection fumbled a little, and her free hand gripped the short hair at the back of his neck, pulling his head up until they were face-to-face.

The wide pupils and parted mouth were a beautiful sight, right before she dove in for a soul-searing kiss that almost had him losing his focus, his fingers briefly losing their rhythm beneath her pants.

"Here's an idea," he said, his voice throatier than he would have liked. "Let's see who can stay the most focused."

Eyelids wide, she said, "Clothes stay on?"

"Deal."

Matt knew he was in trouble when Callie stopped kissing him and pulled back to look at his face. Her lips—ruddy from being consumed by his—curled into a grin and, before Matt could figure out what she had in mind, her hand slipped beneath his briefs and made contact, closing around his erection. Her soft palm encircled his hard length.

For a moment, his mind went blank and his heart flatlined.

"Callie." This time her name came out more of a groan. "I can't—"

Callie writhed against him, encouraging his fingers to get with the program again. Desperate, he used his free hand to ruck her shirt up to just beneath her breasts before he caught himself, remembering their deal.

Why'd he come up with this torture?

Matt bent forward and captured the tip of her breast with his mouth again, cursing the two layers of fabric between them. Callie's hand stroked him faster, and the need building low in his back began to increase in intensity, his movements less about teasing and more about pushing them both over the edge. And the devouring of her with his lips and teeth and tongue became as much about satisfying his need as hers.

Callie's lids went wide, her mouth partially open as she sucked in breath after breath, and her hand began to falter, the rhythm of her strokes stuttering. When she arched her back, her body giving one final shudder, she dragged her thumb directly over his sensitive tip. Matt's spine went stiff, the orgasm shooting through him, stripping the strength from his limbs.

Matt had no idea how many minutes passed before

his endorphin-soaked brain became aware of his surroundings again. A breeze gently rocked the hammock and cooled their sweat-slicked skin. The smell of sex hung in the air, and the feel of Callie's soft body pressed against Matt's lulled him into a sense of peace. In fact, he might have sworn never to move again.

"That was definitely the most fun I've ever had with my clothes on," he said, his eyes still closed. "I haven't done the third-base-only thing since high school."

"Third base. Really? Do people still use the term?"

He looked down at Callie with a grin. "Only perverts like me."

She tipped back her head and laughed, and the movement sent their slick torsos sliding against each other.

"Um..." Callie wiggled against the mess between them as a small smile crept up her face. "I think we're going to need to go for another dip in the water."

CHAPTER FIVE

THE NEXT MORNING, Callie leaned back in the chair in her office and stared blankly at her laptop, currently parked on her desk. She'd come to work early to get some planning done, but after the hot moment in the hammock yesterday, her mind hadn't been the same. Her *body* hadn't been the same. How could she concentrate on creating a medieval menu for a wedding reception when all she could think about was Matt?

Especially getting Matt…*naked.*

They'd driven back to the city, and the parting had been full of untapped potential. Unfortunately she'd had a meeting with a client last evening, so she couldn't invite him up to her condo. And no matter how far things had gone between the two of them, she still felt awkward asking him to come to her place once she was free. A request synonymous with asking him over for a night of sex.

Not that there was anything wrong with *that.*

After all, they were two consenting adults.

However, if her current mind frame were any indication, having Matt Paulson around would surely slow down her progress at work.

Callie set her elbow on her sleek cherrywood desk

and propped her chin in her hand. Perhaps Matt was right. Maybe she should stop avoiding the extended family. Maybe if she simply started showing up to the various family functions her relatives would stop continuing to file her away under the to-be-pitied category. Avoiding the family while waiting for time to take care of the issue hadn't helped.

For God's sake, ten years surely would have cured the problem by now.

But continuing to avoid the family amounted to everyone thinking she was hiding in shame, which couldn't be further from the truth. She needed to show up, hold her head high and let everyone see that she was exactly where she wanted to be in her life, past mistakes be damned.

Callie sat up and fired off an email to her aunt, accepting the invitation to the family reunion. If she was lucky, maybe Matt would still be around and she could ask him to come with her. A little steadying presence by her side would be welcome for sure. Of course, having him around meant they could actually make it beyond the juvenile label of third base.

Unfortunately, the thought of Matt in her bed sidetracked her again.

"Callie."

Startled, she looked up. Colin stood on the other side of her desk, looking down at her with a bemused expression on his face, dark hair curling a bit just above his ears. How had he entered her office without her even hearing him? After a quick check of her watch, she realized fifteen minutes had passed by without her knowledge. Good Lord, she'd never get anything done at this rate.

"I knocked, but you didn't answer," Colin said.

"Sorry." Callie sat up and pretended to shuffle through a few files on her desk. "What have I done to warrant a visit from my favorite ex-boyfriend?"

Colin let out a huff of humor and dropped into the seat across from her. "I'd take that as a compliment if you had more exes running around."

Callie lifted a brow dryly, determined to remain unaffected by the efficiently targeted, well-meaning jab. Unfortunately, when Colin went on, remaining unaffected became impossible.

Colin crossed his arms. "The Paulson thing is turning into a bigger deal than I thought."

Oh, God.

Stunned, Callie stared at her ex, hoping to read exactly what he was talking about in his expression. But nothing in his blue eyes gave away his thoughts. Had he already guessed she was slipping quickly into a *thing,* for lack of a better word, with Matt? Callie racked her brain trying to figure out how she'd given everything away. Short of Matt leaving handprints on her body she was at a loss to explain the turn of events. Unless Colin had suddenly developed psychic powers she didn't know about.

"Uh…bigger deal?" she said.

"Yes. Like nationally televised newsworthy deal."

Television?

Matt *would* look good on a sex tape.

"Wait, *what?*" She shook her head and leaned back in her seat, trying to pry her mind out of the gutter. "I'm confused."

Clearly Colin was talking about something other than her relationship with Matt. Their sexual exploits, while hot in a kind of innocent way, were hardly the stuff of tabloids.

"The *Dungeons of Zhorg* community caught wind of the Paulson wedding," Colin said. "And there are people clamoring to come for some of the events."

Callie stared at her ex, her heart working overtime to supply enough blood to her brain. She'd only been gone for a day. One day. She'd enjoyed lunch with Matt, taken a swim and indulged in an erotic, fully clothed moment with a handsome guy. When the heck had everything become so crazy?

Being caught up in a sex-tape scandal suddenly seemed appealing in comparison.

"The LARP event was to be for the wedding guests only," Callie said.

"That was the original idea. But someone at Gamer's World got wind of the plans and now they want in on the action, too. I called and spoke with Tommy Paulson myself, and he and his fiancée are in favor of making this as big as we want, as long as Rainstorm Games foots the bill for all the extras. Our publicist is contacting the local networks and several of them are interested in running a human interest piece about Tommy and Penny's story."

Gamer's World? Networks?

Holy hell.

"Colin." Her voice came out weak. News cameras? At a wedding she'd arranged? "I only agreed to handle this wedding because the smaller scale made it doable. Money isn't the only issue here. I'm just one person, plus a part-time assistant."

And while the businesswoman in her considered the additions an opportunity of a lifetime, the woman who wanted to have time to eat and sleep over the next two months had issues with the idea. Not to mention how would she even find two minutes to see where yesterday's foray into hotness with Matt would lead? And see where the relationship would take her?

"Don't worry," he said. "I have plenty of experience with these types of events. I've launched several popular games, remember?"

"What I remember best was you arranging a zombie invasion of a wedding your wife and I planned," she said dryly.

Colin sent her an unapologetic grin.

Despite everything, she smiled. "It was an epic ending to a fabulous wedding."

Callie had gone all out in helping Colin's then-fiancée plan a spectacular Mardi Gras wedding. She'd grown pretty close to Jamie in the process. And even though Callie wished them well in their marital bliss, a little part of Callie envied them, as well. The closest Callie had ever come to anything serious had been with Colin, and their relationship ended ten years ago.

I'd take that as a compliment if you had more exes running around.

The realization suddenly made her love life seem a little pathetic. But she'd been so busy pouring all her energies into her business, determined to turn her negative into a positive that she hadn't had time for a relationship.

She hadn't lived the life of a monk. She wasn't *that* insane. Callie had dated and enjoyed herself along the way. But she'd passed on actively pursuing anything serious because she wanted to be in the right place in her life. And while she'd been building her business, her social life had lagged behind, stuck in the old days.

Hanging out with old friends was well and good, but what about making new ones?

Case in point, one of her best friend's was her ex from ten years ago.

Unfortunately, Colin seemed oblivious to her brutal personal epiphany as he went on.

"I checked out the park you chose and spoke with the people in charge," he said. "They have plenty of room and more than adequate parking."

Right. They were in the middle of discussing how her work life had just gotten hellaciously complicated. Did he have any idea what he was asking of her?

Colin went on. "I don't think we'll need that much room, but the park said they could handle up to a thousand people."

"A thousand?" she said weakly, trying to force her mind back to the concerning turn of events. Her private party wedding suddenly going public…

"Colin, that's way more work than I signed on for."

"I know you've been trying to prove to your parents how successful your business has become. I assumed you'd jump at the chance to do exactly that."

"True. But televising a wedding I've only had two months to arrange isn't exactly how I figured to pull this off."

"If anyone can do this, it's you."

"You mean if anyone is crazy enough to *try,* it's me."

"Listen, Callie—" Colin leaned forward, his blue eyes on hers "—I trust you. I know you can pull this off in a manner that will live up to the newly expanded LARP event."

I trust you.

Damn, here she was resenting the fact he'd just increased her workload by a hundred and he had the nerve to utter those words she rarely heard other than from her clients.

I trust you.

The twinge in her heart was impossible to ignore.

After her spectacular fail in college, the one person she'd directly affected the most had been Colin. She hadn't asked him to come up and bail her out. But he'd come. Because that was the kind of guy he was. And the trip had cost him greatly.

Still, he'd been the first to forgive her. The first to embrace her crazy decision to start her own business arranging themed weddings, and he even managed her website. And if that wasn't enough, he participated in the *Ex Factor* blog because it helped *her,* not him. He remained anonymous, which meant he received nothing in return, other than the satisfaction of seeing his friend succeed and her massive gratitude.

Callie stared at Colin. Obviously Colin considered the turn of events an opportunity not to be missed, for both her business and his. And Tommy and Penny appeared thrilled, as well.

"When it comes to work, no one is more focused than you, Callie."

I was until Matt Paulson landed in my life.

"Uh, thanks."

Clearly the man didn't remember how distracted she'd been when he'd arrived at her office. And all of this meant that, damn, she probably should try to tone things down with the brother of the groom. How could she give this event the proper attention while preoccupied by the potential for more with Matt Paulson?

"You know I'll give it my all," she said.

"You always do." Colin reached across her desk and gave her a friendly cuff on the arm. "I'll have my publicist coordinate things with you. And if you need any extra help, don't hesitate to holler."

She sent him a smile she didn't quite feel. "Sure."

Callie watched Colin exit her office, and the moment he disappeared Callie flopped back against her seat. The question remained, how good was she at pulling off the impossible? And how was she going to convince Matt to return to a hands-off relationship?

More important, how was she going to convince herself?

CHAPTER SIX

"THIS REALLY ISN'T necessary, Mr. Croft." Callie pressed the elderly man's handkerchief to the cut on her forehead, hoping the blood had stopped oozing down her face. The E.R. was packed and it was only seven-thirty in the evening. The hour they'd spent in the waiting room so far felt like the tip of the iceberg.

Callie tried again. "It was kind of you to drive me here, but I don't need to see a doctor."

A trickle of blood ran down her hand as she applied pressure to her forehead, and she cursed the timing. How could she convince the man she didn't need medical attention with her arm bringing to mind a horror flick? Served her right for being so distracted.

She'd gone to the costume shop today to rummage around and check out the crucifix she'd spied on the shelf the first day she'd visited the store. Focusing on her work hadn't come easy, especially with the dressing room in her line of sight. And then, while standing on the shelf, she'd received a call from Matt, asking her to dinner.

No wonder she'd dropped the stupid crucifix on her head.

A drop of blood landed on her thigh, and she swiped

the spot with her sleeve before the shop owner noticed. "I'm fine. Really. I can take care of this at home."

The balding man's forehead looked permanently creased with concern. "But that crucifix is heavy. You might need a CAT scan."

That crucifix was heavy, indeed. Hurt like heck on the way down, too. Reaching for the sucker on the top shelf had been a stupid plan. Maybe Matt was right. Maybe she should stick to the cheaper, less authentic, less *heavy* props from here on out. Unfortunately, that didn't solve her problem now. She kept hoping to convince the shop owner to leave, so she could leave, too. When she'd agreed to meet Matt for dinner tonight—to discuss the wedding *only,* she'd stressed to Matt—showing up bleeding wasn't exactly the professional image she'd wanted to project.

A shout from down the hallway caught the attention of the entire waiting room. A man with handcuffs was kicking and screaming and shouting profanities, being escorted by two policemen. One of the cops sported a pretty impressive bloody nose.

Callie sighed and addressed Mr. Croft. "At least go on home to your wife."

So that I can leave this E.R.

"Not until you get checked out by a doctor," Mr. Croft said.

Callie bit back the groan. She hated being forced to go with her last resort but, at this point, she had no choice. She had to call Matt anyway, because making their dinner date looked impossible at this point. And she still hadn't decided how to tell him she was putting their personal relationship, such as it was, on ice.

Callie pulled out her cell phone and placed the call, and Matt answered on the second ring.

"Hey. It's Callie." She turned in her seat to face away from where Mr. Croft was pacing and lowered her voice. "I'm sorry to bother you, but I need your help."

"Does it involve another impossible deal involving sex with our clothes on? Because I'm not sure I'm up for torturing myself tonight."

Despite everything, Callie bit back the smile and went on, "No, nothing like that. I went to Mr. Croft's shop to check out a crucifix for an *Interview with the Vampire* wedding I'm planning."

"Vampires?"

She grinned at the doubtful tone of his voice. "Set to take place at midnight. In a graveyard."

"That's just creepy."

Callie laughed. "Anyway…" She glanced at Mr. Croft, who was now speaking with the clerk again, gesturing anxiously back at Callie.

The poor man was going to have a stroke at the thought of her keeling over from head trauma.

"I reached up to grab the crucifix and managed to knock the thing down on my head." She purposefully didn't share exactly why she'd been so distracted. "And it's, um, a lot heavier than it looks."

"Are you okay?"

"I have a little cut on my forehead. But Mr. Croft is freaking out. I think he's afraid I'm going to keel over and die. He refuses to leave until I get checked out by a doctor."

She could hear the grin in Matt's voice.

"And you just happen to know one," he said.

"I hate asking you for a favor like this. But—"

"Which E.R.?"

"St. Mathews."

"I'm leaving right now."

The next half hour passed by painfully, and Callie was no closer to deciding how to handle Matt. Not only that, the waiting room looked set to explode, every seat full. A couple was arguing and several kids were crying and Callie thought she was going to lose her mind. When the double doors whooshed open and Matt entered, relief swamped Callie, even as awareness shimmied up her spine.

He strode toward her with the look she remembered from the first night they'd met. Focused and intent on solving a problem.

Matt knelt in front of Callie, and she ignored the ridiculous catch in her chest as he lifted the bandage on her forehead, examining the cut.

"How long ago did it happen?" He ran his finger gently down the edge of her tender skin, and she sucked in a breath. The scent of spicy soap hit her nose, and she took in his hair, damp and curling a bit at the edges. Clearly he'd just gotten out of the shower. And the thought of a naked Matt soaping himself made her squirm in her seat.

She'd had the pleasure of having that hard length pressed along her hip…

Mr. Croft appeared beside Callie. "Two hours ago. The crucifix is heavy. I shouldn't have kept it on the top shelf."

Matt sent Callie a conspiratorial wink before assuming a serious face again, looking up at Mr. Croft. "Was there any loss of consciousness?"

"No."

"Any vomiting or slurred speech? Have you noticed her acting or saying anything odd?"

Mr. Croft visibly relaxed a bit. "No."

Good thing the man wasn't privy to her crazy thoughts about Matt.

Matt turned back to Callie. "Feeling dizzy?"

Heck, yeah. Because you're so close, and you smell so good and—oh, my God—those hands.

The feel of his fingers and that hot hazel gaze bringing back the moment on the dock.

"No," she said instead. "No dizziness."

"I don't see a need for a CAT scan." Matt stood, keeping a reassuring hand on Callie's shoulder, and Callie fought the urge to lean into the comforting gesture. "Why don't you let me take her home, Mr. Croft? I can keep an eye on her tonight. If any concerning symptoms crop up, I can bring her back here."

Poor Mr. Croft looked incredibly earnest. Callie could tell the older man wanted to leave, but the worry just wouldn't let him go. "But what about her cut. Shouldn't she get that sutured?"

"The edges are clean." Matt pulled out something shaped like a marker from his pocket, with a clear tip. "We have a special kind of glue we use to close these kinds of lacerations. I can take care of this at home."

"You're sure?"

Matt's face adopted that perfect combination of soothing authority and self-assurance that inspired confidence. "Absolutely."

"Okay. But you'll call if something happens?"

"Of course." Matt sent Mr. Croft a smile that said, "I've got this."

Callie watched the shop owner make his way back

through the automatic doors, not allowing herself to relax until the man disappeared from sight.

She let out a sigh and turned to Matt. "*Thank* you. I thought he'd never leave."

"Guilt." His lips twisted wryly. "The damn emotion is a powerfully motivating force. And, speaking of the emotion, shouldn't you be feeling a little of the same?"

When she looked at him stupidly, he went on.

"You promised a night out on the town, showing me the best that New Orleans has to offer. To make up for the nuclear, skin-melting étouffée I had to eat at your aunt's place. I think I remember something about fine dining. Maybe a little dancing. I believe your condo was mentioned, as well."

Shoot, she'd forgotten all about that. How was she going to get out of this gracefully?

She licked her lips nervously. "Oh, well—"

"I'm only kidding." He gently pulled her to her feet. "A hot night out loses a bit of its appeal when your date is actively hemorrhaging."

"I'm not bleeding anymore." She touched the sore spot with her fingers. "At least not very much."

"How about I get you home, close up that cut and we order takeout?" He cupped her elbow, and she tried to ignore the skin-on-skin contact. "And when you start to vomit profusely, slur your words and your left pupil dilates, I'll call Mr. Croft and tell him I'm dragging you back to the E.R. for a CT scan and emergency brain surgery."

She sent him a sarcastic look.

Matt simply grinned. "Maybe next time you should wait for the proprietor to retrieve the item on the top shelf for you."

"Would you want to watch Mr. Croft crawl up a rickety old ladder?"

"Hmm," he said. "Point taken."

Another shout came up as a State Trooper hauled in a man that appeared to be flying high on something. Sirens wailed outside as an ambulance pulled up to the side ramp. Callie couldn't wait to leave the hectic scenario behind. But Matt? Well, Matt was looking around with an expression of…

Good Lord. Was that *affection?*

"You like the craziness of the E.R., don't you?" she asked.

The little boy grin he sent was adorable. "Love it."

Callie tipped her head. "Does your job in Michigan get this crazy?"

Matt's gaze slid from hers to the overflowing waiting room, the staff bustling about. The chaos in the E.R. appeared to be reaching some sort of zenith. Instead of appearing overwhelmed by the sensory input, Matt looked sorry to be leaving. A nurse came out to announce there was a three-car pileup, with several patients on the way, asking the less urgent patients to please be patient. Matt looked as if he were itching to join in the mayhem and help out.

"Manford E.R. has its moments," he said. "But never anything like this."

So if he didn't stay in Manford for the job, or because he loved the town, why didn't he move? Before she could ask, he linked his fingers with hers, and the contact did crazy things to her pulse. Ridiculous, really, after everything they'd done in the hammock. The simple feel of palm against palm should not be so stimulating.

Matt squeezed her hand lightly. "Time to take you home."

The words zipped through Callie's brain, lighting little fires in their wake. She hesitated. If Matt took her home to fix her cut and keep an eye on her, despite his previous words, the risk of a repeat in the hammock was great.

After informing the clerk to take Callie off the waiting list, they made their way out the door into the night. The air muggy and warm and, after dealing with Mr. Croft for the past hour and a half, Callie had never been so grateful to leave an air-conditioned building. Regrettably, leaving also meant she had to make up her mind how to tell Matt.

And soon.

Thirty minutes later Callie opened the door to her condominium and tried hard not to show just how torn she was by his presence. But she needed to be honest with Matt. No doubt the man expected to finish what they'd started. And, God knows, Callie longed for the same thing.

Just tell him while he cleans up your cut, Callie.

Sure, she'd just wait until he was touching her with those fabulous hands. Nothing wrong with that plan, *at all.*

Her throat tight, Callie set her purse on the foyer table and then led Matt into her kitchen. Matt came to a stop in the middle of the room, scanning the dark wood cabinets, the marble counters and the top-of-the-line kitchen appliances. Despite the small size, her upscale condo had everything she needed, including being located in the fabulous Arts District.

“Not bad for a former tomboy who used to catch crawdads,” he said.

Callie smiled. “How about a drink before we get started?”

Lord knows she needed one.

“Scotch?” she asked.

“Absolutely.”

Hopefully a bit of alcohol would take the edge off, so she poured two, rehearsing her lines for the conversation that was about to take place.

Handing Matt his drink, she said, “I suppose you heard about Colin and Tommy’s big plans to take the DoZ weekend and go public.”

Matt sighed and threaded his fingers through his hair, leaving sandy-colored spikes in his wake. “I’m sorry.”

She let out a soft huff, amused. “Not your fault.”

“You could have said no. Tommy and Penny were already getting what they wanted.”

“Colin asked.”

Matt said nothing in response, so she handed Matt his drink and he simply followed her down the hall of hardwood floors and into the bathroom containing the same dark wood cabinets and marble counters as the kitchen. The mere fact that Matt hadn’t commented meant she had some explaining to do. Callie leaned her hip against the cabinet and watched Matt pull out everything he needed from his bag, totally focused on his task.

She’d experienced firsthand the chaos of the E.R. waiting room. God only knows how much worse the noise and confusion had been in back, which explained a lot about Matt’s ability to focus. Obviously the man had learned to block out unnecessary stimuli, concentrating on the task in front of him. And the memory of having all that attention directed at her sent heat crawling up her back.

"I'm curious what kind of hold Colin has over you," Matt said.

"I told you before, I owe him."

"Yeah, but I considered your debt more of an 'I'm going to organize this weekend party for him' kind of obligation. Not an 'I'm going upgrade the whole shindig to a blowout publicity stop' kind of obligation."

He'd stopped, a package of gauze in his hand as he watched Callie closely.

"I'm assuming this has something to do with your college blunder," he went on.

Callie almost laughed at the benign-sounding title he'd given her mistake.

"When I got dragged to the police station, Colin made the long drive to come bail me out. Colin was livid, and I was angry because I hadn't even asked for his help. He just assumed and came." Her voice dropped a notch. "And, unfortunately, the trip wound up screwing up his finals. He..." She looked away for a moment. "He almost flunked that semester."

She took a deep breath, pushing the horrendously shameful memories away. She'd alienated herself from her parents, her boyfriend and most of her friends in one awful day. Not to mention losing the scholarship.

Coming back to New Orleans was the hardest thing she'd ever done, but she didn't regret the move for a moment.

"And now that this weekend has morphed into the party that just won't stop growing, this is a massive opportunity for Rainstorm Games," she said. "And, hence, Colin. The added publicity is also good for my business."

She took a deep breath and met Matt's gaze again, forcing the words out. "I can't pull off doing my job and sorting through—" she gestured her hand between the two of them "—this, whatever *this* is, at the same time."

A hush descended in her bathroom, and the pause felt big enough to swallow her whole. In fact, she kind of wished it would.

Matt set the gauze on the counter and stepped closer, and her awareness of him increased to distracting levels. "You're telling me that you're going to let your guilt keep you from enjoying our time together?"

"It's not guilt."

God, she hated that word. She'd spent the first few years back in New Orleans drowning in a murky sea of remorse. She'd promised herself, *promised,* she'd have nothing more to do with the emotion. But still…

Matt cocked his head and continued to say nothing, and the burn in her belly brought a frown to her mouth.

Damn.

"Okay," she said. "Maybe I do have some leftover guilt."

She hated admitting that to herself, much less to Matt. It was bad enough her parents still brought up her moment of shame, reminding her of all she'd done. She'd been struggling for years to prove to her parents she'd successfully moved on. And how disappointing to realize she'd subjected herself to the same treatment, even if unconsciously done.

Callie sighed and rubbed her forehead. There were

better ways to spend her time than to engage in endless self-flagellation.

"From what you told me, you're partially responsible for bringing him and his wife together," Matt said. "Shouldn't a happy ending release you from your debt?"

"I can't screw up this wedding and the promotional event—"

"You won't," he said, stepping so close she could see those beautiful flecks in his eyes.

"See?" Heart doing crazy somersaults in her chest, she pressed back against the cabinet. "I can't think when I'm so distracted."

He lifted a hand to her face. "First, I'll be happy to provide lessons on how to remain focused despite distractions. I think the fact that I'm capable of holding this conversation with you…alone…in your condo… a bed just a room away, proves my point. Second, if I promise to let you get plenty of sleep tonight, will that convince you?"

The conflicting desires—the need to prove herself and the need to feel Matt's hands on her again—went to war in her head again. If she cut out all the bare essentials, she could do this. Her gaze dropped to the T-shirt stretched across Matt's chest, hugging the lean muscles beneath. How much sleep did one need, anyway?

"I think you sold me when you mentioned the lessons," she said.

"Good." The sexy smirk on his face just about did her in, and he stepped back. "Just so we're clear, I'm going to clean up your cut and take you to bed. So if you still have a problem with that, you need to let me know now."

How could he say those words so calmly? Especially

with her pulse striving to achieve record rates? The man had stated his plans to take care of her injury and take her to bed, both declarations delivered with the same nonchalant tone as if the two activities were somehow on the same par with each other. She envied his ability to pull the coolly collected demeanor off.

She felt the need to throw him off guard, to keep him on his toes.

"Just so we're *clear...*" Now that the matter had been decided, she pulled off her bloodstained blouse and tossed the garment aside. "Not only did the corset embellish the goods, the push-up bra I wore that day on the dock made me look bigger than I really am."

Holding his gaze, she reached around her back to unfasten her bra, heart thumping hard, record rates achieved. But her pulse shot higher when Matt reached around and gripped her hand, stopping her efforts and putting about an inch of space between their torsos. She stared up at Matt, those beautiful hazel eyes boring into hers. Heat radiated from his body. Or maybe the one generating the scorching temperatures was her.

His voice low, Matt said, "There is absolutely no way I'll be able to take care of that laceration with you bare-chested. So leave the bra on." A muscle in his jaw ticked, and she had the absurd urge to ease the spot with her tongue. "At least until I'm done."

This last was delivered with a light in his eye that could melt metal.

"Nice to know I can at least warrant being labeled a distraction," she said.

"Never fear. You definitely fall into the category of a distraction. A major one. Not only did I bring the necessary equipment to clean and close up the laceration on your forehead, I brought a box of condoms, too, just in case you didn't have any here."

Her heart stopped, and then restarted with a stutter. Unfortunately, the faster rate made concentrating on the conversation difficult. She squirmed and he shot her a mock chastising look.

"You're going to have to be still," he said. "All that wiggling is…distracting."

Callie closed her lids. Best not to stare up into those hazel eyes. "Do you always have trouble focusing when closing up a woman's cut?"

"No, but they are usually dressed in more than a bra." His voice dropped an octave. "And it's never been you before."

His fingers gently traced around the bruised area briefly and she prided herself on her patience. On her ability to keep her eyes closed with that face and those dreamy eyes so close to hers. She felt his breath warm her forehead, and she gripped the counter, fighting the urge to lean up and take that fabulous mouth with hers.

She was too distracted by the memory to worry much about the sound of rustling, as if he were searching for something, but then came a brush of something soft and wet, followed by a sharp sting.

Callie's lids popped open as she sucked in a breath. "My God."

"Sorry."

An antiseptic smell drifted from the cotton ball in his hand, and he leaned in and pressed a kiss close to the wound before pulling his head back.

She stared up at those lips so close. "What are you using to clean the cut? Hydrochloric acid?"

The chuckle that followed brought a wry twist of her lips. "How did you guess?"

Callie studied Matt's face as he gently pinched the skin around the cut and applied the liquid skin adhesive. She concentrated on breathing, the sound of the air conditioner humming, anything to keep herself from rising up on tiptoe to kiss Matt, which wasn't easy. She had firsthand knowledge that he kissed like a dream. He hadn't needed much to bring her to her knees that day on the dock, just his mouth and those fabulous hands.

When he finished, he dropped his hand. "Now, be careful not to open that up until it has time to dry."

"Is that going to interfere with you taking me to bed?"

"Hell, no," he said, and then he covered her mouth with his.

At first it was just a damp press of skin against skin, his mouth slotted against hers. The heat in Callie's belly increased, seeping along her veins, and she rose up on her toes, taking more. With a groan, Matt opened his mouth, forcing Callie's open and tasting her with his tongue. He tipped his head to the right, and then to left, as if comparing how they best fit together. Heart thumping, Callie was just about to pull back and suggest moving things to the bedroom when Matt leaned down, gripped her behind the thighs and lifted her.

Callie pulled her head back. "Wait," she said with a gasp that contained both humor and desire, clutching his shoulders for balance. "What's your plan for providing lessons on how to remain focused despite distractions?"

The crooked smile on Matt's face sent anticipation and heat curling up in her stomach, and she wrapped her legs around his waist. With one hand against her bottom, he supported her weight as he pulled the box of condoms from his bag.

"No worries." He exited the bathroom, heading up the hallway and into her bedroom. He placed her on the bed, staring down at her with a heated look that sent her stomach searching for her toes. "I'll think of something."

His gaze swept down her body, the hazel eyes growing dark, and goose bumps fanned across her skin. Without a word, he pulled off her sandals and stripped her of her clothes, until all that remained were her panties and bra.

She pushed up on one elbow and reached for his shirt. "Let me help."

Matt gently pushed her back down, the crooked smile sinfully sexy. "No," he said. "Wouldn't want you to hurt yourself and pull that head wound back open."

"Then what am I supposed to—?"

Matt gripped her wrists and raised her hands over her head, curling her fingers around the wooden slats of her headboard. He leaned down and pressed a gentle kiss next to her cut.

"Your job is just to hold on and not move," he said.

A stab of desire sliced through her, heating her between the legs. "Not move?" she asked. "But how am I supposed to—"

Matt reached for the button on his shirt, and she watched, mesmerized, as he undid the row of buttons one by one and tossed the shirt aside. His eyes on hers, he reached for the front of his jeans, and Callie's heart picked up its pace. The muscles in his arms and chest rippled as he flicked open his pants and pushed everything down. Lean hips, well-muscled thighs and a heart-attack-inducing erection left Callie struggling to continue the act of breathing.

"Matt..."

The words died as he knelt at her feet, removing her bra and panties. She waited for him to kiss her. Instead, Matt picked up her leg, pressing openmouthed kisses up her shin, her thigh, and then landing on her hip bone.

"The key to keeping that incision safe," he murmured against her skin, "is to remain completely still."

She arched her back, hoping to encourage him to head south. Instead, he trailed higher until his tongue dipped in her navel, sending a skitter of sparks up her spine. He cupped her between the legs and shifted higher, his mouth moving up until it landed on a nipple.

Shock and desire shot through her limbs, and she arched her back, seeking more of that mind-blowing mouth against her skin. Matt circled the tip with his tongue, and Callie sucked in a breath. But just as she was melting at the caress, he ran his tongue down her abdomen, across her hip and landed between her legs.

Heat and pleasure blasted through her. "Oh, my God, Matt," she said, tipping her head back.

When Matt flicked his tongue against her, Callie whimpered, "Please..."

She wanted to wrap her arms around his back and pull his body down. She wanted his naked skin stretched out across the top of hers. She wanted to reach down and clutch his head, pulling him closer.

Fingers tight around the headboard, she said, "Can I let go yet?"

"Nope," he said. At least this time his voice sounded harsh, as if he were wound up tight and needed release.

Jeez, she knew how he felt.

"Not yet," he said.

He sat up on his knees, and Callie's breath escaped with a protesting sound. Palms damp against the wooden slats of the headboard, she watched Matt apply a condom, her fingernails digging into her palms. Eyes homing in on hers, he swooped up her body and buried himself deep between her legs. His pace relentless, he rocked into her.

Mind spinning, muscles straining, she struggled to keep her hold of the headboard as he moved. The intensity in his gaze and the dark, focused look on his face brought her closer to the edge. His body hard, Matt drove her higher, the muscles in his arms lengthening and bulging from his efforts.

"Matt."

"Okay."

His one-word response brought a cry of relief, and Callie wrapped her arms around his back, her legs around his hips, holding him close. Urging him on. Hanging on tight. The heat of pleasure burned hotter, brighter, until Callie was sure she'd burst into flames. Feeling out of control, she gripped his shoulders harder. The orgasm burst outward, shock waves moving through her body, and she closed her eyes, relishing the sensation, barely aware as Matt gave one final thrust, calling out her name.

CHAPTER SEVEN

THE NEXT MORNING, awareness came to Matt in layers, each one better than the one before. Slowly he became cognizant of a comfortable bed, of soft sheets and Callie's hair tickling his cheek, his hand resting on her hip. Her body lay lax, her breathing deep and even as she slept. For a moment he enjoyed the simple pleasure of holding a beautiful woman in his arms. A lazy morning where he had nothing he needed to do and no place he needed to be. Even better?

The potential for a repeat of last night.

He felt more relaxed than he had in a long time and not just because of the sex. Although the activities went a hell of a long way at taking the edge off the tension he'd been carrying around since he'd first laid eyes on Callie. The great sex left his body humming.

A buzzing sound caught his attention, and he peered over Callie's shoulder. His cell phone vibrated madly, inching across the nightstand in its efforts to get his attention. When it went to voice mail, his phone flashed. Five missed calls.

Damn.

Panic punched him, and he bolted upright in bed, picturing Tommy calling for help. The emergency room trying to contact him about his brother being brought in for an overdose. The police calling to deliver the tragic news…

The house was dark when Matt entered—not a peaceful stillness, but the eerie kind that filled him with dread. Suffocating. Terrifying. Anxiety crawled up his spine as he headed up the hallway and called out Tommy's name, getting no answer. He knew his brother was home because his car was in the drive.

When he spied his brother's bedroom door cracked open, Matt's steps slowed, his pulse increased and goose bumps prickled his neck, spreading throughout his limbs. His heart hammered in his chest as he slowly pushed the door open, and certainty slid into place when he saw Tommy lying on the floor, pale, as still as death.

Matt slammed his eyes shut against the memory, nausea rising in his stomach and tightening his chest. How could he have forgotten to check in with Tommy last night?

Matt fought to control his breathing, cursing under his breath, mindful of Callie sleeping next to him. He glanced down. Fortunately, she still appeared to be deep in sleep. Matt rolled out of bed and stood, reaching for the phone. As he scrolled through the missed calls, his heart continued to pound, no matter how much he told himself to calm down.

Every voice message was from Tommy, which meant he wasn't dead. At least not yet.

Relief poured through Matt, and he leaned against the wall, bracing his hands on his knees. Willing himself to friggin' get a grip.

Once he felt steadier, he padded down the hallway

and into Callie's living room. Hitting Tommy's number, Matt collapsed onto the couch and braced for the topic.

Tommy voice sounded worried. "Where the hell have you been?"

Matt rubbed his eyes and let out a self-directed scoff of ridicule.

"Sorry, Tommy. I got distracted."

Matt's mind drifted back to Callie

Yep, very distracted.

Tommy's huff sounded more amused than annoyed. "Yeah, well, when my worrywart of a big brother didn't check in like usual, I got concerned. And with every unreturned call, I thought you'd been mugged and knocked unconscious or something."

The bark of laughter held more bitterness than humor. Hopefully Tommy wouldn't notice.

"Sorry, Tommy. Long story. Wound up making a trip to the E.R. last night."

"You okay?"

"I'm fine. Just…helping out a friend."

"A friend?"

Matt ignored the implied inquiry beneath his brother's tone. "I'm heading back home tomorrow."

His return to Manford was long overdue.

"Good," Tommy said.

The relief in Tommy's voice had Matt sitting up right. For the first time, Matt noticed the tension underlying his brother's voice, a tension that didn't relate to his brother's worries about Matt.

"Are you, uh…?" Being a moron meant Matt's question came out incredibly lame. "Okay?" Matt finished.

Okay, of course, meaning many different things.

Are you sleeping all right?

Having trouble at work?

Using again?

Matt bit back the groan and dropped his head into his hand, phone still pressed to his ear. They'd been skirting the edges of this issue since the last time Matt had picked Tommy up from a thirty-day stint in rehab. And the two years of tiptoeing were tiresome. Because, seriously, how many ways could two men have the same conversation?

If you don't quit, you're going to wind up dead, Tommy.

I've given it up for good, Matt, I swear.

And in Tommy's defense, Matt knew his brother meant the words every time he repeated them.

Tommy's voice brought Matt back to the conversation. "No, everything's fine."

There was an awkward pause. "Good," Matt said, wondering what Tommy was *really* thinking.

"Penny and I will have a couple of steaks on the grill waiting for you when you get off the plane."

As always, Tommy managed to bring a smile to Matt's lips, despite the tension. "Sounds perfect."

Matt signed off and leaned his head back against the couch, closing his eyes. Wishing he could recapture that feel-good, peaceful moment this morning when he'd first woken up. The lingering pleasant buzz from a night of fantastic sex. The lack of the ever-present uneasiness eating away at his stomach. He was too young to feel this damn old.

The residual panic-induced adrenaline still coursed through his limbs. Normally he needed several cups of coffee before being fully awake in the morning. Today, the scare had left him supercharged, and the tension in Tommy's voice still weighed on Matt's mind.

Something had upset his little brother. And if Matt didn't get back soon and get to the bottom of whatever was going on, he might wind up dragging Tommy back to rehab again.

His gut clenched and he felt sick to his stomach.

Jesus, don't throw up.

Callie's voice broke through the unpleasant thought. "So you're heading out tomorrow?"

Matt opened his eyes and spied Callie leaning in the living-room doorway. She didn't look fully awake, with her honey-colored hair tousled and her eyes sleepy. She was in a T-shirt that just covered her bottom, her long legs bared—legs that had spent a good portion of the night wrapped around him.

Longing surged through him. The urge to pick her up and carry her back to bed was strong.

"Sorry." She pushed the hair out of her face. "I didn't mean to eavesdrop."

"No problem. And, yeah," he said. "I have several shifts I have to work this coming week."

And a brother to check in on.

Callie tipped her head. "Will you be coming back before the wedding?"

Six weeks without seeing Callie again seemed like cruel and unusual punishment. But Matt knew the tightness in his chest wouldn't ease completely with just a quick check on his brother, not with the tension he'd heard in Tommy's voice.

The playful light in Callie's eyes eased the tension until Matt had to fight a smile as he tried to sound serious. "Depends."

Clearly, she caught the underlying tease in his tone. "On what?"

"On whether or not you'll make it worth my while."

"Does a good party hold any merit?" Callie said. "I was hoping you would come to my family reunion with me. You can sit back, relax and enjoy the loaded comments bestowed upon me by some of my relatives. And if that doesn't tempt you—" her lips twisted wryly "—there'll be some great food, too. I just happen to be related to the woman who makes the best shrimp étouffée in two counties. Nice and spicy."

Matt laughed, enjoying the way Callie's dry humor eased that residual tightness in his chest. "That's not the kind of spicy I was hoping for."

Her warm gaze lit with mischief, Callie uncrossed her arms and came closer. And with each step she took every cell in Matt's body became tighter and tighter, focused on the enticing expanse of skin, the tension now of a different sort. And far more welcome.

She came to a stop in front of him. "So will you do a girl a favor and come back for a visit before the wedding?"

Matt looked up at Callie. He'd be crazy to plan a return visit when he had so much on his plate already. Two weeks of work at Manford Memorial, with a four-day stint in one of the busiest emergency rooms in Miami in between. Between travel, the need for sleep and the upcoming wedding, there wouldn't be much in the way of spare time. Adding in an unnecessary trip back to New Orleans clearly bordered on insane.

"I promise you can crash here during your stay," Callie said.

Hell, who could say no to that kind of offer?

Matt gave up, the grin creeping up his face as he

reached for Callie's thigh, pulling her into his lap. "I'll do my best to make it happen."

One week later

At ten o'clock in the evening, Matt let himself into the split-level house he'd grown up in and now shared with Tommy and Penny. Matt tossed his keys on the kitchen counter and rolled his shoulders to ease the tension of a long, boring shift in the E.R. Heading toward his side of the house, he was careful not to wake the sleeping occupants located at the other end. The arrangement had worked out better than he'd originally hoped.

One side of their shared home belonged to Tommy and Penny, providing them plenty of room for privacy. The space contained a bedroom, a family room and a guest-room-turned-gaming-room. The latter had been Tommy's childhood bedroom and, years later, served as his retreat during the worst of his getting-clean stages.

Matt had spent years tiptoeing past the room and hovering outside the closed door, watching and wondering and worrying about Tommy. Even if Tommy had moved out, there was no way Matt could ever enter the room without feeling that sick churn in his stomach, a nausea that always left him longing to vomit, just to purge himself of the feeling. During the worst times, darkness and despair had seemed embedded in every nook and cranny, oozing from the walls and carpet. The lingering echoes of those emotions still pressed in on Matt. Even now he felt the hair rise on the back of his neck every time he glanced up the hallway.

Matt lived on the other side of the house where he

had a bedroom and an office large enough to afford him some private space of his own. The kitchen and living room provided a common area in which Tommy, Penny and Matt could choose to hang out together at the end of the day. Since Matt traveled so much, he rarely spent more than a week at a time at his home base.

Clearly the current living situation wasn't a permanent solution, but for now the arrangement worked. When Penny had joined the Paulson household, Matt had offered to move into one of the nicer apartment complexes up the street. But Tommy had refused to kick Matt out of his home. With Tommy's track record, most of the decent rental properties would refuse to take him on as a tenant. Unfortunately, Penny's history ruled out even some of the shadier places in town. In truth, Matt hadn't fought the setup, mostly because the two couldn't hide much if Matt occasionally occupied the same home.

So they existed in this state of limbo, a lot like the limbo of his and Callie's relationship.

Sighing, Matt entered his bedroom and toed off his shoes. He gripped the hem of his scrub top and wearily pulled it over his head before reaching for his pants. He needed a shower, food and a good night's rest. But mostly, he needed to see Callie again.

Yesterday's sketchy night of sleep had started with dreams of her in a wet T-shirt, Matt's hands roaming freely over the thin cotton, tracing the lace of her bra. As if by magic, then he'd been stroking the bare curves of her breasts. Tasting her skin. Reaching for her shorts. And because everything came easy in a dream, suddenly she'd been naked, squirming beneath him with an endless amount of enticingly silky skin, and he'd been licking his way down her flat stomach and to her inner thigh…

He needed to get a grip.

Last week's flight back home had been delayed and he'd been stuck in the Minneapolis airport for twelve hours and, instead of catching a much-needed nap, he'd spent the entire time fantasizing about being back in Callie's bed. Not exactly the way to encourage grabbing some shut-eye on the plane, either. By the time he'd arrived home in Michigan, it was almost 3:00 a.m. and he was dead-tired, frustrated and ready to turn around and head back to New Orleans. Instead, he'd dropped into bed and tossed and turned, missing Callie even more. He'd finally fallen into an exhausted sleep and slept until nine in the morning, which meant he'd missed seeing Tommy before his brother left for work.

An anxious twist in Matt's chest had him clutching his dirty clothes, and he dumped his scrubs into the wicker hamper with more force than necessary.

At first glance, everything had seemed fine at home. Tommy looked good, Penny looked good and both appeared to be continuing on the path of the straight and narrow. Dinner that first night together had included steaks on the grill, as promised, but Tommy's behavior seemed off. The nagging feeling wasn't anything Matt could put a decisive finger on. There was a distance Matt wasn't used to, especially since they'd been living in each other's pockets for the past two years. And the tension had now been gnawing at Matt's insides for days.

Matt pondered the possible causes as he showered

and dressed in sweatpants and a T-shirt. He padded into the kitchen. Standing at the kitchen counter, he ate delicious leftover pasta, thanks to Penny, who knew how to cook. Adding her to the mix had definitely improved the cuisine in the Paulson house.

Two of his three requirements met, and with sex with Callie disappointingly out of the question, he knew sleep was still a long way off. Matt headed for his office and dropped onto the leather couch, turning on his laptop on the coffee table.

An icon popped on his screen, indicating Callie had just flipped on her computer. With her a time zone behind him, the late hour wasn't quite as bad for her as for him. He hesitated for a moment and then hit the call button.

The moment Callie's image appeared on screen, he felt his tension ease. She was sitting cross-legged on her bed, wearing pajamas. Unfortunately, the fifteen-inch screen on his laptop didn't do her beautiful eyes justice.

"This is a surprise," she said.

"A pleasant one, I hope."

"Absolutely."

He couldn't see the playful light in her gaze, but he knew of its presence because of her tone. And for a moment, all he wanted was to climb onto a plane and fly back to New Orleans where everything seemed so much easier and simpler.

And certainly a hell of a lot more fun.

"Did I interrupt anything?" he asked.

"Nothing exciting."

Files and small patches of fabric samples surrounded Callie on the bed. A silk robe clung to her shoulders but remained open in front. Matt spied a lacy tank top and what looked like a feminine pair of…

"Are those boxer shorts?" he said.

"You can take the tomboy out of the country, you know, but…" Smiling, she finished the sentence with a shrug and reached for her bedside table, picking up a glass of white wine. "At least they're hot pink and edged with lace. Besides, I haven't had to entertain company this late at night since you left."

A twinge of possessiveness flared, and Matt tamped it down and concentrated instead on the twinkle in her eyes on the monitor.

Her hair hung in a gentle loop at the nape of her neck, gathered in some sort of casual twist that managed to look comfortable and pretty and sexy, all at the same time. An empty plate on her nightstand suggested she'd just finished her dinner. Clearly she'd eaten in bed.

He wished he'd eaten in her bed, too.

Matt glanced at the files scattered on her comforter. "What are you working on?"

Her smile held more than a hint of mischievousness. "Just sitting down to compose my reply to an *Ex Factor* reader for my blog. Actually, you're the perfect person to help me with my response."

Matt let out a soft scoff. "I doubt that. I thought this was Colin's department."

Callie laughed. "He's responsible for the man's view, yes. But I wanted your thoughts before I replied."

"What's the question?"

Two seconds ticked by before she answered.

"A bride-to-be asking for advice on how to convince her future brother-in-law to walk her down the aisle," she said.

The one-two punch to his conscience came out of the blue, shocking the hell out of him.

Matt let out a groan. "You're making that up."

Callie shifted some paperwork and fabric swatches aside, settling back against her headboard with her glass of wine in hand. She stretched those toned, silky legs in front of her, bringing to mind when they'd been wrapped around his waist. The inside of his chest grew hot, heating the blood shooting through his veins.

When would he get a chance to hold her again?

He pushed the hopeless thought aside and concentrated on Callie, who was currently eyeing him over the rim of her wineglass. An expression like that meant trouble for sure.

She took a sip and carefully set her drink on the nightstand. "I had a long talk with Penny yesterday."

Of course she had.

"She was desperately trying to come up with someone to walk her down the aisle," Callie said. "And I told her she should ask you again."

Matt shifted uneasily on the couch, propping his feet on the coffee table just to the left of his laptop. Might as well get comfortable for the conversation ahead.

"Yeah?" he replied in his best noncommittal voice.

He knew Tommy was disappointed Matt hadn't told Penny he'd give her away. His brother hadn't come out and said as much, but Matt knew. The closer they drew to the date of the wedding, the tenser things had grown. Still, compared to all the other issues brewing between them, Penny's request seemed minor in comparison.

Callie's lighthearted tone was long gone. "Matt, you said yourself that I should be grateful for the family I have. That I should get over myself and go to that reunion because wasting the family I have was stupid."

His brow crinkled. "Those are *not* the words I used."

"No," she said, her chuckle drifting over the speaker. "You were definitely more tactful. But that's what you meant. And you were right. Going to the reunion is the right thing for me to do. I have a family. One that wants to see me, even if they do make the occasional callous remark." Callie sat up a touch, her brown eyes earnest, her voice soft. "You don't have that choice because your parents are dead, and that's a tragedy. But Penny doesn't have a choice, either. Her parents refuse to have anything to do with her." She paused before going on. "And that's a tragedy, too."

"I know."

Several beats passed by before Callie went on, tipping her head. "Do you not like Penny?"

He resisted the urge to bring the video chat to a close. He could sign off and close the lid to the laptop and be done with this conversation. But no matter the topic, the sight of Callie in her sexy boxer pj's was impossible to resist.

"It's not that." Matt wearily scrubbed his hand down his face. "Penny's fine."

And he meant the words, he seriously did. They weren't just a platitude he pulled out of his ass when convenient. He admired anyone who could fight an addiction and win. He knew better than most just how hard that battle could be. Penny was bright, capable and, if nothing else, she clearly loved Tommy.

"Are you against this marriage?" Callie asked.

"No." He winced at the force behind his words. He

dropped his hands into his lap, and his voice dropped several octaves, as well. "Maybe."

In response to Callie's hiked brow, Matt let out a sigh. "Yes."

Despite the harsh word, it felt good to get the sentiment off his chest. From the very moment Tommy had introduced Penny to Matt, Matt had been fighting the part of him dying to find a way to send the woman packing. He let out a soft scoff at the thought. As if he held *that* kind of power in his hands.

But the overwhelming urge had nothing to do with Penny personally and *everything* to do with the need to protect his brother, no matter what.

Matt felt like a dirtbag for admitting he didn't want Tommy and Penny to marry, but Callie's gaze remained free of judgment. And as he studied those beautiful brown eyes, relief slowly washed over him because he knew he could be absolutely, brutally honest with Callie. No matter how ugly his feelings, she wouldn't hate him for the truth.

He definitely could have used her steady presence during the worst of Tommy's addiction years.

"Tell me," she said softly.

The tight knot in his chest unwound a bit. "Jesus, Callie," he groaned out. "It's like taking the potential for disaster and multiplying the bloody thing by a hundred."

"What are you talking about?"

He dragged a hand through his damp hair, knowing he was leaving tufts sticking out in all directions. "I'm talking about Tommy relapsing and dragging Penny down with him." He scowled in an attempt to mask the all-consuming fear as he considered the alternative.

"Or vice versa. If she starts using again, how is Tommy going to resist temptation?"

Fear gripped him, and he hated himself for succumbing to the familiar emotion.

He shifted on the couch again. Now that he was on a roll, the words spilled out. "Or let's say they do manage to stay clean while they're together. What happens if the relationship tanks? Because let's face the facts here. Two former users probably aren't the most stable of sorts. How would Tommy handle the stress of a breakup and not be tempted to slip?"

Callie pursed her lips in thought as she reached for her glass and took another sip of wine. "Every relationship has the potential to tear a person down." She set her drink aside and met Matt's gaze again. "And this one is no different."

He briefly pressed his lids closed, wishing the logic helped. "I know."

But how many ran the potential to lead to something so dark? So permanent? Because nothing was more permanent than *death*.

Callie crossed her arms across her chest. "Tommy and Penny understand each other better than anyone else ever could. Yes, they could bring each other down. There's no doubt about that." She didn't sugarcoat the words, even allowing more time for them to sink deep before going on. "But I happen to believe they'll hold each other up."

He hiked a brow dryly. "Yeah, well, you arrange weddings for a living. Your favorite character is Elizabeth Bennet, a woman who conveniently managed to fall in love with a man who could save her family from destitution. A fairy tale."

"*Pride and Prejudice* is not a fairy tale."

Matt hiked a brow. "Close enough. Seriously, Callie, real life rarely works out like that." He let out a self-directed scoff. "You see happily ever after around every corner, but I get to patch people up after they beat the crap out of each other."

I get to be the lone family member left to pull my brother out of the gutter, over and over again.

"Did you have a bad shift tonight?" she asked.

Hell, yeah.

"Kind of," he said instead. Despite the topic of conversation, Matt fought a smile, his lips twitching at the memory. "The chief of staff argued with the head of E.R. about transferring a patient, a divorcing couple had a screaming match in triage and two best friends showed up because they'd beat the crap out of each other over a computer game."

Callie rolled her eyes. "The friends were guys, I'm assuming."

"Yeah. It started out as a joke and ended up fairly ugly," Matt said. "To be fair, a case of beer had been consumed, so I'm not sure you can hold them completely accountable for their stupidity."

"Of course you can hold them accountable," she said. "There's no excuse for being stupid enough to drink so much alcohol that a computer game becomes more important than a friendship."

Callie leaned forward and came closer to the screen, lying on her belly and folding her arms on the bed. The new position brought her close enough for him to see the light in her eyes. This time the spark was earnest, nothing playful about it at all.

"Penny needs you right now, Matt. She's going to be

a sister of sorts, and you owe it to your brother to start this relationship out on the right foot." A line appeared between her brows. "Don't make Penny keep paying for the same mistakes over and over again."

Callie was right. He *knew* she was right. Penny and Tommy both deserved Matt's unconditional support. But so far, he'd let fear rule his reactions. The habit would be difficult to break because the fear ran so deep that nothing short of a scalpel could cut the sucker out, and even that would take a significant piece of Matt during the process.

He'd just have to carry on with the fear firmly in place.

Matt blew out a breath and studied the woman on the screen, wishing like hell they were in the same room. "Man, I wish I could touch you right now."

A glimmer appeared in her eyes. "Tell you what," she said. "If you agree to at least have a conversation with Penny about the wedding, I'll let you watch me touch myself."

The bark of shocked amusement slipped out even as Matt's heart set up a pounding pace beneath his sternum. "Are you freaking kidding me?"

"I'm deadly serious."

He eyed Callie's cleavage, the potential blooming and bringing all sort of delicious scenarios to mind. "How many glasses of wine have you had?"

"I just had a conversation with my mother," she said dryly, "which rarely goes well. The numbing effects of two glasses of wine are about the only way I can survive our conversations. Unfortunately, that's just enough alcohol to also make me reckless—" a huge grin crept up her mouth "—but not enough to excuse me from my stupidity."

Callie dropped the robe down her shoulders and tossed it aside, leaving her lacy tank and the curve of her breasts displayed. The view on Matt's screen improved considerably.

"I'll touch mine if you'll touch yours," she said smoothly.

The libido-punching words and the seductive look on her face morphed his blood into flaming rivers of fire, licking along his limbs. He fisted his hand, fighting the groan.

He'd give anything to able to reach through the screen and pull Callie onto his lap. His mind filled with images of his time with Callie: the wet shirt plastered against firm breasts, her cheeks flushed, her mouth parted as she convulsed around his fingers in the hammock.

Even better? Callie beneath him as she'd urged him on in her bed.

On screen, she reached for the hem of her lacy tank and pulled the fabric over her head.

Callie now sat there, beautiful breasts exposed, her top dangling from her finger. "So what do you think?"

His voice hoarse, he said, "I think what they say about cameras is right."

"What do they say?" she said as she tipped her head curiously, a lock of honey-colored hair falling across her cheek.

And a bare-chested woman had no right looking so innocently adorable and sexy and sophisticated, all at the same time.

"The lens does add five pounds." A teasing grin tried

to hijack his mouth. "Specifically, 2.5 to each side. You look bigger, even without the corset."

She threw back her head and laughed, and the sound soothed away the lingering bits of his bad mood, courtesy of a shift with patients who'd brought their arguments into his E.R. Matt's muscles relaxed as the tension slipped away.

Callie scooted forward and propped her elbows on the bed, her breasts now hanging in full view of the camera. The immediate reaction of Matt's libido almost did him in, tenting his sweatpants in an embarrassing way, and he tried to discreetly ease the pressure by tugging on his waistband.

"Careful," Callie said, "or I'll hit the minimize tab on the screen, and you'll look much smaller."

A hoarse chuckle escaped. "Don't you dare."

Though God knows he had bigger worries to be concerned about, like the fact that moving air in and out of his chest suddenly felt complicated.

"I haven't been sleeping well." Her tone husky, she slowly slid a hand down her stomach. "You?"

His voice felt raw. "No."

"If you agree to talk to Penny, I'll let you watch me masturbate."

His already straining erection strained some more, and his groin grew so tight he thought he'd crack in half. Christ, every muscle was tensed and ready and willing and able, urging Matt to do exactly whatever Callie asked.

But wouldn't he be better off calling a halt to this impossible relationship now? Every interaction led him further and further down a slippery slope. He'd shown up in New Orleans to find a wedding planner and leave, but had wound up staying for two weeks. He'd left for home with the plan of returning for the wedding, and moved heaven and earth to free up some time for another trip back. Until eventually breaking things off felt impossible.

"And then I can watch you do the same," she said.

"You want me to masturbate on camera for you?"

"Why not?" she said. "We're both grown-ups. If I sign off now, what will you do?"

"Take care of this myself."

"What's a little video sexting other than a way to challenge ourselves? You know, up the ante on our third-base event on the dock."

"So now, instead of third base we're…what?" He quirked a teasing eyebrow. "Hitting zero base?"

"You wouldn't want to deprive me of the pleasure of watching, would you?"

Desire shot through his limbs, his heart slamming in his chest, and he tugged on the leg of his briefs, dying to provide a little relief.

"Why are you so intent on this little endeavor, anyway?" he asked.

"You look like you've had a crappy day."

"I did."

The arguing of the administrators had been prolonged and, as with most management types, full of a lot of hot air as both sides seemed intent on hearing themselves speak. Matt just wanted to provide appropriate care for the patient. But the scene had morphed into Matt being thrown into the mix of two men running for political office. And between the fighting friends and the divorcing couple, the evening had ended on a truly sucky note.

A little sexual release seemed a small pleasure to ask.

But part of him wondered about the point of this little, well, *exercise,* for lack of a better word. Callie lived in New Orleans. Callie *loved* New Orleans. And her business clearly thrived in a city that provided ample opportunity for themed weddings. Matt knew few couples, if any, would travel to Manford, Michigan, to fulfill their adventure wedding fantasies. And he certainly couldn't move because Tommy lived here.

The last time Matt had left his little brother for too long, Tommy had almost died....

Matt slammed his eyes closed, torn between what he wanted now and what he feared would be too hard to let go of later.

"Matt."

He opened his eyes and found Callie had shifted on her bed.

"Okay," he said. "I can't promise anything, but I'll think about having a conversation with Penny."

"That's all a girl can ask," Callie said.

A palm cupped her breast and her seeking hand finally slid beneath the front of her boxers. "I have a thing for your broad shoulders," she murmured. "I have ever since the dressing room." Her honey words rolled over him, and her thumb began to circle the tip of her breast. "I love the feel of your hard chest against mine when you move on top of me." The bud hardened and swelled, and blood *whooshed* annoyingly in his ears. He didn't want to miss even the tiniest inflection in the drawl.

Her eyes glazed over. "Picture me spread beneath you."

His chest struggled to suck in enough oxygen.

She looked like every adolescent's wet dream.

Granted, she didn't have as lush a figure as most centerfolds. But he craved the feel of her skin, her taste on his tongue and the toned legs. The gentle flare of her hips was just enough to entice a man. Her breasts were perfectly formed. As her breath came faster, the tips rose and fell faster with every breath. The hand down her panties moved faster. The fact that he couldn't see exactly what was going on was almost hotter for the secrecy.

The only thing he knew for certain was that she was ready for him. If he was in her bed right now, he could pull her beneath him and thrust deep, no foreplay needed. Good God, he closed his eyes and remembered sliding between those silken thighs and into her wet heat.

With a groan, he reached into his pants and grasped his erection. He ignored the thoughts swirling in his head as he began to stroke himself.

"Matt—" Callie's voice cracked.

"I know."

"Hurry," she said.

His hand pumped a little harder as he watched her eyes glaze over, her hips start to roll with every movement of the hand between her legs. He grew so tight he thought he'd crack.

"That's really…" Her voice trailed off. She sounded out of breath. "Hot," she drawled.

"Is *hot* the agreed upon safe word?"

"Do we need a safe word?"

"With you around, hell, yeah."

Nothing was safe with Callie around, most of all his sanity.

Even on screen he could see the flush on her cheeks

and her lips part as she began to pant for breath. And while his gaze remained locked on hers, every once in a while he saw her tick her gaze down. To watch what he was doing.

Frustrated by the constricting fabric, Matt gave up on restraint and tugged his sweatpants down to his thighs before returning his hand to his erection, his hand beginning an intense rhythm. His attention drifted between memories of Callie moving beneath him in bed and the live picture of her on screen. Sweat dotted his upper lip, and the pleasure wound tighter. He remembered the scent of her shampoo and the sounds she made as she clutched his back. Callie whimpered—even that tiny sound held a hint of the South. A second ticked by before he realized the noise had come from Callie and not just his memories.

"Oh, my God, Matt. I can't—" Callie's voice gave out.

He glanced at her, and suddenly Matt couldn't suck in the oxygen fast enough.

Matt had the overwhelming urge to lean forward and lick the computer screen, a sad substitute for the sweet taste of Callie's skin. Instead, he imagined taking her nipple into his mouth and sucking hard, picturing her writhing against him. He could almost smell the scent of sex, the feel of sweat-slicked skin against sweat-slicked skin. An electric energy pulsed in his groin, demanding to be released.

Don't you dare finish first, Paulson.

"Callie," he whispered, his voice hoarse.

The single, desperate word had the intended effect. Callie arched her back and let out a long, low moan.

Despite the soft tone, the sound slammed into Matt, and he closed his eyes, following on her heels.

Matt had no idea how much time ticked by before he could focus again. Slowly he became aware of his heaving breaths, and he lifted his head to stare at the computer screen. Callie had a dreamy look on her face and a slight smile on her lips.

"Hey," she said softly.

"Hey, yourself."

Her smile grew bigger. "Aren't you glad you agreed?"

A chuckle escaped. "Callie, hitting zero base with you is a hundred times better than hitting a home run with someone else."

CHAPTER EIGHT

CALLIE WEAVED HER way through the crowded baggage terminal of the Louis Armstrong New Orleans International Airport, dodging passengers and carts loaded with luggage as she looked for Matt. Because of the location of the airport and her condo in relation to her family reunion, he'd insisted on taking a taxi to her place because picking him up would have been out of her way. And they'd be cutting the timing close enough.

She'd finally pretended to give in. But surprising him as he gathered his bags had been her plan all along. Because Matt had decided to make the trip back to New Orleans again. A special trip, just to see her. And she had every intention of making the most of the three-day weekend.

She knew how hard he'd worked to clear his schedule so he could come back for her family reunion. The effort he'd exerted on her behalf generated a lovely feel-good buzz, along with an anticipation and hope that left her alarmed at her own stupidity.

Don't expect too much, Callie.

She shoved back the warning voices in her head, promising herself not to think negative thoughts. Matt hadn't gone out of his way to steal an extra couple of days with her just so she could wallow in doubt about the future. She spied a broad back and sandy hair that curled a little at the collar, and pleasure flushed up her back.

Nope, not a chance. She intended to enjoy every second they spent together.

She grinned as she tapped one side of a very nice set of shoulders. "Excuse me, sir. Do you have the time?"

Matt turned, and, if she'd been holding out for a smile, she'd have been disappointed.

Instead of responding, he hooked his hand behind her neck and dragged her close, her body crash-landing into his. He kissed her without apology, nothing tentative or hesitant about the maneuver. Hot and hungry and brimming with heat, his hard lips moved across hers as if he'd been thinking of nothing else for the entire flight down. Perhaps since last night.

Maybe for the past two weeks.

Callie gripped his shirt and pulled him close, moaning into his mouth as she plastered her torso tighter against his. She met him turn for turn, taste for taste. Despite the crowd, she did her best to show him she'd missed him, too. His tongue rasped against hers, want and need and determination stamped in his every action. Like a gentle assault she couldn't quite fend off, not that she had any desire to do such a ridiculous thing.

When the need to inhale grew too great, Callie pulled back.

"Though my appreciation for Skype has skyrocketed, I much prefer face-to-face encounters." Matt grinned and looked down the front of her blouse, no doubt seeing the lacy cups of her push-up bra. "You hiding a watch down there?"

"Nope." She held up her wrist. "Today I'm wearing one like everybody else."

His lips quirked. "How disappointing."

"No worries," she said, mimicking his favorite phrase. "I'll make it up to you later."

"You mean after I eat lunch with the LaBeau family and start sweating cayenne pepper out of my pores?"

Callie laughed. "I can't wait." Though the thought of the entire LaBeau family being present left her nibbling on her lip in concern. All those aunts and uncles and cousins she hadn't seen in so long, swarming around her…

The day had started out cloudy and cool and stayed so for most of their two-hour drive. Fortunately, the sun finally broke through the clouds just in time for Callie to arrive at the outdoor park by the Mississippi River, Matt by her side. The crowd of LaBeaus had already gathered around the tables set up lengthwise, enough food to feed the town of New Orleans, and then some.

Callie eyed the crowd, a swell of nausea slaying the last of her appetite. "I'm thinking we should do this in small doses."

He frowned in confusion. "You mean eat?"

"No," she said. "Meet my relatives."

"If I can survive Aunt Billie's étouffée then I can definitely handle your relatives."

"Oh, they'll love you." Callie's smile felt tight. "It's me they might have a problem with."

Aunt Billie stopped by first, and Callie was grateful her aunt was so reliable. A few teasing comments later, and Callie knew she was blushing, and then a warm welcome for Matt was delivered with a hug and an offer to bring him some of her étouffée herself. Promising, of course, to bring him the milder version this time.

The next thirty minutes passed uneventfully. A few aunts and uncles and distant cousins wandered by, not to mention a few people she couldn't pin down her relationship to. Callie made the introductions and there were a few wayward comments about how long it'd been since she last came to the reunion. Several questions about her business, and one or two that were an indirect reference to her past. All in all, mostly just a whole lot of chitchat that didn't mean much. But, in some ways, meant *everything*. Slowly, her tension eased to bearable levels, and she stopped bracing every time another family member approached.

And then her parents arrived.

Callie watched her mother make her way across the grass in Callie's direction. They had the same figure, except her mother's hips reflected her love of the homemade biscuits she had perfected years ago.

"Hey, Mama."

She leaned in to kiss her mother on the cheek, even as dread curled up in her stomach and took up more than its fair share of room.

"I just heard about the weekend event you're arranging for Colin," her mother said. "A friend of mine heard about it on the radio."

Callie bit back the sigh and plastered a smile on her face. "Actually, I'm arranging the weekend for a *client,* Mama." She gestured at Matt, grateful for his steady presence at her side. "Matt Paulson hired me to help with his brother's wedding. Tommy and his fiancée met online playing one of Colin's games."

"What a lovely story," her mother said with a nod at Matt.

The way her mom eyed him made it clear she couldn't care less about the engaged couple. The brother of the groom, on the other hand…

"Callie's doing an excellent job," Matt said.

"I'm sure she is," her mother said. She turned to look at Callie. "Your little party business does seem to be doing quite well."

Your little party business…

Her mother always qualified Callie's business in such a way as to make her feelings known. As if being a themed wedding planner was okay, but only if you had no other options.

Callie's heart slipped lower in her chest as her face strained to maintain the smile, and she ignored Matt's gaze as his brows tented curiously over his eyes. He opened his mouth as if to say something, and then pressed his lips into a firm line. Apparently, in five seconds Matt had surmised the best way to deal with Callie's mother.

The proverbial biting of the tongue.

Though Callie wished she was biting his instead.

Heaven help her, not the thought to be having while holding a tricky conversation with her mother. Matt reached out and settled his hand in the small of her back, and Callie sent him a grateful look. The smile he responded with calmed her nerves and she returned the smile.

"Callie is quite bright," her mother said to Matt before turning back to Callie. "Imagine what you could have done if you'd applied the same energy to a law practice."

Her heart slipped to her toes. She knew how proud her parents had been when, in high school, she'd announced she wanted to go to law school. They'd proudly shared the news every time they'd gone back to visit their old hometown. There wasn't a single relative, distant or otherwise, that hadn't been invested in her progress at college.

And then she'd gotten arrested and lost her scholarship and…

Dear God.

Callie tried to come up with a response. "Mama—"

But that was it, because what else was there to say?

"She's the best themed wedding planner in New Orleans," Matt said smoothly.

Jeez, why was she standing here so tongue-tied? She should say something to her mother. She should defend her business, her life, her *choices.* Instead, she let Matt come to her defense.

"Of course she's the best," Callie's mother said. "But there really isn't that much competition." She tipped her head and met Matt's gaze. "Are you two dating?"

Callie's heart attempted to leap from her chest and she lightly gripped her mother's elbow. *"Mama."*

"What?" Belle LaBeau said, as if she didn't understand why Callie was so upset.

Callie shot Matt an apologetic smile. "Matt, will you excuse us for a moment please?"

The amusement twinkled in Matt's eyes. "No worries."

Callie began to drag her mother in the direction of a flat, grassy spot overlooking the river.

"Mama," Callie said, careful to keep her voice low. "What are you doing?"

"When my daughter brings a man to our family reunion, I have to assume he's more than just a client."

"Matt is—" Callie wearily swept her hair from her face. "He's not—" She dropped her hand to her side, frustrated by her inability to identify what Matt was, not only to her mother, but to herself, as well. "He's just...a friend."

Good Lord. She'd been reduced to a lying, babbling idiot.

"Does Matt live in New Orleans?" her mother asked.

The question landed like a well-placed barb in Callie's gut. What was it about mothers that gave them the ability to sniff out the painful heart of a matter in 3.3 seconds flat?

"No," Callie said, and her face felt like it would crack from the effort to keep from frowning. "He lives in Manford, Michigan."

"Never heard of it," Belle said.

"Neither had I before meeting Matt," Callie said.

"Does he have family around these parts?"

"No," Callie said, gritting her teeth.

"No ties to New Orleans at all?"

"None whatsoever, Mama."

The longer the back and forth went, the more tense Callie's spine became, until she'd thought she'd snap in half. The fact her mother was verbalizing Callie's secret concerns only made matters worse.

Thankfully, Callie's mother paused. But before Callie's tight muscles could lessen even a smidgen, Belle LaBeau opened her mouth to speak again, and Callie interrupted her.

"Is this really necessary, Mama?"

When they reached the far end of the grassy spot, Callie let go of her mother's arm.

"It's just a simple question, Callie. Surely Mr. Paulson doesn't mind? You two are either dating, or you're not." She hiked a brow. "So?"

Callie opened her mouth. "I—"

Belle LaBeau's brow shifted even higher.

"I don't know," Callie finished in a rush.

The disappointment in her mother's eyes was a familiar look. "Callie," she said with a defeated tone. "When are you going to do more than arrange *other* people's weddings and find a man of your own?"

And with that, her mother pivoted on her heel and headed back to the pack of relatives in the park. Callie stared after her.

Are you two dating?

How come she didn't have an answer to her mother's question? But there were also more important questions at hand. The wedding weekend was coming up quickly, and once the event was over, what would happen then?

Matt swung the handle with everything he had, and the ax rotated through the air and struck the wood with a solid *whump,* well outside his intended target. The small crowd gathered around the booth moaned in sympathy. Matt propped his fist on his hip, frowning at the bright red bull's-eye, the blade buried a good two feet from the outside ring.

Clearly he wouldn't be winning any awards today.

"Good thing you have other skills to recommend you, because I'm not sure you'd do so well in the Middle Ages."

At the sound of Callie's voice from behind, Matt smiled and turned to facc her.

Dressed in a simple medieval barmaid dress, Callie grinned up at him. Friday had been pure chaos as the wedding guests who'd arrived early at the designated hotel had gathered for dinner at a local restaurant. Matt's time with Callie had been disappointingly limited since he'd arrived in town for the wedding, too much of Callie's days taken up with last-minute details or impromptu meetings with Penny and Tommy.

And Matt refused to be amused by the sight of Callie's and Tommy's heads bowed together, both getting excited over some ridiculous detail about the weekend. Last evening he'd caught the two of them huddled together in a corner, engaged in an earnest debate about how to set up the ax-throwing competition so as many people as possible could enjoy the view.

Unfortunately, at the time, Matt had had no idea this would be to his disadvantage.

"I think I just lost the first round," he said as he headed for Callie.

She smiled and stepped closer, closing the gap between them. "You need someone to cheer you up?"

Matt linked his fingers with hers and led Callie a few steps away, pulling her beneath the awning of a neighboring tent that wasn't quite as crowded and offered a bit of privacy. Fortunately the heat wave had ended long ago, and while the skies were clear and sunny, the cool breeze meant Matt wouldn't be needed to treat the participants for heat stroke.

A definite plus in his book.

Grateful for the rare moment alone, he leaned in to nuzzle Callie's ear, enjoying the scent. Her hair smelled of magnolias and her skin smelled like…well, like *Callie.* And how he recognized the scent after only two months, with only two actual weeks together, was beyond him.

"Cheer me up? What did you have in mind?" he said.

Callie placed her hand on his chest and leaned in close. "I'll tell you tonight if you stop by my place before heading back to the hotel."

"I could skip going back to my hotel room altogether."

"You could. However, if you spend *all* night at my place I won't be at my best tomorrow."

"So?"

He kissed his way up her neck and lightly nipped the delicate shell of her ear before stealing a hard kiss. But the simple contact felt majorly insufficient. He returned to delve deeper, tasting her tongue with his, enjoying the way she gripped the hair at his neck, as if needing the stability to stay upright.

"Just how much sleep do you need in order to pull tomorrow off, anyway?" Matt asked against her mouth.

"I'm not sure," she whispered back.

The sound of a throat clearing broke the spell.

Matt looked up and found Tommy staring at them both with the hugest grin on his face, his arm wrapped around Penny. With her black, pixie cut hair and petite frame, she looked fragile enough to break. That she'd survived what she'd done to her body never ceased to amaze Matt. Tommy was taller than Matt by an inch, but thinner by twenty pounds. At least he no longer appeared gaunt. Neither one looked as if they were nervous about the wedding tomorrow. In fact, in their medieval outfits they looked like just two of the guests enjoying the day.

Tommy's gaze shifted from Matt to Callie and then back again. "Can I steal Callie for a second, Matt?"

Matt fought like hell to pretend that heat wasn't rising up his face at his little brother catching him necking like a stupid schoolkid. Tommy looked intensely amused, if not a little shocked. Not surprising given Matt hadn't been forthcoming about his relationship with Callie. Mostly because he knew there would be questions. Questions he didn't know how to respond to.

Questions he didn't know the answer to himself.

Matt's voice came out gruffer than he'd planned. "No problem. Have at it. I'm sure you both have stuff to discuss about tomorrow."

Callie didn't look embarrassed at all. Instead, she seemed to find something in Matt's face humorous.

She reached up to plant a kiss on his lips. "I'll meet you at the LARP tent at two?"

"Sure."

Tommy and Callie instantly launched into a debate about a problem with this afternoon's schedule for the live-action role-playing as they headed in the direction of the LARP tent. Penny turned to look up at Matt, and he felt her gray gaze all the way to his medieval-approved work boots.

Wasn't dealing with a kid brother enough? Must he endure his soon-to-be sister-in-law's amusement, too?

But Penny's eyes were somber as she looked at Matt. "I want to thank you again for agreeing to walk me down the aisle."

Matt bit back a groan and shifted on his feet. He'd almost prefer being mocked for acting like a schoolkid who couldn't keep his hands to himself. When he'd decided to tell Penny he'd changed his mind, he chose to make the announcement with as little fanfare as possible. So two nights after his conversation with Callie, and the spectacular Skype call, Matt had mentioned at dinner that he'd be fine with walking Penny down the aisle, if she still wanted him to.

Tommy had looked speechless, and Penny had barely managed to let out a shocked yes before Matt had picked up his plate and concentrated on the cleanup. Too bad he didn't have any pressing activities he could bury himself in now. Somehow, he didn't think signing up for a second try at ax-throwing qualified as pressing.

Especially given his hideous lack of skills.

He swept his gaze across the field of white tents, the setting like the base encampment prior to one of the many epic battles in *The Lord of the Rings*. A crowd of people milled about in their costumes. But, unfortunately, nothing required Matt's immediate attention.

He aimed for a nonchalant shrug, hoping he pulled it off. "No biggie."

Penny let out a small laugh, but Matt got the impression that there was zero humor in the act. "It's a very big deal for me. I mean, I know I'm not exactly the girl you had in mind for Tommy."

Despite everything, Matt let out an amused scoff. "That's assuming I even gave the matter much thought. I was too busy trying to keep him alive."

He hadn't meant to let the last bit slip out.

"I know you were." She stepped forward and laid a hand on Matt's arm. "I love him, Matt. I really do."

Oh, God. How had he suddenly become the trusted

sidekick in a chick-flick movie, slated as the confidant he never wanted to be? Ever. In this life, or the next.

"I know how close you two are, and I just wanted to say…" her lips twisted, and she paused before going on "…thanks."

He cleared his throat. "Well, whether you want to be or not," he said, his voice gruffer than he'd planned, "you're part of the family now."

Tears welled in her eyes and left Matt dying to escape. Before he could figure out how to make that happen gracefully, Penny pulled him into a hug that caused the sword at his hip to jab him in the abdomen. Two of the longest seconds of his life later, Penny pulled back and reached on tiptoe to plant a kiss on Matt's cheek.

Which was nicer than he'd thought it would be, but all he really wanted was to find Callie and grab a few minutes alone. Penny shot him a beautiful smile, spun on her heel and took off.

Feeling a little lighter, he watched his soon-to-be sister-in-law thread her way through the crowd. At least the weekend weather appeared to be behaving for tomorrow's wedding. The sunny days came complete with a cool breeze and mild temperatures. Good thing, too, seeing how most of the guests were dressed for the times. No shorts or tank tops or T-shirts, just tunics and cloaks and surcoats, not to mention petticoats and peasant dresses.

He scanned the sea of colors, looking for Callie, when a hand clapped him on the back.

"Can I buy the best man a beer?"

Thwarted again.

Matt turned and hiked a brow at his kid brother. Tommy swept the brown waves of hair from his face—a nervous habit since he'd been a little kid. The sight never failed to trigger a swell of affection in Matt's heart.

"Mead," Matt said. "Callie very specifically instructed me to call it mead."

"Yeah." Tommy's brown eyes crinkled at the corners. "About Callie—"

"Beer," Matt said, fighting the scowl and hoping to put off any further questioning. Mentioning Callie's name had been tantamount to asking for his kid brother's harassment. "I'm definitely up for a beer."

Tommy shot Matt a look that screamed, "Nice try, sucker," clearly communicating that Tommy was on to his big brother's deflection technique and was only humoring him.

For now.

Matt wasn't entirely sure why he didn't want to discuss Callie with Tommy. They'd been living in each other's pockets for so long the reluctance felt strange. But something about his time in New Orleans felt too personal to discuss. A private time Matt didn't want to share with anyone.

Including his brother.

Regardless, a small knot of tension curled low in Matt's gut as they weaved their way through the crowd of people, passing the strolling minstrels on their way to the largest tent set in the middle of the field. A meeting place, of sorts, with a crowd clearly intent on reliving the feel of a medieval tavern.

Tommy found two empty stools at the end of a crudely constructed wooden table. A barmaid arrived to take their order and, as soon as she returned with two mugs of beer, the two of them were left alone with nothing but the noise around them and several years' worth of unresolved issues between them.

Sticking with the matter at hand seemed best.

"To you and Penny," Matt said, lifting his mug.

Tommy grinned and toasted Matt back. When his brother took a drink and set his beer down, the determined look on his face left Matt wishing he could go back to throwing another ax, even if it meant risking getting booed by a large crowd.

"There's something I've wanted to ask you," Tommy said.

Matt felt like a fool for not meeting his brother's eyes. "Fire away."

"What's up with you and Callie?"

Matt lifted his gaze to his brother's brown eyes—puppy eyes, their mother had called them. Funny how Matt had forgotten about that until just now. But she'd been right. Tommy had the same look that managed to look happy and sad, wise and innocent, all at the same time.

Matt shrugged. "We've decided not to label the relationship just yet."

Long-distance was the only label that fit. But the idea totally sucked. He'd been down the long-distance relationship road before. He couldn't imagine this time would end any prettier.

"But you're sleeping with her," Tommy said.

Frowning, Matt ran his thumb up his mug, staring at the trail left behind in the condensation. Not being the kind to kiss and tell left him in a bit of a quandary. He only had two choices, to either share too much or lie. And neither sat right with Matt.

Tommy let out a laugh. "Never mind. Your silence is good enough. Actually, I'm kind of relieved."

"Really?" Sleeping with Callie certainly made Matt feel better. But why the heck would Matt's relationship make *Tommy* feel better? "Why?"

A grin crept up his kid brother's face. "Because all that time you were down here in New Orleans, arranging this shindig, I felt bad that you had to be the one working out how to pull this weekend off. When a few days turned into almost two weeks…" Tommy ruffled his shaggy brown hair. "I don't have to tell you I was feeling pretty guilty."

"No worries, sport." Matt reached across the table and gave Tommy's shoulder a cuff. "You just owe me your undying allegiance for the rest of your life. Simple enough."

Matt's attempt at dodging a heavier discussion with a lighthearted response didn't work. Tommy's expression remained fixed on Matt and serious. And the look never went well for Matt.

"But before you stand up beside me tomorrow," Tommy said. "I want to say it again." Tommy leaned his elbows on the table. "I'm sorry for everything I put you through."

More than just the words, the expression on his little brother's face left Matt on edge.

Matt didn't look away, and every ounce of tease in his tone disappeared. "I know you are."

"But I also need to know that you forgive me," Tommy said.

Well, hell.

Matt sat back and stared out at the chaos beyond the tent. Forgiveness, he'd found, had been harder and harder to come by. The first relapse had been easy. The second, not so much. By the third round of rehab, forgiveness had been a huge struggle. A battle Matt had sometimes thought he wouldn't win.

But here they sat, two years later…

You can't make them keep paying for the same mistakes over and over again.

Callie was right. Even if they had been in this very spot before, and Tommy had screwed up again. And clearly Tommy needed a truthful answer and not a glib response. Maybe Tommy had put his brother through an emotional wringer, but his hard work this past twenty-four months meant he deserved nothing less than an honest answer.

That and the fact the man was set to get married tomorrow.

Matt delivered the words while staring at his mug. "I'm not gonna lie, Tommy. It hasn't been easy." He lifted his gaze to his brother. "But…come on." Matt leaned forward and folded his arms on the table. "Why would I help arrange this weekend if I still had even a trace of resentment left? All I want is for you to be happy. I mean, look around you." He gestured toward the scene that included knights, and maidens, and trolls. Matt let out a huff of humor as he looked at his kid brother. "You think I'd go to all this trouble otherwise?"

Sam's serious face didn't budge. "Yeah, you would. You *totally* would." Despite the words, a grin slowly spread across Tommy's face, bringing the same the response from Matt. "But it's good to know that's not the case."

Matt blew out a breath, and the tension in his shoulders eased. "Well, now that we have all that cleared—"

"I'm not done, Matt. I need you to lighten up a little."

"Lighten up?"

"You know what I'm talking about," Tommy said.

The noise of the tent filled the air between them, and tension curled in Matt's gut. He watched a juggler wander by, wishing he could avoid the upcoming conversation.

"Look," Tommy said, "I'm getting through this, day by day. Both Penny and I. And yeah, sure—" Tommy pushed his hair back from his face "—some days it takes all I have to make it through. But I'm clean." He stared at Matt. "I'm *clean*."

Matt blinked back the pain, hating the words that needed to be said, even after all this time. He'd spent ten years watching Tommy, struggling to help him fight this demon that had him firmly in its grip. He'd never said the words before, because the sentiment had felt like a betrayal. But they needed to be said now.

I'm clean.

Because how many times had Matt heard those words?

Matt's words came out rough. "Yeah, I know you are, Tommy," he said. Two sharp heartbeats thumped by. "But for how long?"

Tommy barely registered a flinch on his face.

Jesus, Matt. You're such a bastard.

"You have to stop hovering, Matt," Tommy said. "I'm not a kid anymore."

"I know you're not."

Tommy went on as if Matt hadn't spoken. "Because you and I know there is no end point here. I'll always be at risk. Some days are so damn hard I want to curl up in a corner and cry." Tommy leaned closer, and Matt's chest ached so hard he thought his ribs would fracture. “I know you have this intense need to fix things. I know you see a problem and your first extinct is to swoop in, tough love and all. But you *can't* fix this for me. This is something I have to do all by myself.”

“Maybe so.” Matt set his mug on the wooden table with a *thump.* “But I can damn sure be around if you start to slip again.”

Be around, stuck in a job where the typical day left Matt wishing he watched paint dry for a living. What was the point of this conversation? What could it possibly solve? Matt had been examining Tommy's problem from every possible angle for the past ten years. And as far as he figured, there was only one solution.

“Now if were done with the best man talk,” Matt said, easing his words with a gentle pat on Tommy's back. “I've got another ax-throwing competition to lose.”

CHAPTER NINE

OVER THE PAST ten years, Callie had sometimes wondered if she'd been fooling herself about her life. Today Callie had determined with absolutely certainty that her mistake all those years ago had been both the worst and the best turning point of her life.

If she hadn't blown that scholarship she'd probably be working for someone else right now, because that would have been the safer, easier route to take. But when her choices had been limited to only one—that one choice being whatever she could build herself from the ground up—she'd set about and done just that.

With the most important event in the history of Callie's business currently taking place right before her eyes.

The day of the Paulson-Smith wedding began just as beautifully as the day before. The grassy field was dotted with white tents that flapped in the cool breeze, providing a sharp contrast against the crystal-blue sky. A crowd of guests dressed in their best medieval fair, maidens and princesses and knights stood next to wizards and trolls. Penny's silver silk gown shimmered around her slender figure and made her look like an elegant elf.

Gorgeous.

The crowd had grown from online gaming friends to several hundred interested well-wishers. From the three news cameras mixed in with the crowd, clearly the publicity would be bigger than even Colin had guessed. With her ex, along with Penny and Tommy, set to be interviewed during the reception, the day clearly promised to be a boon for Callie's business.

So how come all she could focus on was Matt?

With about eight other things she should be checking on, Callie shaded her eyes from the sun, grinning as a chain-mail-wearing Matt walked Penny down a makeshift aisle composed of friends dressed as knights, swords drawn and creating an arch over a red carpet leading to the front of a gorgeous canopy. The sight created a happy thrum in Callie's veins. Publicity aside, the scene was the single most satisfying event in her life to date.

But Matt wearing chain mail would never cease to be Callie's favorite part. And while he protested that he was no one's knight in shining armor, she begged to differ. The smile on the bride's face, and the almost embarrassed look on Matt's, brought about a pressure in Callie's chest.

An emotion she couldn't name.

Feeling like a sappy fool, Callie grinned as she discreetly wiped the tears gathering at the corners of her eyes. Tommy looked happy. Penny positively beamed. And Matt, the man who played the largest role in ensuring this ceremony happened, looked adorably embarrassed and charmingly put out. He'd stuck by his brother and refused to give up when things got tough. And, no matter how silly Matt thought the whole affair, he'd thrown himself into making sure today took place just how Tommy and Penny wanted.

A buzzing started in her chest, creating a warmth that had nothing to do with the sun or the crowd pressing in around her.

Standing on the other side of the makeshift aisle, Colin discreetly waved at Callie and then pointed at his watch. They'd caught up earlier and planned on running through the best way to handle the news interviews set to take place after the ceremony. Which she was about twenty minutes late for.

She knew she should slip away and meet up as planned, but she couldn't force her feet to move. Callie blinked and glanced back up the aisle, unable to shift her gaze from Matt as he leaned in for Penny's kiss. Or when he stepped forward to stand by Tommy.

The buzzing grew stronger. Callie pressed her hand to her chest as the pressure became a physical ache, the realization washing over her with all the gentleness of a tidal wave.

She loved him.

The terrifying and wonderful and life-altering realization kept her rooted in place. Even as Colin managed to unobtrusively weave his way through the crowd of people craning to watch the small three-person bridal party make their way beneath the white awning covering the wooden platform—a last-minute addition ensuring the larger than expected crowd could see the ceremony.

But all Callie wanted to watch was Matt, in his chain mail and leggings and boots and the sword hanging at his side. A small grin on his face as he watched Tommy take Penny's hand and step in front of the officiant dressed as, of all things, a wizard.

And falling for the man who lived a thousand miles away felt significantly more terrifying than failing at this publicity event.

Jeez, what had she done?

A hand lightly gripped her elbow, but she didn't budge as Colin whispered in her ear.

"We were supposed to meet twenty minutes ago," he said.

"I know."

Still, she didn't move. No matter how many times she told her feet to start walking.

"What's the matter?" Colin leaned forward, his gaze landing on her face. "Good God, Callie. What's gotten into you?"

She stared up at Colin, her mind still stuck on her personal epiphany. And then she felt a drop of water hit her cheek. Concerned, Callie glanced up at the sky. Still no clouds. She touched her face and finally realized she was still crying.

Despite her ridiculously romantic ideals, she'd never cried at a wedding before. Of course, realizing she'd fallen hard for the brother of the groom was a first, too.

Concern clouded Colin's voice. "Are you okay?"

Callie didn't respond, simply watched Tommy and Penny begin to repeat their vows. And the signal that the ceremony was quickly coming to a close provided the impetus to move. With one last lingering look at Matt on stage, hands clasped behind his back, eyes fixed on his little brother, Callie turned and followed Colin silently through the throng of people to a quiet spot well away from the crowd and the ceremony.

Colin still looked at her as if she were about to go off the deep end. "Callie, are you sick?"

"No." She shook her head, hoping the motion would clear her spinning brain.

No such luck.

Colin crossed his arms, a skeptical look creeping up his face. "I know you love weddings. But this is kind of over the top, even for you."

She wiped her cheek again and found her cheek just as wet as before. Good grief, she felt as if she'd sprung a leak.

"So what's wrong?" Colin asked.

She stared up at her ex, a million responses flitting through her brain before the only one that fit came out.

"I love him."

Colin suddenly looked as though he'd prefer to be identified as the evil Zhorg and taken into custody by the crowd to be hanged by the neck until dead. And then drawn and quartered. Followed by a massive festival as the townsfolk danced while he burned, his body cremated just to be sure the deed was done.

Her ex's eyes shifted from Callie's face to the focus of her gaze, the small party standing on stage, and then back to Callie again.

Worry laced his tone. "I hope you're talking about Matt and not Tommy."

Forcing back the bubble of hysterical laughter, mostly triggered by panic, Callie rolled her eyes. "Of course I'm talking about Matt."

"Good." Colin winced. "Because falling for a man who just walked down the aisle probably wouldn't end well."

A surge of fear hit. "Matt lives in Manford, Michigan. A thousand miles away."

"I'm sure y'all can work something out."

She wished she felt so optimistic. And why hadn't she concerned herself with this detail before? Suddenly pulling off a fabulous event without losing her focus seemed a terribly stupid reason for avoiding a relationship with Matt. But this? Falling in love with a man who lived so far away? One who clearly felt responsible for his brother?

She'd only just begun to realize how complicated their relationship was.

Callie had ten years—and most of her identity—invested in Fantasy Weddings. Her business wasn't portable. She couldn't just pick up and start over again. And she loved New Orleans. Her family was here. Her friends were here.

The tension in Callie's stomach expanded.

"Hey." Colin laid his hand on Callie's shoulder. "Now's not the time to fall apart, okay?"

The concern in his face only highlighted how truly screwed she was. She wiped her cheeks and forced herself back to the matter at hand. "Of course not. I can handle this." She tried for a confidence-inspiring smile, hoping it didn't feel as weak as it felt. "Let's go talk to the news crew and figure out the best place for the interviews."

Right.

Interviews.

Medieval wedding reception.

Dungeons of Zhorg.

Callie turned her back on the end of the ceremony—and the view of Matt standing on stage—and followed

Colin in the direction of the news crews. Focusing on getting through the rest of the day appeared to be her only option.

The sun was setting as Callie forced herself to focus on the staff taking down the tents. When Matt came up beside her, she gave strict instructions to her heart to calm down. Much to her distress, her instructions went ignored when he slipped an arm around her waist.

"You okay?" he asked.

"Absolutely."

Her smile felt forced, and Callie knew Matt suspected something, but she concentrated on remaining calm so she could finish her job. During the reception, Tommy and Penny's brief interview had come out really cute, mostly because they were both so ridiculously happy. Callie had no doubt their two minutes of fame would be well received by viewers. As the maker of the video game, Colin's interview was less emotional. But Colin was more than just a geeky gamer. He excelled as the marketing guru, as well. His smooth, well-polished blurb mentioning Fantasy Weddings and the *Dungeons of Zhorg* sounded casual and didn't come across rehearsed at all.

"How much longer before I can get you alone again?" Matt murmured, a crooked smile on his face.

She discreetly fished her small pocket watch from the bodice of her princess dress, her favorite costume to date. The overdress of robin's-egg-blue split in front, forming an inverted V to showcase the design of the white satin and gold brocade pattern beneath.

And, despite the fear now curled around her spine

and setting up house, she had to laugh at the expression on Matt's face.

"I was thinking I'd like to get you out of that dress and see how you'd look in chain mail." His sex-filled smile started a thrumming vibration in her belly and spread outward. "With nothing underneath. So..." he said.

He leaned in close, sending a spike in her pulse, heat between her legs and anxiety twisting in her stomach.

"How long?" he finished.

"My assistant volunteered to oversee the cleanup," she said. "And I already spoke to the vendor who supplied the table and chairs, so I'm free to go."

Free to go.

Free to go where? Back to her place with Matt and have sex? Or free to go back to her regularly scheduled life, the one without Matt in it?

"Perfect," Matt said, steering her in the direction of the parking lot.

Swallowing hard, she glanced down at her dress and smoothed a hand down her skirt. "How did your week at Manford Memorial go?"

"As uneventful as ever," Matt replied.

She pounced on the one thing she knew for sure. Matt held no deep abiding affection for his job or his hometown. Surely that meant he'd be willing to move? No matter how much she loved him, she simply couldn't afford to start all over again.

Desperate for something to do with her hands beside reach for Matt, she picked up her skirt as she walked. "Have you ever thought about living somewhere other than Manford?"

Matt shot her a guarded look, the expression doing

little to ease her nerves. So she hurried on before she lost her courage completely.

"You know, find a new job?" she said.

"Why should I?" His steps slowed a little, making it easier to match his stride. But his tone was wary. "It's home."

Her feet fumbled, and Matt reached out briefly to steady her. Jeez, his hand on her arm wasn't helping to calm her down. But she couldn't just take him home to her bed without finding out more.

Callie opened her mouth to speak but failed at making a sound. She swallowed hard, forcing her mouth to cooperate. "But have you ever considered taking a part-time job somewhere else?" She glanced at him out of the corner of her eye. "Moving your home base?"

Matt kept his eyes firmly ahead. "Like where?"

The loaded question felt like a shotgun aimed at her heart. Was he avoiding her gaze because he wasn't sure of the direction of the conversation? Or did he know and simply wanted to avoid the topic altogether? One thing she knew for sure, she'd never know unless she asked. And sleeping with Matt now that she'd figured out she loved him would make letting him go harder in the end.

"Like here," she said. "In New Orleans."

Several seconds passed with only the sound of the gravel beneath their shoes, and Callie felt every crunch like a kick to the chest.

"I could certainly look into doing recurrent shifts as a traveling doc in their E.R.," he said.

Not exactly the answer she wanted to hear. But the response felt encouraging.

"How often could you get down this way?" she asked.

"I could pull off six, maybe seven days a month."

Six days a month? And he'd be working busy shifts. What kind of life would that be for the two of them?

Callie came to a stop and stared up at him. "That's not much time."

A small breeze kicked up, and the setting sun finally sank beneath the tops of the oak trees, casting a shadow across them both.

"Callie." With a sigh, Matt turned to face her, and she could see the conflict in his expression. "I can't leave Manford."

The words sliced through her like a sharp blade through whipped cream cheese.

"Why not?" she asked.

Matt looked out across the parking lot. Several seconds ticked by. Callie expected him to come up with something noteworthy, given the amount of time he spent formulating his response. But when the words came they were incredibly disappointing in their simplicity.

"It's my home," he said.

Callie slowly inhaled, searching for strength, before blowing out her breath in one long exhale.

"People move all the time, Matt," she said. "And it's not as if you love your job there." She waited for him to look at her again. When he kept his eyes on the park, the trees fading as dusk claimed the rest of the landscape, she went on, "I know you don't. So don't even try to pretend that you do."

"I never said I did."

She stepped closer. "So move down here." Callie longed to get some sort of a response from the man. When nothing was forthcoming, she tried again. "Make

New Orleans your home base. Tommy's married now, Matt. He's moving on with his life."

Callie died a million deaths waiting for him to respond.

"I know," he said.

Did he? Tommy seemed to be moving on with his life. But not Matt.

"Are you planning on going on the honeymoon with them?" she asked dryly.

"Jesus, of course not."

Fear and frustration made her words harder than she'd intended. "Then why not move?"

Matt strode several feet away before stopping, his back to her. He shoved his hands into his hair, leaving sandy tufts sticking up. When he finally turned to face her again, the look on his face was one she'd never seen before.

"The last time I left Tommy for too long I came home and found him unconscious on the couch." He stared off in the distance, and she knew by the look on his face he was seeing now what he'd seen back then. "He'd gone through rehab number four and had been doing well for months. But I knew right away he wasn't just sleeping. Everything was off. The room felt wrong. Tommy looked wrong. Damn, the very air in the room felt wrong. I couldn't wake up him up. And—"

His voice grew so hoarse it died out, and Callie reached out to gently wrap her fingers around his wrist, the look on his face heartbreaking.

"For two seconds I couldn't find a pulse," he said.

A chill swept up her spine and traveled out her limbs. Goose bumps pricked her arms, the hair at the back of her neck standing on end. Matt's words came out rushed.

"And suddenly all the tough love you've come to accept as necessary just doesn't matter anymore," he said.

"He's been clean for two years, Matt," she said softly.

"Which is why I started taking the occasional locums jobs in Miami and Los Angeles. But I can't be gone that long."

"I'm in love with you."

The stunned look on Matt's face would have been funny if she hadn't been hurting so much. She hadn't meant to say the words yet. And she certainly hadn't meant for them to come out the way they did. So plain. With no lead-in. Nothing, no sign from her to prepare Matt for what would follow. But maybe the simple statement would knock some sense into the man.

Callie stared at Matt, her mind spinning as she tried to make sense of the words. At first she thought his resistance simply meant he didn't feel as much for her as she felt for him. But the look on Matt's face now told her the truth. He did care about her. No telling how much, but enough that he clearly didn't want to leave. But he just couldn't let his worries about Tommy go.

Matt had suffered so much through the years, and his fear for Tommy was deeply entrenched. There'd be no reaching the man with easy words. She was going to have to be brutally, brutally honest with him to get him to see reason. He loved his brother too much, had suffered too much to let the issue go easily.

And, as hard as it was going to be, she had to fight. She deserved a chance at happiness. And Matt deserved so much more than he had in his current life.

She steeled herself against the pain she knew was sure to follow. "So that's what this is about."

Matt's expression grew guarded. When he said nothing, she went on, no matter how much it hurt him in turn. Matt couldn't be allowed to continue to sacrifice himself, not when her bluntly harsh words had a chance of getting him to see how much more he deserved out of life. "What is with you and this martyr complex?" she said.

"I don't know what you're talking about."

"Yes, you do," she said softly.

"Look, is this really necessary? I'd hoped to enjoy the rest of my time in New Orleans with you."

Anger flared, pushing the tender feelings to the back of the line. "And that will be…what? Two, maybe three days?" She forced herself to maintain his gaze. Heart thumping, she tried to keep the bitterness at bay, but his unwillingness to even consider a change hurt like hell. "I understand you want to stick around and be there for Tommy if he needs you. And I suppose you have to do what you think is right. But I can't do this anymore."

"Do what?"

"Love you. Settle for a few days here and there. I've put my life on hold and now that I've rediscovered how much life there is to live outside of work, I don't want to settle anymore."

Matt stared off into the shadows growing along the trees lining the park. A muscle in his jaw ticked, and, for the second time that day, Callie fought the tears of frustration and anger and pain that were gathering at the corners of her lids. He didn't look torn, signaling she at least had some room to convince him to change his mind. He looked resigned.

And that hurt worst of all.

"You're right," he said. "You shouldn't have to settle for whatever time I get to snatch here and there. You deserve a full-time relationship, not a part-time one. You also deserve better than to continue to endure your mother's insinuation that you've settled for less with your job. Maybe you should tell her exactly how you feel instead of letting your guilt keep you silent."

Matt unlocked her car and opened the door for her. Muscles tight, head aching, heart hurting, she gathered up her dress and slid into the driver's seat, fabric billowing around her legs. She gripped the steering wheel and willed herself to calm the heck down so she could at least say goodbye without sounding like a total wreck.

Hand on the roof her car, Matt leaned in to press his lips to hers.

"Goodbye, Callie. Thanks for making Tommy and Penny's day special."

Matt straightened up and stared down at her for three more heartbeats. And then he turned and headed across the parking lot.

CHAPTER TEN

ONE WEEK LATER, Callie sat in her office and twisted off the top of her bottled water, staring at her laptop in the center of her desk. As she tried to compose a reasonable answer to her latest *Ex Factor* question, she avoided looking at the tiny camera eye centered at the top of the computer screen. And desperately tried not to remember how Matt had looked the night of their Skype sex.

She pressed her palms over her eyes. Maybe if she pushed hard enough she could force the images from her brain. Unfortunately, her brain was still filled with visions of Matt wearing nothing, long muscular legs stretched out before him. The broad shoulders and the hard chest and the flat abdomen. She loved the way his sweatpants had been slung low over his lean hips. Better still? Those sexy hands satisfying his body while she urged him on with her words. The sight of the successful conclusion would be her undoing for some time to come.

Throat dry as yesterday's leftover toast, she reached for her bottle of water and swallowed gratefully.

She might never be able to sit through a video conference again without thinking of that moment. A fact that would prove incredibly inconvenient today when she'd had a Skype session with the mother of the bride of next week's *Pride and Prejudice* wedding.

But of all the things she missed about Matt, many a sexy episode aside, she missed his smile the most. The sexy half smirk, that teasing hint of a grin. And her favorite? The smile accompanied by that spark of full-on humor in his eyes. She wished she could hang a poster on her wall with all the various looks. But that would only remind her of what was missing in her life.

And that something was Matt.

Callie slumped in her seat. The first few days after the wedding, she'd hoped that he'd call her up to say he'd rethought his position. But as one day slipped into the next, she began to wonder if she should consider moving. But leaving New Orleans, her family and her business?

She couldn't imagine life so far away from the city, the bayou of her childhood and Aunt Billie. As strained as their relationship was, she'd even miss her parents. And she'd just started reconnecting with the extended family she hadn't seen in years. She couldn't leave now.

A knock sounded on her door and a head full of brown hair poked through.

Callie sat up in surprise. "Mama."

Her mother rarely came to visit at the office. Usually it was Callie making the trip across town to see her parents.

"Hi, honey. You look…off," her mom said.

A sad smile crept up Callie's face. "I'm feeling very off."

Her mother settled into the seat across from Callie and folded her arms across her lap. She looked ready to wait until Callie explained.

"The Paulson wedding was a huge success," Callie said

"So I heard. That's nice."

Nice.

Snippets of the event had been broadcast on two local cable channels. Tommy and Penny's brief interview had been picked up by a syndicated news channel and been aired across the country. Callie had received more business inquires in the past week than ever before. Business was booming, and Callie would probably need to hire extra help to keep up with the work.

But all she got from her mother was *nice.*

"What happened with that doctor you brought to the reunion?" her mother said.

The muscles in Callie's stomach clinched. Something in her mother's voice rubbed Callie wrong. It was the same tone she'd used the first time they discussed Callie's screwup in college. The tone that held an implied "What now?" Ten years later and her mother still expected bad news at every turn. And, as bad news went, this was the worst Callie had ever experienced.

Matt…*gone.*

And if she could blurt out the truth to Matt, there seemed no point in keeping anything from her mother now. "I'm in love with Matt Paulson."

Something flickered in her mother's eyes, but her expression didn't budge. "I figured out as much on my own."

"You did?"

"Well, I am your mother." Her mother shrugged, as if the act of giving birth to Callie somehow had provided Belle LaBeau a peephole into Callie's heart. "And it's not like you did a very good job of hiding the fact. I could tell by the way you looked at him at the reunion. When he laughed, your whole face would light up." She hesitated and then smoothed a hand down her pants. "You certainly never looked at Colin like that."

This time Callie did groan. Good God. How long before her mother let this issue go? Callie had recovered from the breakup years ago. Did her mother need therapy to get past this and move on?

"Mama, Colin and I have been over for years. He's happily married to a woman I consider a friend."

"I'm well aware of that." A soft smile appeared on her mother's face. "I happen to know the woman who planned the wedding."

In the end, Callie lost her battle with a wry grin.

"I'm not stuck on Colin," her mother went on.

The news surprised Callie, because she sure couldn't tell by her mother's action. Every single visit with her mom had ended with Colin being mentioned at some point in time.

Callie sat up straighter in her seat. "Then why are you constantly bringing him up?"

"Only because he's the last man you've brought around to visit your family. At least, he was until Matt came along."

The mention of Matt's name brought a fresh wave of pain, her heart aching. Callie shifted her focus to the window that overlooked the warehouse district of New Orleans. The day sunny and bright, but inside Callie's office felt dark.

"You're happy arranging weddings for other people, yet you haven't had a serious relationship in ages," her mother said. "What happened with Matt?"

Callie's voice sounded as hollow as she felt. "He went

back home to Michigan. And he's kind of stuck living in Manford. It's..." Callie paused trying to think of an explanation that wouldn't be an invasion of Matt's and Tommy's privacy. "It's complicated."

Her mother crossed her legs and studied Callie for a moment. And in one of those moments known horribly well by kids the world over, Callie knew her mother was about to offer advice. Whether Callie wanted it or not.

"You could move up to Michigan," she said. "Maybe even finally realize your dream of finishing college."

Callie's heart slowly slipped to her toes.

"I don't want to go back to college," Callie said.

"But that was all you talked about in high school."

"That was the dream of an eighteen-year-old who had no real idea what she wanted to do with her life," Callie said. "It was always more your dream than mine."

Her mother looked knocked flat, and a stab of guilt struck Callie again. She never meant to be quite so truthful.

"Look, Mama," Callie said. "I'm sorry you and Dad sacrificed so much to get me into a great school."

Her mother straightened her shoulders. "Your dad and I sacrificed so you could make something of yourself."

Callie dropped her head into her hands. "Mama." Callie managed not to let out a moan. Barely. She looked up again. "I love my job." She dropped her hands to her desk and met the brown gaze of her mother sitting on the other side. "This is exactly where I want to be. I'm my own boss and I have a very successful business. I appreciate all you and Dad have done for me, but—"

It was past time she told the truth and stopped letting this issue slide. She couldn't continue to remain silent.

Callie sucked in a breath and gathered her courage. "But I'm not sorry about how things turned out. I wouldn't change anything even if I *could.* If I could climb into a time capsule and undo all I'd done in college, I wouldn't." She should have spoken these words ages ago. Callie steadily held her mother's gaze. "I'm exactly where I want to be," Callie said, "doing exactly what I want to do."

The strength of the conviction in her words reminded her exactly why she couldn't drop her life and move up to Michigan. Both her mother's brows arched in surprise, and Callie let the words settle a little deeper before going on.

"This isn't my second-choice life, Mama. This is my very *best* life."

Or at least it had been until she lost Matt.

Callie pushed the crushing thought aside and concentrated on meeting her mother's gaze. "And I need—"

When Callie's voice gave out, her mother set her purse on the floor beside her chair. "What do you need?"

"I need to stop feeling like y'all are just waiting for me to screw up again."

Silence filled the room and Callie did her best not to shift her gaze away from her mother. It felt as if Callie had lived and died a thousand lives as she waited for her mother to speak.

"Okay," her mother said.

Callie blinked. *Okay?* Just like that?

"Now you need to do me a favor, Callie."

Callie fought to keep her breathing steady. "What's that?"

Her mother leaned forward, her eyes intent. "Stop

avoiding relationships. Get serious about finding someone, about sharing your *future,* with someone."

Callie's lungs stopped functioning, and she longed to take a deep breath. Problem was, she had finally gone out and gotten serious about someone.

But he was gone for good.

"Why are you still here?"

Tommy's voice echoed off the walls of the garage, and Matt turned from his task of sorting through his tools. "Excuse me?"

Matt had been banging around the garage for the past two hours, trying to pack for the move to an apartment that held little appeal, yet grateful for the mindless task of sorting through his stuff. He'd tossed the things he didn't need—a pile that wasn't as big as it should have been—and stacked the stuff yet to be packed, which was larger than need be. Boxes covered the floor of his bedroom and living room and perched on the counters in the kitchen. He couldn't seem to decide what to keep and what to throw away. So two hours ago Matt had come out to the garage, frustrated by his inability to focus, thinking that dividing the supply of tools in half would be an easier process.

He'd never had trouble focusing before. If anything, his focus had always been a problem. But with his mind stuck on missing Callie, and the impossible situation a relationship with her presented, he'd come out to sort through his problem the only way he knew how: banging the wrenches and screwdrivers and the various-size hammers around. The process offered him some satisfaction.

But zero relief.

"You heard me," his brother said.

Tommy stepped down into the garage. His wavy brown hair and brown eyes always made him look a bit like an overgrown puppy. Well, an overgrown puppy with serious issues.

His brother came to a halt beside Matt and leaned his hip against the workbench.

"How long are we going to tiptoe around this, Matt?"

Silence had been working for them so far. And Matt wasn't sure he knew how to change the status quo.

"I don't know what you're talking about," Matt said.

But he did. The dark thoughts plaguing him since he'd left New Orleans had been following him around like a black cloud hell-bent on raining down on his head, complete with lightning bolts and thunder and the foul mood.

Tommy let out a scoff. "You don't want to be here." He waved his hand to encompass their current surroundings, but Matt knew he was referencing something much bigger than a garage located in Manford, Michigan. "You want to be in New Orleans." Brown eyes gazed at Matt. "With *Callie.*"

The familiar ache in his chest friggin' hurt.

"Maybe," Matt said.

Yes, his mind screamed.

Matt turned away from his brother and concentrated on repacking the tools in a manner worthy of the most diehard of obsessive compulsives. Matt knew the statistics; crystal meth addicts had one of the highest relapse rates of all the drug users.

There was no answer to this one.

Just like Tommy's addiction, this wasn't a problem Matt could fix. There was no treatment to be applied that cured the disease. Frustration burned through Matt and he randomly picked up a wrench and rubbed his finger on the cool metal.

"But my home is here," Matt said.

"It doesn't have to be."

Matt closed his eyes, his fingers curling around a Phillips head screwdriver.

"Manford doesn't have to be your home base anymore," Tommy went on. "In fact, you could take a permanent job in New Orleans. The emergency rooms there have to be busy enough to satisfy the adrenaline junky in you."

"I could," Matt said. "But I won't."

"Why not?"

Matt stared out the window at the bleak view that only appeared that way because he was in freaking *Manford.* Anxiety coiled in his stomach, and he decided to voice the words that had been bouncing around his head for years.

"Because when I walked in on you two years ago, for several seconds I thought you were dead."

The ache in his chest was all-consuming, and he met his brother's brown eyes again. They'd never discussed that day. The event had been too painful. Matt took in the way Tommy's hair flopped on his forehead, just like it had as a kid.

"And I can't bear to go through that again," Matt said.

"So what does that mean?" Tommy cocked his head. "Tough love until the day I die?"

Matt's lips twisted. "*Tough* is a pretty good word for it," he said. But as the moment lingered between them, Matt finally went on, "No matter what, you're my brother. That comes before everything else."

Tommy cleared his throat as his eyes grew suspiciously bright. "I told you before, you can't save me from myself, Matt," he said softly. And then he let out a humorless huff. "Though God knows you've tried." He rolled his head, as if releasing the tension in his neck. "You can't put your entire life on hold anymore," Tommy continued. "You have to let it go, Matt."

Anger, bright and hot, surged from his core. "What the hell?" Matt braced himself as he faced Tommy. "You're my brother, Tommy. How am I supposed to just let you go?"

"Not me," Tommy said. "The guilt."

The word slammed into Matt, leaving him gut-punched and short of breath. His ribs squeezing his heart so hard Matt was sure the pressure would crush him.

What is with you and this martyr complex?

Jesus, he'd told Callie to fully let go of the past, and here he was clinging to his. But Tommy didn't know about the thoughts he'd had…

Matt let out a self-deprecating scoff, wishing Callie was here with him with that playful spark in her eyes and her honey-tinted drawl. And the kind of nonjudgmental understanding that let a person share even the worst truths about themselves without fear.

Because how could he share that brutal news with his kid brother? He opted for the easier explanation instead.

Matt left the tool bench and headed for the stairs leading to the kitchen, dropping down to sit on the bottom step. "I should have been around more in the beginning."

"You had a medical degree you were trying to earn." Tommy took a seat beside Matt.

"But Mom and Dad were gone, and we were alone."

And God knows wading through the days, trying to figure out how to deal with Tommy and be an adult all at the same time hadn't been easy.

They sat there, side by side, and Matt tried to push the memories of the first time he'd found Tommy passed out on the floor. Of a Tommy so gaunt, so thin, his color so unhealthy that it physically hurt to look at him. Sure, Matt had been checking in by phone. But only so much information can be gleaned from the sound of a voice.

He couldn't remember the precise moment he began to have his suspicions something was off. The little niggles of doubt had always been easily rationalized away.

He's having an off week.

He's stressed.

He's just not hungry today.

Of getting the call he'd wrecked his car again, and this time not being sure Tommy was going to pull through. Perhaps the time had come to explain to Tommy exactly how much Matt didn't deserve his kid brother's devotion.

Matt stared straight ahead. He couldn't meet Tommy's eyes, not with what he was about to say.

"The third time you walked out of rehab and waded back into that mess it took everything in me not to leave." Matt closed his eyes as he remembered the turbulent thoughts from that day. Angry. Petrified. And knowing he just couldn't live this life anymore.

Tommy remained quiet beside him while silence engulfed the garage. Matt couldn't bring himself to look at his brother. The confession was hard enough to express without those wide, brown eyes staring at him. He felt like crap for sharing the thoughts with his brother. If they'd just been a fleeting thought Matt wouldn't feel so guilty. But since that day, every morning he'd woken up with the same thought.

Leave.

Get out of town.

Save yourself.

He scrubbed his face with his hands, exhausted from the mental war being waged in his head. And so friggin' sick of living his life in limbo he didn't know what to do. With every one of those thoughts came the opposing thought. Tommy was all the family Matt had. Walking away felt impossible, even during those times Matt was sure he was drowning.

"God, you have no idea just how badly I wanted to pack up and get the hell out of Dodge. Go to the farthest city that I could." He turned to meet his brother's gaze. "Because I just couldn't bear the torture of waiting around for you to finally kill yourself. Watching you waste away into someone I didn't recognize anymore."

Always braced for the next slip. The next call from the E.R. The next night Tommy didn't come home and Matt was sure that he'd overdosed, unconscious.

Or dead.

"I just couldn't stand to have my heart broken again," Matt said.

Tommy's voice sounded raw. "But you didn't go."

Matt's lips twisted at the words. They might as well be inscribed on his tombstone.

"But it's time," Tommy said. "You've got to get on with your life and stop worrying about your kid brother. Go back to Callie, Matt." Tommy's brown gaze held

Matt's hostage, and then his brother grinned. "Before you become a grumpy old man no one wants to be around anymore. Cuz, you know, you're already half-way there."

Matt slowly sucked in a breath. He'd told Callie to get over the guilt, maybe it was time he followed his own advice.

He let out a scoff. "Is this my kid brother giving me advice?"

"This is your kid brother showing you some tough love, dude, because it's my turn. You need to leave. I need you to leave." Tommy crossed his arms and leaned back against the railing. "How can I ever be sure I've made it on my own if you're always around to help me out? I've kicked the ugly addiction. Every day I'm concentrating on staying clean. I know you've tried to ease my way in the world by smoothing out the bumps along the way. Now it's time for me to handle life on my own."

Matt's chest shook with the force of the pounding beneath his ribs.

"Go back to New Orleans. Take a job there. You can visit whenever you like. This will always be your home, too." Tommy stood up, looking down at Matt. "But you belong with Callie."

Tommy climbed the last two steps and entered the kitchen, closing the door behind him. Matt stared at the door, his brother's parting words echoing in his brain.

CHAPTER ELEVEN

THE WALTZ STARTED, and the bride and groom headed for the center of the room, the ballroom of the Riverway plantation transformed into an eighteenth-century ball. Callie watched, holding her breath as the bridal party joined in. They'd only had two days to rehearse the dance, and certainly no time to practice in their Regency-era wedding outfits.

With the bride's dark hair upswept and adorned with baby's breath, curls pinned to her head, imagining her as Elizabeth Bennet required very little stretch of the imagination. The groom, however, wasn't quite tall enough to pull off a convincing Fitzwilliam Darcy. But the man wore the cravat and waistcoat with pride.

Callie was enjoying the results of her hard work when a voice interrupted her thoughts.

"So, will there be zombies invading this reception?"

Callie whirled and came face-to-face with Matt, and the sight sent Callie's senses soaring. In a waistcoat, white linen cravat and pantaloons, he looked unusually formal yet still good enough to eat.

"Could be a fitting end, don't you think?" he finished with an easy smile.

Callie tried to reply, her mouth parting, but no words formed.

Was he here to convince her to reconsider a long-distance relationship? Or was he here to tell her he'd changed his mind and that he was ready to let his little brother go? Maybe he was finally ready to move on from a life that including the two brothers living in a constant state of protector and the protected. Callie knew the situation had been necessary during the beginnings of Tommy's recovery days—the by-product being two men who didn't know how to simply be brothers, instead of recovering addict and responsible older brother.

Callie fisted her hand behind her back, resisting the urge to grip the lapel of Matt's coat and haul him closer. She longed to ask him the questions swirling in her brain, questions like *Why are you here?* or *Have you changed your mind?*

Or more important: *Do you love me as much as I love you?*

"No," she said. "No zombies."

"That's too bad," he said.

"Depends on who you ask."

Not the conversation she'd have predicted would take place upon seeing Matt again. Not only did she not know where to start, she was almost afraid to find out the answers. If he was here to convince her to change her mind and accept less, she just might cave.

And even as her head was telling her to be strong, her heart was breaking a little more.

"Walk with me a moment?" he asked.

Pulse picking up its pace, she said, "Sure."

Callie followed Matt out the French doors and onto the veranda, trying to convince herself to stay true to her goals.

But the past few weeks had only gotten harder, not easier, and she wasn't entirely sure she had the strength to resist a part-time relationship offer again. Not when every morning started with her missing Matt, his laugh and his dry sense of humor. And every evening ending up with her staring up at the ceiling of her room, dreaming of having him back in her bed. In her life.

But all that seemed too much to ask after two weeks of no contact.

"How did you pull off the outfit?" she asked instead.

He turned and leaned against the wrought-iron railing, the branches of the oak tree beyond lit by the light from the ballroom.

"I phoned Colin and spoke with Jamie," Matt said. "Turns out your ex's wife was very eager to help me arrange a romantic meet up with you. She insisted this would be an opportune moment. Even phoned the bride and groom to ensure I'd be welcome."

A small laugh escaped Callie. "That explains the looks they were giving me at the rehearsal dinner last night."

Matt grinned. "Beware the romantic musings of those who are about to get married. Unfortunately—" he looked down at his clothes "—everyone thought it best I blend in."

"Why are you here, other than to make the most delicious Fitzwilliam Darcy ever?"

She probably shouldn't have added in the last part.

She should be playing it cool. She should be holding her feelings closer to her chest. But she couldn't.

"I came tonight hoping to make an impression," he said.

Afraid to breathe, Callie asked, "What kind of impression?"

Matt stepped closer, instantly swamping her senses. The warm breeze ruffled his sandy hair and held a hint of magnolias, but all Callie could register was Matt's scent of fresh citrusy soap. The heat from his body. The sizzle in those hazel eyes.

His eyes never left hers. "'I have been meditating on the very great pleasure which a pair of fine eyes in the face of a pretty woman can bestow.'"

Two seconds passed before the words fully registered in her brain.

Stunned, Callie reached out and gripped the sleeve of Matt's waist coat. "You read *Pride and Prejudice?*"

A slow smile crept up his face.

"How else is a man supposed to impress a woman who arranges fantasy weddings for a living?" he asked. "Quoting Darcy seemed like a good place to start."

Too afraid to hope, Callie remained silent, her grip on his sleeve growing tight.

"I just got started on the paperwork to obtain privileges at St. Matthews Hospital," Matt went on. "Turns out they have a need for a few more E.R. docs."

Heart hammering, she had to ask, "For locums work?"

"Nope," he said. "Full-time. Well, 80 percent time, anyway. Because that will leave me some room to do an occasional locums shift up in Manford."

Afraid to burst the budding hope in her heart, Callie hiked an eyebrow, and Matt smiled.

"Only one week every three months or so. That will give me plenty of time to visit my brother and his wife." His lips twitched, as if holding back a smile. "Especially now that I'm going to be an uncle."

The last was delivered so nonchalantly that several seconds passed before the news registered.

Callie let out an embarrassing whoop and launched herself into Matt's arms. He folded his arms around her, and she realized her feet were still dangling off the ground. But she didn't care. She basked in the feel of his embrace and the ever-growing realization that finally, *finally,* Matt was in New Orleans for keeps. Matt appeared in no hurry to let her down. Callie had no desire to ever let him let her go.

She buried her face in his neck and inhaled, enjoying the smell of warm skin and the feel of Matt's arms around her again. "What changed your mind?"

"Well," he said, his voice rumbling though his chest to hers. "You said you wanted me here. Tommy wanted me here. And I wanted to be here. Ultimately not being here seemed kind of stupid."

"I love your logic."

"I figured you would."

Matt set her back on her feet, but kept his arms wrapped firmly around her back, her chest pressed against his hard torso.

She looked up at him. "Did Tommy have to beat you off with a stick?"

"No." Matt's hazel eyes grew serious, and he gazed through the French doors at the couples now waltzing across the floor. "He used his own brand of tough love on me. And he agreed with your assessment. That I was good at the tough love while he was using, but I sucked after he'd quit."

"Remind me to send Tommy a huge present every year on his birthday."

"Yeah? Well, he told me he planned to send you a gift every month for getting me out of his hair. And it wasn't only logic that brought me back."

"No?"

"Yeah, there was also this little issue of me falling in love with you."

Tears gathered the corners of her eyes, and she blinked, forcing them back. How would she maintain the professional demeanor with tears in her eyes? Matt swept a strand of hair from her cheek, his fingers taking their time, and then cupped her face.

"I'm sorry it took me a while to get my head on straight," he said. "I didn't mean to make things so hard on you."

She sniffed and sent him a watery smile. "'You must learn some of my philosophy. Think only of the past as its remembrance gives you pleasure.'"

"Ah," Matt said, his lips twitching. "I love that line. And I admire Elizabeth Bennet and her practical approach to life." He eyed the front of her dress. "But I have to confess, the clothing of her era leaves a lot to be desired. Though you look beautiful, this isn't my favorite costume."

"Yeah, the A-line style doesn't exactly flatter the figure. Don't worry," she said, grinning up at Matt. "They aren't as flat as they look in this dress."

With a crooked smile, Matt leaned in and nuzzled

her neck. “No worries,” he said. “I’m thinking that admiring your occasional kooky attire will keep me happily entertained for the rest of my life.”

* * * * *

THE BEST MAN & THE WEDDING PLANNER

TERESA CARPENTER

This book is dedicated to my editor
Carly Byrne for her patience, understanding,
speed and good cheer. I never see her sweat.
Even when I do. Thank you for everything.

Teresa Carpenter believes that with love and family anything is possible. She writes in a Southern California coastal city surrounded by her large family. Teresa loves writing about babies and grandmas. Her books have rated as Top Picks by *RT Book Reviews* and have been nominated Best Romance of the Year on some review sites. If she's not at a family event, she's reading or writing her next grand romance.

CHAPTER ONE

"Now boarding, first-class passengers for Flight 510 to Florence."

Lindsay Reeves's ears perked up. She glanced at her watch; time had gotten away from her. She closed her tablet folio, tucked it into her satchel and then reached for the precious cargo she was personally escorting across the ocean. She hooked the garment bag holding the couture wedding dress for the future Queen of Halencia over her shoulder and began to move as the attendant made a second announcement. "First-class passengers now boarding."

"Welcome aboard." The attendant looked from the second ticket to Lindsay. "I'm sorry, both passengers will need to be present to board."

"We're both here. I bought a seat for this." She held up the garment bag.

The woman smiled but her eyes questioned Lindsay's sanity. "You bought a first-class ticket for your luggage?"

"Yes." She kept it at that, not wanting to draw any further attention. With the wedding only a month away, the world was alive with wedding dress fever.

"We have a storage closet in first class that can hold it if you want to refund the ticket before takeoff," the attendant offered.

"No, thank you." Lindsay pressed the second ticket into the woman's hand. "I'm not letting this bag out of my sight."

On the plane she passed a nice-looking older couple already seated in the first row and moved on to the last row where she spied her seats. She draped the garment bag over the aisle seat and frowned when it immediately slumped into a scrunched heap on the seat.

That wouldn't do. She pulled it back into place and tried to anchor it but when she let go, it drooped again. The weight of the dress, easily thirty pounds, made it too heavy to lie nicely. She needed something to hold it in place. After using her satchel to counter the weight temporarily, she slid past a young couple and their two children to speak to the flight attendant.

"We have a closet we can hang the dress in," the male attendant stated upon hearing her request.

"I've been paid not to let it out of my sight," she responded. True enough. Her reputation as a wedding planner to the rich and famous depended on her getting this dress to the wedding in pristine condition without anyone seeing it but her, the bride and her attendants.

"Hmm," the man—his name tag read Dan—tapped his lips while he thought.

"Welcome aboard, sir." Behind Lindsay another attendant, a blonde woman, greeted a fellow passenger.

Out of the corner of her eye Lindsay got the impression of a very tall, very broad, dark-haired man. She stepped into the galley to give them more room.

"You're the last of our first-class passengers," the attendant advised the man. "Once you're seated, please let me know if you need anything."

"Check," the man said in a deep, bass voice and moved down the aisle.

Goodness. Just the one word sent a tingle down Lindsay's spine. She sure hoped he intended to sleep during the long, red-eye flight. She wanted to get some work done and his voice might prove quite distracting.

"I've got it." Dan waved a triumphant hand. "We'll just put the seat in sleep mode and lay the bag across it."

He poured a glass of champagne and then another. "Will that work?"

"Yes, that will be perfect. Thank you."

"Seats aren't allowed to be reclined during takeoff. Once we reach cruising altitude I'll be along to put the seat down. And I'll look for something to secure it in case the flight gets bumpy."

"Great. You've been very helpful."

Lindsay headed back to her seat. Halfway through first class she caught sight of the newcomer and her breath caught in the back of her throat. He was beautiful. There was no other word for it. Long, lean features with high cheekbones, dark, slanted eyebrows and long, black eyelashes. Dark stubble decorated his square jaw.

Suddenly her eyes popped wide and she let out a shriek. "Get up!" she demanded. "Get up right now!"

He was sitting on the dress!

A frown furrowed his brow. He slowly opened lambent brown eyes so stunning she almost forgot why she was yelling. Almost.

"Are you talking to me?" he asked in a deep, rasping voice.

"Yes." She confronted the man, hands on hips. "You're in my seat. Sitting on my dress. Get up!"

"What's the problem here?" The other attendant appeared next to her.

"He's in my seat." She pointed an accusing finger. "Sitting on my garment bag. Make him move."

Behind her a young child began to cry. Lindsay cringed but held her ground.

The beading on this dress was intricate, all hand-sewn. If it had to be repaired it would cost a fortune. And she'd already paid a pretty penny to make sure nothing happened to it. How could someone sit on a garment bag without noticing it?

"Let's all calm down." The blonde attendant squeezed by Lindsay. "Sir, can I ask you to stand, please?"

The man slowly rose. He had to duck to the side to avoid hitting the overhead compartment. He must be six-four, maybe six-five; a long way to glare up from five feet four. She managed.

"I'm not sitting on anything." He gestured across the aisle. "I moved it there because it was in my seat."

Lindsay looked to her left. The garment bag rested in a heap on the seat with her heavy satchel dumped on top. She jumped on it, removing her bag and smoothing the fabric. It was all mushed as though it had been sat on.

"May I see your tickets, please?" Dan requested.

Lindsay pulled hers from the front pocket of her satchel and waited to be vindicated.

"Actually, you're both in wrong seats. My fault, I'm afraid. I'm used to a different plane. I do apologize. Ms. Reeves, you are on the left and, Mr. Sullivan, you need to move forward a row."

Lovely. She couldn't even blame the beast. Except she did.

At least he'd be in the row ahead of her so she wouldn't have to have him next to her the entire flight.

His brown gaze went to the toddlers in the row in front of the one the attendant indicated. "I'd prefer the back row." He pasted on a charming smile. "Is it possible to trade seats?"

No. No. No.

"Of course." The blonde gushed, swayed, no doubt, by his dimples. "There was a cancellation so no one else is boarding in first class. Is there anything I can get you before we continue boarding?"

"A pillow would be nice."

"My pleasure, Mr. Sullivan." She turned to Lindsay. "Anything for you, ma'am?"

Ma'am? Seriously? "I'd like a pillow. And a blanket, please."

"We'll do a full turndown service after the flight gets started." She gave Sullivan a smile and disappeared behind the curtain to the coach area.

Lindsay stared after her. Did that mean she didn't get a pillow or a blanket? This was her first time flying first-class. So far she had mixed feelings. She liked the extra room and the thought of stretching out for the long flight. But Blondie wasn't earning any points.

Lindsay draped the garment bag over the window seat as best she could until the seat could be reclined. Unfortunately that put her in the aisle seat directly across from Mr. Tall, Dark and Inconsiderate.

Nothing for it. She'd just have to ignore him and focus on her work. It would take the entire flight to configure the seating arrangement for the reception. She had the list of guests from the bride and the list of guests from the groom. And a three-page list of political notes from the palace of who couldn't be seated next to whom and who should be seated closer to the royal couple. What had started as a private country wedding had grown to include more than a hundred guests as political factors came into play.

It was a wedding planner's nightmare. But she took it as an opportunity to excel.

Before she knew it she was being pushed back in her chair as the plane lifted into the air. Soon after, Dan appeared to fold down the window seat. He carefully laid the heavy garment bag in place and secured it with the seat belt and a bungee cord. She thanked him as she resumed her seat.

She glanced out of the corner of her eye to see Sullivan had his pillow—a nice, big, fluffy one. Ignore him.

Easier thought than done. He smelled great; a spicy musk with a touch of soap.

Eyes back on her tablet, she shuffled some names into table seats and then started to run them against her lists to see if they were all compatible. Of course, they weren't. Two people needed to be moved forward and two people couldn't be seated together. That left four people at the table. She moved people to new tables and highlighted them as a reminder to check out the politics on them. And repeated the process.

A soft snore came from across the way—much less annoying than the shrill cry of one of the toddlers demanding a bandage for his boo-boo. Blondie rushed to the rescue and the boy settled down. Except for loud outbursts like that, the two boys were actually well behaved. There'd been no need for Sullivan to move seats.

"Would you care for a meal, Ms. Reeves?" Dan appeared beside her.

She glanced at the time on her tablet. Eight o'clock. They'd been in the air an hour. "Yes, please."

"You have a choice of chicken Cordon bleu or beef Stroganoff."

"I'll have the beef. With a cola."

He nodded and turned to the other side of the aisle. Before he could ask, Sullivan said he'd have the beef and water.

Her gaze collided with his. Brown eyes with specks of gold surveyed her, interest and appreciation sparkled in the whiskey-brown depths, warm and potent.

Heat flooded her, followed by a shiver.

"What's in the bag?" he asked, his voice even deeper and raspier from sleep. Way too sexy for her peace of mind.

"None of your business." She turned back to her table plan.

"Must be pretty important for you to get so upset. Let

me guess, a special dress for a special occasion?" He didn't give up.

"Yes. If you must know. And it's my job to protect it."

"Protect it? Interesting. So it's not your dress."

She rolled her eyes and sent him a droll stare. "I liked you better when you were snoring."

He grinned, making his dimples pop. "I deserve that. Listen, I'm sorry for my attitude earlier and for sitting on the dress. I had wine with dinner and wine always gives me a headache."

Lindsay glared at Sullivan. "So you did sit on the dress." She knew it. That had definitely been a butt print on the bag.

He blinked, all innocence. "I meant I'm sorry for dumping it over there."

"Uh-huh."

His grin never wavered.

"Why did you have wine with dinner if it gives you a headache?"

The smile faded. "Because dinner with my folks always goes better with a little wine. And I'm going to have a headache at the end either way."

"Okay, I get that." Lindsay adored her flighty, dependent mother but, yeah, dinners were easier with a little wine. Sometimes, like between husbands, a lot of wine was required.

A corner of his rather nice mouth kicked up. "You surprise me, Ms. Reeves. I'd have thought you'd be appalled."

"Parents aren't always easy." She closed her tablet to get ready for her meal. "It doesn't mean we don't love them."

"Amen. Respect is another matter."

That brought her attention around. He wore a grim expression and turmoil churned in his distracted gaze. The situation with his parents must be complicated. It was a sad day when you lost respect for the person you loved most in the world. She understood his pain only too well.

Thankfully, Dan arrived with a small cart, disrupting old memories. He activated a tray on the side of her seat and placed a covered plate in front of her along with a glass of soda. Real china, real crystal, real silverware. Nice. And then he lifted the cover and the luscious scent of braised meat and rich sauce reached her.

"Mmm." She hummed her approval. "This looks fantastic."

"I can promise you it is," Dan assured her. "Chef LaSalle is the pride of the skies."

She took her first bite as he served Sullivan and moaned again. She couldn't help it, the flavors burst in her mouth, seducing her taste buds.

"Careful, Ms. Reeves," Sullivan cautioned. "You sound like you're having a good time over there."

"Eat. You'll understand." She took a sip of her drink, watching him take a bite. "Or maybe not. After all, you've already eaten."

"I wasn't hungry earlier. Damn, this is good." He pointed to the video screen. "Shall we watch a movie with our meal?"

She was tempted. Surprising. After the disaster of last year, work had been her major consolation. She rarely took the time to relax with a movie. She was too busy handling events for the stars of those movies. A girl had to work hard to make the stars happy in Hollywood. And she had to work harder than the rest after allowing an old flame to distract her to the point of putting her career at risk. But she'd learned her lesson.

Luckily she'd already signed the contract for this gig. And she planned to make the royal wedding of the Crown Prince of Halencia, Antonio de l'Accardi, to the commoner, Christina Rose, the wedding of the century.

Thirty days from now no one would be able to question her dedication—which meant returning to the puzzle of the table seating.

“You go on,” she told Sullivan. “I have to get back to my work.”

“What are you doing over there? Those earlier moans weren’t as pleasant as your dinner noises.”

“It’s a creative new form of torture called a seating arrangement.”

“Ah. It sounds excruciating.”

“Oh, believe me. It’s for a political dinner and there are all these levels of protocols of who can sit with whom. And then there’s the added element of personal likes and dislikes. It’s two steps back for every one step forward. And it’s a lot of manual double-checking…talk about a headache.”

“Politics usually are.” The grimness in his tone told her there was something more there. Before she had time to wonder about it, he went on. “The information isn’t on spreadsheets?”

“It is, but there are more than a hundred names here. I have to seat a table and then check each name to see if they’re compatible.”

“You know you can set up a program that can look at the information and tell you whether the table mates are compatible at the time you put the name in.”

She blinked at him. “That would be wonderful. How do I do that exactly?”

He laughed, a deep, friendly sound, then rattled off a string of commands that had her eyes glazing over. “The setup will take a few minutes but will likely save you hours overall.”

“Yeah, but you lost me at the word ‘algorithm.’” She wiped her mouth with the cloth napkin. “You really had my hopes up for a minute there.”

"Sorry, tech talk. I own a company that provides software for cyber security. A program like this really isn't that difficult. Let me see your computer after dinner and I'll do it for you. It'll take me less than an hour."

This man was tempting her left and right. She weighed the hours she'd save against the confidentiality agreement she'd signed and sadly shook her head.

"Thank you for offering but I can't. This is a special event. I'm not allowed to share information with anyone except my staff, designated officials and pre-approved vendors."

"This is for the royal wedding of Prince Antonio of Halencia, right?"

Her eyes popped wide. How could he know that?

"Come on, it's not hard to guess. The wedding dress, the seating chart. We're on a flight to Florence. And I know they have an American event planner. Hang on, I'll take care of this."

He pulled out his cell phone and hit a couple of buttons.

"What?" she challenged. "You're calling the palace in Halencia? Uh, huh. I don't think so. You can hang up now."

"Hey, Tony." He raised a dark eyebrow as he spoke into the phone.

Tony? As in Antonio? Yeah, right.

"I got your text. Don't worry about it. I'm here for a month. I'll see you next week." He listened for a moment. "Yes, I had dinner with them. They were thrilled with the invitation. Hey, listen, the wedding planner is on my flight and she needs some programming to help her with the seating chart. She's bound by the confidentiality agreement from letting me help her. Can you give her authorization? Great, I'm going to put her on."

He held the phone out to Lindsay. "It's Prince Antonio."

CHAPTER TWO

LINDSAY ROLLED HER eyes at the man across the way, wondering how far he meant to take this joke and what he hoped to achieve.

"Hello?"

"*Buona sera*, Ms. Reeves. I hope you are having a nice flight."

"Uh, yes, I am." The voice was male, pleasant and slightly accented. And could be anyone. Except how had he known her name? Sullivan hadn't mentioned it.

"Christina is thrilled to have your services for the wedding. You have my full support to make this *il matrimonio dei suoi sogni*—the wedding of her dreams."

"I'll do my best." Could this actually be the prince?

"Duty demands my presence at the palace but I look forward to meeting you at the rehearsal. Zach is my best man. He will be my advocate in Monte Calanetti for the next month. He is available to assist you in any way necessary."

She turned to look at the man across the aisle and quirked a brow at his evil smirk. "Zach…Sullivan?"

"Yes. We went to college together. He's like a brother to me. If he can assist with the meal plan—"

"The seating chart." She squeezed her eyes closed. *OMG, I just interrupted the royal prince.*

"Of course. The seating chart. If Zach can help, you must allow him to be of service. He is quite handy with a computer."

"Yes. I will. Thank you."

"It is I who thanks you. You do us an honor by coming to Halencia. If I can be of further assistance, you have access to me through Zach. *Buona notte*, Ms. Reeves."

"Good night." Instead of giving the phone back to Sullivan she checked the call history and saw she'd spoken to Tony de l'Accardi. She slowly turned her head to meet chocolate-brown eyes. "You know the Prince of Halencia."

"I wouldn't take on the best man gig for anyone else."

The flight attendant appeared with the cart to collect his meal and sweetly inquire if he'd like dessert.

Lindsay rolled her eyes, barely completing the action before the blonde turned to her.

"Are you done, ma'am?"

Ma'am again? Lindsay's eyes narrowed in a bland stare.

Her displeasure must have registered because the woman rushed on. "For dessert we have crème brûlée, strawberry cheesecake or a chocolate mousse."

Lindsay handed off her empty plate and, looking the woman straight in the eye, declared, "I'll have one of each."

"Of course, ma… Ms. Reeves." She hurriedly stashed the plate and rolled the cart away.

Lindsay slowly turned her head until Sullivan's intent regard came into view. Okay, first things first. "I'm only twenty-nine. Way too young to be ma'am."

He cocked his head.

She handed him his phone. "Why didn't you tell me you were the best man?"

He lifted one dark eyebrow. "Would you have believed me?"

She contemplated him. "Probably. I have a file on you."

His slanted eyebrow seemed to dip even further. "Then I'm surprised you didn't recognize me. You probably have profiles on the entire wedding party in that tablet of yours."

She lifted one shoulder in a half shrug of acknowledgment. "I've learned it's wise to know who I'll be working with. I didn't recognize you because it's out of context.

Plus, you don't have an eight-o'clock shadow in your company photo in which you're wearing glasses."

"Huh." He ran the backs of his fingers over his jaw. "I'll have to get that picture updated. I had Lasik eye surgery over a year ago. Regardless, I didn't know you were involved in the wedding until you started talking about the meal arrangements."

"Seating arrangements," she corrected automatically.

"Right."

The flight attendant arrived with dessert. She handed Zach a crystal dish of chocolate mousse and set a small tray with all three desserts artfully displayed in front of Lindsay.

"Enjoy," she said and retreated down the aisle.

"Mmm." Lindsay picked up a spoon and broke into the hard shell of crystalized sugar topping the crème brûlée. "Mmm." This time it was a moan. "Oh, that's good."

"Careful, Ms. Reeves, you're going to get me worked up if you continue." Zach gestured at her loaded tray with his spoon. "I see you like your sweets."

"It's a long night." She defended her stash.

"I guess you don't plan on sleeping."

"I have a lot of work." She gave her usual excuse then, for some unknown reason, confessed, "I don't sleep well on planes."

"It may help if you relaxed and watched the movie instead of working."

No doubt he was right. But work soothed her, usually. Over the past year she'd found it increasingly more difficult to believe in the magic of her process. She blamed her breakup with Kevin last year. But she hoped to change that soon. If a royal wedding couldn't bring back the magic in what she did, she needed to rethink her career path.

"Thank you for that insightful bit of advice. What don't you like about being best man? The role or the exposure?"

"Either. Both. Seems like I've been dodging the limelight since I was two."

"Well, you did grow up in a political family." That brought his earlier comment and reaction into context. Her research revealed he was related to the political powerhouse Sullivans from Connecticut. "Never had any aspiration in that direction?"

The curse he uttered made her glance worriedly toward the toddlers. Luckily the lack of sound or movement in that direction indicated they were probably asleep.

"I'll take that as a no."

"I wished my father understood me so well."

She empathized with his pain. She felt the same way about her mother. Perhaps empathy was why she found him so easy to talk to. "I've found parents often see what they want to see. That addresses the exposure…what do you have against the role of best man?"

"I hate weddings. The fancier the event, the more I detest them. There's something about the pomp and circumstance that just screams fake to me." He licked his spoon and set the crystal dish aside. "No offense."

No offense? He'd just slammed everything she stood for. Why should she be offended?

And he wasn't done. "It's like the couple needs to distract the crowd from the fact they're marrying for something other than love."

"You don't believe in love?" It was one thing for her to question her belief in what she was doing and another for someone else to take shots at it.

"I believe in lust and companionship. Love is a myth best left to romance novels."

"Wow. That's harsh." And came way too close to how she felt these days.

The way his features hardened when he voiced his feelings told her strong emotion backed his comment. Kind of at odds with his family dynamic. The Sullivans were touted as one of the All-American families going back for generations. Long marriages and one or two kids who were all upstanding citizens. They ranked right up there with the Kennedys and Rockefellers.

The attendants came through the cabin collecting trash and dirty dishes. They offered turndown service, which Lindsay turned down. She still had work to do.

"Just let us know when you're ready."

Across the way Zach also delayed his bed service and got the same response. Once the attendants moved on, he leaned her way.

"Now you know you can trust me, are you ready for me to work on your spreadsheet? I'd like to do it before I start my movie."

"Oh. Sure." Could she trust him? Lindsay wondered as she pulled out her tablet. Just because she knew who he was didn't mean he was trustworthy. Too charming for her peace of mind. And a total flirt. "Do you want to do it on mine or should I send it to you?"

"Little Pixie, I'd like to do yours." His gaze ran over her, growing hotter as it rolled up her body. Her blood was steaming by the time his gaze met hers. "But since I have to work, you should send it to me."

"It'll do you no good to flirt with me." She tapped in her password and opened her spreadsheet. "What's your email?" She keyed in the address and sent it. "This wedding is too important to my career for me to risk getting involved with the best man."

"Oh, come on. The best man is harmless." Zach had his laptop open. "Got it. He's shackled for the whole event."

"The best man is a beast. His mind is all wrapped up in the bachelor party and strippers. He feels it's his duty to show the groom what he'll be giving up. And more than half the time he's on the prowl for some action just to remind himself he's still free, whether he is or not."

Zach flinched. "Wow. That's harsh."

Oh, clever man. "With good cause. I have a strict 'no fraternizing with the wedding party—including guests'—policy for my company and the vendors I work with. But, yeah, I've had to bolster a few bridesmaids who took it too far and expected too much and went home alone. Or refer them back to the bride or groom for contact info that wasn't shared."

"That's a lot of blame heaped on the best man."

"Of course, it's not just the best man, but in my experience he can be a bad, bad boy."

"It's been a long time since I was bad."

"Define long."

He laughed.

"Seriously, I just want you to rewind the conversation a few sentences and then say that again with a straight face."

His gaze shifted from his laptop to make another slow stroll over her. Jacking up her pulse yet again.

He needed to stop doing that!

Unremorseful, he cocked an eyebrow. "I'm not saying I don't go after what I want. But I'm always up front about my intentions. No illusions, no damages."

Sounded like a bad boy to her.

"Well, you have fun, now. I'm here to work."

He shook his head as he went back to keying commands into his computer. "All work and no play makes Ms. Reeves a dull girl."

"I'm not being paid to have fun." And that was the problem right there—the one she'd been struggling with for nearly a year.

Her work wasn't fun anymore.

And the cause wasn't just the disillusionment she suffered in her love life. Though that ranked high on the motive list. She'd started feeling this way before Kevin had come back into her life. Instead of being excited by the creative endeavor, she'd gotten bogged down in the details.

Maybe it was Hollywood. Believing in the magic of happily-ever-after got a little harder to do with each repeat customer. Not to mention the three-peats. And the fact her mother was her best customer. Hopefully, husband number six would be the charm for her.

Seriously, Lindsay crossed her fingers in the folds of her skirt. She truly wished this marriage lasted. She liked Matt and he seemed to get her mom, who had the attention span and sense of responsibility of a fourteen-year-old. There was nothing mentally wrong with Darlene Reeves. She could do for herself. She just didn't want to. Darlene's dad had treated her like a princess, giving her most everything she wanted and taking care of all the little details in life. He'd died when she was seventeen and she'd been chasing his replacement all her life.

She'd had Lindsay when she was eighteen and then she learned to get the wedding ring on her finger before they lost interest. In between love interests, Lindsay was expected to pick up the slack.

She loved her mother dearly. But she loved her a little easier when she was in a committed relationship.

"Did you fall asleep on me over there?"

His question called her attention to his profile. Such strong features—square jaw dusted with stubble-defined cheekbones, straight nose. He really was beautiful in a totally masculine way. Too much temptation. Good thing her policy put him off limits.

"No. Just going over what I need to do."

"Perfect timing then." He swirled his finger and hit a single key. "Because I just sent your file back to you."

"So soon?" She reached for her tablet, excited to try the

new program. The file opened onto a picture of circles in the form of a rectangle. Each circle was numbered. She'd refine the shape once she viewed the venue. She ran her finger across the page and as it moved over a circle names popped up showing who was seated at the table.

"Cool. How do I see everybody?"

"You hit this icon here." He hung over his chair, reaching across the aisle to show her. He tried showing her the other features, but his actions were awkward. Being left-handed, he had to use his right hand to aid her because of the distance between the seats.

"This is ridiculous." Unsnapping her seat belt, she stood. "Do you mind if I come over there for a few minutes while we go over this?"

"Sure." He stood, as well, and stepped aside.

Standing next to him she came face to loosened tie with him. She bent her head back to see him and then bent it back again to meet his gaze. "My goodness. How tall are you?"

"Six-four."

"And the prince?"

"Six-one." Long fingers tugged on a short dark tendril. "Does this brain never stop working?"

"Not when I get a visual of a tall drink of water standing next to a shot glass."

"I'm not quite sure what that means, but I think there was a compliment in there somewhere."

"Don't start imagining things at fifty thousand feet, Sullivan. We're a long way from help." She tugged on his blue-pinstriped tie. "You can ditch this now. Was dinner a formal affair?"

The light went out of his eyes. He yanked the tie off and stuffed it in his pants' pocket. "It's always formal with my parents."

She patted his chest. "You did your duty, now move on."

"Good advice." He gestured for her to take the window seat.

She hesitated for a beat. Being trapped in the inside seat, surrounded by his potent masculinity, might be pushing her self-control a little thin. But his computer program blew her mind. From the tiny bit she'd seen, it had the potential to save her hours, if not days, of work.

"Ms. Reeves?" His breath wafted over her ear, sending a shiver racing down her spine. "Are you okay?"

"Of course." She realized he'd been talking while she fought off her panic attack. "Ah…hmm." She cleared her throat to give herself a moment to calm down. "Why do you keep calling me by my last name?"

"Because I don't know your first name," he stated simply.

Oh, right. The flight attendants had used their last names. The prince had given her Zach's name and then she'd read it on her spreadsheet.

"It's Lindsay."

A slow grin formed, crinkling the corners of his eyes. "Pretty. A pretty name for a pretty girl."

So obvious, yet the words still gave her a bit of a thrill. She pressed her lips together to hide her reaction. "You can't help yourself, can you?"

"What?" All innocence.

"Please. That line is so old I think I heard it in kindergarten."

She expected to see his dimple flash but got an intent stare instead. "It's not a line when it's true."

A little thrill chased goose bumps across her skin. Oh, my, he was good.

She almost believed him.

Shaking her head at him, at herself, she slid past him and dropped into the window seat.

He slid into his seat, his big body filling up the small

space. Thankfully they were in first class and a ten-inch console separated their seats, giving her some breathing space. Until he flicked some buttons and the console dropped down.

"That's better."

For who? She leaned away as he leaned closer. Just as she feared, she felt pinned in, crowded. When he dropped the tray down in front of her, the sense of being squeezed from all sides grew stronger. Not by claustrophobia but by awareness. His scent—man and chocolate—made her mouth water.

"So is it easy for you?" He half laughed, going back to their previous conversation. "To move on?"

"It's not, actually. My mom problems are probably just as bad as or worse than your parent problems. Yet, here I am, jetting off to Italy."

Mom's words, not hers. Darlene couldn't understand how Lindsay could leave and be gone for a month when Darlene's next wedding was fast approaching. It didn't matter that Lindsay had booked this event well before Darlene got engaged or that it was the wedding of the year—perhaps the decade—and a huge honor for Lindsay to be asked to handle it.

"I doubt it."

"Really? My mother is my best customer."

"Oh-hh." He dragged the word out.

"Exactly. Soon I'll be walking her down the aisle to husband number six."

"Ouch. Is she a glutton for punishment?"

"Quite the opposite. My mother loves to be in love. The minute a marriage becomes work, it's the beginning of the end. What I can't get her to understand is that you have to work on your marriage from day one. Love needs to be fostered and nourished through respect and compromise."

"Honesty, communication and loyalty are key."

"Yes!" She nudged him in the arm. "You get it. Maybe you won't be such a bad best man, after all."

He lifted one dark eyebrow. "Thanks."

"Anyway. I can waste a lot of time worrying about Mom or I can accept that it's her life to live. Just as my life is mine to live." She didn't know why she was sharing this with him. Her mother's love life wasn't a secret. Far from it. But Lindsay rarely talked about her mother. "Until the next time she comes crying on my shoulder, I choose the latter."

"At least she lets her suckers off the line."

"What does that mean?"

"Nothing." He ran a hand around the back of his neck, loosening tight muscles. "It's hard to let my parents just be when they keep harping on me to join the campaign trail."

"They want you to run for office?"

"Oh, yeah. I'm to stop messing around with my little hobby and turn my mind to upholding the family name by running for the next open seat in congress."

"Hobby? Didn't I read an article that your company just landed a hundred-million-dollar government contract to upgrade electronic security for the military?"

"You did." While he talked he opened the seating arrangement program. "And between that contract and Antonio selling me his share of the business, I've met a goal I set the day I opened my business."

Clearly, resignation overshadowed pride, so she ventured, "You exceeded your father's net worth?"

He shifted to study her. "So you're psychic as well as a wedding planner?"

"When you work with people as closely as I do, you get to know how they think."

"Hmm."

"It's an impressive accomplishment."

The Sullivans came from old money made from banking and transportation. Their political dynasty went back several generations. "Your parents must be proud of you."

"They didn't even mention it. Too focused on when I'd leave it all behind and fall in line with my family obligations." He tapped a few keys and her seating arrangement popped up on the screen. "Feels kind of hollow now."

"I'm sorry."

He didn't look up. "It doesn't matter."

"You mean it didn't matter to them."

He gave a negligent shrug. "I'm a big boy. I can handle it."

"Well, I officially call the parent battle a draw. I know it's not the same but…congratulations."

That earned her a half smile and a nod. Then he started to run her through the features of the computer program.

"This is fabulous." All she had to do was type a name into a seat slot and all the notes associated with that name appeared sorted by category and importance. "You have saved me hours of work."

His eyes gleamed as he went on to show her a few additional options. "And if you do this—" he punched a couple of keys "—it will auto-fill based on a selected category." He clicked social standing and then pressed Enter. Names popped into assigned seats.

She blinked. "Wow. What do the colors mean?" Many of the names were in red and blue.

"Blue means there's a conflict with someone else at the table. Red means there are two or more conflicts."

While he showed her how to access the conflicts, she impulsively pressed the button to call the attendant. The blonde appeared with impressive speed, her smile dimming slightly when she saw Lindsay seated with Zach.

"How can I help you?"

"We'd like two glasses of champagne, please. And some strawberries if you have them."

"I think I can find some. Be right back."

"Champagne?" He cocked his head. "You turned it down earlier."

"That was before. Now we have things to celebrate. I have this to help me finish my seating plan and you met a career-long goal."

The attendant arrived with a tray, setting it down between them. "*Buon appetito!* Ms. Reeves, would you like us to do your turndown service now?"

"Sure." Maybe the champagne would help her sleep. The woman turned away and Lindsay lifted a flute of bubbling gold wine. "To you. Congratulations and thank you."

Zach lifted his flute and tapped it against Lindsay's. "To you." A crystal chime rang out as pretty as the sound of her laughter. Her simple gesture almost undid the butcher job his parent's self-absorption had done to his pride. He didn't get them, probably never would. They couldn't spare the smallest show of affection. But this prickly little pixie put her animosity aside to toast his success.

She didn't know him except as a helpful jerk and a few dry facts on paper. Heck, she hugged the window in an attempt to maintain her distance yet she still celebrated his accomplishment.

It almost made him feel bad about sabotaging the wedding.

CHAPTER THREE

IT WAS A drastic plan. One Zach took no pleasure in. But he'd do whatever necessary to ensure his friend didn't suffer the frigid existence his parents called marriage. Antonio was already sacrificing his life for his country; selling off his business interests in America to Zach. He shouldn't have to give up all chance of happiness, too.

Zach reluctantly agreed to be best man. He didn't believe in big, lavish weddings. And he didn't approve of Tony's insane sacrifice. So why would he agree? Because Tony was the closest thing he had to a brother. Of course, he had to support him.

And of course he felt compelled to talk him out of throwing his future away.

Zach knew the circumstances of Antonio's marriage and it made him sick to think of his honorable, big-hearted friend locked into a miserable existence like his parents had shared.

He wasn't thinking of doing anything overt. Certainly nothing that would embarrass the royal family, especially his best friend. But he could cause a few delays. And earn enough time to talk his friend out of making the biggest mistake of his life.

Tony had a lot on his plate taking on the leadership of his country. Halencia had reached a state of crisis. Antonio's parents were gregarious, bigger-than-life characters madly in love with each other one moment and viciously in hate the next. There'd been public affairs and passionate reconciliations.

The country languished under their inattention. The

king and queen lived big and spent big, costing the country much-needed funds.

The citizens of Halencia loved the drama, hated the politics. Demands for a change had started years ago but had become more persistent in the past five years. Until a year ago when the king was threatened with a paternity suit. It turned out Antonio wasn't getting a new sibling. It was just a scare tactic gone wrong.

But it was the last straw for the citizens of Halencia.

The chancellor of the high counsel had gone to Antonio and demanded action be taken.

Antonio had flown home to advise his father the time had come. The king must abdicate and let Antonio rule or risk the monarchy being overthrown completely.

The citizens of Halencia cheered in the streets. Antonio was well loved in his home country. He lived and worked in California, but he took his duty as prince seriously. He returned home two or three times a year, maintaining a residence in Halencia and supporting many businesses and charities.

Everyone was happy. Except Tony, who had to leave everything he'd worked to achieve and go home to marry a woman he barely knew.

Zach knew the truth behind Tony's impromptu engagement four years ago. He was one of a handful of people who did. And though it was motivated by love, it wasn't for the woman he'd planned to marry.

Tony was a smart man. Zach just needed a little time to convince him that marriage was drastic and unnecessary.

Lindsay seemed like a nice person. She'd understand when this all played out. Surely she wouldn't want to bring together two people who were not meant to be a couple. Plus, she'd get paid either way. And have a nice trip to Italy for her troubles.

Once he was in Halencia and had access to Tony and

Christina, he'd subtly hound them until one or the other caved to the pressure. And maybe cause a snag or two along the way so the whole thing just seemed like a bad idea.

Of course he'd have to distract the pretty wedding planner with a faux flirtation to keep her from noticing his shenanigans. No hardship there. He was attracted enough to the feisty pixie to make it fun, but she was way too picket-fence for him so there was no danger of taking it too far.

He saw it as win, win, win. Especially for those not stuck in a loveless marriage.

She lifted her glass again. "And thanks again for this program."

"I hope you like puzzles, because there's still a lot of work there."

"Not near what there was." She picked up a strawberry, dipped it in her flute and sank dainty white teeth into the fruit. The ripe juice stained her lips red and he had the keenest urge to taste the sweetness left behind. "In fact, I may actually watch the movie."

"Excellent." He all but had her eating out of his hand with that act of kindness. And he'd needed something after stumbling onto the plane half blind with a migraine and sitting on the blasted dress. He'd popped some over-the-counter meds just before boarding. Thank the flight gods the headache had finally eased off.

He needed to stick close to her if this sabotage was going to work. He'd do his best to protect her as he went forward, but if it came down to a choice between her job and the happiness of the man who meant more to him than family, he'd choose Tony every time. No matter how pretty the wedding planner.

He'd revealed more about himself than he meant to, than he ever did really. But her attitude toward parental problems appealed to him: do what you can and move on. How refreshing to find someone who understood and accepted that not all parents were perfect. Many people didn't get along with their parents but most loved and respected them.

He tolerated his parents, but he wasn't willing to make a total break, which probably meant he harvested hope for a better relationship at some point. He couldn't imagine what might bring it about so he pretty much ignored them except when he was on the east coast or at a family function requiring his presence.

Next to him Lindsay sipped champagne and flipped through the movie choices. The dim lights caught the gold in her light brown hair. She had the thick mass rolled up and pinned in place but soft wisps had broken free to frame her face. He wondered how long the confined tresses would flow down her back. Her creamy complexion reminded him of the porcelain dolls his mother collected, complete with a touch of red in the cheeks though Lindsay's was compliments of the champagne.

She shot him a sideways glance, a question in her pretty baby blue eyes.

He realized she'd asked a question. "Sorry. I got lost in looking at you."

A flush added to the red in her cheeks and a hand pushed at the pins in her hair. "I asked if you preferred the comedy or the World War One drama." She turned back to the screen, fidgeted with the buttons. "But maybe I should just go back to my seat."

"No. Stay. This is my celebration, after all."

She glanced at him through lush lashes. "Okay, but you'll have to behave."

"I'll have you know my mother raised me to be a gentleman."

"Uh-huh." She made the decision for them with the push of a button. "That might be reassuring, except I doubt you've been under your mother's influence for quite some time."

He grinned and reached up to turn off the overhead light. "Very astute, Ms. Reeves."

Lindsay came awake to the rare sense of being wrapped in warm, male arms. She shot straight up in her seat, startling the man she cuddled against. His whiskey-brown eyes opened and blinked at her, the heat in his slumberous gaze rolling through her like liquid fire.

Escape. Now. The words were like a beeping alarm going off in her head.

"Can you let me out?" She pushed away from him, gaining a few inches and hopefully reinforcing the message to move. Now.

"Is the movie over?" He reined her in with an easy strength. His broad chest lifted under her as he inhaled a huge breath and then let it go in a yawn.

"Yes. This was fun." Too much fun. Time to get back to the real world. "But I need to get past you." He tucked a piece of her hair behind her ear instead of moving. The heat of his touch called for desperate measures. "I've got to pee."

He blinked. Then the corner of his mouth tipped up and he stood. "Me, too." He helped her up and gestured for her to go first.

"You go ahead," she urged him. "I want to grab a few things to freshen up with."

"Good idea." He opened the overhead compartment and grabbed a small bag. "Can I help you get anything?"

"Thank you, no." She waited until he wandered off to gather what she needed from her tote.

The attendants had performed her turndown service so both beds were down for the night. She automatically checked the garment bag holding the royal wedding dress.

It lay nicely in place, undisturbed since the last time she checked. She bent to retrieve her tote from under the seat in front of hers and decided to take the bag with her. Strap looped over her shoulder, she hurried down the aisle.

It was after one and the people she passed appeared to be out for the count. Even the attendants were strapped in and resting. Good. Lindsay intended to take her time. She wanted Zach to be back in his seat and sound asleep when she returned.

He was too charming, too hot, too available for her peace of mind. She hadn't needed to hear his views on marriage to know he was single. From her research she'd already gathered he had commitment issues. The only hint of an engagement had been back in his college days.

She'd found that snippet of information because she'd been researching his history with the prince. They'd both been going to Harvard's school of business but they'd met on the swim team. They both broke records for the school, Zach edging out Antonio with a few more wins. Antonio explained those extra wins came from Zach's longer reach. In the picture accompanying the article it was clear that Zach had at least three inches on all his teammates.

Tall, dark and handsome. Tick, tick, tick. The stereotype fit him to a tee, but did little to actually describe him. He was brilliant yet a terrible flirt. Could apologize when he was wrong and laugh at himself. But it was the touch of vulnerability surrounding his desire for his parents' approval that really got to her. She understood all too well the struggle between respect and love when it came to parents.

Bottom line: the man was dangerous. Way out of her league. And a distraction she couldn't afford. She may be headed for one of the most beautiful places on earth, but this was so not a vacation. She needed to stay sharp and focused to pull off the wedding of the century.

Face washed, teeth brushed, changed into yoga pants and a long-sleeved T-shirt, she glanced at her watch. Twenty minutes had passed. That should be enough time. She gathered her clothes and toiletries and tucked them neatly into her tote before making her way quietly back to her seat.

Zach lay sprawled on his bed. He was so tall he barely fit; in fact, one leg was off the bed braced against the floor. No doubt he had a restless night ahead of him. For once she'd sleep. Or pretend to. Because engaging in middle-of-the-night intimacies with Zach Sullivan could only result in trouble. Trouble she couldn't afford.

Climbing into her bed, she pulled the covers around her shoulders and determinedly closed her eyes.

She had this under control. She'd just ignore the man. If she needed something from the groom, she'd get it from the palace representative or Christina. There was no need for her to deal with Zach Sullivan at all. That suited her fine. She'd learned her lesson.

No more falling into the trap of self-delusion because a man paid a little attention to her. But more important—work and play did not go together.

"There must be some mistake." Lindsay advised the car-rental clerk. "I made my reservation over two months ago."

"*Scusa.* No mistake. My records show the reservation was canceled."

"That's impossible," Lindsay protested. Exhaustion tugged at her frayed nerves. This couldn't be happening. With everything she needed to do for the wedding, she absolutely required a vehicle to get around. "I had my assistant confirm all my reservations a week ago."

The clerk, a harried young man, glanced at the line behind her before asking with exaggerated patience, "Perhaps it is under a different name?"

"No, it is under my name." She gritted her teeth. "Please look again."

"Of course." He hit a few keys. "It says here the reservation was canceled last night."

"Last night? That doesn't make any sense at all. I was in the middle of a transatlantic flight." Enough. Arguing did her no good. She just wanted a car and to get on the road. "You know it doesn't matter. Let's just start over."

"*Scusa*, Ms. Reeves. We have no other vehicles available. Usually we would, but many have started to arrive for the royal wedding. The press especially. And they are keeping the vehicles. We have requested more autos from other sites but they won't be here for several days."

"There you are." A deep male voice sounded from behind her.

She glanced over her shoulder to find Zach towering over her. Dang, so much for losing him at the luggage carousel. Assuming her professional demeanor, she sent him a polite smile. "Have a good trip to Monte Calanetti. I'll keep you posted with updates on the arrangements. I'm going to be here for a bit." She smiled even brighter. "They've lost my car reservation."

"They didn't lose it. I canceled it."

"What?" All pretense of politeness dropped away. "Why would you do that?"

He held up a set of keys. "Because we're going to drive to Monte Calanetti together. Don't you remember? We talked about this during the movie last night."

She shook her head. She remembered him asking her what car-rental company she'd used and comparing their accommodation plans; he'd rented a villa while she had a room at a boutique hotel. Nowhere in her memory lurked a discussion about driving to Monte Calanetti together. There was no way she would have agreed to that. Not only did it go against her new decree to avoid him whenever possible, but she needed a vehicle to properly do her job.

"No," she declared, "I don't remember."

"Hmm. Must be champagne brain. No problem. I've got a Land Rover. Plenty of room for you, me and the dress." He grabbed up the garment bag, caught the handle of her larger suitcase and headed off. "Let's roll."

"Wait. No." Feeling panicked as the dress got further out of her reach, she glared at the clerk. "I want my reservation reinstated and as soon as a car is available, I want it delivered." She snatched up a card. "I'll call you with the address."

Dragging her smaller suitcase, Lindsay weaved her way through the crowd, following in Zach's wake. Luckily his height made him easy to spot. She was right on his heels when he exited the airport.

Humidity smacked her in the face as soon as she stepped outside; making her happy she'd paired her beige linen pants with a navy-and-beige asymmetrical short-sleeved tunic.

Champagne brain, her tush. What possible motive could he have for canceling her reservation if she hadn't agreed?

This just proved his potent appeal spelled danger.

Okay, no harm done. She handed him her smaller case and watched as he carefully placed the garment bag across the backseat. It should only take a couple of hours to reach Monte Calanetti. Then she could cut ties with the guy and concentrate on doing her job.

"How long to Monte Calanetti from here?" she asked as he held the door while she slid into the passenger seat.

"I've never driven it, but I can't imagine it's more than a few hours." He closed her in, rounded the front of the Land Rover and climbed into the driver's seat. A few minutes later they were in the thick of Florence traffic.

The old world elegance of the city charmed her, but the stop and go of the early evening traffic proclaimed work-force congestion was the same worldwide. She could admit, if only to herself, that she was glad not to be driving in it.

"Have you've been to Tuscany before?" she asked Zach.

"I've been several times. A couple of times with Antonio and once with my parents when I was twelve."

"So you know your way around?" She smothered a yawn.

"I do." He shot her an amused glance. "Enough to get us where we're going."

"I was just going to offer to navigate if you needed me to."

He stopped at a traffic light, taking the time to study her. "Thanks." He reached out and swept a thumb under her left eye in a soft caress. "You're tired. I guess relaxing didn't help you sleep."

She turned her head away from his touch. "I slept a little, off and on."

"Disrupted sleep can be less restful than staying awake." He sympathized. "Are you better at sleeping in a car?"

"Who can't sleep in a car? But I'm fine. I don't want to miss the sights. The city is so beautiful."

He drove with confidence and skill and a patience she lacked. He'd shaved on the plane; his sexy scruff gone when she woke this morning. The hard, square lines of his clean-cut jaw were just as compelling as the wicked shadow. The man couldn't look bad in a bag, not with a body like that.

Unlike her, he hadn't changed clothes, he still wore his black suit pants and white long-sleeved shirt, but the top two buttons were open and the sleeves were rolled up to his elbows. The suit jacket had been tossed onto the backseat.

"Florence is beautiful. The depth of history just draws me in. Halencia is the same. Since I'll be here for a month, I'm really hoping to get a chance to play tourist."

"Oh, absolutely. They have some really fantastic tours. I plan to stay after the wedding and take one. I'm torn between a chef and wine-tasting tour or a hiking tour."

"Wow, there's quite a difference there."

"I'm not going to lie to you. I'm leaning toward the pasta and wine tour. It goes to Venice. I've always wanted to go to Venice."

"Oh, yeah," he mocked, "it's all about Venice and nothing about the walking."

"Hey, I'm a walker. I love to hike. I'll share some of my brochures with you. There are some really great tours. If you like history, there's a Tuscan Renaissance tour that sounds wonderful."

"Sounds interesting. I'd like to see the brochures."

"Since technology is your thing, I'm surprised you're so into history."

"I minored in history. What can I say? I'm from New England. You can't throw a rock without hitting a historical marker. In my studies I was always amazed at how progressive our founding fathers were. Benjamin Franklin truly inspired me."

"You're kidding."

"I'm not." He sent her a chiding sidelong look. "I did my thesis on the sustainability of Franklin's inventions and observations in today's world. He was a brilliant man."

"And a great politician," she pointed out.

"I can't deny that, but he didn't let his political views define or confine him. I respect him for that. For him it wasn't about power but about proper representation."

"I feel that way about most of our founding fathers. So tell me something I probably don't know about big Ben."

"He was an avid swimmer."

"Like you and Antonio. Aha. No wonder you like him—" A huge yawn distorted the last word. "Oh." She smothered it behind a hand. "Sorry."

"No need to apologize." He squeezed her hand. "Don't feel you have to keep me company. Rest if you can. Jet lag can be a killer."

"Thanks." He'd just given her the perfect out from having to make conversation for the next hour. She'd snap the offer up if she weren't wide-eyed over the sights. Nothing in California rivaled the history and grandeur of the buildings still standing tall on virtually every street.

Zach turned a corner and the breath caught in the back of Lindsay's throat. Brunelleschi's Dome filled the skyline in all its Gothic glory. She truly was in Italy. Oh, she wanted to play tourist. But it would have to wait. Work first.

Riding across a beautiful, sculpted old bridge, she imagined the people who once crossed on foot. Soon rural views replaced urban views and in the distance clouds darkened the sky, creating a false twilight.

Lindsay shivered. She hoped they reached Monte Calanetti before the storm hit. She didn't care for storms, certainly didn't want to get caught out in one. The turbulence reminded her of anger, the thunder of shouting. As a kid, she'd hated them.

She didn't bury her head under the covers anymore. But there were times she wanted to.

Lightning flickered in the distance. Rather than watch the storm escalate, she closed her eyes as sleep claimed her. Her last thoughts were of Zach.

Lack of motion woke Lindsay. She opened her eyes to a dark car and an eerie silence. Zach was nowhere in view. Stretching, she turned around, looking for him. No sign. She squinted out the front windshield.

Good gracious, was the hood open?

She pushed her door open and stepped out, her feet crunching on gravel as a cool wind whipped around her. Hugging herself she walked to the front of the Land Rover. Zach was bent over the engine using a flashlight to ineffectually examine the vehicle innards. "What's going on?"

"A broken belt is my best guess." He straightened and directed the light toward the ground between them. "I've already called the rental company. They're sending a service truck."

She glanced around at the unrelenting darkness. Not a single light sparkled to show a sign of civilization. "Sending a truck where? We're in the middle of nowhere."

"They'll find us. The vehicle has a GPS."

Relief rushed through her. "Oh. That's good." She'd had visions of spending the night on the side of the road in a storm-tossed tin can. "Did they say how long before they got here? *Eee!*" She started and yelped when thunder boomed overhead. The accompanying flash of lightening had her biting back a whimper to the metallic taste of blood.

"As soon as they can." He took her elbow and escorted her to the passenger's-side door. "Let's stay in the car. The storm looks like it's about to break."

His big body blocked the wind, his closeness bringing warmth and rock-solid strength. For a moment she wanted to throw herself into his arms. Before she could give in to the urge, he helped her into her seat and slammed the door. A moment later he slid in next to her. He immediately turned the light off. She swallowed hard in a mouth suddenly dry.

"Can we keep the light on?" The question came out in a harsh rasp.

"I think we should conserve it, just in case."

"Just in case what?" It took a huge effort to keep any squeak out of her voice. "The truck doesn't come?"

"Just in case. Here—" He reached across the center console and took her hand, warming it in his. "You're shaking. Are you cold?" He dropped her hand to reach behind him. "Take my jacket."

She leaned forward and the heavy weight of his suit jacket wrapped around her shoulders. The satin lining slid coolly over her skin but quickly heated up. The scent of Zach clung to the material and she found it oddly comforting.

"Thank you. You won't be cold?"

She heard the rustle of movement and pictured him shrugging. "I'm okay right now. Hopefully the tow truck will get here before the cold seeps in. Worst case, we can move into the backseat and cuddle together under the jacket."

Okay, that option was way too tempting.

"Or you could get another one out of your luggage."

His chuckle preceded another crash of thunder. "Pixie girl, I don't know if my ego can survive you."

Maybe the dark wasn't so bad since he hadn't seen her flinch. Then his words struck her. "Pixie girl? That's the second time you called me that."

"Yes. Short and feisty. You remind me of a pixie."

"I am average," she stated with great dignity. "You're a giant."

"You barely reach my shoulder."

"Again, I refer you to the term 'giant.'" She checked her phone, welcoming the flare of light, but they were in the Italian version of Timbuktu so of course there was no service.

"Uh-huh. Feisty, pretty and short. Pixie it is."

Pretty? He'd called her that before, too. Pleasure bolstered her drooping spirits. She almost didn't care when the light faded again. Not that his admission changed her feelings toward him. He was a dangerous, charming man but she didn't have to like him just because he thought she was pretty. He was still off limits.

Hopefully he took her silence as disdain.

Right. On the positive side, the bit of vanity served to distract her for a few minutes. Long enough for headlights to appear on the horizon. No other vehicles had passed them in the twenty minutes she'd been awake so she said a little prayer that the approaching headlights belonged to their repair truck.

"Is the repair service coming from Monte Calanetti? How far away do you think we are?" She feared the thought of walking, but she didn't want to stay in the car all night, either.

"We're nowhere near Monte Calanetti," Zach announced. "By my guess we're about ten miles outside Caprese."

"Caprese?" Lindsay yelped in outrage. Caprese was the small village where the artist Michelangelo was born. "That's the other direction from Monte Calanetti from Florence. What are we doing here?"

"I told you last night. I have an errand to run for Antonio before I go to Monte Calanetti. It's just a quick stop to check on his groomsmen gifts and do a fitting."

"You so did not tell me."

"I'm pretty sure I did. You really can't hold your champagne, can you?"

"Stop saying 'champagne brain.' When did we have this conversation? Did I actually participate or was I sleeping?"

"You were talking, but I suppose you might have dozed off. You got quiet toward the end. I thought you were just involved in the movie. And then I fell asleep."

"Well, I don't remember half of what you've told me.

You should have reminded me of the plans we supposedly made this morning. I need to get to Monte Calanetti and I need my own car. I know you're trying to be helpful but..."

"But I got you stuck out in the middle of nowhere. And you're already tired from the flight. I'm sorry."

Lindsay clenched her teeth in frustration watching as the headlights slowly moved closer. Sorry didn't fix the situation. She appreciated the apology—many men wouldn't have bothered—but it didn't get her closer to Monte Calanetti. She had planned to hit the road running tomorrow with a visit to the wedding venue, the Palazzo di Comparino and restored chapel, before meeting with Christina in the afternoon.

Now she'd have to reschedule, move the interview back.

"Lindsay?" Zach prompted. "Are you okay?"

"I'm trying to rearrange my schedule in my head." She glanced at her watch, which she'd already adjusted to local time. Seven-fifteen. It felt much later. "What do you think our chances are of getting to Monte Calanetti tonight?"

"Slim. I doubt we'll find a mechanic willing to work on the Land Rover tonight. We'll probably have to stay over and head out tomorrow after it's fixed."

"If they have the necessary part."

"That will be a factor, yes. Here's our help." A small pickup honked as it drove past them then made a big U-turn and pulled up in front of them.

Zach hopped out to meet the driver.

Lindsay slid her arms into Zach's jacket and went to join them.

"Think it's the timing belt." Zach aimed his flashlight at the engine as he explained the problem to the man next to him. Their savior had gray-streaked black hair and wore blue coveralls. The name on his pocket read Luigi.

"Ciao, signora," the man greeted her.

She didn't bother to correct him, more eager to have

him locate the problem than worried about his assumption that she and Zach were married.

The driver carried a much bigger flashlight. The power of it allowed the men a much better view of the internal workings of the Land Rover. The man spoke pretty good English and he and Zach discussed the timing belt and a few other engine parts, none of which Lindsay followed but she understood clearly when he said he'd have to tow them into Caprese.

Wonderful.

Luigi invited her to sit in his truck while he got the Land Rover hooked up to be towed. She nodded and retrieved her purse. Zach walked her to the truck and held the door for her. The interior smelled like grease and cleanser, but it was neat and tidy.

"From what I remember from my research of Italy, small is a generous adjective when describing Caprese. At just over a thousand residents, 'tiny' would be more accurate. I'm not sure it has a hotel if we need to stay over."

"I'm sure there'll be someplace. I'll ask Luigi. It's starting to rain. I'm going to see if I can help him to make things go faster." He closed the door and darkness enveloped her.

The splat of rain on the windshield made her realize her ire at the situation had served to distract her from the looming storm. With its arrival, she forgot her schedule and just longed for sturdy shelter and a warm place to spend the night.

A few minutes later the men joined her. Squeezed between them on the small bench seat, she leaned toward Zach to give Luigi room to drive. The first right curve almost put her in Zach's lap.

"There's a bed-and-breakfast in town. Luigi's going to see about a room for us there." Zach spoke directly into her ear, his warm breath blowing over her skin.

She shivered. That moment couldn't come soon enough. The closer they got to town, the harder it rained. Obviously they were headed into the storm rather than away from it.

Fifteen minutes later they arrived at a small garage. Lindsay dashed through the rain to the door and then followed the men inside to an office that smelled like the truck and was just as tidy. Luigi immediately picked up the phone and dialed. He had a brief conversation in Italian before hanging up.

He beamed at Lindsay and Zach. "*Bene, bene*, my friends. The bed-and-breakfast is full with visitors. *Si*, the bad weather—they do not like to drive. But I have procured for you the last room. Is good, *si*?"

"*Si. Grazie,* Luigi." Zach expressed his appreciation then asked about the repairs.

For Lindsay only two words echoed through her head: one room.

CHAPTER FOUR

THE B AND B WAS a converted farmhouse with stone walls, long, narrow rooms and high ceilings. The furniture was sparse, solid and well worn.

Lindsay carried the heavy garment bag to the wardrobe and arranged it as best she could and then turned to face the room she'd share with Zach. Besides the oak wardrobe there was a queen bed with four posters, one nightstand, a dresser with a mirror above it and a hardback chair. Kindling rested in a fireplace with a simple wooden mantel, ready to be lit.

The bathroom was down the hall.

No sofa or chair to sleep on and below her feet was an unadorned hardwood floor. There was no recourse except to share the bed.

And the bedspread was a wedding ring quilt. Just perfect.

Her mother would say it was a sign. She'd actually have a lot more to say, as well, but Lindsay ruthlessly put a lock on those thoughts.

Lightening flashed outside the long, narrow window. Lindsay pulled the heavy drapes closed, grateful for the accommodation. She may have to share with a near stranger and the room may not be luxurious, but it was clean and authentic, and a strong, warm barrier against the elements.

Now why did that make her think of Zach?

The rain absorbed the humidity and dropped the temperature a good twenty degrees. The stone room was cool. Goose bumps chased across her skin.

She lit the kindling and once it caught added some wood. Warmth spread into the room. Unable to wait any longer, she made a quick trip down the hall. Zach was still gone when she got back. He'd dropped off her luggage and had gone back for his. She rolled the bigger case over next to the wardrobe. She didn't think she'd need anything out of it for one night.

The smaller one she set on the bed. She'd just unzipped it when a thud came at the door.

Zach surged into the room with three bags in tow.

"Oh, my goodness. You are soaked." She closed the door and rushed to the dresser. The towels were in the top drawer just as the innkeeper said.

Zach took it and scrubbed his face and head.

She tugged at his sopping jacket, glad now she'd thought to give it back to him. "Let's get this off you."

He allowed her to work it off. Under the jacket his shirt was so damp it clung to his skin in several places. He shivered and she led him over to the fireplace.

"Oh, yeah." He draped the towel around his neck and held his hands out to the heat.

"Take the shirt off, too," she urged him. She reached out with her free hand to help with the task, but when her fingers came skin to skin with his shoulder she decided it might be best if he handled the job himself.

To avoid looking at all the tanned, toned flesh revealed by the stripping off of his shirt, Lindsay held the dripping jacket aloft. What were they going to do with it? He handed her the shirt. With them?

A knock sounded at the door. Leaving Zach by the fire, Lindsay answered the knock. A plump woman in a purple jogging suit with more gray than black in her hair gave Lindsay a bright smile.

"Si, signora." She pointed to the dripping clothes, "I take?"

"Oh. *Grazie.*" Lindsay handed the wet clothes through the door.

"And these, too." From behind the door Zach thrust his pants forward.

Okay, then. She just hoped he'd kept his underwear on.

"Si, si." The woman's smile grew broader. She took the pants while craning her head to try to see behind Lindsay. She rolled off something in Italian. Lindsay just blinked at her.

"She said the owner was sending up some food for us."

As if on cue, Lindsay's stomach gurgled. The mention of food made her realize how hungry she was. It had been hours since they'd eaten on the plane. *"Si."* She nodded. *"Grazie."*

The woman nodded and, with one last glance into the room, turned and walked down the hall.

"You have a fan." Lindsay told Zach when she closed the door. "Oh, my good dog." The man had his back to her as he leaned over the bed rummaging through his luggage. All he wore was a pair of black knit boxer briefs that clung to his butt like a lover. The soft cloth left little to the imagination and there was a lot to admire.

No wonder the maid had been so enthralled.

And Lindsay had to sleep next to that tonight.

"What about a dog?" He turned those whiskey-brown eyes on her over one broad, bare shoulder.

Her knees went weak, nearly giving out on her. She sank into the hard chair by the fire.

"Dog? Huh? Nothing." Her mother had taught her to turn the word around so she didn't take the Lord's name in vain. After all these years, the habit stuck.

He tugged on a gray T-shirt.

Thank the merciful angels in heaven.

"I'm going to take a quick shower. Don't eat all the food."

"No promises."

He grinned. "Then I'll just have to hurry."

He disappeared out the door with his shaving kit under one arm and the towel tossed over his shoulder.

Finally Lindsay felt as though she could breathe again. He took up so much space. A room that seemed spacious one moment shrank by three sizes when he crossed the threshold. Even with him gone the room smelled of him.

She patted her pocket. Where was her phone? She needed it now, needed to call the rental agency that very moment and demand a car be delivered to her. They should never have allowed a party outside the reservation to cancel. They owed her.

The hunt proved futile. Her phone wasn't in her purse, her tote or either suitcase. She thought back to the last time she'd used it. In the Land Rover, where it had been pitch-black. It must still be in the vehicle.

That was at the garage.

There'd be no getting her phone tonight. Dang it.

Stymied from making the call she wanted to, she took advantage of Zach's absence to gather her own toiletries and yoga pants and long-sleeved tee she'd worn on the plane. And a pair of socks. Yep, she'd wear gloves to bed if she had any with her. And if she had any luck at all, he'd wear a three-piece suit.

There'd be no skin-to-skin contact if she could help it.

Loosen up, Lindsay. Her mom's voice broke through her blockade. *You're young and single and about to share a bed with one prime specimen. You should be thinking of ways to rock the bed not bulletproof yourself against an accidental touch.*

How sad was it that her mother was more sexually aggressive than she was?

Her mom was forever pushing Lindsay to date more, to take chances on meeting people. She'd been thrilled when Lindsay had started seeing Kevin again. She'd welcomed him; more, she'd invited him to family events and made a point of showing her pride in Lindsay and her success.

Right, and look how that turned out.

To be fair, Mom had been almost as devastated as Lindsay when Kevin showed his true colors. She may be self-absorbed but Lindsay never doubted her mom's love. She wanted Lindsay to be happy and in her mind that equated to love and marriage. Because for her it was—at least during the first flush of love.

Lindsay wanted to believe in love and happily ever after, but it was getting harder to do as she planned her mother's sixth wedding. And, okay, yeah, Mom was right; Lindsay really didn't make an effort to meet men. But that wasn't the problem. She actually met lots of interesting men. While she was working, when it was totally inappropriate to pursue the connection.

The problem was she was too closed off when she did meet a nice guy. After stepfather number two, she'd started putting up shields to keep from being hurt when they left. She and Kevin had been friends before they were a couple and when they'd split up, her shields just grew higher.

She hadn't given up on love. She just didn't know if she was brave enough to reach for it.

You're in Italy for a month with a millionaire hunk at your beck and call. It's the perfect recipe for a spicy summer fling. Every relationship doesn't have to end with a commitment.

Mom didn't always practice what she preached.

The food hadn't arrived when Zach returned smelling of freshly washed male. He wore the same T-shirt but now his knit boxers were gray. She could only thank the good Lord—full-on prayer, here—that the T-shirt hung to his thighs, hiding temptation from view.

"Bathroom is free," he advised her.

Her stomach gurgled, but he looked so relaxed after his

shower and the storm had her so on edge she decided to get comfortable. Grabbing up the cache she'd collected, she headed for the door.

"Don't eat all the food," she told him.

"Hey, you get the same promise I did."

She stared at him a moment trying to determine if he was joking as she'd been. His features were impassive and he cocked a dark brow at her. Hmm. She better hurry just in case.

The bathroom was still steamy from his visit. As she pulled the shower curtain closed on the tiny tub she envisioned his hard body occupying this same space. His hard, wet, naked body. Covered in soap bubbles.

Oh. My. Dog.

She forced her mind to the nearly completed seating chart to remove him from her head. But that, too, reminded her of him so she switched to the flowers. Christina had yet to decide between roses and calla lilies or a mix of the two. Both were beautiful and traditional for weddings.

It may well depend on the availability. Christina wanted to use local vendors and merchants. She'd said it was for the people so should be of the people. Lindsay still puzzled over the comment. *It* was obviously the wedding, but what did she mean "it was for the people"?

Was the royal wedding not a love match?

Lindsay could ask Zach. He'd know.

No. She didn't want to know. It was none of her business and may change how she approached the wedding. Every bride deserved a fantasy wedding, one that celebrated the bond between her and the groom and the promise of a better future together. It was Lindsay's job to bring the fantasy to life. The reality of the relationship was not in her hands.

Her musings took her through the shower, a quick attempt at drying her hair, brushing her teeth and dressing. Fifteen minutes after she left the room, she returned to find

Zach seated on the bed, his back against the headboard, a tray of food sitting beside him.

The savory aroma almost brought her to her knees.

"Oh, that smells good." She dropped her things into her open case, flipped the top closed and set it on the floor before climbing onto the bed to bend over the tray and the two big bowls it held. She inhaled deeply, moaned softly. "Soup?"

"Stew."

"Even better. And bread." She looked at him. "You waited."

He lifted one shoulder and let it drop. "Not for long. It just got here. Besides, we're partners."

Her eyebrows shot up then lowered as she scowled at him. "We are so not partners." She handed him a bowl and a spoon. Tossed a napkin in his lap. Then settled cross-legged on her pillow and picked up her own bowl. "In fact, I think I should arrange for my own car tomorrow. I need to get to Monte Calanetti and you have to wait for the Land Rover to be repaired, which could take a couple of days."

"Getting a car here could take longer yet. You heard the rental clerk. All the vehicles are being taken up by the media presence here for the wedding."

"Oh, this is good." No point in arguing with him. She was an adult and a professional. She didn't require his permission to do anything.

"Mmm." He hummed his approval. "Are you okay with sharing?"

"The room?" She shrugged. "We don't really have a choice, do we?"

"The bed," he clarified and licked his spoon. She watched, fascinated. "I can sleep on the floor if you're uncomfortable sharing the bed."

"It's hardwood." She pulled her gaze away from him. "And there isn't any extra bedding."

"I can sleep near the fireplace. It won't be comfortable, but I'll survive. We're still getting to know each other, so I'll understand."

Crack!

Thunder boomed, making Lindsay jump and spill the bite of stew aimed for her mouth.

"Dang it." She grabbed her napkin and scrubbed at the stain on her breast. "Are you uncomfortable?"

"No." He took her bowl so she could use both hands. "But I'm a man."

Oh, yeah, she'd noticed.

"If something happened between us, I'd be a happy man in the morning. You, on the other hand, would be satisfied but regretful."

She glared at him. "Nothing is going to happen."

He held up his hands, the sign of surrender blemished by the bowls he held. "Of course not."

"So there's no reason not to share."

"None at all."

"It's settled then."

"Yep." He handed her bowl back. "Now you want to tell me what your deal is with storms?"

Zach watched the color leech from Lindsay's cheeks, confirmation that his suspicions were right that her reaction to the thunderstorm exceeded the norm.

She was nervous and jumpy, which was totally unlike her.

Sure she'd gone ballistic when he'd sat on the wedding dress, but considering the cost of the gown she could be forgiven for hyperventilating.

Generally he found her to be calm and collected, giving as good as she got but not overreacting or jumping to conclusions. Efficient but friendly. The storm had her shaken and he wanted to know why.

"Nothing." She carefully placed her bowl on the tray. "I'm fine."

"You're jumpy as hell. And it started before we got to the room so it isn't the sleeping arrangements. It has to be the storm."

"Maybe it's you." She tossed the words at him as she slid from the bed. "Did you consider that?"

"Nope." His gaze followed her actions as she put the suitcase back on the bed and began to organize the things she'd dumped in. "We're practically lovers."

Ice burned cold in the blue glare she sent him. "You are insane."

"Oh, come on." He taunted her. "You know it's going to happen. Not tonight, but definitely before the month is up."

"In your dreams. But I live in reality."

"Tell me about the storms."

"There's nothing to tell." The jerkiness of her movements told a different story.

"Okay. Have it your way." He relaxed back against the wall and laced his arms behind his head. "I like storms myself."

"You like storms?" The astonishment in her voice belied her indifference. "As I said, insane. I'm going to take the tray downstairs."

Zach grabbed the bread and wine from the tray and let her escape. Pressing her would only antagonize her.

He'd had nothing to do with the engine failure, but he approved of the results. If he were a man who believed in signs, he'd take it as karma's righteous nod.

He'd been playing with her when he'd alluded to them being lovers. Or so he thought. As soon as the words had left his mouth, he'd known the truth in them. He generally preferred leggy blondes. But something about the pixie appealed to him.

Her feistiness certainly. At the very least it was refreshing. With his position, family connections and money, people rarely questioned his authority and never dismissed him. She'd done both. And still was.

He had no doubt she'd try to make a break for it tomorrow.

He sipped at the last of his wine, enjoyed the warmth as it rolled down his throat. The fire had burned down to embers and he stirred himself to get up and feed it. The thick stone walls and bare wood floors kept the room cool so the fire gave nice warmth to the room. Plus, he imagined Lindsay would find it a comforting offset to the storm.

She was more pretty than beautiful, her delicate features overshadowed by that lush mouth. His gut tightened as heat ignited his blood just as flame flared over the fresh fuel.

Oh, yeah, he wanted a bite of that plump lower lip.

He'd have to wait. He'd put her off limits when he concocted the sabotage plan. He couldn't use her and seduce her, too. That would be too much. But she didn't need to know of his restraint. Just the thought of him making a move on her would keep her on edge, making it easier for him to cause a little chaos.

A glance at his watch showed the time at just after nine. Early for him to go to bed most nights but tonight, fatigue from travel, the time change and the concentration needed to drive an unfamiliar vehicle on unfamiliar roads weighed on him.

The room held no TV so it was sleep or talk.

He wouldn't mind getting to know his companion better but somehow he knew she'd choose the escape that came with sleep. Whether she actually slept or not. His feisty little pixie had a bit of the ostrich in her.

The door opened and she slipped inside.

"You're still up?" She avoided his gaze as she crossed to the bed and zipped the case that still sat on her side.

"Just feeding the fire."

She lifted the case and he stepped forward to take it from her.

"I can do it," she protested, independent as always.

"So can I." He notched his chin toward the bed. "You're falling asleep on your feet. Go to bed."

"What about you?" Caution filled her voice and expression.

"I'm going to tend the fire for a bit. I'll come to bed soon."

Relief filled her blue eyes and he knew she thought she'd gotten a reprieve; that she hoped to be asleep before he joined her in the far too small bed.

Truthfully, he hoped she fell asleep, too. No point in both of them lying awake thinking about the other.

Lindsay pretended to be asleep when Zach came to bed. His presence kept her senses on edge. Between him and the storm that still raged outside her nerves were balanced on a fine-edged sword.

She tried to relax, to keep her breathing even so as not to disturb Zach. The last thing she wanted was another discussion on why storms bothered her. It was a weakness she preferred to ignore. She usually plugged in her earphones and let her playlist tune out the noise.

Tonight there was nothing in the still house to disguise the violence of the weather outside the window. Everything in her longed to press back into the strong male body occupying the other half of the bed. Instead she clung to the edge of the mattress determined to stay on her side.

Thunder boomed and lightening strobed at the edges of the closed drapes. Lindsay flinched then held herself very still.

"Oh, for the love of dog, come here." Long, muscular arms wrapped around her and tugged her against the hard planes of a male chest.

Shocked by both action and words, Lindsay chose to focus on the latter. She glanced over her shoulder into dark eyes. “What did you say?”

“Woof, woof.” And his lips settled softly on her cheek, a simple human-to-human contact that left her wanting more.

She sighed and made a belated attempt to wiggle away. Her body and nerves might welcome his touch but her head shouted, *Danger!* “I know it’s silly. It’s something my mom taught me when I was little. It kind of stuck.”

“I think it’s cute.”

She went still. “I’m not cute. I’m not a pixie. And we’re not going to be lovers. You need to let me go.” One of them needed to be smart about this.

His arms tightened, pulled her back the few inches she’d gained. “Tell me about the storms.”

“There’s nothing to tell!”

His silence was a patient demand.

“What’s to like about them? They’re angry and destructive.”

“A storm is cleansing. It can be loud, yes, but it takes the old and washes it clean.”

She thought about that. “Destruction is not cleansing.”

“It can be. If something is rotten or breaking, it’s better to come down in a storm than under a person’s weight. You might have to finish the cleanup but life is fresher once you’re done.”

“I doubt people who have lost their homes to a hurricane or tornado would agree with you.”

“Hurricanes and tornadoes are different. This is a simple summer thunderstorm. Nothing to get so worked up over.”

“I know.” She lay with her cheek pressed against her hand. She should move away, put space and distance between them. But she didn’t. Couldn’t. Having strong arms surrounding her gave her a sense of belonging she hadn’t experienced in way too long. It didn't even matter that it was all in her head. Her body had control right now. With a soft sigh she surrendered to his will and her body's demand.

"It's not even my phobia. It's my mother's that she passed on to me." She blamed the kiss for loosening her resolve. Hard to keep her wits about her with the heat of his kiss on her cheek.

"How'd she do that?"

"She hates storms. They don't scare her, though, they make her cry."

"Why?"

"She was only seventeen when she got pregnant with me. My dad tried to step up and they got married, even though he was barely eightteen. My mom is very high maintenance. Her dad always gave her everything she wanted. Took care of things for her. She expected my dad to do the same. She was too demanding and he finally left. It was during a storm that he took off and never came back. She was left pregnant and alone."

"So she cries when it rains."

"Yes." Lindsay had pieced the story together through the years. She loved her mother; she was fun and free-spirited. But Lindsay also recognized her faults; it had been a matter of self-preservation.

"Her dislike of storms comes from sadness."

She nodded, her hair brushing over his chin. She'd never talked to anyone about this.

"But your jumpiness suggests a fear-based reaction."

A shiver racked her body and she curled in on herself. Everything in her tightened, shutting down on a dark memory. She wanted to tell him it was none of his business, but then he might let her go and she wasn't ready to give up the cocoon of his embrace.

His arms tightened around her and his lips slid over her cheek, giving her the courage to answer.

"It's a lingering unease leftover from childhood. It's distressing to hear your mother cry and know there's nothing you can do to help."

"It seems the mother should be comforting the child, not the other way around."

"She's more sensitive than I am."

A tender touch tucked her hair behind her ear, softly trailed down the side of her neck. "Just because you're tough doesn't mean you don't need reassurance now and again."

She relaxed under the gentle attention. Though she rejected the truth in his words.

"This storm caught me when I was tired. I'm sorry I disturbed you. I usually put my earbuds in but I left my phone in the Land Rover."

"Ah, a sensible solution. I should have known." He shifted behind her, leaving her feeling chilled and alone. And then his weight settled against her again and earbuds entered her ears. "You're stuck with my playlist, but maybe it'll help you sleep."

She smiled and wrapped her hand around his. "Thank you."

His fingers squeezed hers.

She felt the tension drain away. Now she had the music, she'd be okay. She no longer needed the comfort of his arms.

Her eyes closed. In a minute she'd pull away. There was danger in staying too close to him. Already her body recognized his, which made it all too easy for him to hold sway over her. She needed to stay strong, to stay distant…

The last thing she knew was the feel of his lips on her cheek.

CHAPTER FIVE

LINDSAY WOKE JUST before eight with the earbuds still in her ears. The tunes had stopped. She felt around for the phone but came up with the end of the earbuds instead. Her hand hadn't encountered a hard male body, but the stillness of the room had already told her Zach was out and about.

She threw back the covers and her feet hit the floor, her toes curling in her socks against the chill of the hardwood. Padding to the window, she pushed back the drapes to a world awash in sunshine. The ground was still wet but the greenery and rock fences had a just-scrubbed brightness to them.

Or was that Zach's influence on her?

A peek down the hall showed the bathroom was free so she quickly grabbed her things and made a mad dash to claim it. Aware others may be in need of the facilities she kept it short and soon returned to the room to dress and put on her makeup.

Before going downstairs, she packed her things so she'd be ready to leave when a car arrived. In spite of Zach's comfort and kindness last night, or maybe because of it, she fully intended to make her break from him today.

The heavenly scent of coffee greeted her in the dining room. Some fellow occupants of the B and B were seated at the long wooden table, including Zach. Cheerful greetings came her way as she moved through the room.

"Breakfast is buffet style this morning as there're so many of us." A gray-haired gentleman pointed with his fork toward the buffet she'd passed.

"Henry, don't use your utensils to point." An equally

gray-haired woman pushed his hand down. “They’ll think we have no manners.” She smiled at Lindsay with a mouth full of crooked teeth. “That handsome husband of yours made you a cup of coffee he was about to take upstairs. I’m glad you could join us. I’m happy to meet up with some fellow Americans. We’re Wes and Viv Graham from Iowa and the folks there on the end are Frank and Diane Murphy from Oregon.”

“Nice to meet you all.” She sent Zach a questioning look at the husband comment and received a shrug in reply. Right. She’d get him for that. Hopefully they wouldn’t be there long enough for it to be an issue. She backtracked to the buffet.

Croissants, sausage, bacon, quartered oranges and some cappuccino. No eggs. She took a couple of pieces of bacon, one sausage and a few orange wedges.

“I was just about to come wake you.” Zach appeared beside her and took her plate. “I’ve arranged for alternate transportation and it’ll be here in about half an hour. How’d you sleep?”

Huh. If he was leaving in half an hour maybe she’d stick with him, after all. It would take her longer than that to get her phone. “I slept well, thank you.” Truly thanks to him.

“You’re going to want one of these.” He placed a croissant on her plate. “It’s called a *cornetto*. There’s a wonderful jam inside.”

He took off for his seat, leaving her to follow. Their audience watched with avid curiosity. At their end of the table, Lindsay smoothed her hand across his shoulders. “Thank you, sweetie.” She kissed him softly, lingering over his taste for a beat longer than she intended to, then slid into the chair around the corner to his right.

She pressed her lips together. Okay, that bit of payback totally backfired. But playing it through to the end, she glanced shyly down the table. "I'm sorry. We don't mean to be rude. Newlyweds." She rolled her eyes as if that explained everything.

A pleased smile bloomed on Diane's face. "Oh, my dear, don't mind us old folks. Congratulations. You two enjoy yourselves." She turned to her husband. "Frank do you remember on our honeymoon when we—"

"Well done." Zach pushed her coffee toward her. "But that's the first and last time you ever call me sweetie."

She flashed him a provocative look. "We'll see."

Let him stew on that. He was the one to say they'd be lovers, after all.

"Be nice to me or I'll take your *cornetto*."

"I don't think so." She picked up the horn-shaped pastry and bit in. Chewed. Savored. "Oh, my dog."

"I told you so." Satisfaction stamped his features as he leaned back in his straight-backed chair.

"This is wonderful." She pointed at the jam-filled roll. "We have to have these at the wedding."

"We're a long way from Monte Calanetti."

"Oh, I'm aware." Censure met unrepentance. "Tell me again why we're in Caprese and not Monte Calanetti?"

"An errand for the prince."

She waited for more. It didn't come.

"I took care of it this morning. I'm ready to go when the new transportation gets here."

That was a relief. She finished the last of her *cornetto* with a regretful sigh and a swipe of her tongue over her thumb. "Maybe not these exact rolls but definitely *cornettos*."

"I'm all for it, but I suggest you discuss that with Christina."

She nodded, eyeing him speculatively through another bite. "How well do you know Christina?"

"Not well." He glanced down, snagged one of her orange wedges. “I met her once. Theirs has been a long-distance relationship.”

“She seems really nice. And she showed a lot of enthusiasm when we first started planning, but she’s cooled off lately.”

“Really?” That brought his head up. “Do you think she’s having second thoughts?”

Lindsay gave a half shrug. “Very few brides make it to the altar without suffering a few nerves along the way. It’s probably nothing. Or nothing to do with the wedding, anyway.”

“Tony’s been off, too. He got me to come all this way a month in advance of the wedding, but now it feels like he’s avoiding me.”

“I’m sure they both have a lot on their plates right now.” So much for the reassurances she’d been hoping for. The fact Zach had noticed something off, too, gave her some concerns. “I’ll know more after my appointment with Christina, which was supposed to be this afternoon. I’ll have to reschedule. Oh, that reminds me. I need to get my phone out of the Land Rover.”

“Sorry, I forgot.” Zach reached around and pulled something from his back pocket. He set her phone on the table. “I had Luigi bring it by this morning.”

“Thanks.” She picked it up, felt the warmth of the glass and metal against her flesh and tried to disengage from the fact it had absorbed the heat from his hot bum.

A loud whopping sound overhead steadily got louder. Everyone looked up. Then, in an unchoreographed move, they all stood and rushed to the back terrace. Lindsay, with Zach on her heels, brought up the rear.

As she stepped out onto the cobblestone patio, a helicopter carefully maneuvered in the air, preparing to land in the large farmyard.

Zach watched Lindsay’s face as the big bird neared the

ground, knew by the pop of her eyes exactly when she spied the royal insignia on the door. She turned to stare at him as the inn occupants wandered forward to examine the helicopter and talk to the pilot.

Zach surveyed the royal conveyance with a smirk. "Our new transportation."

"You have got to be kidding me."

He liked the look of awe in her eyes. Much better than the fear she'd tried so hard to hide the night before. There was something more to her dislike of storms than a leftover agitation from her mother's distress. Something she wasn't willing to share, or maybe something she didn't fully remember.

He wished he could have done more than just lend her his earbuds.

"It's good to have friends in high places. When I told Tony you were concerned about missing your appointment with Christina, he insisted on putting the helicopter at my disposal in assisting you for the duration."

Actually, Zach had suggested it; still Tony jumped at the chance to accommodate Christina. Forget bending over backward, Tony was doing flips to give Christina the wedding of her dreams. Because he knew their lives were going to suck.

For Zach's part, he figured the sooner he got to Christina, the sooner he could talk sense into her. They'd only met once, but Tony lauded her with being a sensible, caring person. Surely she saw the error in what they were about to do.

He could only hope she'd listen to reason and end things now. Then he and the wedding planner could spend the next month exploring the wonders of Tuscany.

Shock had her staring wide-eyed at the big machine. "I have a helicopter for the next month?"

"I have a helicopter until after the wedding. The pilot takes his orders from me."

"Ah. But you're here to help me." She rubbed her hands together. "So, I have my very own helicopter for the next month. Oh, this is going to make things so much easier."

"I'm glad you're happy." And glad he'd be able to keep tabs on her. Things were falling nicely into place. "I told him I had designs on his wedding planner and I needed something to impress her."

All wonder dropped away in a heartbeat.

His little pixie turned fierce, getting right up in his space.

"Listen to me, Mr. Sullivan." Her blue-diamond eyes pinned him to the spot. "You may not think much of what I do, but it's very important to me, to your friends and, in the case of this wedding, to this country. I was starting to like you, but mess with my business and you won't like me."

Dog, she was beautiful. She may be tiny but she worked that chin and those eyes. He'd never wanted to kiss a woman more in his life. Defensive, yes, but not just for herself. She honestly cared about Tony and Christina. And the blasted country.

He did like her. More than he should. He'd have to be careful not to damage her in his rescue mission.

"Tony is why I'm here. Ms. Reeves. I promise you, I'm going to do everything in my power to make sure this turns out right for him."

"Okay, then." Her posture relaxed slightly. "As long as we understand each other."

"Understand this." He wrapped his hands around her elbows, lifted her to her toes and slanted his mouth over hers.

She stiffened against him for the briefest moment, in the next all her luscious softness melted into him. She opened her mouth to his and the world dropped away. The sparkling-clean farmyard, chattering Midwest tourists and his majesty's royal helicopter disappeared from his radar.

He'd meant the kiss to be a distraction, to focus her on his mythical seduction and away from his actual plan to change Tony's mind about marrying Christina. And vice versa.

But all he knew in that moment, all he wanted to know, was the heated touch of the pixie coming apart in his arms. He wrapped her close, angling the kiss to a new depth. She tasted of berry jam and spicy woman. Her essence called to him, addled his senses until he craved nothing more than to sweep her into his arms and carry her up to their room.

Her arms were linked around his neck and he'd dragged her up his body so they were pressed together mouth to mouth, chest to chest, loins to loins. It wasn't enough. It was too much.

Someone patted him on the arm. "You young ones need to take that upstairs."

The world came crashing back. Zach slowly broke off the kiss. He lifted his head, opened his eyes. Passion-drenched pools of blue looked back at him. Her gaze moved to his mouth. A heavy sigh shifted her breasts against his chest. She looked back at him and blinked.

"You should put me down now."

Yes, he should. The kiss had gotten way out of control and he needed to rein it in. "I don't want to. Christina will understand if we're an hour late."

What was he saying? *Get a grip, Sullivan.*

"I won't." She pushed against him. "This was a mistake. And it won't happen again."

"Why not?" he demanded because that's what he'd want to know if he were seriously pursuing her, which he wasn't. She was too sweet, too genuine for him. He needed someone who knew the rules of non-commitment.

Still, when he set her on her feet, he took satisfaction in the fact he had to steady her for a moment.

"Because I'm a professional. Because you are the best man."

"And you have a policy. You're the boss, you can change policy."

"Not a good idea." She straightened her shirt, smoothing the fabric over her hips. "I have the policy for a reason. I'm the wedding planner. I'm not here to have fun. I'm here to work. You—" she swept him with a glance "—would be a distraction when I need all my wits about me."

"Signor..." The pilot approached. "If you desire to stick to your flight plan, we should leave within the next fifteen minutes."

"Thank you."

"May I assist with the luggage?"

Glad to have this scene wrapping to a close, Zach met her gaze. "Are you ready?"

"I am." She stepped back, composed herself. "I just need to grab my luggage and the wedding dress." She headed into the house. "Do you think they'd mind if I took a few *cornettos* to go?"

Grinning, he followed her inside. He best be careful or this woman was going to turn him inside out.

Lindsay loved traveling by helicopter. She'd been a little nervous to start out with, afraid the heights might get to her. Nope. Whizzing through the air above the scenic vista gave her a thrill.

The helicopter flew over a meadow that looked like gold velvet. She pointed. "It's beautiful. What crop is that?"

"No crop, *signorina.*" The pilot's voice came over her headphones. "Sunflowers."

"Sunflowers," she breathed. She'd never seen a whole field of the big, cheerful flowers.

Zach tapped the pilot on the shoulder and he took them down and did a wide loop so she actually saw the flowers. She'd told Zach she wasn't there to have fun, but, oh, she was.

That didn't mean she could throw caution to the wind and jump into a summer fling. Her blood still thrummed from his embrace. It would have been so easy to let him seduce her. Except she couldn't. She needed to grow a spine, put him in his place. The problem was she melted as soon as he touched her.

If she was honest, the physical attraction wasn't what worried her. She liked him. Way too much for her peace of mind. That made the physical all the more tempting. She wanted love in her life but this was the wrong time, wrong place, wrong man.

Restraint came at a cost, but she wouldn't jeopardize everything she'd built on an overload of hormones. She just needed to resist him for a few weeks and then she'd be back in Hollywood and he'd be back in Silicon Valley.

Zach pointed out the palace as they flew over Voti, Halencia's capital city and Christina's home. The big, yellow palace presented a majestic silhouette with its square shape and the round battlement towers at the corners. The notched alternate crenels screamed castle. The building had a strong, regal presence set on a shallow cliff side overlooking the sea on one side and the sprawling city of Voti on the other.

One of the towers had been converted into a heliport.

"Are we landing at the palace?" She spoke into the microphone attached to the headphones.

"Yes." Zach nodded.

"So I'll get a chance to meet Prince Antonio?"

Now he shook his head. "Sorry, he's in meetings all day. We'll be going straight down and out to a car waiting for us. We'll be just in time for your one-thirty appointment with Christina."

The helicopter made a wide turn then started its descent. Lindsay experienced her first anxious moments, seeing the land rush up to meet her. Without thinking, she reached out and grabbed Zach's hand.

His warm grip wrapped around her fingers and gave a squeeze. She instantly relaxed, feeling grounded. Putting her stringent, no-fraternizing policy aside for a moment, she smiled at him. He'd been gentle and kind last night and was supportive now. No doubt he'd hate the description, but he was a genuinely good guy.

Even though she was essentially a stranger to him, Zach had gone over and beyond the call of duty.

She longed to see some of the interior of the palace, but a palace attendant met them and a very modern elevator took them straight down to the ground level. The attendant led them through a ten-foot portico, which he explained was the width of the castle walls.

Wow, Lindsay mouthed. Seriously, she felt like a little girl at Disneyland. She was so busy trying to see everything at once she nearly tripped over her own feet.

Zach grasped her elbow. Steadied her. "Careful, Tinkerbell."

Caught gawking. But she couldn't care. This was amazing. "We're in a castle. Couldn't I be Cinderella?"

He released her to tug on her straight ponytail. "No changing up now. Tinkerbell is a pixie, right?"

"She's a fairy. And you need to stop. I'm not that short."

"You're a little bitty thing. With lots of spunk. Nothing bad about that."

She rolled her eyes. "If you say so." They exited onto

a round driveway where a car and driver waited. She grabbed Zach's arm to stop him. "Listen, you don't need to come to my appointment with Christina. I can promise you'll be monumentally bored. If you stay here, you may get a few minutes to visit with Antonio."

"I want to come. It'll be good to see Christina again and to let her know Antonio isn't shirking his groom duties." He waved the driver off and held the door open for her himself. "Besides, I'm not hanging around hours just to get a few minutes of Tony's time. We'll connect soon enough."

She should go through her notes on the ride through Voti to be prepared for the appointment. Should, but wouldn't. The city was so charming, not a high-rise to be seen, and the buildings were bunched closely together, creating narrow lanes. The warmth of the earth tones and red-tiled roofs was like an architectural hug. She loved the bursts of color in hanging planters. And the odd little plazas they'd drive through that all had lovely little fountains.

Christina worked not far from the palace. All too soon the car pulled to a stop in front of a three-story building. Lovely, black, wrought-iron gates opened into a cobblestoned courtyard.

"Zach, Ms. Reeves, welcome." The driver must have called ahead because Christina stepped forward to greet them.

She was tall—Lindsay's notes read five nine and her subtle heels added a few inches to that—and stunning with creamy, olive skin and thick reddish-brown hair sleeked back in a French twist. She wore a fitted suit in cobalt blue.

Standing between her and Zach, Lindsay did feel short.

"Christina." Zach wrapped her hand in both of his. "You haven't changed a bit in four years."

"You flatter me," she said in perfect English, her accent charming. She led them through the courtyard and up a curving wrought-iron staircase to an office on the second floor. “We both know that’s not true. Thank goodness. I was barely out of school and quite shy.”

“And soon you’ll be the Queen of Halencia.”

Christina’s eyelashes flickered and she looked down as she waved them into seats. “I prefer to focus on one thing at a time. First there is the wedding.”

“Of course.”

“Thank you, Ms. Reeves, for coming so early to assist in the preparations. I originally intended to continue with the foundation on a part-time basis in their offices here in Halencia, but the prince’s advisors have convinced me I’ll be quite busy. It would be unfair to the foundation to hold a position and not be here to help. It is such a worthy endeavor. I would not want to hamper it in any way.”

“It’s important work. I’m sure, as the queen, your interest will be quite beneficial, so you’ll still be of help.”

“That’s kind of you to say.” Christina inclined her head. A regal gesture if Lindsay had ever seen one. Maybe she’d been practicing.

Lindsay waved toward the open window. “You have a lovely view of the palace from here. It must be amazing to sit here and see your future beckoning for you.”

Christina’s smile slipped a little. “Yes. Quite amazing.”

“It’s a lot to think about, isn’t it?” Zach spoke softly. “All that you’re giving up. All that you’re taking on?”

Appalled at the questions that were sure to rattle the most confident of brides let alone one showing a slight nervousness, Lindsay sent him a quelling glance.

“I am at your disposal to assist in any way I can,” she advised her bride.

“You have been wonderful. My mind is just everywhere these days. I hope you do not mind taking on the bulk of the arrangements?”

“Of course. If we can just make some final decisions, I

can take care of everything. Your attendants are all set, the dresses have been received and a first fitting completed. I just need to know your final thoughts on the flowers, the total head count and whether you want to do indoors or outdoors for the reception. I have some sketches for you to look at." She passed a slim portfolio across the desk. "The palace wants to use the royal photographer, but I know some truly gifted wedding photographers if you decide you want a specialist."

"I am sure the royal photographer will be fine. These are marvelous drawings, Ms. Reeves. Any of these settings will be wonderful."

"Lindsay." She gently corrected the soon-to-be princess, who seemed near tears as she looked at the reception scenes. Lindsay could tell she wasn't going to get much more from the woman. "Every wedding should be special. What can I do to make your day special?"

"You have done so much already. I like the outdoors. I remember playing in the palazzo courtyard, pretending it was a palace. It seems appropriate."

"Outdoors is a lovely choice. Regarding flowers, we passed a meadow of sunflowers on our way here today. Gold is one of the royal colors you listed. I wondered—"

"Sunflowers! Yes, I would love that. And roses, I think. You seem to know what I want better than I do."

"I've done this for a long time. I'll get the final head count from the palace contact. We've covered almost everything. But we never addressed if they do the traditional 'something old, something new, something borrowed, something blue' here in Halencia or if you even want to play along?"

"What is this tradition?" A frown furrowed her delicate brow.

"It's just a fun tradition that originated in England. It

represents continuity, promise of the future, borrowed happiness and love, purity and fidelity."

"It sounds quite lovely. But I do not have any of these things."

"The fun is in getting them. In America the items are often offered by friends and family. If you share you're doing this, you'll get everything you need and it will all have special meaning for you."

"I know of something old." She tapped a finger against her desk. "Yes, I would like to have it for the wedding. It is a brooch that has been in my father's family for many years. It is said that those who wore the brooch at their wedding enjoyed many happy years together. Yes. I must have the brooch."

"Sounds perfect." Pleased to get a positive reaction and some enthusiasm from the bride, Lindsay made a note in her tablet.

"But I do not know where the brooch is." Sadness drained the brief spark of light. "The women of my generation have not chosen to go with the old tradition. Do you think you can help me find it?" Christine's eyes pleaded with Lindsay. "My grandmother or Aunt Pia might know who had it last."

Goodness, Lindsay never liked to say no to a bride, but she couldn't see how her schedule would accommodate hours on the phone tracking down a lost family jewel.

"Sure, we'll be happy to locate it for you."

Zach stole her opportunity to respond. But, sure, it was a good way to keep him occupied and out of her hair.

"We're talking a few phone calls, right?"

Christina shook her head. "The older generation of women in my family are very traditional. They will not talk of such things to a stranger over the phone. And they will not talk to you alone, Zach." She reached for a pen and paper. “I will write a letter you can take with you. *Grazie*, both of you.”

Oh, Zach, what had he got them into? The hope in Christina’s eyes prevented Lindsay from protesting time constraints.

“I wish I could give you more time but with learning the workings of the palace, I am a bit overwhelmed.” Christina handed Lindsay the letter she’d written. “With the two of you helping, I feel so much better.”

“I’m glad.” Lindsay tucked the letter into her tote.

“Lindsay, do you mind if I have a moment alone with Christina?” Zach made the quiet demand and tension instantly radiated from his companion.

“Of course.” Lindsay stood and offered her hand to Christina. “I’ll keep you apprised of the arrangements.”

“Thank you.” Christina used both hands to convey her urgency. “And the progress in locating the brooch.”

“Absolutely.” Lindsay smiled and turned away. With her back to Christina, Lindsay narrowed her eyes at him and mouthed the words, “Do not upset the bride.”

He maintained an impassive demeanor. “I’ll be along in a moment.”

Though Christina watched him expectantly, he waited for the distinct click of the door closing before he addressed her.

“I hope you’ll forgive my concern, but I noticed you seem unsettled.”

“I have much on my mind.”

“I understand. But I also know the circumstances of your…relationship with Antonio.” The situation warranted discretion on so many levels. “And I wonder if you’re having second thoughts?”

Her chin lifted in a defensive gesture. “No.”

“Perhaps you should.”

Surprise showed before she composed her features

into a calm facade. "I can assure you I have considered the matter thoroughly. Did Antonio send you here to test me?"

"No. Tony has asked me to be his advocate in all things wedding related. I take my responsibilities seriously and when I look at this situation, I have to wonder what the two of you are thinking. Marriage is a binding, hopefully lifelong, commitment. The two of you barely know each other. No one would blame you if you changed your mind. Least of all Tony. He knows how much you've already sacrificed for your country."

Her shoulders went back. "Has he changed his mind?"

It would be so easy to lie. To destroy the engagement with a bit of misdirection that resulted in an endless loop of he said, she said. But he had some honor. The decision to end it must be hers, Antonio's or theirs together.

"No. He's determined to see this through. He's very grateful to you."

She nodded as if his words affirmed something for her. "Thank you for your concern. There is much to adjust to, but I will honor my promise. In little over a month, I will marry Prince Antonio."

CHAPTER SIX

LINDSAY WAS STILL puzzling over what Zach felt compelled to talk to Christina about in private as she climbed to her room on the third floor of Hotel de la Calanetti, a lovely boutique hotel situated on a hillside overlooking Monte Calanetti's central courtyard.

Considering his opinion of lavish weddings and how unsettled Christina came across, leaving them alone together made Lindsay's left eyebrow tick. He better not have caused trouble.

In retrospect she wished she'd waited to say goodbye to Christina until after he'd spoken to her. Then Lindsay might have learned what the discussion had been about. Or maybe not. The other woman's natural poise hid a lot. Lindsay had been unable to tell if the woman was upset when she'd walked them out.

Holding the garment bag draped over her arm, Lindsay stepped aside so the hotel manager's teenage son, Mario, could unlock the door.

"Signorina." He ducked his head in a shy move and gestured for her to precede him.

She stepped in to a comfortable, refined room furnished with nice 1800s furniture. Thankfully there was a private bathroom. One large window allowed sunshine to flow in and provided a delightful view of the village and town center.

But it was tiny; smaller than the room at the farmhouse. Though this room included a desk, which she was happy to see, and a comfortable chair, she barely had space to walk around the double bed.

She tipped Mario—who'd lugged her suitcases up the three flights—with some change and a smile.

"Grazie, signorina." He rewarded her with a bashful grin and raced away.

The garment bag took up the entire closet to the point she had to bump it shut with her hip. She'd hoped to leave the dress with Christina, but the bride had nixed that plan. The queen had made a reservation with a favorite *modiste* in Milan and Christina had asked Lindsay to hold on to the dress and bring it to the fitting.

So of course that was what she'd do. And apparently everything else.

When Christina had walked them out, she'd given Lindsay a brief hug and whispered, "I trust you to finish it. Please make the prince proud."

Lindsay got the message. She was on her own for the final push. Luckily her assistant would be arriving in a few days.

Hands on her hips Lindsay surveyed her room. It was lovely. And if she were here on vacation it would be perfect. But where was she going to work?

The desk for computer work was the least of her needs. She'd shipped five boxes of pre-wedding paraphernalia to the hotel. Upon check-in, Signora Eva had eagerly informed Lindsay the boxes had arrived and she'd be sending them up shortly.

Lindsay puffed out a breath that lifted her bangs. She thought longingly of the hillside villa Zach had pointed out as they'd flown over it. He had the whole place to himself. He probably had a room he could donate to the cause. Unfortunately he'd constantly be around. Talking to her. Distracting her. Tempting her.

Better to avoid that trap if she could.

She lifted her suitcase onto the bed and started unpacking. When she finished, she'd walk down to the town center to get a feel for the small city. She may have to find office space; possibly something off the town courtyard would be pleasant and close. In the meantime, she'd ask Signora Eva to hold on to the boxes.

Dressed in beige linen shorts and a cream, sleeveless tunic, Lindsay strolled down the hill. There was no sidewalk, just the ancient cobblestoned street. Charming but not the easiest to walk on.

A young man zipped by her on a scooter, followed closely by his female companion. Lindsay watched them until they turned a corner and vanished from view. She hadn't heard from the car-rental company yet. Monte Calanetti was a lovely little city, but not small enough she could do all her business by foot.

The zippy little scooter looked promising. It wouldn't hold anything, but she could have things delivered. But where? Not the hotel. She'd get claustrophobic after a day.

She reached the city center; not a courtyard, but a plaza. Oh, it was lovely. In the center an old fountain bubbled merrily, drawing Lindsay forward. Businesses ringed the plaza, many with hanging pots of flowers. It was bright and colorful and had probably looked much the same a hundred or even five hundred years ago.

Well, minus the cars, of course.

History in Tuscany wasn't something that needed to be brought to mind. The past surrounded you wherever you went, influenced your very thoughts. Already Lindsay was contemplating how she could make it a part of the wedding.

"Buon giorno, signorina," a male voice greeted her. "May I assist you in finding your way?"

She swung around to confront a large, barrel-chested man with a full head of black hair dusted gray on the sides. His bushy mustache was more gray than black. Friendly brown eyes waited patiently for her assessment.

"Hello." She smiled. "I'm just wandering." She waved her hand around. "I'm spellbound by the beauty of Monte Calanetti. You must be so proud the royal wedding will be performed here."

"Indeed we are. I am Alonso Costa, mayor of this fair city. I can assure you we have much to offer those who stay here. Amatucci's is one of the best boutique vineyards in the world, and Mancini's restaurant is superb. I fully expect Raffaele to earn an Italian Good Food Award this year. What is your interest, *signorina*? I will direct you to the best."

Oh, she was sure he could. She liked him instantly. He'd be a great source to help her.

"It's nice to meet you, Alonso, I'm Lindsay Reeves and I'd like to learn more about your beautiful city. Would you like to join me for coffee?"

White teeth flashed under the heavy bush of his mustache. "I would be most delighted, *signorina.* The café has a lovely cappuccino."

"Sounds wonderful." She allowed him to escort her across the plaza to an outdoor table at the café. He went inside and returned with two cappuccinos and some biscotti. She began to wonder if they had a gym in town. All this wonderful food, she'd be needing one soon.

She introduced herself more fully to the mayor and he proved a font of information. As she'd expected the media, both print and electronic, had already landed heavily in Monte Calanetti.

Alonso rubbed his chin when she asked after office space. "I will ask around. But I must warn you most available space has already been rented or reserved. The wedding has proved quite prosperous for the townspeople. Many have rented out spare rooms to house the paparazzi or provide work space as you have requested."

He named a figure a family had asked for the rental of their one-car garage and her mouth dropped open.

"Si," He nodded at her reaction. "It is crazy. But the press, they bid against each other to get the space."

"Well, it's more than I can afford. I'll have to figure out something else."

The empty chair next to Lindsay scraped back and Zach joined them at the table. He laid one arm along the back of her chair while holding his other hand out to Alonso. "Zach Sullivan. I've rented the De Luca villa."

"Ah, the best man." Alonso shook hands. "A palace representative provided a list of VIPs who would be visiting the area for the wedding. Your name is on the top."

Zach grinned. "It's good to know Tony has his priorities straight."

The casual reference to the prince impressed the mayor. He puffed up a bit as he gave Zach the same rundown about the town he'd given her. Except he offered to arrange a tour of the vineyard and make reservations at the restaurant. With great effort she restrained an eye roll.

"Tell me about the fountain," she asked to redirect the conversation.

Alonso gave her a bright smile. "The legend is that if you toss a coin and it lands in the clamshell you will get your wish. We recently learned that the sculptor of the nymph was Alberto Burano. The fact that the nymph wore a cloak caught the attention of an art historian. She recognized Burano's style and researched the fountain and Burano until she linked the two."

"That's amazing. And brings more value to the fountain and the city. Do you know anything more about the legend?"

"Actually, Lucia's search inspired me to do one of my own and I found that nymphs are known to be sensual creatures of nature, capricious in spirit living among humans but distant from them so when one presents an offering, such as the clamshell, it means the nymph has found true love and the offering is a gift of equal love."

"It's a lovely legend of unselfishness and love." The romance of it appealed to Lindsay.

"But does it work?" Zach questioned.

"Before I did the research I would have said half the time. Now, when I think back to the stories I've heard, success always involved matters of the heart. I believe when the coin lands in the clamshell it activates the gift and the wish is granted when true love is involved."

Zach quirked one dark eyebrow. "You're a romantic, Mr. Mayor."

Alonso smiled and shrugged in a very Italian gesture. "This is what I have observed. Does it make me a romantic to believe in the legend? Maybe so. But the tourists like it."

"I'm sure they do," Lindsay agreed. "Who doesn't like the thought of true love? Wouldn't it be cool to have a replica of the fountain at the reception?"

"*Si*. There is a mason in town that makes small replicas he sells to tourists. I'll give you his number. He might be able to make something bigger."

"That would be great. Thanks."

The mayor's cell phone rang. "Excuse me." He checked the display. "I must take this call. It has been a pleasure to meet you both. *Il caffè* is my treat today."

"Oh, no," Lindsay protested. "I invited you."

"And I am pleased you did. Allow me to welcome you both to Monte Calanetti with this small offering. You can reward me by thinking of local resources when planning this illustrious wedding."

"I already planned to do so."

"Ah—" he made a show of bowing over her hand "—a woman who is both beautiful and clever. You are obviously the right person for the job."

"You flatter me, Alonso. But I must be truthful. The bride insists that I use local goods and people whenever I can."

"Molto bene." He nodded, his expression proud. "Already our princess looks after the people. But I think maybe you would do this anyway, *si*?"

"I've found that local talent is often the best."

"*Si, si.* As I say, a clever woman. *Buona giornata.* Good day to you both. Ms. Reeves, I will get back to you with a referral. *Ciao.*" He made his exit, stopping to yell something inside the café. Then with a salute the mayor hurried across the square.

"I thought the French were supposed to be the flirts of Europe," Zach mused.

"I liked him."

"Of course. He was practically drooling over you. Clever woman."

She laughed and batted her lashes. "Don't forget beautiful."

His eyes locked on hers, the whiskey depths lit with heat. "How can I when you're sitting right next to me?"

Held captive by his gaze, by a quick and wicked fantasy, it took a beat to compose herself. She cleared her throat as she chased the tail of the topic. Oh, yeah, the mayor. "You can tell he cares about his town and his people. I respect that. Excuse me."

She grabbed her purse and made her escape. Whew, the man was potent.

"Where are we going?" He slid into stride next to her.

And apparently hard to shake.

"*We* are not going anywhere." She reached the fountain and began to circle the stone feature, making the second answer unnecessary.

"I thought I made it clear, I'm here to assist you."

She flashed him a "yeah, right" glance.

"I appreciate the offer, but my assistant will be arriving at the end of the week." She continued circling.

"What are you doing?"

"I'm checking out the fountain, choosing the best place to throw a coin." The fountain was round, about twelve feet wide with a rock formation rising from slightly off center to a height between seven and eight feet. The cloaked nymph, reclined across two rocks from which the water flowed, reached forward, displaying one nude breast as she offered the clamshell to the side of the rushing water so some of it ran over the stone dish. If you threw too far to the left, the flow of water would wash your chance away, too far to the right and an over-cropping of rock would block the coin.

"You're going to make a wish? For true love? I thought your schedule didn't allow for such things."

"It doesn't." He was right about that. "It's not for me."

"For who then? Your mother?"

"Now there's a thought. But…no." Unfortunately she didn't know if her mother would recognize true love if she found it. She was so focused on the high, she rarely made it past the first few bumps. Even true love required an effort to make it work. "I'm making a wish for Antonio and Christina."

He stopped following her and planted his hands on his hips. "Why? They're already headed for the altar. They don't need the nymph's help."

"Really?" she challenged him. "You're that sure of them?"

His expression remained set. "I think fate should be allowed to take its course."

"And I think it needs a little help." She dug out her coin purse. Hopefully American coins worked as well as euros. Choosing a spot a little to the left because she was right-handed, she tossed her coin. Too light. It fell well short of the clamshell. She tried again. This one went over the top. A third got swept away by the water. "Dang it. That one was in."

"You're not going to make it in. It's set up to defeat you."

"Hey, no advice from the galley." Maybe a nickel? Oh, yeah, that had a nice heft. "What did you talk to Christina about earlier?"

"If I'd wanted you to know, I wouldn't have asked you to leave."

"Tell me anyway." The nickel bounced off the rock.

"No. Try a little twist at the end."

"I'd share with you," she pointed out as she tossed her last nickel. And missed.

"It's none of your business."

She fisted the dime she was about to throw and faced him. "Wrong. I'm here to plan the royal wedding, which makes the bride very much my business. She was already unsettled. And I know you're not a big fan of lavish weddings. I need to know if you upset her."

"I didn't upset her," he said too easily.

"Good. Great. So, tell me, what did you talk about?"

He just lifted a dark eyebrow at her.

"Seriously, I need to know. Just because she didn't look upset doesn't mean she wasn't."

"You're being a nutcase."

"And it'll all go away if you just tell me."

"Okay." He shoved his hands into his pockets. "I picked up on her uneasiness, as well. I asked her if she was having second thoughts."

"Zach!"

"What? This is my best friend. If she's going to bolt, now would be the time to speak up. Not when he's standing at the altar."

"I told you, all brides go through a bit of nerves. Unless you're the M-O-B, pointing out their shakiness only makes it worse. Even then it can be iffy."

His features went blank. "M-O-B?"

"Mother of the bride."

"Oh. She's probably the last person Christina would confide in."

"Why do you say that?"

"My impression is the two aren't particularly close."

"Hmm. Good to know." Lindsay had already noted Christina's reluctance to include her mother in the planning.

Mrs. Rose made her displeasure quite well known, which brought Mr. Rose out to play. Lucky for Lindsay the palace official had taken over dealing with the Roses.

"All the more reason to show Christina support rather than undermine her confidence," Lindsay advised Zach.

"Rest easy. She assured me she would be marrying Tony."

"Okay." She read his eyes and nodded. "Good. Thanks." She turned back to the fountain. "My last coin. What kind of twist?"

"You're still going to make a wish? I just told you Christina's fine."

"I want more than fine. I want true love."

"You do know most political marriages aren't based on love." Something in his tone had her swinging back to him. The late-afternoon sun slanted across his face, casting his grim features into light and shadow.

"Yes," she said softly, "but is that what you want for your friend?"

He moved closer, brushing her ponytail behind her shoulder. "So what is your wish?"

"I'm wishing for true love and happiness for the bride and groom." With the words, she pulled her arm back. As it moved forward Zach cupped her hand and, as she released the coin, gave it a little twist.

The dime flew through the air and plopped with a splash right in the middle of the clamshell.

"We did it!" Lindsay clapped her hands then threw her arms around Zach's neck and kissed his cheek. "Thank you."

He claimed a quick kiss then set her aside. "Don't celebrate yet. We still need to see if it works. Which should only take—what?—the next fifty years."

"Nope." Flustered from the kiss, Lindsay stepped back shifting her attention from him to the fountain. What had he said? Oh, yeah. How did it work? "Now we have faith."

The first attempt to find the brooch was a bust.

Lindsay tried insisting she could handle finding the brooch herself. It was something she could do while she waited for her assistant to arrive and figured out her work space situation. And she needed a break from Zach, especially after the kiss at the fountain. His casual caresses were becoming too common and were definitely too distracting for her peace of mind.

A little distance between them would be a good thing.

Unfortunately, as he pointed out, Christina's grandmother lived in a tiny house in a village halfway between Monte Calanetti and Voti, and Lindsay didn't have transportation without him. A new rental hadn't showed up and the helicopter flew at his discretion. Plus, he'd offered to interpret for her. Since Mona didn't speak much English and Lindsay didn't speak much Italian, she was stuck.

Mona Rose was small with white hair, glasses and lots of pip. She greeted them warmly as Christina had called to say they would be coming. Lindsay sat on a floral-print couch with crocheted lace doilies on the arms while Zach lounged in a matching rocking chair.

Mona served them hibiscus tea and lemon cake while she chatted with Zach.

Lindsay smiled and sipped. After a few minutes of listening, she discreetly kicked Zach in the foot.

He promptly got the clue. "She's very pleased Christina wishes to wear the brooch. She wore the brooch for her wedding and had many happy years with her Benito. Her daughter, Cira, chose not to wear the brooch and now she's divorced with two children."

"I'm sorry to hear that." Lindsay accepted a plate of cake. "Does she know where the brooch is?"

Zach conveyed the question.

Mona tapped her chin as she stared out the window. After a moment she took a sip of her tea and spoke. "Sophia, my youngest sister, I think was last to wear *le broccia*." She shook her head and switched to Italian.

Zach translated. "Pia is her older sister. Her daughter was the last to get married. She didn't wear the brooch, either, but Mona thinks Pia may have it."

"Grazie." Lindsay directed her comments to Mona, smiling to hide her disappointment. She was hoping this chore could be done.

"Would you be willing to do a quick look through your things while we're here? Just to be on the safe side."

Zach translated both the question and Mona's answer.

"*Si*. I will look. Christina is a good girl. And Antonio, he is good for Halencia. But they will both need much luck."

The next morning Lindsay struggled to get ready while shuffling around five large boxes. When she'd returned to the hotel last night, all five boxes had been delivered to her room. As predicted, she'd had a hard time getting around the bed. She'd actually had to climb over it to get to the bathroom.

When she'd asked about it at the front desk, Signora Eva apologized but explained a delivery of provisions had forced her to reclaim the space she'd been using to store Lindsay's boxes. That had meant the boxes needed to be delivered to Lindsay's room. This morning she'd managed to arrange them so she had a small aisle around the bed, but she had to suck in a breath to get through.

The thought of unpacking everything in this limited space made her cringe. She'd be tripping over her samples every time she turned around.

Frustrated, she left the room for some breakfast. Later she wanted to view the palazzo and chapel where the wedding and reception would take place. But she hoped to rent a scooter before making the trip to the other side of town.

If any were still available.

The press truly had descended. On her way to breakfast she fended off two requests for exclusive shots of the wedding dress. She informed them the dress was under lock and key at the palace and suffered no remorse for her lie.

When Signora Eva came by to refill her coffee, Lindsay asked if she knew of any place she might rent for a work space and received much the same response as she'd gotten from the mayor.

She was processing that news when her cell rang.

With a sinking heart she listened to her assistant advise her she wouldn't be joining her in Halencia, after all. While Mary gushed on about the part she'd landed in a situation comedy all Lindsay could think about was how she'd manage without an assistant.

Lindsay needed to be out in the field a lot. She counted on her assistant to keep track of all the details of a wedding, do follow up and advise Lindsay of any problems. She'd quickly become bogged down if she had to take on the extra work.

Because she cared about Mary, Lindsay mustered the enthusiasm to wish her well. But as soon as she hung up she had a mini meltdown. Stomping over to the sideboard, she plopped an oversize muffin onto her plate and returned to her seat, her mind churning over her lack of options…

As Lindsay made the hike up the hill to Zach's villa she contemplated the obvious answer to her space problem. Much as she preferred to avoid Zach, after two short days she seriously considered asking him for help.

Her hesitation wasn't worry over his answer. He'd been ordered to assist her and he genuinely seemed to take his duty seriously.

The problem would be in dealing with him.

From the air, the villa had looked vast enough to provide a small corner for her without causing her to trip over him at every turn. But she wouldn't know until she saw the inside, which is what had prompted this little trip.

She wiped her brow with the back of her hand. Only eight in the morning and already the day had some heat to it. The blue, cloudless sky offered little relief from the relentless sun. But it also meant no humidity.

"Good morning, partner." Zach's voice floated on the air.

She paused and shaded her eyes to seek him out. He stood on a terrace of his rented villa. The big, stone building rested right up against the old protective wall that ringed the city. From this vantage point it looked huge. Three stories high, the bottom floor created the terrace where Zach stood. The top floor was a pergola with windows on all sides.

"Good morning." She waved.

"You missed the street." He gestured for her to backtrack a bit. "It's a narrow drive right by the pink house."

She followed his directions, turning at the pink house, and there he was coming to greet her. He wore khaki shorts and a blue cotton shirt untucked. The sleeves were rolled to expose his muscular forearms. He looked cool, calm and competent.

How she envied him.

The trees thinned as they neared the villa. He took her

hand and led her down a steep set of steps and a walkway along the side of the house. When they rounded the corner, her breath caught in her throat.

The small city spread out below them, a backdrop to the green lawn that covered the hillside. Oak, olive and pine trees provided shade and privacy. To her right a table and chairs sat under a covered patio, the ivy-covered trellis lending it a grotto effect while a stone path led to a gazebo housing white wicker furniture.

To the far side rosebushes lined a path leading to an infinity pool.

Forget the palazzo. This would make a beautiful setting for a wedding. Well, if you weren't a royal prince.

She took pride in the large, lavish weddings she'd planned for hip and rising celebrities, but she took joy in putting together weddings that were cozy gatherings. Yup, give her intimate and tranquil over pomp and circumstance any day of the week.

"Come up with me." A spiral wrought-iron staircase took them to the terrace he'd been standing on when he'd hailed her. She followed his tight butt up the steps.

Good dog, he was fine. His body rivaled any sight she'd seen today. Even the view from the terrace that provided a panoramic vista of everything she'd seen.

"Impressed yet?" Zach asked behind her left ear.

"I passed impressed before I reached the pool."

"I had my coffee out here this morning. I don't think I've ever spent a more peaceful moment."

"I'm jealous." She stepped away from the heat of his body. She needed her wits about her when she presented her proposition. His assertion they'd be lovers haunted her thoughts. And dreams.

Oh, she was a weak, weak woman in her dreams.

As heat flooded her cheeks she focused on the view

rather than his features. “I’m afraid I’m about to disrupt your peace.”

“Pixie, just looking at you disrupts my peace. In the best possible way.” He punctuated the remark by tracing the armhole of her sleeveless peach-and-white polka dot shirt, the backs of his fingers feathering over sensitive flesh.

She shivered, shaking a finger at him as she created distance between them. “No touching.”

He grinned, again unrepentant. “What brings you by today?”

“I wondered if you wanted to go to the cake tasting with me.” She tossed out her excuse for the spy mission. Men liked cake, right?

As soon as the words left her mouth, she thought better of her desperate plan. If she worked here, it would be more of his charming flirtation and subtle caresses until she gave in and let him have his wicked way with her. Or she stopped the madness by seducing him on the double lounge down by the pool. Enticing as both scenarios were, neither was acceptable.

“You know…never mind. I’ve already taken advantage of your generosity. Enjoy your peace. I can handle this on my own.” She turned for the stairs. “I’ll catch you later.”

The chemistry between them nearly struck sparks in the air. The force of the pull buzzed over her skin like a low-level electrical current. She had it banked at the moment, but the right word or look and it would flare to life in a heartbeat.

Her best bet was to walk away and find another solution to her problem. One that didn’t tempt her to break her sensible rules and put her company at risk. She purposely brought Kevin to mind, remembered the pain and humiliation of his betrayal and recalled the looks of pity and disapproval on the faces of her friends and colleagues.

She'd never willingly put herself in that position ever again.

"Cake." Zach caught her gently by the elbow. "You can't tease me with cake and then walk away. It's one of the few chores regarding this wedding gig I'd actually enjoy."

She studied him for a moment before replying. He met her stare straight-on, no hint of flirting in his steady regard. She appreciated his sincerity but still she hesitated.

"Okay. You're in. But we have to go now. I have an appointment to view the palazzo this afternoon. Has the rental company replaced your car yet?"

"No. I have my assistant following up on it. Do we need the helicopter?"

She shook her head. "The bakery is in town." She supposed she'd have to follow up on her own rental now. Pulling out her phone, she made a note. "But it's hot out. My plan is to rent a scooter."

A big grin brought out a boyishness in his features. "You don't have to rent a scooter. There are a couple downstairs in the garage along with something else you might find useful."

"What?"

"Come see." He strode over to a French door and stepped inside.

Trailing behind him, she admired the interior almost as much as the exterior. The bedroom they moved through displayed the comfort and luxury of a five-star hotel. Downstairs it became apparent the villa had gone through a modern update. The lounge, dining room and gourmet kitchen opened onto each other via large archways, creating an open-concept format while exposed beams and stone floors retained the old world charm of a Tuscan villa.

Oh, yeah, she could work here. Too bad it was a no-go.

Off the kitchen Zach opened a door and went down a

half flight of stairs to the garage. He flipped a light and she grinned at what she saw. A sporty black golf cart with a large cargo box in the back filled half the space. On the far side were two red scooters.

"Sweet. This will work nicely."

"Dibs on the cart."

She lifted her eyebrows at him. "What are you, ten?"

"No, I'm six-four. I'd look foolish trying to ride the scooter."

Running her gaze over the full length of him, she admired the subtle muscles and sheer brawn of his wide shoulders. She saw his point. He'd look as though he were riding a child's toy.

He grunted. "Work with me here, Lindsay. You can't tell me no touching and then look at me like that."

"Sorry," she muttered. She claimed the passenger seat. Caught.

Turned out wedding planning could be quite tasty. Zach finished the last bite of his sample of the white amaretto cake with the vanilla bean buttercream icing. And way more complicated than it needed to be.

The baker, a reed-thin woman with a big smile and tired eyes, had six samples set out for them when they'd arrived at the quaint little shop on a cobblestoned street just off the plaza. She'd dusted her hands on her pink ruffled apron and explained what each sample was.

Lindsay explained Christina had already chosen the style and colors for the cake; their job was to pick out the flavors for the three different layers. It took him five minutes to pick his three favorites. Lindsay agreed with two but not the third. He was happy to let her have her preference, but…no. The baker brought out six more samples, which were all acceptable.

The fact was they couldn't go wrong whatever choice

they made. There was no reason this appointment needed to be an hour long. But Lindsay insisted the flavors be compatible.

They were finally done and he was finishing off the samples of his favorites while Lindsay completed the order with the baker up at the counter.

He'd be taking a back seat on the hands-on stuff from now on. He was a stickler for attention to detail, but efficiency had its place, too.

The little bell over the door rang as two men strolled in, one tall and bald, the other round and brown-haired. They eyed the goods on display and Zach heard a British slant to their accent.

He knew immediately when they realized who Lindsay was. They closed in on her, obviously trying to see the plans for the cake. Their interest marked them as two of the media horde invading the town.

Lindsay politely asked them to step back.

Baldy moved back a few inches but Brownie made no move to honor her request.

Zach's gaze narrowed on the two, waiting to see how Lindsay handled herself. His little pixie had a feisty side. She wouldn't appreciate his interference. And this may well blow over. All press weren't bad, but he knew money could make people do things they'd never usually contemplate.

Ignoring the looming goons, Lindsay wrapped up her business and turned toward him. The media brigade blocked her exit, demanding details about the cake, pestering her for pictures. She tried to push past them but they went shoulder to shoulder, hemming her in.

In an instant Zach crossed the room.

"You're going to want to let her by."

"Wait your turn." Brownie dismissed him. "Come on, sweetcakes, show us something."

Sweetcakes?

"It's always my turn." Zach placed a hand on either man's shoulder and shoved them apart.

They whirled on him like a mismatched tag team.

"Back up," Brownie snarled at Zach's chest. And then he slowly lifted his gaze to Zach's. Even Baldy had to look up.

Zach rolled his thick shoulders. That's all it usually took. Sure enough, both men took a large step back.

"Ms. Reeves is with me." He infused the quiet words with a bite of menace. "I won't be pleased if I see you bothering her again."

"Hey, no disrespect." Baldy quickly made his exit. Brownie clenched his jaw and slowly followed.

"Thank you." Lindsay appeared at his side. "Those two were more aggressive than most."

"Are you okay?" He pulled her into his arms. "Do you put up with that often?" He couldn't tolerate the thought of her being hassled by those media thugs on her own.

"All the time." For a moment she stood stiffly, but with a sigh she melted against him. "One of the guys at my hotel offered me a hundred-thousand dollars for a picture of the wedding dress, which means the tabloids are probably willing to pay a million for it."

"That explains why you've lugged it halfway across the world."

"I said it was locked up at the palace. But for a million dollars, I don't doubt someone might try to check out my room anyway."

That did it. He may not support this wedding, but he had his limits. He wouldn't put his plan, or Tony's happiness, before Lindsay's safety. The thought of her vulnerable on her own at the hotel and someone forcing their way into her room sent a primitive wave of rage blasting through him. He had to fix this.

"You should give up your room at the hotel and stay with me at the villa. It would be safer for you."

CHAPTER SEVEN

"UH, NO." LINDSAY pushed away from the safety of his arms. Yes, she'd been spooked by the menacing media jerks, but was Zach totally insane? "That is not an option." She even thought better of asking for work space at the villa. "This—" she waved between the two of them, indicating the chemistry they shared "—makes it a bad idea."

"Even I'm picking up on what a big deal this is for the press." He led her back to their table. "It didn't really strike me at first. I'm used to photographers hanging around hawking at Antonio for a picture. Some of them can be unscrupulous in their bid for a shot." He sat back crossing his arms over his chest his gaze intent, focused on her, on the problem. She had a sudden, clear vision of what he'd look like sitting at his desk. "It's the only solution that makes sense."

She sent him a droll stare. "You're just saying that to get in my pants."

"Not so."

The bite in the denial sent embarrassed heat rushing through her.

"Yes, I want in your pants, but not at the expense of your safety."

She blinked at him, her emotions taking a moment to catch up with her hearing. Obviously she'd touched a nerve.

"Okay."

"Excellent." Satisfied, he leaned forward in his chair. "It's settled. You'll move into the villa. We'll find a secure spot for the dress and you can choose a room for yourself and one of the spare rooms for your office. Or you can use the sunroom if you prefer."

"No. Wait." Panicked, she made a sharp cut-off gesture with her hand. "I was acknowledging your comment not agreeing to move in. We need to talk about this."

"We just did."

"Yes, and I appreciate your putting my safety ahead of your libido, but what does that mean? I've told you how I feel about maintaining a professional distance with all members of the wedding party, especially the best man."

A raised eyebrow mocked her. "I remember."

She gritted her teeth. "Well, you're a touchy-feely guy and I can't deal with that in a professional relationship."

A stunned expression flashed across his well-defined features but was quickly replaced with a contemplative mask.

"You have my promise I'll try to keep my hands to myself."

"The problem with that sentence is the word *try*."

He ran a hand over the back of his neck, kneading the muscles and nerves as if to relieve tension, studying her the whole time. Then he flexed his shoulders and faced her.

"Here's the deal. I'm not a touchy-feely guy. Not normally. I go after what I want, but I respect boundaries and I can handle being told no."

Yeah, like that happened.

"For some reason it's different with you. I like my hands on you, like the touch and taste of you to the degree it's instinctive to seek it."

OMD. That is so hot.

"So, yes. I promise to *try*."

She gulped. "Okay."

His eyes flashed dark fire. "Is that okay you'll stay or—"

"Yes. Okay, I'll move in." It may be insane to move in

with him, but she would feel safer. Plus, it solved her work problem. "But I'm keeping my room at the hotel. Space is already at a premium here in Monte Calanetti and I need a place I can retr—uh…go to if things don't work out."

"Fair enough. And as a gesture of my commitment, I'll pay for the room since you won't be using it."

"That's not necessary."

"It is to me. I'll feel better with you at the villa, and I want you to know you can trust me."

She slowly nodded. "Okay. I'll go pack."

"I had your boxes delivered up here, but if you choose this space, you'll need a proper desk. It has a bar and a billiard table, but that's it."

"I don't need anything new," Lindsay protested.

"I doubt the owners will object to us leaving behind an extra piece of furniture."

"That's not the point." He'd warned her that the space lacked a desk or table for her laptop. But, seriously, she didn't see the problem; she sat with it in her lap half the time.

"Pixie." He stopped in the upper hallway and swung to face her. His hand lifted to touch but he caught himself and curled the fingers into a fist that he let drop to his side. "Didn't you look at the numbers? The government contract will lift me to billionaire status. I can afford a desk."

He opened a door she'd thought was a linen closet. It revealed a staircase of stone steps. His hand gestured for her go ahead of him.

"First of all—" she paused in front of him "—congratulations."

A pleased smile lit his eyes. The simple expression of joy made her glad she'd put that first.

She got the feeling he received very little positive reinforcement in his personal life. The business world recognized and respected his genius, and his employees obviously appreciated his success and most likely his work ethic. But as an only child whose parents ignored his personal business interests in favor of their own agenda for him to join his father in politics, who did he have that mattered to tell him job well done?

She shook the thought away. He was not a poor, unfortunate child, but an intelligent, successful man.

And he'd hate her pity.

"Second—" she started up the stairs "—it's not for you to buy me a desk."

"The duties of a best man are unlimited. But you could be right. Do you want me to call Tony and ask him? Because I can pretty much guarantee his response will be, 'If the wedding planner needs a desk then buy her a desk. And don't bother me with such trivial things.'"

Aggrieved, she rolled her eyes, making sure he saw as she rounded the bend in the stairs. "Please, even if he blew off the request that easily, he wouldn't add that last bit."

"Not only would he say it, Pixie, that was the clean version. Tony doesn't have a whole lot of patience these days."

"He must be dealing with a lot—oh, I love, love, *love* this."

She strolled into the middle of the bright room and did a slow turn. The room was a long octagon. Three walls were made of glass and windows, two others were of stone and one held a fireplace. The last was half stone, the other half was a stained-glass mural of a Tuscan hillside; a bar with brown-cushioned stools ran almost the full length of the wall. At the far end there was a door. She checked it out and found it opened onto another spiral staircase that led to the terrace below.

"A separate entrance."

"Yes, I'll give you a set of keys. When your assistant gets here, she can still have access if we're gone."

"That'd be great but my assistant won't be coming."

"What happened?"

"My practical, poised, ever-efficient assistant finally landed a part in a sitcom."

"Ah, the joy of proprietorship in Hollywood."

Still feeling deserted, Lindsay nodded. "It's the third time it's happened to me. Of course, I'm thrilled for her. But seriously? Worst timing ever."

"Hey, listen. I'm the first to admit this wedding stuff is not my thing, but I'll help where I can."

"Thanks, but you've done enough by offering me this space. I'll finally be able to put up my wedding board. And the help I need involves a hundred little things, well below your pay grade." She really couldn't see him playing secretary. And she may appreciate the space and assistance, but the last thing she needed was to have him constantly underfoot.

"There's no help for it. I'll have to hire someone local. Maybe Alonso knows someone he can recommend. On the plus side, it will be good to have someone who knows the area and the people, who speaks the language and knows the cost of things."

"Alonso will know someone. In the meantime, I'm sticking with you. I'll get a locksmith in to reinforce the locks on all the doors."

She wanted to protest the need for him to shadow her. Instead she nodded, knowing he was reacting out of concern for her. And she was happy to have the extra security for the dress. It might seem a bother for something they'd only have for another week, but she'd be more comfortable knowing the villa was secure.

She strolled further into the room. In soft beige and sage green, the furniture looked sturdy and comfortable. A U-shaped couch invited her to sit and enjoy the amazing view. The billiard table Zach had mentioned was on the right and her boxes were stacked on the green felt. Past it was the fireplace wall with a bookshelf that offered a wide selection of reading material. Another door hid a bathroom.

The ceiling was high, the beams exposed, and a large fan circulated the air in the room.

There were only two low-slung tables. One in front of the large couch and one between the swivel chairs near the fireplace.

"Oh, yeah, I can work here. No hardship at all."

She'd totally make do.

Hands on his hips, Zach surveyed the room. "You'll need a desk." He repeated his earlier decree. "And you mentioned a wedding board. Is that a whiteboard?"

"A whiteboard would be nice, too. My wedding board is usually a corkboard. I need to be able to tack things to it."

He had his phone in his hands and was making notes. She sighed, knowing there'd be no shaking him until she hired an assistant. In one sense it was reassuring to know she wasn't on her own, but it made her plan to avoid him a no-go. It was almost as if fate were working against her.

"I guess we have our shopping list, then. What do you want to do now? Unpack your boxes? You said earlier that you wanted to check out the palazzo."

"Yes. The boxes can wait." Better to have the boards when she went to do that, anyway. "But, honestly, there's no need for you to accompany me. Stay. Enjoy your day."

"I'm coming with you."

Of course he was. At this point, it was easier to agree than to argue. "Fine. Let me call Louisa and remind her I'm coming then we can go."

"Who's Louisa?"

"The owner of the palazzo. We've spoken a couple of times. She seems nice. Did you hear they discovered a fresco when they were restoring the chapel?"

"No. That's quite a discovery. It has to add to the property value."

"You are such a guy."

"Pixie, were you in any doubt?"

"Hello, Louisa, it's so nice to finally meet you. Thank you for allowing us to tour the property today." Lindsay greeted the owner of the palazzo.

It surprised Zach to see Louisa was an American. The two women were close to the same age but dissimilar in every other way. Louisa topped Lindsay by four or five inches and wore her white-blond hair in a messy knot on top of her head. Her willowy frame and restrained posture gave her a brittle appearance.

Funny, she held no attraction for him because she fit his type to a tee: long, lithe, and blond. Sure he recognized she was a beautiful woman, but she appeared almost fragile next Lindsay's vibrancy.

"Louisa, I have to say I'm a little concerned. I thought the renovation would be further along." Lindsay swept her hand out to indicate the overgrown vegetation and construction paraphernalia strewed through the courtyard and surrounding grounds.

"I can see why you'd be confused." Louisa's smile was composed. "But we're actually right on schedule. They've just completed the interior restoration. The construction crew will be back today to finish clearing out their equipment and trash. The next step is the landscapers, but I was actually thinking of hiring some men from town first, to just clear all this out."

"That might be a good idea," Lindsay agreed. "Just level it and start fresh."

"Exactly. I can see some rosebushes, lavender and a few wild sunflowers. But it's so overgrown it's hard to know if they'd be worth saving if we took the time and effort to clear the weeds around them."

Lindsay nodded as the other woman talked. "I think you have the right idea."

Zach enjoyed watching them interact. He liked how Lindsay's ponytail bobbed as she talked and the way the sunshine picked up golden highlights in her hair.

He almost forgot his purpose in shadowing her every move.

Mostly because it was against his nature to be covert, to be less than helpful. Case in point: this morning. When he saw Lindsay being intimidated by the press, he jumped right into fix-it mode and invited her to move into the spacious villa. And he'd provided her with a prime workspace. Hell, he fully intended to get her a desk.

All of which went against his prime objective of keeping Antonio from a life of misery. With that thought Zach took out his phone and texted his friend, tagging him for a meeting time.

Right now his biggest problem was the blurring line between his mock flirtation with Lindsay and his honest reactions. There'd been too much truth in his arguments to get her to stay at the villa. She was too comfortable to be around, too soft to the touch, too easy to imagine in his bed.

And too dangerous to succumb to.

He hadn't felt this way about a woman since…ever. And he wasn't going there.

From here on out he was back on his game.

"Thanks for talking it through with me." Louisa folded her arms in front of her. "I'm very grateful to the monarchy for doing the renovation of the palazzo and chapel. I certainly couldn't have afforded anything this elaborate all at once. Probably never, come to that. But it's been a pretty intense process. It's good to have someone to discuss a decision with."

"I bet." Lindsay grinned. "Call on me anytime. I'm great at discussion."

"I can see you are." A friendly sparkle entered Louisa's light blue eyes. "And probably pretty good at decisions, too."

Lindsay rocked on her heals. "Yeah, it's kind of part of the job description."

The composed smile held a little more warmth as Louisa gestured to the chapel. "Shall we do a walk-through? I'm afraid we'll have to make this fairly quick. I have an appointment in Florence tomorrow. I'm driving over tonight so I'll be there in the morning. I've booked passage on the two o'clock ferry."

"That's fine. Today I just want to get a feel for the place and take some pictures so I know what I'm working with. And—oh, this is beautiful." Lindsay surveyed the interior of the chapel with a mix of wonder and calculation on her face. "So charming with the arched windows and the dark wood pews. I can come back on another day to get actual measurements and check out the lighting. I love how the jewel colors flow over the stone tiles from the stained-glass windows. Christina has chosen an afternoon wedding and evening reception. She wants to have it outdoors, so the landscaping will be important."

"I won't be able to hire the workers to clear the grounds until I return from Florence," Louisa informed her, "but I'll make it a priority when I get back."

"Why don't I handle that for you?" Zach offered, seeing an opportunity to cause a few days' delay. He'd simply tell the workers to be careful to preserve any original flowers. "I'll talk to the mayor to get some referrals."

"Thank you. I appreciate it. They did a wonderful job with the restoration," Louisa stated. "It was quite a mess in here. Stones were missing, the stained-glass windows were broken and some of the walls had wood covering them. Here's the fresco that was uncovered." Louisa moved to a shallow alcove and Zach followed Lindsay over.

He understood her gasp. The ancient painting of Madonna and child took his breath away. The colors were vibrant, the detail exquisite. It was almost magnetic—the pull of the fresco, from the pinky tones of Jesus's skin and the color of Mary's dark blue robe, to the white and yellow of the brilliant beam of light encasing them and the greens of the surrounding countryside bright with orange and red flowers. The details were so exact, every brush stroke so evident, it seemed it could have been painted a week ago rather than five hundred years.

"Look at the love on their faces." Lindsay breathed. "The artist caught the perfect expression of Mary's unconditional love for her child and Baby Jesus's childlike wonder and awe for his mother. It shows the full bond between mother and child. This will certainly add to the ambience of the wedding."

With the beauty and love inherent in the fresco, Zach could see how she'd think so. But with his friend's future and happiness at risk, he couldn't take that chance.

Zach surprised Lindsay with his patience and insight the next day as they toured four nurseries. She had a whole list of requirements from bouquets and boutonnieres to centerpieces and garlands and more.

Lindsay planned to use roses for the groomsmen, sunflowers over linen chair covers for the reception and a combination of the two for everything else.

To bring about a sense of intimacy in the courtyard and to define the separate areas for eating and dancing, she planned to have rustic scaffolding erected. Lights, flowers and silk drapery would blend rustic with elegance to create a sense of old and new. She actually appreciated Zach's male point of view and his logistical input.

The helicopter came in handy as they buzzed around the countryside. Deciding on the second vendor she spoke with, Lindsay asked to return to the nursery to put in her order. Zach made no argument. He simply directed the pilot and helped her aboard.

Zach waited patiently in an anteroom of the magnificent palace. He stood at the terrace doors overlooking a section of the rose garden. Curved benches spaced several feet apart created a circle around a marble fountain of a Roman goddess.

Lindsay would love it. He had to hand it to her, that woman worked. He could practically hear her discourse on what a lovely venue the rose garden would be for a wedding, how the circle represented the ring and the ring represented the commitment made between bride and groom, who once joined together there became no beginning and no end, just the unity of their bond.

"Yeah, right."

"Talking to yourself, *amico mio*?" a gruff voice said before a hand clapped on his shoulder.

"Just keeping myself company waiting for you."

"I'm glad you came." Tony pulled Zach into the hug he'd learned to endure through the years. Tony was a demonstrative man, how could he not be with such passionate parents?

"Yeah, well, it became clear if I wanted to see you, I'd have to come to you."

"I only have thirty minutes. I wish I had more time to give you. Hell, I wish we were at Clancy's eating wings, drinking beer and catching a game."

"We could be there in fourteen hours," Zach said, hoping it would be that easy.

Tony laughed. "I'm tempted." He opened the terrace door and stepped outside. To the left stood a table with comfortable chairs. And a bucket of beers on ice.

"What, no chicken wings?"

"They are on the way."

Zach sat across from his friend and leaned back in his chair. Tony looked tired. And harassed. Zach knew Tony had to be busy for him to put Zach off. They were as close as brothers, too close for the other man to brush him aside.

"How are things going with the wedding?" Tony asked.

"Let's just say I could tell you in excruciating detail and leave it at that."

Tony grinned. "Thanks, bro. I mean that."

"Only for you," Zach assured him. "How are things going here?"

"Slowly." Tony grabbed a beer and opened it. "Everyone has a different opinion of how the monarchy should be run."

"And you have to learn the worst-case scenario for each before you'll make a determination," Zach stated, knowing that's how his friend operated. In working security protocols he liked to work backward to make sure the worst never happened.

"It doesn't help that I constantly have to address some question or concern about the wedding or coronation. It's a lot to juggle."

"So maybe you should put the wedding off." Zach took the opportunity presented to him. "Get the monarchy stabilized first and then revisit the idea of marriage when you can choose someone for yourself."

"Are you kidding me?" Tony laughed again. "Instead of cheering me, the people would be rioting in the streets. I think they want this wedding more than anything else."

"Because it's a Cinderella story?"

Tony shrugged. “Because I’ve made them wait so long.”

“Because you never intended to marry Christina.”

“Shush.” Tony glanced around the terrace. “We won’t speak of that here.”

“Someone needs to speak of it before it’s too late to stop it.”

“That time is long gone, my friend. Christina will make a good queen. The people love her.”

“They don’t know her any better than you do. She’s been off in Africa.”

“Taking care of sick children. It plays well. Ah, the chicken wings. *Grazie*, Edmondo.”

The servant bowed and retreated.

Zach quirked a brow at his friend. Tony shrugged and they both reached for a chicken wing.

After a moment Tony sighed. “Man, I needed this.” He upended his beer, drinking the last. “I don’t know anything about running a country, Zach.”

“You know plenty. You’ve been training for this your whole life. Even while living in California,” Zach reminded him.

“That’s different. I always planned to hand over control to a republic, but I’m not sure that’s what the people want. They are all behind this wedding and I can’t let them down. I just need to do the opposite of what my dad would do and I’ll be doing a better job than has been done.”

“A little harsh, don’t you think?”

“No.” Tony shook his head and reached for another beer. “I love my parents, but their relationship is messed up. I don’t ever want to love anyone so much it messes with my head. Better a business arrangement than a volatile, emotional mess.”

Zach plucked a bottle of beer from the bucket, knowing he’d gotten as far as he was going to get tonight. He reached out and clicked bottles with Tony. "To the monarchy."

Tony's statement about a business arrangement only made Zach more determined to see him freed from a loveless marriage. Because his friend was wrong. At least a volatile, emotional mess inferred someone cared. You didn't get that guarantee with a business arrangement. What you got was a cold, lonely life.

CHAPTER EIGHT

WHAT A DIFFERENCE a week made. As she flew through the air on the way to Milan, Lindsay thought about all she'd accomplished since her last flight in the helicopter. She had her wedding board up and she'd made contact with all the local vendors she'd lined up before coming to Halencia, confirming plans and reevaluating as necessary.

She'd talked to the landscapers and she had an appointment at the end of the week to meet at the palazzo to go over her needs for the wedding and reception. On the mayor's recommendation, Zach had hired a crew to clean up the palazzo and chapel grounds. They should be well done by the time she met with the landscapers.

Yesterday she'd hired an assistant. Serena was twenty-two, fresh out of university and eager to assist in any way she could with the royal wedding. Lindsay worried a little over the girl's age, knowing she'd have to be strong enough to say no to outrageous offers for inside information about the wedding, and mature enough to know when she was being played. But Serena was Mayor Alonso's daughter and she had his glib tongue and a no-nonsense attitude that convinced Lindsay she could handle the job.

Plus, she just plain liked the young woman.

She'd gone a little googly-eyed over Zach but, seriously, who wouldn't? It was a fact of life she'd have to put up with.

"We are coming up on Milano," the pilot announced.

Lindsay leaned forward to get a view of the northern city. Two prominent pieces of architecture caught the eye. A very modern building of glass and metal that twisted well into the air and an ancient cathedral dramatically topped with a forest of spires. Both buildings were stunningly impressive.

She glanced at Zach and found his gaze on her. Smiling, she gestured at the view. "It's spectacular."

"It is, indeed," he agreed without looking away from her.

She turned her attention back to the view, pretending his focus on her didn't send the blood rushing through her veins.

He'd kept to his promise not to touch her. Well, mostly. He didn't play with her hair or take her hand, but he stayed bumping-elbows close wherever they went. And he still liked to put his hand in the small of her back whenever he directed her into or out of a building or room.

Serena had asked if they were together, so Lindsay knew the townspeople were speculating about their relationship. She'd given Serena a firm no in response and hoped the word got out about the true state of things.

They landed at a heliport on a mid-rise building not far from the Duomo di Milano. Downstairs a car was waiting to take them to a shop along Via Monte Napoleone. Lindsay checked her tablet to give Zach the address.

She looked forward to handing the dress over to Christina and the queen's seamstress. Providing security for the gown had proved more stressful than she'd anticipated. Having it off her shoulders would allow her to focus on the many other elements of the wedding demanding her attention.

"There it is. Signora Russo's. Christina and the queen are meeting us there. I already spoke to Signora Russo about the damage to the beading. She said she's a master seamstress and she would fix it."

"I'm glad to hear it."

A valet took the car and she and Zach were escorted inside. An attendant took the garment bag and led them to a plush fitting suite. A large, round couch in a soft ivory with a high back topped by an extravagant flower arrangement graced the middle of the room.

The bride and queen stood speaking with a petite, ageless woman in a stylish black suit. Lindsay walked across the room with Zach to join them.

Christina made the introductions. It might have been Lindsay's imagination, but the other woman seemed quite relieved to see them.

"Zachary!" exclaimed Her Royal Highness Valentina de l'Accardi, Queen of Halencia when she saw Zach. "As handsome as ever." She glided forward and kissed him on both cheeks. "*Mio caro*, thank you for helping Antonio. He is so busy. Many, many meetings. We do not even see him at the palace."

"Valentina." Zach bent over her hand. "You are ever youthful. I thought for a moment Elena was here."

"Zachary!" Valentina swatted his forearm and giggled. Yes, the matriarch of Halencia giggled. And flushed a pretty rose. "Such a charming boy. Be careful, Ms. Reeves, this one knows what a woman wants to hear, be alert that he does not steal your heart."

"Yes. I've noticed he's a bit of a flirt."

"*Si*, a flirt." Warm brown eyes met hers with a seriousness her lighthearted greeting belied. The woman clasped her hand and patted it. "I am so pleased you were able to come to Halencia to plan Antonio and Christina's wedding. I wanted only the best for them."

"Now, you flatter me." Lindsay squeezed the queen's hand before releasing her and stepping back. "It is I who is privileged to be here. And to be here in Signora Russo's shop. I may have to steal a moment to shop for my own dress for the wedding."

"Oh, you must. My friend will take the best care of you. Giana, Ms. Reeves needs a dress. Charge it to my account. It shall be my treat for all her hard work."

Appalled, Lindsay protested. “Your Highness, I cannot—”

“I insist.” The queen waved her objection aside. “I only wish I could stay and help you shop. And see Christina in her gown!” She sighed with much drama. “Regretfully, I must leave. One of Antonio’s many meetings draws me away. Christina—” Valentina moved to the bride’s side and Christina bowed to receive a kiss on the cheek. “Worry not. Giana has made many women look like a princess. She will do her *magia* and make you a *bella* bride.”

For an instant Christina seemed to freeze, but in a blink it passed and she bowed her head. “*Grazie*, Your Highness.”

“But you, Christina, will be a real princess. And that demands something special from a woman. The reward is something special in return.” She picked up an ornate, medium-size box from the couch and slowly lifted the lid. A glimmering tiara rested on a bed of white velvet.

Christina put a hand to her throat. “Valentina.”

“I wore this when I married Antonio’s father. It must stay in my family, but you would honor me if you wore it when you marry my son.”

Tears glistened in Christina’s eyes. “It’s beautiful.” Diamonds and sapphires swirled together in gradually bigger scrolls until they overlapped in the front, creating a heart. “It’s too much.”

“Nonsense. A princess needs a tiara,” Valentina insisted. “It would please me very much.”

Christina sent Lindsay a pleading look. What should she do?

Lindsay gave a small shrug. “It’s something borrowed and something blue.”

“Oh, my.” Christina gave a small laugh. “You said the items would come.”

“I must go.” Valentina handed the box to Christina.

"Try it on with your dress and veil, you will see. A security officer will stay behind to collect it until the wedding."

"Valentina." Christina gripped the other woman's hand. *"Grazie."*

"*Ciao*, my dears." With a wave of her fingers, the queen breezed out the door.

Immediately the room felt as if a switch had been flipped and the energy turned off.

Giana Russo excused herself and followed behind Valentina.

Christina sighed, her gaze clinging to Zach. "And I'm supposed to follow that?"

Lindsay's gut tightened. She'd soothed many a nervous bride. But a nervous queen-to-be? That was out of her league. She sent Zach a pleading look.

He didn't hesitate. He went to Christina and wrapped her in a warm hug. "She's a force of nature, no denying that. Everyone likes Valentina. She's fun and vivacious." He stepped back at the perfect moment. "But what Halencia needs now is warm and constant. And that's you."

"*Grazie*, Zach." Christina's shoulders relaxed with his words. "I am glad you came today."

"Of course. Hey, listen. I'm sorry for sitting on your dress. I'll pay for all the repairs and alterations."

"You sat on my dress?" Christina's surprise showed on her face. "Lindsay said some beading came loose during the travel."

"With a little help from my butt." He glanced at Lindsay over his shoulder, gratitude warming his whiskey eyes. "She seems to think Signora Russo can do *magia* and fix it."

"*Si, si.* I can fix." Giana blew back into the room. An attendant followed behind and carried Christina's beautiful gown into one of the dressing rooms. "I have looked at the damage. It is not so bad. A little re-stitching will solve everything."

"Nonna!" A little girl ran into the room. Adorable, with big brown eyes and a cap of short, wild curls, she clutched a bright pink stuffed dog under arm. She came to a stop when she spotted three strangers with her grandmother.

"Ah, Lucette. *Scusa il bambina.*" Giana tried to pick up the toddler but she squealed and ducked behind Christina. "My apologies. We had a small emergency and I was recruited to babysit. My daughter should be here shortly to get her. Lucette, come to Nonna."

"Oh, she's no trouble. *Ciao*, Lucette." Christina bent at the knees so she was on the same level as the little girl, who stared at her with big, beautiful eyes. "What's your doggy's name?"

Lucette giggled and held out the dog. She jabbered a mouthful of words that made no sense to Lindsay at all. She looked at Zach but he shook his head, indicating he didn't understand the words, either.

"What a lovely name." Christina apparently made the dog's name out or pretended to. She chatted with the child for another few minutes, making the girl laugh. From her ease with the little one, it was obvious Christina loved children. Her gentleness and genuine interest delighted Giana's granddaughter until a harried assistant hurried into the room and swept the girl up.

"Scusa." The young assistant bobbed her head and left with the little girl.

Giana sighed. "Such excitement today. Are you ready, Signorina Rose, to try on your dress?"

Christina nodded. She and Giana disappeared into one of the dressing rooms.

Lindsay and Zach looked at each other.

"Do we stay or go?" Zach asked.

"I'm going to stay until she comes out." Lindsay sat

facing the occupied dressing room. "She may want company for the whole appointment. You can go if you want. I'm sure she'd understand."

"I'll wait to see how long you're going to be." He settled next to her. Way too close. His scent reached her, sensual and male, distracting her so she almost missed his question. "Have you ever come close to being the bride?"

"Not really." She smoothed the crease in her pale beige pants. "The one time I even contemplated it, I found out the relationship existed more in my imagination than in reality."

Interest sparked behind his intelligent gaze.

"How about you?" She tried to sidetrack him.

"Once," he admitted. "How do you get to marriage in your imagination? You're too levelheaded to make up what's not there."

"Thanks for that." She uncrossed and then re-crossed her legs, creating distance between them on the couch though her new position had her facing him. "He was my high school sweetheart. We got split up during our senior year when his parents moved away."

"That's tough."

She chanced a quick peek at him through her lashes to see if he truly understood or was simply saying what he thought she wanted to hear. The intensity in his regard showed an avid interest, encouraging her to go on.

"It was tough. We just understood each other. I lost my best friend as well as my boyfriend." The crease on her right leg got the same smoothing action as her left. "I always felt he was the one who got away."

"But you reconnected."

"We did. When the royal wedding was announced last year, he saw a piece where it mentioned I was the event planner, so he looked me up in Hollywood."

"And you had fonder memories of him than he had for you?"

"You could say that." The gentle way he delivered the comment made it safe to look at him as she answered. "I was so surprised and happy to see him. My mom, too. She's always on me to find a man. At first it was as though Kevin and I'd never been apart." Because of their past connection, he'd skipped right under her shields. "We were having lots of fun just hanging out and catching up. But I was so busy. Especially after word I'd been chosen to handle Antonio's wedding started to get around.

"Kevin was a freelance writer, so his schedule was flexible and he offered to help. I didn't want to take advantage, but I wanted to be with him. I let him tend bar at a few of the smaller events. That went well, so he started pushing to work the weddings."

"This is where the but comes in?"

Lindsay nodded, went back to plucking at her crease.

Zach's hand settled over hers, stilling the nervous motion.

She calmed under his touch. Under the sympathy in his eyes.

It still hurt to recall what a fool she'd been.

"First I got a warning from one of my vendors. He didn't know we were involved and he said I should keep an eye on the new bartender. He'd seen him outside with one of the guests."

"Bastard."

"It gets worse. And it's my own fault."

"How is it your fault when he's the one cheating?"

Good question. Too bad she didn't have a good answer.

"Because I let him charm me. When I asked him about what the vendor had seen, he didn't get defensive or act guilty. He had a story ready that the woman told him she was feeling sick so he'd walked her outside, hoping fresh air would help. I had no reason not to believe him. It explained what the vendor saw and…Kevin could be very solicitous."

"But it happened again."

Her head bobbed; perfect representation for the bobble-head she'd been.

"He tried to explain that one away, too. But I was starting to wise up. I should have ended it then." But that ideal from the past lingered in her heart, overriding the urging of her head. "Before things started going south, I'd been invited to a big wedding of a studio head and asked Kevin to go with me. I didn't want to go alone and I wasn't working so I thought it would be okay." She blinked back tears. "I should have known what he wanted. The clues were there."

"He was using you."

"Oh, yeah. He always wanted to know who everyone was. I thought he was just starstruck by the movers and shakers of Hollywood. The truth was he had a script he was shopping. I found him messing around with a well-known producer."

"Male or female?"

That surprised a bark of laughter from her; the moment of levity easing her rising tension. "Female. But thanks for that perspective. I guess it could have been worse."

"Bad enough. He hurt you."

"Yes. But only because I saw what I wanted to see."

"The possibility of a wedding for the wedding planner?"

"How is it you can see me so clearly?" she demanded.

It was uncanny how he saw straight to her soul. She hadn't been half as sad at losing Kevin as she had been to lose a boyfriend with marriage potential. She wanted what she gave to all her clients. A lovely wedding, in a spectacular venue, with friends and family surrounding her as she pledged her love. She longed for it with all her heart.

Kevin had stolen that from her. He'd given her hope, dangled the reality within her reach, only to yank it away. He was a user with no real affection or respect for her.

He'd seduced her for her contacts. And, yeah, that hurt. Her pride had taken a huge hit and the experience had left her more relationship-shy than ever. But it had taken less than a week for her to recognize it was more work-related than personal. He could have damaged her reputation. She'd worked twice as hard since the breakup to make sure it didn't happen again.

And she shored up her defenses to keep from letting anyone close enough to use her again. Or hurt her.

"Because it's all right here." Zach responded to the question about seeing her so clearly by stroking his thumb over her cheek. "There's no deception in you, Lindsay. You're open and giving and articulate."

"You're saying I'm an open book. How flattering." Not.

"I'm saying there's no artifice in you. When you interact with someone, they know they're getting the real you—straightforward good or bad. Do you know what a gift that is? To know you can trust what's being presented to you without having to weigh it for possible loopholes and hidden agendas?"

"Politics," she said dismissively.

"School. Business. Friends. Dates." He ran down a list. Then, too restless to sit, he rose to pace. "For as far back as I can remember I've known not to take anything at face value. My nannies used to praise me for being a good kid then lie about my behavior to get a raise."

"That's terrible." What a sad lesson for a child to learn. "You said you almost got close to a wedding. What happened? Is it what put you off big, fancy weddings?"

"It never got that far." He fell silent and fingered a wisp of lace edging a floor-length veil. Then he moved to one glittering with diamonds and, finally, to one of lace and the opalescence of pearls.

As the silence lengthened, she knew an answer wasn't coming. And then he surprised her.

"Luckily I learned before it was too late that it wasn't me she wanted but the Sullivan name." The lack of emotion in his reply spoke volumes.

He didn't add more. He didn't have to. After a childhood of indifference, he'd fallen for a woman only to learn she had more interest in his family name than in the man who carried that name.

Lindsay felt his pain. Shockingly so. Meaning he was getting under her skin. That shouldn't be happening; her shields were firmly in place. Zach just refused to acknowledge them. And he was getting to her.

She wanted to know more, to ask what happened, but she'd been wrong to get so personal. They weren't on a date. They were working. She had no right to dig into his past when she insisted theirs was a professional relationship.

Yet she was disappointed. She rarely talked about herself, never exposed her heart like that. And he'd responded, obviously reluctant to share but reciprocating just the same. How unfair that life should send her this man when all her attention needed to be focused on her job.

He lifted the lace-and-pearl veil and carried it to her.

"What are you doing?" she breathed.

Pulling her to her feet, he turned her and carefully inserted the combs of the veil in her hair. The exquisite lace flowed around her, making her feel like a bride even in a sleeveless beige-linen pant suit.

"Imaging you as a bride." His breath whispered over her temple. "What would you choose for yourself, Lindsay?"

"I'm like you," she said as he led her toward a three-way mirror. Why was she letting him do this? "I want small, intimate."

"But with all the trimmings?"

"Of course. Oh, my." The pearls on the lace gave it a glow. He'd placed the veil just under her upswept bun. The lace caressed her arms as it fell down her back in an elegant waterfall of tulle and lace and pearls. It had such presence it made her beige pantsuit appear bridal.

The picture in the mirror stole her breath. Made her longing for what eluded her come rushing back.

She'd hoped coming to Tuscany, managing the royal wedding, would help her get her wedding mojo back. Peering into the mirror she realized that would only happen when she opened herself to love again. Sweat broke out on her upper lip at the very notion of being that vulnerable.

"I love the pearls against your sunshine-brown hair." Zach brushed the veil behind her shoulder and met her gaze in the mirror. "You're going to make a beautiful bride."

With him standing beside her in his dress shirt and black pants the reflection came too close to that of a bride and groom. Her heels brought her up to his shoulder. They actually looked quite stunning together.

She swallowed hard and took a giant step backward, reaching up at the same time to remove the veil. She was in so much trouble.

"I'm the planner, not the bride," she declared. "I don't have time to play make-believe." Handing him the veil, she retreated to the couch and her purse. Time to put fanciful thoughts aside and call Christina's aunt to set up an appointment on their way home.

Because she'd liked the image in the mirror way too much for her peace of mind.

Just Lindsay's luck. Christina's aunt Pia couldn't meet with them until five in the evening. She ran through her current to-do list in her head, looking for something she could check off.

"Oh, no, you don't." Zach tugged on her ponytail. "You've worked nonstop this past week. We are due some rest and relaxation. We're in the lovely city of Milan. I say we play tourist."

Okay, there were worse ways to spend the afternoon than wandering the streets with a handsome man on her arm.

Lunch at an open café on the Naviglio Grande—a narrow canal with origins in the 1100s used to transport the heavy marble to the middle of the city where the Duomo di Milano was being built—was a true delight. As was strolling along the canal afterward and checking out the antique stores and open-air vendors.

A lovely candleholder at a glassblower's stall caught her eye. How perfect for the reception tables. They had a flat bottom and five-inch glass petals spiked all the way around to create a floral look. The piece had presence but was short enough to converse over without being in the way. And she loved that it came in so many colors. She wanted the one with spiking gold petals. It reminded her of sunflowers.

"I'd like to order two hundred, but I need them within two weeks. Can you do that?" The young artist's eyes popped wide.

"Si. Si," he eagerly assured her. "I have ready."

"Why so many?" Zach asked. "And don't you already have candleholders with the royal crest on them?"

"Yes, but I think the clear glass bowls etched with the royal crest will sit nicely right in the middle of these and be absolutely gorgeous with a candle inside. A win-win." She got a beautiful, unique presentation that was both fragile and bold, and the palace got their staid, boring candleholders used.

"That's pretty genius." He applauded her.

"It's my job to mix the styles and needs of the bride and groom into a beautiful event that's appealing to them individually and as a couple."

"I'm learning there's more to this wedding planning stuff than I ever would have believed."

"Yeah. I'll convert you yet."

"Now, that's just crazy talk."

She sent him a chiding glance. "I want two hundred because I want plenty for my reception tables, but I also think the candleholders will make good gifts for the guests. What do you think, best man? Christina has pretty much left the decisions up to me and you're Antonio's stand-in. Do you think this would make a good gift for the guests to take away?"

He blinked at her for a moment, clearly surprised to have his opinion sought. He rubbed his chin as he contemplated the candleholder she held. "It's a pretty sophisticated crowd, but, yeah. Each piece is unique. That will appeal to the guests while the piece will also act as a reminder of the event."

"Then it will have served its purpose."

She turned back to the vendor. "In two weeks," she repeated, needing to know his excitement wasn't overriding his capabilities.

"*Si, si…due* weeks. I work night and day."

Given he would be working with heat and glass, she wasn't sure that was a good idea. She made a note in her tablet to check on his progress in a week. If he wasn't going to make it, she'd adjust her order to cover the tables only. And just give the royal crest candleholders away as a gift. But she really hoped he could pull it off.

She gave him her card with her email, asked him to send her a purchase order and advised him he'd have to sign a confidentiality agreement. His hand shook as he took the card, but he nodded frantically and handed Zach the package containing the sample she'd bought.

Zach made the next purchase. A Ferrari California T convertible. She thought they were just window shopping when he dragged her to the dealership. There was no denying the cars were sexy beasts. And it seemed the height of luxury to have the showroom on the fifth floor.

Even when Zach started talking stats and amenities, she blew it off. Nobody walked into a Ferrari dealership and walked out with a car. Or they shouldn't. It was a serious investment and required serious thought.

But Zach stood, hands on hips, surveying the slick car and nodding his head to whatever the salesman was saying. The portly man spoke English with such a thick accent she didn't know how Zach understood him.

"What color?" Zach asked her.

Her turn to blink at him in surprise at having her opinion sought. "What?"

"What color do you like better? The red or the black?"

"Are you insane? You can't just walk in here and buy a car."

"I'm pretty sure I can."

"But—"

"I've been thinking of buying one," he confessed. "I'm stoked at the idea of buying it here in Italy, from the original dealership. And it'll be nice to have a car since the rental company hasn't replaced the Land Rover yet."

She eyed the beautiful, sleek cars. "They'll probably have it replaced before they can deliver one of these."

"Pixie, they could have a car ready in an hour. But they have one downstairs with all the amenities I want. I could drive it back to Monte Calanetti if I wanted."

"Oh, my dog. You're serious about this."

He grinned, flashing his dimple and looking younger and as satisfied as a teenaged boy getting his first car.

"It's the California T series. I have to have one, right? I deserve something for closing the government deal. What color?" he demanded again.

Okay, she got it. He sought a physical treat for recent accomplishments because he wasn't getting any emotional accolades. Who could blame him? Not her.

"Indeed you do." Adjusting her mood to his, she glanced around the show room. "You don't want red or black. Too cliché."

"I'd use the word classic."

"I like that pretty blue. It reminds me of the sea around Halencia. If you're taking a souvenir home, it should represent where you've been."

"The blue." His inclined his head, his brown eyes reflecting his appreciation of her comeback. "Hmm." He strolled over to look it over better. "I'm not really looking for pretty."

"Is rockin' a better adjective? More masculine? We can use that if you prefer, because it's a rockin' pretty blue."

"I like rockin'."

"But do you like the blue?"

"I do. Though the classics are nice, too."

"They're cliché for a reason."

"Signora." The salesman flinched, unable to stay silent any longer. "*Per favore*, not say cliché."

"Scusa," she apologized, sending Zach an unrepentant smirk.

He said something in Italian to the salesman, who nodded and stepped away.

"I have to do this," he said, lifting her chin on his finger and lowering his mouth to cover hers as if he couldn't wait another moment to taste her.

CHAPTER NINE

THE FLAVOR OF him filled her senses. Oh. Just, oh.

She should protest, step away, remind him of their professional status. She did none of those things. Instead she melted against him, lifting her arms around his neck.

How she'd missed his touch. She thrilled at his hands on her waist pulling her closer, at his body pressed to hers from mouth to knees, the two of them fitting together like cogs and grooves. This was more dangerous than watching their reflection in the mirror at Signora Russo's. By far.

Didn't matter. She sank into sensation as she opened to him. More than she should in a Ferrari dealership. Or maybe not. They were hot cars, after all.

A throat clearing loudly announced the return of the salesman.

Zach lifted his head, nipped her lower lip.

"Hold on." She ducked her head against him, turning away from the salesman.

"What are you doing?" He spoke gently and cradled her head. Perfect.

"Saving you some money. Tell our friend over there that you're sorry, but I'm totally embarrassed and want to leave."

He rattled off a few words of Italian. Predictably the salesman protested.

She pushed at Zach, making a show of wanting to leave. "Tell him you'll have to buy the car when you get back to the States because we're leaving Milan tonight and probably won't make it back here."

While he conveyed her message, she grabbed his hand

and began pulling him toward the exit, carefully avoiding the salesman's gaze.

The salesman responded in a conciliatory tone, his voice growing closer as he spoke.

"He just dropped the price by ten thousand dollars," Zach advised her.

She frantically shook her head and, holding his hand in both of hers, she bracketed his arm and buried her face in his shoulder. "Let's see if we can get him to twenty. Shake your head sadly, put your arm around me and head for the elevator."

"You know I can afford the car."

"So not the point."

"What was the point again?"

"Trust me. He's not going to let you walk away."

He sighed, then she felt the movement of his head and his arm came around her. She leaned into him as they walked toward the elevator.

"I can't believe I'm leaving here without a car."

"You can always order it online and have them deliver it. If he lets you walk away."

"You owe me dinner for this."

They got all the way to the elevator before the salesman hailed Zach. He rushed over, all jovial and solicitous, giving his spiel as he approached. The elevator doors opened just as he arrived next to them. The man opened his arms wide in a gesture that welcomed Zach to consider what a good deal was being offered.

Zach nodded. *"Si, avete un affare."*

"You took the offer?"

"I have. And you're invited to visit the gift shop and pick out a gift while I finalize things here."

"Oh. Nice touch. Okay, you can buy the car." She stepped into the elevator. "Don't be long."

Thirty minutes later he collected her from the gift shop

and they headed out. On the street he pulled her into his arms and gave her a long, hard kiss. Then he draped his arm around her shoulders and started walking.

"That's the most fun I've had in a long time."

"How much?"

"For twenty-five thousand less than quoted."

"Aha! So you owe me dinner."

"You have skills, Pixie."

"I have a few tricks. I'm always working with a budget whether it's five hundred dollars or five million, so I've learned to negotiate for my job. I enjoy the challenge. You have money. You're used to buying what you want without worrying about the cost."

"I've negotiated for my business."

"But that's different, isn't it? You're on the sales side then, demanding value for services. When it comes to buying—"

"I want the best regardless of price. It's how I was raised."

"You were fortunate." As soon as the words left her mouth she remembered what he'd said about people in his life always having an agenda even when he was a young child and how his parents brushed aside his success to make demands of him. Money didn't make up for everything. She quickly changed the subject.

"So, are you driving home? Am I visiting Christina's aunt on my own?"

"I'm going with you. I went with the blue car, which needed modified for some of the upgrades I wanted. They'll be delivering the car in a couple of days. We have an hour before we need to meet the helicopter. Do you want to go see the cathedral?"

He was right. Today had been fun. She couldn't remember when she'd last let go and played for a day. She liked playing tourist. Wanted it to continue.

She sighed, knowing she needed to rein them in. A bell kept pinging in her brain, warning her to stop the foolishness, reminding her of the danger of surrendering to his charm. Hadn't she already rehashed all this with herself at the fitting?

Yes, and she knew what she risked if she continued to let her emotions rule her actions.

Yet she still reached up and tangled her fingers with his at her shoulder.

"It'll be rushed, but it sounds like fun."

"Okay, let's go." He stepped to the curb and waved down a taxi. "At least we'll get to see it. And if we really want to see more, we can plan a day when we can come back and do a full tour."

Her heart soared at the way he linked them into the future.

She deserved this time. Work always came first and because the nature of it was so party central she experienced a faux sense of having an active social life. For too long she'd suppressed her loneliness. Just this once she'd let loose and enjoy the history and charm of an ancient city in the company of a gorgeous man totally focused on her.

Sliding into the back of the cab, she smiled when Zach linked their hands. And sighed when he leaned in for a kiss.

Tomorrow could take care of itself.

Zach in a Speedo was a piece of art.

He swam once or twice a day. She remembered from her research that he'd met Antonio on the Harvard swim team. Obviously he still enjoyed the water. And she enjoyed him.

Funny how his swims always seemed to coincide with her need for a break. Uh-huh, a girl was allowed her illusions.

And she could look as long as she didn't touch.

The man was grace in motion. Watching that long, tanned, toned body move through the water gave her a jolt that rivaled caffeine. It was one fine view in a villa full of spectacular views and it made Lindsay's mouth water with want.

Now that she knew how it felt to brush up against that fine body, she longed for more. But she was back in the real world so she turned away from the sight of Zach striding confident and wet from the pool.

She took a sip from her soda, needing the wet and the cool. And drained it before she was through. Leaving the empty can on the bar she joined her assistant at the lovely oak table Zach had purchased for her use.

She pulled up her email and sent Christina a message to let her know they were still on the hunt for the brooch. As Christina had warned her Aunt Pia had been leery about talking to them, but with Christina's note she'd finally softened. She'd given the brooch to her daughter, but the younger woman hadn't worn it for her wedding, either. Pia had called her daughter while they were there and she couldn't recall what had happened to the brooch. Pia suggested Sophia might know.

Lindsay would be meeting with Sophia tomorrow, two weeks from the wedding.

"Serena, can you call and remind Louisa that Zach and I will be meeting the landscapers at the palazzo this morning."

The two of them were set to leave in a few minutes and she needed work to help her get the visual of his nearly nude body out of her head.

"Already done. And I sent the information to the glassblower as you requested. He already confirmed delivery for a week before the wedding."

"Excellent."

Serena turned out to be a godsend. She looked cool and competent in blue jeans and a crisp white tee, her long black hair slicked back in a ponytail that nearly reached her waist. And she was every bit as efficient as she appeared.

"Let's put it on the calendar to check with him in a few days to be sure he's on schedule. If I have to find another gift, I'd rather know sooner than later."

"*Si*, I put a note on your calendar."

"Perfect."

They went over a few other items, scratching off two on the to-do list and adding three. "The palace rep is supposed to take care of ordering the table and chairs, but can you call to make sure they have and confirm what they've ordered."

Her brown eyes rounded. "You want me to check the palace's work?"

"Yes. There's no room for misunderstandings. I need to know every detail is covered."

The girl nodded. "*Si*, I will call them."

"Good. I know this may be a hard concept for you, Serena, but until this wedding is over, your first loyalty is to me. It's my job to give the prince and Christina a beautiful wedding that will represent the house of L'Accardi well. You have no idea how many errors I've found by following up on details handled by other people. Some have been innocent mistakes, but others were outright sabotage."

"That's terrible!"

Lindsay nodded. "If I hadn't caught the mistakes, intentional or otherwise, not only would the bride and groom have been disappointed and possibly embarrassed, but my reputation would have suffered badly."

"*Si*. I will check every detail."

"*Grazie.* And don't forget to find a nice, understated dress for the occasion. Something in light blue."

Serena's brown eyes rounded even bigger than before. "I am to attend the royal wedding?" It was a near squeak.

"You'll be working it with me, yes."

"Oh, my goodness! I have to shop!"

Lindsay smiled. "After you check on the table and chairs."

"Si." Serena nodded, her eagerness offset by a desperate look in her eyes.

"And bring me the receipt. It's a work expense."

Relief flooded the girl's features. *"Grazie."*

"Are you ready to go?" A deep male voice filled the room.

Zach stood in the doorway to the house, thankfully fully dressed in jeans and a brown T-shirt that matched his eyes.

"Ready." Lindsay grabbed her purse and dropped her tablet inside. "Let's go."

The wind whipped through her hair as Zach drove them across town in the golf cart. He pulled straight into the drive.

Two things struck her right away. Louisa was in the middle of a heated discussion on her doorstep. Her opponent towered over her smaller frame. He had dark hair, broad shoulders and a wicked-fine profile.

And second, construction paraphernalia had been cleared away but the grounds were only a quarter cleared.

"What the heck, Zach?" Lindsay demanded as she climbed out of the golf cart. "I thought you hired someone to clean this all out."

"I did and I take full responsibility for the mess-up. I hired the crew the mayor recommended and I told them to clear out all the weeds but to save the original plants."

"No, no, no. Everything was supposed to be cleared out."

He grimaced. "I'm hearing that now, at the time I was answering a text from my office. I got it wrong. I'm sorry."

"They didn't even do what you asked." She stomped forward, scanning the dry brush and overgrown ground cover. "The landscaping team is going to be here any minute. The construction team is scheduled to start the day after they're done. This needed to be done already."

This couldn't be happening. She'd had everything planned down to the last minute. There were acres to clear. The whole property needed to be in shape, not just the area around the chapel and palazzo.

"Lindsay, I'm sorry."

Lindsay swung around to Louisa. The other woman stood huddled into herself, the tall man she'd been arguing with at her side.

"This is my fault," Louisa said. "I've been distracted the past few days. I should have noticed the grounds weren't being cleared out like they should be."

"No. It's mine. I should have been checking on the progress." Follow up on every detail. Hadn't she just pressed that fact home with Serena? She'd been the one to drop the ball.

"Placing blame does no good." Zach refused to play the role of dunce. He'd made this mess. It was up to him to clean it up. "We need to focus on a solution."

"He's right." Hands on his hips, the tall man Louisa had been arguing with surveyed the grounds. "You must be Lindsay Reeves, the wedding planner. Nico Amatucci." He held out his hand as he introduced himself. "I own the vineyard next door."

"Right." She shook his hand, appreciated the firm grip. "We're serving your wine at the reception. I've sampled some. It's very good."

"Zach Sullivan, best man." Zach inserted his hand between the two of them, not caring for the admiration in

Amatucci's gaze as it ran over Lindsay. Some distance between the two suited Zach fine.

No way was Zach letting the other man play hero while he chafed under the restraint of his plan. It didn't help that his gut roiled with guilt at seeing Lindsay so upset.

He was making her work harder than she needed to on the most important event of her career. Watching her blame herself for something he'd done didn't sit well, no matter how well-intentioned his plan had been.

Especially when he had nothing to show for it.

Neither Tony nor Christina showed any signs of backing out of the wedding. The two of them had managed to distance themselves from what went on in Monte Calanetti so any delays Lindsay suffered were mere blips on their radars.

Zach had only managed one meeting with Tony, but whenever he broached the topic on their hurried calls, Tony shut him down. Christina did the same when Zach got a few minutes alone with her at the fitting, though he had to give her points for being much more polite about it.

"I'm not sure how this happened." Zach gritted his teeth as he played his part for his audience of three. "I was telling Lindsay I hired the crew Mayor Alonso recommended. He mentioned the owner had just broken up with his girl, but I didn't figure that signified."

"Are you talking about Fabio?" Nico ran his hand through his dark hair. "He gets *molto* messed up when he and Terre are fighting, and he is no good for anything."

"I need to call him, get him out here." Lindsay took out her tablet. "This needs to be finished today. If he can't get it done, I need to get someone who can."

"Let me talk to him, *signorina*," Nico offered, his tone grim. "His girl is *incinta*. Fabio needs the work. I will make sure it gets done."

Lindsay hesitated then slowly nodded.

Seeing the despair in her indomitable blue eyes shredded Zach. He decided right then to stop messing with her. Why should she suffer for Tony and Christine's stubbornness?

She shouldn't.

No more than he should be forced to play the fool.

The trip to Milan rated as one of the best days of his life. He'd enjoyed spending time with Lindsay, more than anyone he could remember in a long time. She was smart and fun, and too restrained, which challenged him to loosen her up. And she constantly surprised him. He marveled at her performance at the Ferrari dealership.

Her ex had given her enough grief. Zach wouldn't add to it.

He'd still try talking sense into the couple. For all the good it would do him. But no more messing with the wedding.

"Fabio's going to need help getting this all done," Zach announced, feeling the need to fix the problem. "Who else can we get to help?"

"I can call my men over to lend a hand for a few hours," Nico offered.

"Thanks, that's a start. I'm going to call the mayor."

"I'll help," Louisa stated. "It'll feel good to get outside and do some physical labor for a change."

Zach lifted his brow at that. The temperature topped eighty and the palazzo was in a valley. There was little in the way of a breeze to offset the mugginess from the clouds overhead.

"It is too hot for you," Nico told her bluntly. "You will stay inside."

Wrong move, buddy. Zach watched the storm brew in the palazzo owner's light blue eyes. She was almost guaranteed to work harder and longer than she would have if the other man had kept his mouth shut. But her offer gave him an idea.

"No," Louisa informed Nico, her chin notched up, "I will not. I'm partially responsible for this situation and I want to help."

"Me, too," Lindsay piped in. "Louisa, do you have an extra pair of gloves? We can get started while Nico contacts Fabio."

"I do. I have a scarf, too. You'll want to put your hair up."

The women wandered off. Nico glared after them. "She never listens."

Zach cleared his throat and clapped Nico on the shoulder. "My man, let me give you some advice. Rather than order a woman about, it's better to make her think it's her idea to start with."

Nico grimaced. "I know this. But she drives me… *pazzo*."

"Crazy? I know the feeling. Perhaps when she starts to weary you can casually mention how thirsty the workers look and she'll go inside to provide refreshments."

"You misunderstand. There is nothing between us," Nico clarified with more emphasis than necessary. "As there is between you and Ms. Reeves."

"If you asked her, she would say there is nothing between us, either."

Nico scowled.

Zach laughed. "You should call me Zach, as we'll be working together." And they got to work.

The whole town came out to help. Or so it seemed. The mayor arrived shortly after a remorseful Fabio. Alonso didn't ask what needed to be done. He wore khaki pants and an old denim shirt with the sleeves rolled up to his elbows. He picked up a shovel and got to work.

Lindsay called Serena and she showed up with a few

friends, four of Nico's men arrived in a pickup, including his brother Angelo. Eva's son, Mario, and a pack of early teens pitched in. The barber closed his shop to help. And on and on it went. Even the landscaping crew joined in, helping to haul debris and refuse away.

Everyone was happy and laughing.

At some point Lindsay was introduced to Vincenzo Alberti, the director of tourism. When she expressed her gratitude, he explained that the whole town was proud the royal wedding was happening there. That they wanted their city to be represented well and that they were all excited to be a part of it in some way.

Lindsay wiped at the sweat on forehead with a towel she'd tucked into her waistband and surveyed their progress. Another hour should see it done. A good thing as it would be dark not long after.

She was hot and sticky, tired and sore. And hungry.

She imagined everyone else was, too. But no one was leaving. They all meant to see it finished. Nico and Louisa had put their animosity aside to coordinate the workers' efforts.

"Almost done." Zach appeared beside her, his tanned and muscular chest on full display. As had many of the men, he'd ditched his shirt somewhere along the way.

She resisted the urge to run her palm down his sweaty abs. More than once she'd caught herself admiring the flex and flow of muscle and tendon under smooth flesh. Dark and tanned, he fit right in with the Halencians. Fit and toned, he matched the laborers pace for pace.

He was poetry in motion and she had a hard time keeping her attention fixed on her chore. Especially with him standing in front of her.

"I'm amazed by the support we got from everyone." Rather than look at him she watched the landscapers fill their truck with bags of weeds. "I wish there was something we could do for them."

"I was thinking the same thing." He took her towel and wiped the back of her neck, sending tingles down her spine where his fingers trailed over her skin. "I thought about hosting a party at the villa, but I prefer to reward everyone now, so I asked Alonso for a suggestion. He mentioned Mancini's. I called and talked to the owner. Raffaele Mancini said he'd open up the patio for us and put a nice meal together."

"'Nice' is the operative word there, champ. Mancini's is catering the wedding. Eva also told me about Mancini's as an option for an upscale meal. I'm not sure I can afford that."

"I'm covering it."

"You don't have to do that."

"I insist. I feel this is mostly my fault. Paying for dinner is a small enough thing to do. Plus, Mancini heard about what happened and apologized for not making it over here to help out. So he's giving us a discount."

The spirit of this town just kept amazing her.

"Shall we start passing the word? Mancini's at eight. That'll give Raffaele time to cook. And the rest of us time to clean up."

Dinner turned into a party. When Lindsay stepped inside, assisted by Zach's hand at the small of her back, she got pulled into a big hug by the maître d', who was a curvy blonde with bright gray eyes and a smile so big she beamed.

"Hello. Welcome to Mancini's." Surprisingly the bubbly blonde was American. Then she announced why she was so excited, "Winner of the Italian Good Food Award!"

"Wow." Lindsay knew the award was on par with the

Michelin Star in France. "Congratulations. That's fantastic."

Zach echoed her. "Raffaele didn't mention it when I spoke to him earlier."

"We just heard an hour ago. You must be Lindsay Reeves and Zach Sullivan, the wedding planner and best man. I'm Daniella, Rafe's fiancée. We have the patio all set up for you. Some people have already started to arrive. You'll have to excuse us if we're a little giddy tonight. We're over the top about the award."

"As you should be," Zach said easily. "I hope you, Raffaele and the staff can join us later for a congratulatory toast."

That smile flashed again. "I'm sure that can be arranged. I'll tell Rafe."

The patio was enclosed but the large windows were wide open, letting in the cool evening air. Wine bottles hung from the overhead beams along with green ivy. Red-checked tablecloths covered two large picnic tables that seated twenty each and three round tables at the far end.

A couple of extra chairs were needed, but everyone shuffled around so everyone got seated. Alonso arranged it so he and Vincenzo sat with Lindsay and Zach along with Nico and Louisa.

Raffaele had "thrown together" a steak Florentine for them that melted in Lindsay's mouth. She was definitely putting it on the wedding menu.

She wondered if Raffaele knew how to make *cornettos*.

"I'm exhausted," Louisa told Lindsay toward the end of the delicious meal when they had the table to themselves. "But it's a good tired."

"It's the same for me." Lindsay sipped her wine. "We accomplished a lot today. The landscapers will start tomorrow and the owner assured me they would make up the lost time."

"That's great. I'm glad we were able to get it done for you."

"I'm so impressed with the townspeople. How they rallied together to help out and were so cheerful even working in the heat and mugginess."

"Well, they're all enjoying dinner. This was a nice gesture."

"Zach's the one to thank. But we were happy to do it. Everyone worked so hard. I can tell you I've decided to order some big fans for the wedding and reception. I want the guests to be comfortable."

Louisa clinked her wineglass against Lindsay's. "I like the way you think. I'm sorry I dropped the ball."

"Don't sweat it. You worked as hard as anyone today." Lindsay eyed Zach talking with Nico, Alonso and a couple of other men near the bar. "And I know how easy it is to get distracted."

"Are the two of you involved?" Louisa asked.

Lindsay's gaze whipped back to her fellow American.

"There's a…tension between the two of you," the woman explained.

"He'd like there to be." Lindsay rolled the stem of her wineglass between her fingers, watched the liquid swirl as her thoughts ran over the past two weeks. "But I need to stay focused on the job. As today clearly proved."

"He can't take his eyes off you."

"And Nico keeps you in his sights. Is there something between the two of you? You seemed to be arguing this morning."

"We're always arguing." Louisa's gaze flicked over the man in question. Her expression remained as composed as always, but there was no hiding the yearning in her pale eyes. "That is why it's good there's nothing between us."

A loud cheer went through the patio. Lindsay glanced around to see Rafe and Danielle had joined the party. Another round of cheers sounded as waiters flowed through the room with trays of champagne glasses.

Alonso grabbed a flute and held it high. "*Primo*, a huge *grazie* to Raffaele and Mancini's for hosting us tonight on such short notice. And for the wonderful meal he provided." More cheers. "*Secondo*, we are all excited to be here to share in the joyous news of Mancini's receiving the Good Food Award!" He held his glass high. "We had no doubts, *amico mio*, none at all. *Complimenti!*"

"Complimenti!" The crowd clapped and cheered, lifting their glasses and sipping.

Rafe stood on a chair. "*Grazie, grazie.* I am happy so many of my friends could be here to share this with me tonight. Business picked up when Mancini's was chosen to feed the royal wedding guests. Now, we have the Good Food Award the tourists will come even more. Monte Calanetti is on the map!"

A roar of approval rose to the roof.

"Nice touch, sharing his success with the citizens." Zach slid into his seat. "Classy."

"Raffaele is good people," Louisa affirmed. "I'm going to congratulate him on my way out. Good night. Zach, thank you for dinner."

"My pleasure."

Louisa walked away, leaving Lindsay and Zach alone together. He picked up her hand. "You look tired."

"I am." Too tired to fight over possession of her hand. She really needed to tell him the day in Milan had been a mistake and they needed to regroup to where they'd been before the trip. But every touch weakened her resolve.

"I'm sorry I messed up." There was a quality to his voice she couldn't quite pinpoint. She dismissed it as fatigue and the fact he probably didn't have to apologize for his work effort very often. Like never.

"You thought you were hiring the best crew," she reminded him. "And, you know, I really enjoyed today, getting to know more of the local people, seeing how they all rallied around each other to help. It was an inspiring experience. As you said before, too often people are all about their own agendas. Today reinforced my view of humanity."

"Sometimes those agendas can be well-meaning." Again his tone was off.

"You mean like Fabio obsessing over his girl and their baby? I get that, but look at how many lives he impacted by not honoring his contract. Yes, I enjoyed the day, but the landscaper is still going to have to make up lost time, and I lost a whole day. Life is so much easier when people are up front with each other."

He brought her hand to his mouth and kissed her knuckles. "Let's go home and soak our aches away in the Jacuzzi."

Oh, goodness, that sounded wonderful.

And dangerous.

She'd promised herself she'd get her head on straight today, put her infatuation aside and focus on the job. It was the smart thing to do. All he wanted was a summer fling. She had only to recall how he'd clammed up after she'd shared her humiliating history with Kevin to realize his interest was strictly physical.

And still she tangled her fingers with his. "Let's go."

CHAPTER TEN

AFTER THE INTENSE heat of the day, the balmy softness of the night air caressed Lindsay's shoulders with the perfect touch of cool. The rest of her, submerged in the hot, roiling water of the spa, thanked her for her foolish decision.

"I really did need this." She rolled her neck, stretching the tendons.

Strong hands turned her and began to work at the tightness in her shoulders. "So much stress."

The low timbre of Zach's voice made her whole body clench in need. She tried to shift away, but he easily held her in place.

"I never would have thought a wedding would be so much work."

She bit her bottom lip to suppress a moan, not wanting to encourage him. "Why, because it's just a big party? It's more than that, you know. It's two people creating a life together. That requires the meshing of many moving parts. The bride and groom, family members, attendants and, in this case, palace representatives and dignitaries. And that's just on the day. Before that there's flowers, food, wine, cake, photographers, seating in the chapel, setting up for the reception. Seating arrangements. Thank you, once again, for your help with that. I got the final approval from the palace today."

"My pleasure."

There was that tone again. She glanced at him over her shoulder. "You stopped listening after family members, didn't you?"

"You caught me." He let her float away a bit before turning her so she faced him.

"What's up with you?" She brushed the damp hair off his furrowed brow. "You've been slightly off all night."

"Today was my fault."

So that was it. Zach was so laid-back with her she sometimes forgot he ran a multibillion-dollar company. He was used to being in control and being right.

"We already talked about this. Stop feeling guilty."

"You know how I feel about large weddings."

"So what? You deliberately hired someone you knew couldn't do the job? You're just feeling bad because you're a problem solver and today it took a lot of people to fix the problem. It's okay. You repaid them all with a very nice dinner. And they all got to celebrate Mancini's award with Raffaele. I didn't hear a single gripe from anyone today, so cut yourself some slack."

"It's not that. I can't help but think Tony and Christina are making a mistake."

"So you subconsciously sabotaged the cleanup?"

He looked away, staring out at the lights of Monte Calanetti. "Something like that. They barely know each other."

"They've been engaged for four years."

"And he's lived in America the whole time."

This was really tearing him up. So often since they'd met he'd been there for her when she'd needed him. She wished she had the magic words that would ease his concerns.

"They have no business getting married."

"Zach—" she rubbed his arm, hoping to soothe "—that's not for you to say."

"They're going to end up hating each other." The vehemence in his voice reinforced his distress. "I watched it happen to my parents. I can't stand to watch it happen to a man I think of as my brother."

She cupped his cheek, made him look at her. "No matter how much we love someone, we can't make their decisions for them. We wouldn't welcome them doing so for us and we owe them the same respect."

He sighed then pulled her into his lap, nuzzling the hair behind her ear. She wrapped her arms around him and hugged him tight. His arms enfolded her and they sat there for a while just enjoying the closeness of each other.

"She threw me over for my father."

Lindsay went still. "Who?"

"The woman I once got close to marrying."

"Oh, Zach." She tightened her grip on him and turning her head slightly, kissing him on the hard pec she rested against. "I'm so sorry."

"We met in college. My name didn't intimidate her, which was a real turn-on. It seemed all the girls I met were supplicants or too afraid to talk to me. Julia was a political science major. She said that was to appease her parents, that her real love was her minor, which were arts and humanities."

"She targeted you."

"Oh, yeah, she played me. Right from the beginning." He suddenly rose with her in his arms. "It's time to get out."

"I suppose we should." Her arms ringed his neck as he climbed out. She longed to hear more but had the sense if she pushed, he'd close down on her. So she kept it light-hearted. "I'm starting to prune."

He claimed her lips in a desperate kiss, holding her high against him as he devoured her mouth. His passion seduced her body just as his vulnerability touched her heart.

He carried her to the cabana where they'd left their towels. He released her legs and let her slide down his body. In her bare feet he towered over her, a dark shadow silhouetted by the nearly full moon. It took him a mere second to bridge the distance before his mouth was on hers again, hot and unsettling.

The right touch and she'd be lost to reason. From the reaction of his body to hers she knew he felt the same.

But he'd started his story and if she let this moment slip away, she may never hear the full tale.

She pulled back, leaning her brow on his damp chest while she caught her breath. "Tell me."

His hands tightened on her and then his chest lifted in a deep breath. He reached for her towel and wrapped it around her before grabbing his own.

She slid onto the double lounge and patted the cushion beside her. He joined her and pulled her into his arms so her back was to his front and the vista of Monte Calanetti spread out before them.

"She showed disinterest to catch my attention. And when I finally got her to go out with me, we just clicked so smoothly. We enjoyed all the same things. Had some of the same friends. She made me feel like she saw me, Zach Sullivan, as more than the son of William Sullivan. I reached the point where I was contemplating marriage. So I took her home to meet the parents. She was so excited. For the first time she asked me why I wasn't studying political science."

"With your family background, you'd think she'd ask that fairly early in the relationship."

"Yes, you'd think. I explained that I wanted nothing to do with politics. That technology was my passion. And I told her what she could expect with my parents. How they married to connect two politically powerful families and how they spent more time with others than with each other."

"And she went after your father."

"She barely spoke to me for the rest of the flight. I thought she was mulling it over, feared I'd put her off."

"You just gave her a new target." She held him tighter.

"She assumed because I grew up surrounded by politics

that I didn't need to study it. And when I let her know I had no interest in it, and revealed my father liked to play discreetly, she went for the big guns. I caught them kissing in his study."

"I'm so sorry. I know how debilitating it is to walk in on a scene like that. The shock, the embarrassment, the betrayal. But I can't imagine how much worse it must hurt for her to be with your father."

With a double betrayal of this magnitude in his past, she kind of got why he didn't like big weddings. And why he was concerned for his friend.

"I just wanted out of there. My dad stopped me and said she'd be the one leaving. She'd come on to him, surprised him with the kiss. He wasn't interested. After she stormed off, he told me he may not be the best husband, but he'd never put a woman before his son."

"Well, that was good, to know he didn't betray you. Still, it's not something you can unsee."

He rested his head against hers, letting her know he sympathized with her, too. "It meant a lot. It's the single incident in my life I can look back on and know he put me first."

Wow, how sad was that? And yet when she looked at her own life, she couldn't find one instance that stood out like that. The difference was that her mom may put herself first, but Lindsay knew her mother loved her. From what Zach described, his folks rarely displayed affection.

She rolled her head against his chest, letting him know she understood his pain.

"So you've never gotten close to marriage since?"

"No. I've never met a woman I could see myself with five years from now let alone fifty. I don't ever want to end up like my folks. I want someone who will knock me off my feet."

"Good for you. That's what you should want. Hearing you say that about five years down the line, I realize I didn't have that with Kevin, either. I could see myself in a nice house with a couple of kids, but Kevin wasn't in the picture."

"I can see you in my future."

Her heart raced at his words and she had to swallow twice before she could answer. "Do you now?"

"Yes, all the way to tomorrow. I got a call from the dealership. The Ferrari will be here by nine. I thought we could drive to Sophia's."

She bit her lip, waffling a tad because she'd lost so much time today it was hard to justify the drive when the helicopter did the job so fast. Still she didn't want to make him feel even guiltier about today's events.

And, truly, how often did she get the chance to drive through the Halencia countryside in a Ferrari convertible with a handsome billionaire by her side?

This was probably a once-in-a-lifetime adventure. So why not stop fighting the inevitable and let the billionaire seduce her? She only had him for another couple of weeks. Less, really. She didn't want to look back and regret not knowing him fully.

Because she was very much afraid she'd be looking back a lot.

"Do I get to drive?"

"A little pixie like you? I don't think so." He laughed, his body shaking with the sound. The good cheer was wonderful to hear after his earlier despair.

"Come on. We both know it's not the size that matters, but what you do with it." His laughter shook her some more. "I feel I earned the opportunity to drive it at least once."

"We'll see."

"Oh, I'm driving." She snuggled into him. "I can tell it's going to be a lucky day."

"Yeah? How?"

"Well, if you're going to get lucky tonight, it seems only fair I get lucky tomorrow."

He picked her up as if she was no bigger than the pixie he called her and set her in his lap. Using the edge of his hand he tipped her face up to his and kissed her softly.

"Am I getting lucky? What about your strict policies?"

She brushed his hair back, enjoying the feel of the silky strands running through her fingers. "I should stay strong, but you are just too tempting, Mr. Sullivan."

He leaned forward and nipped her bottom lip. "I like the sound of that, Ms. Reeves. Shall we start with a bath in the claw-foot tub?"

How did he know she'd been dying to soak in that tub? It was a modern version of the old classic and could easily hold the two of them. She'd just been waiting for him to be gone long enough to slip into the master bathroom.

Something was still off with him. Why else suggest walking back to the house and risk her coming to her senses? Seated as she was in his lap, there was no doubting his desire for her. Maybe his attempts at humor hadn't quite rid him of his funk in talking about his near miss with wedded bliss.

Unwilling to risk him coming to his senses, she leaned into him, looped her arms around his neck and pressed her lips to his. "Why don't we start here?"

He needed no other prompting. He rolled her so she lay under him. Her head was cradled in one big hand holding her in place for his kiss that belied the fierceness of his embrace by being tender. He cherished her with his mouth; seducing her with soft thrusts and gentle licks until she melted in his arms.

He pulled back, his face unreadable in the darkness of the cabana. A finger traced slowly down the line of her jaw.

"I don't want to hurt you," he said, his breath warm against her skin.

"Then don't," she responded and pulled him back to her.

There were no more words after that, her mind too absorbed with sensation to put coherent thoughts together. The balmy night and towels served to dry them for the most part but she found a few stray drops of water on his side and he shivered when she traced her fingers through the drops, trailing the wet across his smooth skin.

It thrilled her to know her touch affected him as strongly as his did her. He stirred her with his gentleness, but he ignited her when his mouth became more insistent, his touch more demanding. She arched into him, seeking all he had to give.

He grinned against her mouth, assuring her he'd take care of her. A moment later her bikini top slipped away and he lavished attention on the exposed flesh. Her nipple puckered from the rush of heat on damp skin. And the agile use of his tongue.

Wanting nothing between them, she wiggled out of the rest of her suit and pushed at his. Despite her efforts, the damp cloth clung to him.

"Off." She panted against his mouth.

He pushed it down and off without leaving her side. She admired his efficiency almost as much as she admired his form. He was so beautiful she would have liked to see him but he felt too good in her arms for her to regret anything.

Especially when his mouth and fingers did such wicked things to her.

She felt more alive, more energized, more female than any other time in her life.

Being outside made it a hedonistic experience. The night breeze caressed heated skin, while the scent of roses perfumed the air. The rush of emotion compelled her to reach for the moon that hung so heavy in the sky.

Her senses reeled from an overload of sensation. He made her want, made her sizzle, made her mind spin.

When he joined them with an urgency that revealed he was as engaged as she was, she was excited to know she moved him, too. It made her bolder, braver, more determined to drive him insane with pleasure. She loved when he hissed through his teeth, when he kissed her as if he'd never get enough.

When he lost control.

When the connection they shared took her to a whole new level.

Never had she felt so close to another person, in body, in spirit, in heart. He lifted her higher, higher until together they soared through the stars and she shattered in the glow of the moon.

And later, after they roused and he led her to the house for a warm soak in the claw-foot tub and then landed in the comfort of his bed for a repeat performance, she knew for her this was more than two bodies seeking each other in the night.

Somewhere along the way, she'd fallen in love with the best man.

Lindsay stared out the window of the passenger seat in the Ferrari, brooding to the point where the beautiful countryside flew by unnoticed.

She'd had such a lovely morning with Zach. Waking snuggled in his arms, she'd waited for the regret to hit. But no remorse surfaced. She loved Zach. Being in his arms is where she wanted to be.

That would change when she had to walk away. In the meantime she'd make the most of every moment with him.

Watching him put the new Ferrari through its paces on

the trip to Aunt Sophia's pleased her on a visceral level. Seeing his joy, absorbing his laughter, listening to him explain what made his new toy so special. His happiness made her happy, too.

The return trip was much more subdued, with Zach as quiet as she was.

Christina's aunt Sophia was a lovely woman, but a bit unorganized. Pia had called her, so she knew why they were there. She was so happy Christina wanted to wear the pin. Sophia had worn the brooch and she and her husband were still happily married after thirty-nine years.

Lindsay got her hopes up because Sophia seemed certain she had the brooch somewhere, but she'd already looked through her personal jewelry so she thought she must have stored it in the attic with other family heirlooms. Bad knees kept her from doing the search herself so she'd invited Lindsay and Zach to look all they'd like.

Luckily the attic was clean. And airy, once Zach opened the windows. But there was a lot to look through. She found a standing jewelry hutch and thought for sure the brooch would be there. Unfortunately not. Nor was it in any of the boxes or trunks they'd searched. In the end they'd left empty-handed.

"You okay?" Zach reached over and claimed her hand. "You did everything you could to find the brooch."

"I know." She summoned a wan smile, grateful for his support. "I just hate to disappoint the bride. Especially Christina. I've never had a bride disassociate herself so completely from the process so close to the wedding. It's almost as if she's afraid to invest too much of herself into the wedding."

"She's dealing with a lot."

"I get that. That is why I really wanted to find the brooch." With a sigh she turned back to the window. "It's the one thing she seemed to latch onto. It kills me not to be able to find it for her."

The car slowed and then he pulled to the side of the road. She looked at him. "What's wrong? Is it something to do with the car?"

"I needed to do this."

He cupped her face in his hands and kissed her softly. Then not so softly. Slightly breathless she blinked at him when he lifted his head.

"Much better." He slicked his thumb over her bottom lip.

He surprised her by getting out of the car and walking around the hood. He opened her door and helped her out. She looked around and saw nothing but green rolling hills for miles.

"What are we doing?"

"Well, I'm going to be riding. And you are going to be driving."

"Really?" Squealing in excitement she threw herself into his arms. "Thank you. Thank you. Thank you." She peppered his face with kisses between each word.

"Wait." He caught her around the waist when she would have run for the driver's seat. "You do know how to drive a stick, right?"

"I do, yes." This time she pulled his head down to kiss him with all the love in her heart. She knew he was doing this to distract her from her funk, which made the gesture all the more special because he'd categorically refused to let her drive earlier. "I'll take care with your new baby."

He groaned but released her.

She practically danced her way to the driver's seat. Of course she had to have the roof down. That took all of fourteen seconds. Too cool. He took her through where everything was and she pushed the ignition.

Grinning, she said, "Put your seat belt on, lover."

And she put the car in gear.

Grave misgivings hounded Zach as he stared down at the crystal bauble in his hand. Two hearts entwined side by side. Christina's lucky brooch. He'd given up on finding it, given up on sabotaging the wedding, but he'd opened a small tapestry box in one of the trunks in Sophia's attic and there it was. Tarnished, with a few crystals missing, but unmistakable nonetheless.

He'd had no plan when he'd taken it, but for one bright moment he saw a light at the end of the tunnel of Tony's train-wreck plan to marry a woman he didn't love. Without the brooch might Christina back out of the wedding?

With no more thought than that he'd pocketed the trinket.

Now as he clutched it, he realized what he'd done. Christina wasn't backing out. Tony wasn't listening to Zach's appeals to rethink the madness. And Lindsay would freak if she ever learned he'd taken it. On every level professional, friends, lovers, she'd see it as a betrayal.

How could she not when that's what it felt like to him?

He wished he'd never seen it. Never taken it. Never risked everything he'd come to care so much about. Hell, he'd invested so much time in this wedding, even he cared about it being a success.

If only Tony wasn't the victim in all this.

It killed Zach to stand aside while his best friend set himself up for such a big fail. But there was no going back now. It didn't matter that the brooch was not wearable. Didn't matter that he had regrets. The damage was done.

He thought back to the conversation they'd had in the car on the way back from Sophia's. With the brooch burning a hole in his pocket he'd voiced his concerns for Tony and Lindsay had warned him interference never paid off.

"Do you know how many weddings there are where someone doesn't think it's a good idea for some reason?" she'd asked him. "The timing's not right, someone's too young, someone's too old, their ages are too far apart. They don't know what they're doing. She's all wrong for him. He's too good for her. Every one. Show me a wedding and there will be a dissenter in the crowd somewhere."

"They couldn't all be wrong."

"Oh, yeah. Some of them were spot-on. But has it ever worked out well when they try to intervene? No. Because it's not their decision to make. The heart wants what the heart wants."

"What if it isn't love?" he'd demanded.

"Then the situation that brought them together wants what it wants. If the couple is consenting adults, then it's their decision to make."

He heard the message. Understood that a marriage was between the man and woman involved. Still, it was hard to swallow when he knew this was a wedding that was never meant to be.

Glancing around, he looked for a place to stash the piece. Spying a likely spot, he buried it deep. After the wedding, he'd find a way to return the brooch to the Rose family.

In the meantime it was time he got on board and supported his friend.

"Hey," Lindsay called out to Zach where he still sat sipping coffee on the terrace. "I'm doing laundry today. I'm going to grab your stuff."

She went into his walk-in closet and gathered up the items in the hamper. There wasn't that much and she could easily handle it with her things. Something thumped to the floor as Zach filled the doorway.

A crystal brooch, two hearts entwined side-by-side, lay on the brown-and-rust rug.

Heart racing, she blinked once then again, hoping—no, praying—the view would change. Of course it didn't. Christina's brooch lay on the floor at her feet.

It had been hidden in Zach's dirty laundry. Because it was his dirty secret.

Pain bigger than anything she'd ever suffered tore through her heart.

"Lindsay." He stepped into the room that had seemed so big a moment ago but was now tiny and airless.

"You found the brooch." As if it might bite, she backed away from it. A heavy ball of dread lodged in her gut.

"Let me explain." He reached for her.

She pulled away from him.

"What's to explain? You kept it from me. Hid it." Rather than look at him, she stared down at the crystal pin. The silver was tarnished, a few crystals were missing; a beautiful piece ravished by time. It would need to be repaired before it could be worn again.

She lifted anguished eyes to his. "You lied to me."

"I didn't lie," he denied. "I just didn't reveal I'd found it."

"How is that not lying when our whole purpose for being there was to find the brooch?"

"You have to understand, I just want the two of them to stop and think about what they're doing. A lucky pin is a joke." He bent and picked it up. "This is a bandage at the best and a crutch at the very least."

"I understand perfectly." Her stomach roiled as nausea hit. She circled to the left, wanting out of the closet without touching him. "You haven't been helping me at all. You've been using your position as best man to spy on the wedding preparations. Oh, oh." As realization dawned, she retreated from him. When her back hit the wall she sank and wrapped her arms around her knees.

"It was your fault. I thought you were confessing because you felt bad. But it was your fault. You knew exactly what you were doing when you hired Fabio—or had a good idea, anyway. It was all you."

He went down on his haunches in front of her. She shrank away from him.

"Lindsay, this wasn't about you. You were never meant to get hurt."

She closed her eyes to block him out. "Go away."

"You have to listen to me."

"I can't believe anything you say."

"Antonio is a good guy. Always thinking of others. He's kept up with his duties while working in America. He's invested in a lot of businesses here, supported charities. Now he's giving up his life to be king, devoting his life to his country. He deserves to be happy. He has the right to choose his own wife."

"It's his life, Zach. He made his decision. He trusted you." She swallowed around the lump in her throat. "I trusted you."

"You don't understand" He rolled forward onto his knees. And still he loomed over her. "There's more at play here."

"I don't want to understand. I just want you to go away."

I can't." He sounded as if he had a mouth full of glass shards. "Not until I fix this."

"You can't fix this." She shook her head sadly. These past few days with him had been so perfect; a paradise of working and living together. Finding time to escape for a drive or some loving.

But it had been a fool's paradise.

"There's no undoing what's been done."

"There has to be." He reached for her.

She flinched from him.

His hand curled into a fist and fell to his side. "After the deal with the palazzo grounds I stopped. I saw how upset you were and I couldn't be responsible for that. You were never meant to get hurt."

"Stop saying that. What did you expect to happen when a wedding I was planning fell apart at the seams?" How could he possibly believe she'd come out of the situation unscathed if the prince called off the wedding? She was right in the middle of it. Especially with all the little things that had gone wrong. Starting with him sitting on the wedding gown.

Oh, God.

Had he sat on the dress on purpose? Had he known even then who she was and planned to use her all along?

"No, of course not," he responded, revealing she'd spoken aloud. "I had this idea before I left home." He rubbed the back of his head in frustration. "I didn't know who you were when I boarded the plane. This wasn't about you. It was about saving Tony from a lifetime of misery. The wedding planner got paid either way. But I got the opportunity to save him."

Fury drove her to her feet. "You think I'm worried about getting paid? Damn you." She stormed from the closet, not stopping until she reached her room. Yanking her suitcase from where she'd stored it, she opened it on the bed and began dumping in clothes.

Of course he followed her. For such a smart man, he knew how to do stupid real well.

"Do you think I work for a paycheck? Is that all your work is to you? I bet not." She emptied the drawers into the case and went for her shoes. "I take pride in my work."

The shoes didn't fit. She forced herself to stop and fold. She would not come back here. She went into the bathroom and grabbed what toiletries she'd left down here. She clenched her teeth when she thought of the items now occupying space in the master bathroom. He could have them. No way was she going back in that room.

He still stood in the doorway when she returned to her room. His shoulders drooped and his features were haggard. He looked as though he'd lost something precious.

Good. He'd pulled her heart from her chest and stomped on it. Let him suffer.

"I take satisfaction in giving the bride and groom something special, a day they can look back on with pride and happiness."

She closed the suitcase, pushed on the lid a couple of times to mash it down and then started zipping.

"There's more involved than arranging the flowers and cuing the music." With her suitcase closed, she yanked it from the bed and pulled up the handle. Finally she lifted her chin and faced Zach. "But then, I know you don't put much value in what I do. I really should have listened when you said you hate big weddings."

"Lindsay, no—"

"What did you say?" She talked right over his protest. "Oh, yeah, the couple needs to distract the crowd because they're marrying for something other than love."

"Don't do this. Don't leave. I didn't mean you."

"Oh, and let's not forget, love is a myth best left to romance novels."

He groaned.

"No, it's good this happened. Foolish me. I believed I was falling in love. It's so good to know it's just a myth. In a couple of days I'm sure I'll be fine."

She passed him in the doorway, making certain not to touch him. "But you should know there's nothing fake about what I do. I put my heart and soul into my weddings. And the couple doesn't walk away empty-handed. I make memories, Zach. I intend to give Antonio and Christina a spectacular wedding to look back on."

She turned her back on him and walked out. "Stay out of my way."

CHAPTER ELEVEN

AFTER SEVERAL DAYS of brooding, of waffling between righteous indignation and hating himself for the pain he'd caused Lindsay, Zach finally came to the conclusion the first was really no justification for the second.

She still used the sunroom as her workshop, but mostly Serena worked there and when Lindsay did come by, she kept the doors locked; a clear signal for him to stay out.

As he had for the past two evenings, he sat in the shadows of the patio, waiting to catch her when she left for the day. Hoping today she'd talk to him. He hadn't seen her at all yesterday and his chest ached with missing her.

In such a short time she'd burrowed her way into his affections. Watching her work fascinated him; the way she gathered a few odd items together and made something beautiful. Her expression when she concentrated was so fierce it was almost a scowl. Many times he'd wanted to run his thumb over the bow between her brows to see if her creative thoughts might transmit to him and show him what had her so enthralled.

He missed her wit, her laughter, the way she gave him a bad time.

Steps sounded on the spiral staircase and he surged to his feet, meeting her as she reached the patio level. The sun was setting behind her, casting her in a golden glow. Strands of her hair shimmered as a light breeze tossed them playfully around. In juxtaposition her blue eyes were guarded and the skin was pulled taut across her cheeks.

She made to walk by him and he caught her elbow in a light hold.

"Won't you talk to me for a minute?"

She didn't look at him. But she didn't pull away, either. "There's nothing more to say between us."

"There is." He ran his thumb over the delicate skin of her inner elbow. Touching her fed something that had been deprived the past few days. Still, he forced himself to release her. "I tried to explain, but I failed to apologize. I'm sorry, Lindsay. I didn't think hard enough about how this would affect you. I never meant to devalue what you do."

Her shoulders squared and she half turned toward him. "But you don't value it. You've seen the effort involved, you can respect that. But you don't see the value in a beautiful wedding because you see it as the prelude to a flawed marriage."

"In this case, yes."

She sighed. "Zach, I've heard you talk about your parents enough to know what growing up with them must have been like. And I know you love Antonio, that he's probably closer to you than anyone. Mix that with your dislike of big, fancy weddings, and I'm sure this has been hell for you."

"I meant well," he avowed, grateful she saw what motivated him. "I can't stand the thought of him making this mistake, of him being miserable for the rest of his life. But Tony isn't rational when it comes to Halencia."

"Why? Because he refuses to see things your way?" She shook her head, the disappointment in her eyes almost harder to take than the hurt it replaced. "I think that's a good thing. I think a king should be willing to sacrifice for his country. Considering what his parents have put this country through, I think that's exactly what Halencia needs right now. And I think as his friend and best man, you should start showing him some support."

Hearing it broken down like that made him pause and rethink. Hadn't he had the same thought just days ago?

She took the opportunity to walk away. "I understand

why you want to save Antonio. What I can't forgive is your willingness to sacrifice me to get it."

Unable to take anymore, Zack texted Tony.

Need to see you. I've messed up bad. You may want a new best man.

After sending the message, Tony wandered down to the pool to wait for the helicopter to arrive on the wide lawn they'd been using as a landing area. It would be at least an hour, but he had no desire to sit in the house so full of memories.

He stared at the pool and remembered the night he made love to Lindsay.

He couldn't regret it. Wouldn't.

Having her come alive in his arms was one of the high points in his life. He'd connected with her more closely than with any other woman he could recall. Her honest reactions and giving nature seduced him every bit as much as the silky feel of her skin and hair, the sweet taste of her mouth, the soft moans of her desire.

The few days he'd had her by his side had given him a brief glimpse into what the future could hold.

He wanted to scoff at the notion. To discount it as an indicator he'd been on one wild trip to Tuscany. But the truth was he could all too easily see her in his life. Not just here in Halencia but back in the States, as well.

And it scared the hell out of him.

The only thing that scared him more was the thought of losing her from his life altogether.

He knew the biggest betrayal for her was the intimacy they'd shared while she believed he'd been using her. But that's not what happened. He'd wanted Lindsay before he'd known she was the wedding planner. His attraction for her was completely disassociated from what she did.

Or so he'd thought.

Now he knew better. What she did was a part of who she was. She'd spoken of being disillusioned with her job. Her impassioned speech calling him to task for thinking a paycheck would suffice if the wedding fell apart proved she wasn't as lost as she'd feared. She'd been shaken because she let herself get caught up with Kevin and he'd used her.

It sickened Zach to realize he'd done the same thing.

Time to make it right.

The whoop, whoop, whoop of the helicopter sounded in the distance and grew louder. Finally. In another hour or so he'd see Tony, apologize for the mess he'd made of everything and put this whole fiasco behind him.

Being so close to Lindsay but parted from her drove him insane. He wanted to stay and fix it, but she needed to be here. He didn't. Hell, Tony probably wouldn't want him here when he learned what Zach had done.

He'd go back to the States and wait for her to come home. Then he'd find her and apologize again. No justifications, just a straight-up apology.

Ready to have this done, he strolled toward the helicopter. As he got closer he was surprised to see the pilot headed toward him. And then he knew.

"Tony." He broadened his stride and met his friend in a hug. "You came."

"Si, amico mio." Unselfconscious in showing emotion, Tony gave Zach a hard squeeze then stepped back to clap him on the arm. "Your text sounded serious."

"I've messed up."

"So you said. We must fix whatever you have done. I do not care to have anyone else for my best man."

"You haven't heard what I've done yet."

Tony had given up so much to support his country, would he be able to forgive Zach for messing in his affairs?

He couldn't lose both Lindsay and Antonio. Why hadn't he thought with his head instead of his heart?

"This sounds ominous." By mutual consent they headed toward the house. "You are my brother, Zach. You have seen how far I will go for my sibling. There is nothing you can do that will change my love for you. I need someone I can trust at my back during this wedding."

Zach walked at his friend's side. They were passing near the pool when Tony stopped. He looked longingly at the pool.

"Ah, the water looks good. I have not been swimming since I got to Halencia."

"You want to swim?" Zach grabbed his shirt at the back of the neck and pulled it off over his head. "It's as good a place to talk as any."

He stripped down and dove in. As soon as the water embraced him, he struck out, arm overhead, legs kicking, arm overhead, kick, again and again. He needed the physical exertion to empty his mind of everything but the tracking of laps and the knowledge Tony matched him pace for pace.

Tony tapped his shoulder when they reached fifty. "Let's hit the spa."

Zach slicked a hand over his face and hair and nodded.

In one big surge, he propelled himself up and out of the pool. He walked to the controls for the spa and flicked the switch to generate the jets. After grabbing a couple of towels from a storage ottoman and tossing them on the end of a lounger near the spa, he hit the mini fridge for a couple sodas and joined his friend, sighing as the hot water engulfed him.

"Grazie." Tony took a big swig and closed his blue eyes on a groan as he let his head fall back. "You don't know how good this feels. Hey, I know you're working with the

palace liaison on the bachelor party but can we do it here? Keep it tight and quiet."

"Sure. How about poker, cigars and a nice, aged whiskey?"

"Perfect." Tony laughed. "Now, tell me what's up."

Zach did, he laid it all out, not bothering to spare himself. "The good news is you'll still have a beautiful wedding, but I think I should go."

"It's not like you to run, Zach."

He barked a harsh laugh. "None of this is like me."

"True. You actually let her drive your new car?"

Zach eyed his friend still laying back and letting the jets pound him with bubbles. "Focus, dude. I almost wrecked your wedding."

"But you didn't." Tony straightened and spread his arms along the edge of the spa. He nailed Zach with an intent stare. "You messed up your life instead. You care about Ms. Reeves."

He got a little sick every time he thought about never seeing her again. But that wasn't something he was willing to share.

"She's a good person. And she's really worked hard to give you and Christina an event to be proud of. She found these cool candleholders that merge your two styles—"

"Stop." Tony held up a dripping hand. "I'm going to stop you right there. Dude, you're spouting wedding drivel. Obviously you're in love."

"Shut up." Zach cursed and threw his empty soda can at his friend's head. "You know I don't do love."

"I know you have a big heart or you wouldn't care so much about my future. You deserve to be happy, my friend, and I think the wedding planner makes you happy."

How easily Tony read him. Zach had been happier here in Halencia than as far back as he could remember.

But he'd ruined any chance of finishing the trip in the same vein.

"You deserve happiness, too. That's all I really wanted when I started this mess."

"I appreciate that you want me to be happy. But this is something I have to do. To be honest, the thought of a love match would terrify me. Watching the roller coaster that has been my parents' marriage cured me of that. I will be happy to have a peaceful arrangement with a woman I can admire and respect who will stand by my side and represent my country. Like your Lindsay, Christina is a good woman. We will find our way. You need to do the same."

His Lindsay. That sounded good.

"My being here hurts her. It's best if I leave and let her do her job."

"You mean it's easier. Well, forget it. You're my best man and I'm not letting you off the hook. Relationships take work, Zach."

That's what Lindsay said when she was talking about her mother's many marriages.

"If you care for this woman, and it appears you do, you need to fight for her. Apologize."

"I did. She didn't want to hear it."

Tony cocked a sardonic eyebrow. "Apologize again."

Zach nodded. "Right."

"Tell her you love her."

Love. Zach held his friend's gaze for a long moment, letting unfamiliar emotions—confusion, fear, sadness, exhilaration, joy, hope—rush through him. And finally he nodded. "Right."

A knock sounded at Lindsay's door. She ignored it. Now she was back at the hotel she was fair game for the press who thought nothing about knocking on her door at all hours. So pushy.

Another bang on the door.

She kept her attention on her schedule for the next week. Circled in red at the end of the week was *the* day. The wedding.

The rehearsal was in two days, four days in advance of the actual event because it was the only day everyone could get together. She'd have to see Zach, deal with him. As long as he didn't start apologizing again, she'd be fine.

She knew he'd meant well, that he loved Antonio like a brother. She even admired how far he was willing to go to ensure his friend's happiness.

But she couldn't tolerate the fact that she was acceptable collateral damage.

Why did men find her so dispensable?

She was fairly smart, had a good sense of humor. She worked hard; if anything, too hard. She was honest, kind, punctual. Okay, she wasn't model beautiful, but she wasn't hideous, either.

So what made her so unlovable?

More knocking. Ugh, these guys were relentless.

"Signorina? Signorina?" Mario called out. "Are you there? Mama says you should come."

Oh, gosh. She'd left the poor kid standing out there. Lindsay set her tablet aside and rushed to the door.

"Signorina." Mario greeted her anxiously. "Someone is here to see you. Mama says you must come."

Lindsay gritted her teeth. Zach. Why couldn't he leave her be? "Can you tell him I'm busy?"

His eyes grew big and he frantically shook his head. "No, *signorina*. You must come."

She'd never seen the boy so agitated. Fine, she'd just go tell Zach, once more, to leave her alone. Mario led her downstairs to a room she hadn't seen before. A man stood looking out on the rose garden.

"Zach you need to stop— Oh, sorry." She came to an

abrupt halt when the man turned. Not Zach. "Oh, goodness. Prince Antonio. Your Highness."

Should she curtsy? Why hadn't she practiced curtsying?

"Ms. Reeves, thank you for seeing me." He spoke in slightly accented English and had the bluest eyes she'd ever seen. They twinkled as he took her hand and bowed over it in a gesture only the European did well. "I hope you are not thinking of curtsying. It is entirely unnecessary."

His charm and humor put her instantly at ease. That ability, along with his dark, good looks and the sharp intelligence in those incredible eyes, would serve him well as King of Halencia. She wondered if they'd approached him about running for president.

"You're here to plead his case, aren't you?" Why else would the prince seek her out? He'd showed little to no interest in the wedding plans, even through his advocate.

Anger heated her blood. How dare Zach put her in this position? What could the prince think but that she allowed her personal business to interfere with his wedding preparations? Showing no interest and having none were two different things.

This whole situation just got worse and worse.

"I am." Prince Antonio indicated she should sit.

She perched on the edge of a beige sofa. The prince sat adjacent to her in a matching recliner.

"Your Highness, I can assure you the plans for the wedding are on schedule. And, of course, I will continue to work with Zach as your representative, but anything beyond working together is over. He should not have involved you."

"Please, call me Tony."

Yeah, that wasn't going to happen.

"You are obviously important to Zach and he is important to me, so we should be friendly, *sí*?"

She meant to nod; a silent, polite gesture to indicate she heard him. But her head shook back and forth, the denial too instinctive.

"He does not know I am here."

That got her attention. "He didn't send you?"

"No. In fact he planned to leave Halencia, to concede the field to you, as it were. He wanted to make it easier on you."

"Oh." What did she make of that? He was supposed to be best man. Of course he'd have to tell the prince if he planned to leave. Had he already left? Was that why Antonio was here, to tell her she'd be working with a new best man?

Her heart clenched at the thought of never seeing Zach again. The sense of loss cut through the anger and hurt like a sword through butter.

"But he is my best friend. I do not want another for my best man."

"Oh." Huge relief lifted the word up. The feeling of being reprieved was totally inappropriate. He'd used and betrayed her. That hadn't changed. Just as her foolish love for him hadn't changed. It was those softer feelings that tried to sway her now.

Too bad she'd learned she couldn't trust those feelings.

"I have never seen Zach so enamored of a woman. Is it true he let you drive his car?"

She nodded. And she knew why. In piecing things together she figured that must be the trip where Zach had found the pin. She'd been brooding on the trip back and he'd felt guilty.

As he should.

The prince laughed, drawing her attention.

"He really does have it bad. I wish I could have been here to watch this courtship."

"There's been no courtship, Your Highness. Far from

it." She'd stayed strong for two weeks. Why, oh, why had she let his vulnerability get to her? Because she'd fallen for him. Her mom was fond of saying you couldn't control who you fell in love with. Lindsay always considered that a tad convenient.

Turned out it wasn't convenient at all.

"Antonio," he insisted. "I am hoping I can persuade you to cut him some slack. I am quite annoyed with him myself, but I understand what drove him. Zach is not used to having people in his life that matter to him. He is a numbers man. He would have calculated the risk factors and figured those associated with you were tolerable. If the wedding was called off, you would still get paid."

"So he said, but there's more than a paycheck involved here. There's my reputation, as well."

"Which would not suffer if I or Christina called off the wedding."

"It would if it was due to a jinxed wedding, which I can only speculate is what he hoped to achieve."

"Was it such a bad thing he did? Fighting for my happiness?"

"That's not fair." She chided him with her gaze but had to look away as tears welled. She had to clear her throat before speaking. "People don't use the people that matter to them."

Something close to sadness came and went in his blue eyes. "Yes, we do. We are just more up front about it. Zach told me you have the brooch."

It took a second for her brain to switch gears "Yes. It's in my room. It's damaged so I haven't mentioned we found it to Christina yet."

"This is good. If you please, I'd like to take it with me to see if I can get it repaired in time for the wedding."

"Of course. I'll go get it." She quickly made the trip

to her room and returned to hand him the antique piece. "It's really a lovely design."

"Yes, two hearts entwined side by side." Expression thoughtful, he ran his thumb over the crystals. "You can see why it represents true love and longevity."

"Indeed. I hope you are able to get it repaired in time. More, I hope it brings you and Christina much happiness."

"*Grazie*, Ms. Reeves. I can see why Zach has fallen for you. I think you will be good for him."

She sighed on a helpless shrug. "Your Highness."

"Antonio." He bent and kissed her cheek. "As you think about his sins, I wish for you to consider something, as well."

Cautious, she asked, "What's that?"

"Zach does not let anyone drive his cars."

She opened her mouth on a protest.

He stopped her with a raised hand. "Not even me."

She blinked at him as his words sank in, biting her tongue to hold back another ineffective "Oh."

He nodded. "Zach told you of Julia?"

She inclined her head in acknowledgment.

"Ah. Another sign of his affection for you. He does not talk about himself easily. He does not speak of Julia at all. He thought he should have known, that he should have seen through her avarice to her true motives. He's never been as open or as giving since. Until now."

Antonio stepped to the door. "Please do not tell Christina of the brooch. I do not want her to be disappointed if it is not ready in time." With a bow of his head, he took his leave.

Lindsay continued to look at where he'd been. She wrapped her arms around herself, needing to hold on to something. Because everything she believed had just been shaken up.

The Prince of Halencia had come to see her, to plead

Zach's case after he'd tried to sabotage Antonio's wedding. How mixed up was that? If Antonio could overlook Zach's craziness, could—should—Lindsay?

Hurt and anger gripped her in unrelenting talons, digging deep, tearing holes in her soul. She wanted to think this would let up after a couple of weeks of nursing the hurt as it had with Kevin, but this went deeper, stung harder.

What she felt for Kevin had been make-believe; more in her head than anything else. What she felt for Zach came from the heart. And it hadn't stopped just because he'd hurt her. The wrenching sickness in her gut when Antonio'd said Zach planned to leave proved that.

Seeking fresh air, she slipped out of the house and into the dark garden. Lights from the house showed her the way to a path that led to the back of the garden where a bench sat beside a tinkling fountain.

The earthy scent of imminent rain hung in the air. Lindsay looked up. No stars confirmed clouds were overhead.

Great. A storm. Just what she needed.

But it wasn't fear or an uneasiness that took control of her head. Memories of being stuck in Zach's car and staying with him at the farmhouse B and B in Caprese bombarded her.

He'd held her, a stranger, because she was afraid. He'd listened to her sad tale of being scared because her mother always cried during storms. The truth was her father left during a storm and deep down in her child's psyche, she'd feared her mother would leave, too, and Lindsay would be all alone.

Antonio had asked if Zach's fighting for his happiness was such a bad thing.

And the answer was no. She understood Zach's motivation. He'd grown up a victim of his parents' political alliance and the trip to see them en route to Halencia probably trigged the need to intervene on Antonio's behalf.

If this were just the summer fling she'd convinced herself she could handle, she'd forgive him and move on.

But she loved him.

She dipped her fingers in the fountain and swirled the water around. It was still warm from the heat of the day.

She missed the villa. Missed sharing coffee with Zach in the morning seated out on the terrace watching the city come alive down below. She missed his sharp mind and dry humor and his total ignorance of all things wedding-related.

But most of all she missed the way he held her, as if she were the most precious thing in his world.

And that's what she couldn't forgive.

He'd made her believe she mattered. And it had all been a lie.

She'd never been put first before.

Her dad had walked out before she even knew him. And her mother loved her. But Lindsay had always known her mother's wants and needs came first. Even when it was just Lindsay, work came first.

For a few magical days Zach had made her feel as if she was his everything. It showed in the way he'd touched her and by the heat in his eyes. It was in the deference and care he'd demonstrated, the affection and tenderness.

Maybe it was a facade he assumed and that's how he treated all the women in his life—the thought sliced through her brain like shards of broken glass—but it felt real to her. And she couldn't—wouldn't—accept less just to finish out a summer fling.

No more settling. She'd done that with Kevin and learned her lesson. She'd been willing to settle for a fling with Zach because she'd sensed how good it would be between them. And she'd been right. But she loved him, and a fling was no longer enough. She needed honesty, respect and a willingness to put your partner first.

How often had she watched her mother's relationships fall apart because a little work was involved? Her mom was so used to being the center of her world she didn't see that sometimes she needed to make her husband feel he was the center of her world.

Antonio inferred Zach cared for her. He made it sound as if Zach had planned to leave to make things easier for her. More likely he'd wanted out of this whole gig. But there was the bit about letting her drive his car when he never let anyone drive his cars, not even the man he thought of as his brother.

No. Just stop. She pushed the wistful thinking aside as she headed inside. His actions told the story. He didn't love her. He'd proved that when he'd put his friend before her.

Zach had said he liked storms, for him they washed things clean, made them shiny and new, allowing new growth. A good metaphor for him. He was the storm that allowed her to put the horror of Kevin's betrayal behind her. But would her heart survived the tsunami Zach had left in his wake?

CHAPTER TWELVE

TWO DAYS LATER Lindsay walked with Serena toward the Palazzo di Comparino chapel. The rehearsal started in twenty minutes. Nothing was going right today. She should be totally focused on damage control and all she could think about was the fact she'd be seeing Zach in a few minutes.

Her mind and heart played a mad game of table tennis over him. One moment she was strong and resolute in holding out for what she deserved. The next she was sure she deserved him, that his actions proved he cared deeply for the people in his life and she wanted to be one of those people.

"You just got an email from Christina confirming she will not make it to the rehearsal." Serena jogged to keep up.

Lindsay came to a full stop, causing Serena to backtrack. "What about Antonio?"

"He is still delayed at the palace, but he is trying to get here."

"Okay, we're talking a good two hours. Let me call Raffaele to see if he can move dinner up." Before the big blowup between them, she'd suggested to Zach that he host the rehearsal dinner at the villa. With her taking care of the details, he'd been happy to agree.

It was a no-brainer to put Mancini's in charge of the food. Still moving dinner up an hour would be a challenge. But so worth it if it allowed if at least one of the bridal couple to make it to the rehearsal.

"The prince's email said we should start without him."

"Wonderful. Zach will have to act as the groom and can you play the part of Christina?"

"Oh, Lindsay, I am sorry, but I cannot."

"Sure you can. I know these are high-profile people, but all you have to do is walk slowly down the aisle. No biggie."

"No, remember, Papa and I are meeting the glassblower to pick up the last delivery of candleholders. I have to leave in half an hour."

"Oh, yeah, that's tonight. Well, of course. Why should anything workout tonight?"

"Perhaps Papa can go on his own?" Serena made the offer hesitantly. Generous of her since Lindsay knew the two were looking forward to the road trip. A little father-daughter time before Serena went back to school.

"No, you go. I know this trip means a lot to you. I'll work something out."

"You could play the bride," Serena suggested.

"Uh, no. Thanks, but I have to keep things moving." So not a good idea. The very notion of walking down the aisle to Zach in groom mode messed with her head.

And her heart.

The elderly priest had other ideas. He looked like a monk of days gone by and he held her hand and patted the back ever so gently. He spoke softly, listened carefully, and totally took over the rehearsal. Everything must be just so.

He explained what was going to happen, who was going to go where, who stood, who sat, who would leave first and who would follow. He was quite thorough.

Because she found her gaze repeatedly finding Zach, who looked gorgeous in a white shirt and dark sports jacket, Lindsay ran her gaze over the participants. Everyone listened respectfully. Even Queen Valentina and the king, who sat holding hands. Apparently they were in an "on again" phase of their relationship.

The chapel looked lovely. A rainbow of colors fell through the stained-glass windows and standing candle-holders in white wrought-iron lined the walls from the back to the front and across the altar, illuminating the small interior. For the wedding they would be connected with garlands of sunflowers and roses.

And from what she observed, the palace photographer seemed to be doing a good job. He was the only extra person in the room. Serena had quietly made her departure during the priest's soliloquy.

"Come, come." The priest raised his cupped hands as if lifting a baby high. "Let us all take our places. You, young man—" he patted Zach on the shoulder "—will play the part of the groom. And you, *signorina*—" he looked at Lindsay "—will be our bride today."

No, no, no.

Pasting on a serene smile, she politely refused. "I'm sorry, Father, I really need to observe and take notes to ensure a smooth ceremony the day of the wedding."

"*Si, si.* You will observe as the bride. Come, stand here." He motioned to his right.

Zach stood tall and broad on the priest's left.

She swallowed hard and shook her head. She couldn't do it. She couldn't pretend to be Zach's bride when she longed for the truth of the position with all her broken heart.

"Perhaps Elena can play the bride?" she suggested. Hoped.

"Oh, no. Elena has her own role to play as the maid of honor. You are needed, *signorina*. Come."

There was no protesting after that. Plus, others would begin to make note if she made any more of a scene. Clenching her teeth together, she moved forward, holding her tablet in front of her like a shield, looking everywhere but at Zach.

She was fine while the priest directed the action from the altar, but when he stepped away to help people find their spots, Zach narrowed the distance between them by a step then two.

"Please don't start anything here," she implored.

"I'm not." He put his hands in his pockets and rocked on his heels. "How have you been?"

"We should listen to the Father."

"I've missed you."

"Zach, I can't do this here."

"You have to give me something, Lindsay. You asked me to stay away and I have."

She narrowed her eyes at him. "You've texted me several times every day." Crazy things, thoughtful things, odd facts about himself. She'd wanted to delete them without reading them, but she'd read every one, came to look forward to them, especially those that revealed something about him.

"I needed some link to you. I'm afraid I'm addicted."

"You're not going to charm me, Zach." She frantically searched out the priest. When was this show going to get on the road? When she looked back, Zach was closer still.

He bent over her. "You smell so good. Do you miss me at all?"

"Every minute of every day." Her hand went to her mouth. Oh, my dog. Did she just say that out loud?

"Lindsay—"

"The priest is calling me." Heart racing, she escaped to the back of the chapel where the wedding party congregated. The priest nodded when she appeared, as if he'd been waiting for her.

"*Si, si.* We will start with the procession. Just as I described. *Signorina*, you will be last with Signor Rose."

Lindsay took her place by the robust man who made no

effort to disguise his disapproval of Christina's absence. She wasn't Lindsay's favorite person at the moment, either.

Oh, gosh, instead of settling, her heart raced harder. Zach stood at the altar waiting for her to come to him. It felt too real. And, sweet merciful heavens, she wished it were real.

It mattered what he'd done. Yes, he'd meant well. And no, he hadn't known her when he initiated his plan. But it mattered.

The procession began to move. She closed her eyes and stepped forward. Her foot slipped on the uneven ground, so, okay, that wasn't going to work. She opened her eyes and concentrated on the smooth stones of the chapel floor.

He had apologized. And he'd honored her request to stay away. But he hadn't let her forget him, or the time they'd spent together.

Had that been him fighting for her? Or was that wishful thinking?

Suddenly, Mr. Rose stopped and Zach's strong, tanned hand came into view. She fought the urge to put her hands behind her back. All eyes were on her, on them, but this was for Antonio and Christina's wedding. Nobody cared about her or Zach; they didn't care that touching him would be a huge mistake.

She hated how her hand shook as she placed it in his.

He set her hand on his arm and led her to stand in front of the priest. And then he covered her hand with his warm hold and leaned close to whisper, "No need to be nervous. I'm right here by your side."

For some odd reason she actually found his promise reassuring. Facing the priest, not so much.

"Well done, well done." He motioned for the wedding party to be seated. "Lindsay, Zach, if you will face each other. Next I will begin the ceremony. I'll share a few words and then we'll go through the exit procession."

Lindsay turned to face Zach and he took both her hands in each of his. It was the most surreal moment of her life.

The priest began. “Today is a glorious day which the Lord hath made, as today both of you are blessed with God’s greatest of all gifts, the gift of abiding love and devotion between a man and woman. All present here today, and those here in heart, wish both of you all the joy, happiness and success the world has to offer—”

“Stop. I can’t do this.” Lindsay tried to pull away. This hurt too much.

“Lindsay, it’s okay.” Zach’s voice was calm and steady. His hold remained sure and strong as he moved to shield her from the audience. “Father, may we have a moment?”

“Of course, my son.” The priest bowed and moved away.

“Breathe, Lindsay. It’s going to be okay.” Zach leaned over her. “I felt it, too. How right those words were between you and me.”

Lindsay clutched at Zach’s hands, clinging to him as emotions raged through her heart and head.

“I can’t do this. I’m sorry.” Aware her behavior embarrassed both her and him, she lifted bleak eyes to meet his gaze. What she saw made the breath catch in her throat.

His eyes were unshielded and in the dark, whiskey depths shone a love so big and so deep it seemed to go on forever. She felt surrounded in a cushion of caring, lifted on a throne of adoration.

“Zach,” she breathed.

“I love you, Lindsay.” The words echoed everything his eyes already revealed.

Hope slowly swelled through her as her love surged to the surface eager for all his gaze offered. Already weakened, her self-preservation instincts began to crumble as unleashed longing filled her heart.

"I hurt you and I'm more sorry than I can say that I let the fears of my childhood control my common sense when it came to Tony's wedding. You opened my eyes to what I was doing and he hammered it home. But even when I finally accepted the truth and apologized, something still nagged at me, a sense of wrongness that grew rather than diminished."

Behind him she was aware of movement and whispers, reminding her they were not alone. But all she heard, all she saw, was Zach and the raw pain filling eyes that had been overflowing with love just moments ago.

"And then the truth came to me. I couldn't get past how my actions hurt you. I wronged you, not just by disrespecting what you do and by making you work harder, but by putting Tony's needs before yours. That's when I knew the happiness I take in your company and the joy that consumes me when I touch you is actually love."

Now his hands were tight on hers. She ran her thumbs softly over the whites of his knuckles. Everything he'd said was just what she'd longed to hear. She let the last of her concerns melt away.

"Zach." She squeezed his hands. "I love you, too."

Relief flooded his features and he rested his forehead against hers. "Thank God. Because this is bigger and more terrifying than anything I've ever known."

A laugh trilled out of her. "Yes. I'm glad to know I'm not alone."

"You'll never be alone again." He raised his head and his love rained down on her. "Watching you walk down that aisle to me felt more right than anything else in my life. I love you, Lindsay Reeves. Will you marry me?"

"Yes." No hesitation, no need to think. Her misery had come from that same sense of rightness. She longed to spend the rest of her life with this man. "I would love to marry you."

"Right now?" His brown gaze danced with love and mischief.

She blinked at him. "What?"

"Will you marry me right now, in this beautiful chapel we refashioned together?"

Her mind slowly grasped what he wanted, and then her heart soared with excited anticipation. Still, she couldn't get married without her mother. "What about our friends and family?"

"We can have a lavish ceremony back in the States. As big as you want. But I don't want to wait to claim you as mine. So I made sure everyone who truly matters is here."

He stepped back to reveal the chapel filled with people. She saw Louisa sandwiched between Nico and Vincenzo. Raffaele and Daniella sat next to Eva and Mario. Alonso and Serena were here instead of on the road. And many more of the townspeople she'd met and worked with over the past month filled the pews, including the King and Queen of Halencia.

And standing with the grinning priest was Prince Antonio and…her mother.

"Mom?"

"I knew you'd want her here." Zach's hand rested warm and familiar in the small of her back.

"You must have been planning this for days."

"It's the only thing that's kept me sane." He lifted her chin, his mouth settling on hers in restrained urgency. When he raised his head, his eyes gleamed with the heat of desire, the steadfastness of love. "Shall we do this?"

She nodded slowly. "Yes."

Her answer ignited a flurry of activity. Antonio stepped forward while her mother grabbed her hand and hustled her back down the aisle and out the door. In an instant she was in her mom's arms being hugged hard.

"I'm so happy for you, baby. Zach is a force of nature.

If he loves you anywhere near as much as his actions indicate, you will have a long and joyous marriage." She sighed. "For all my marriages, I've never had anyone look at me with so much love."

Lindsay was too excited to have her mother here to care that her special day had circled around to focus on her mom's feelings.

"I'm so glad you're here. You look beautiful." Her mom wore a lovely, pale green silk suit that went well with her upswept brown hair and green eyes. "And you're wrong. Matt looks at you like that. You've just been too focused on yourself to notice."

"Lindsay!" her mother protested, but a speculative glint entered her eyes. "I'll let that slide. We need to get you ready."

"I think I'm as ready as we have time for." Lindsay glanced down at her flowing ivory dress that came to just below her knees in the front and to her ankles in the back and knew she'd been set up. Serena had insisted the dress was perfect for today; business moving into party mode. Of everything she owned this would have been her choice for an impromptu wedding gown.

"Oh, we have time for a few special touches." Darlene pulled Lindsay around the side of the chapel where a full-length, gold-framed mirror leaned against the side of the building, next to it was a garment rack with a flow of tulle over one end and a stack of shelves hanging from the other.

"Something old." From the shelves her mother lifted out a set of pearl-and-sapphire earrings.

"Grandma's earrings." Darlene had worn them for her first wedding and Lindsay recalled saying wistfully she'd wear them at her wedding someday. Her mother had remembered. Her hands shook a little as she put them on.

"Something new." A beaded belt and matching shoes adorned in pearls and crystals shimmered in the late-afternoon sun. While Lindsay traded her sandals for the high-heeled pumps, Darlene stepped behind her and clipped it into place at her waist. They both fit perfectly.

"Something borrowed." Mom smiled. "I saved this because you loved it so much." The tulle turned out to be a full-length veil scalloped on the edges in delicate pearl-infused embroidery. "Close your eyes and face the mirror."

Lindsay's heart expanded; she hadn't realized her mother had been paying such close attention to her reactions through the years. She closed her eyes against a well of tears while Darlene fussed with the veil and the lovely floral hair clip that went with it.

Next she felt a rouge brush dust over her cheeks and some gloss being dabbed on her lips. A tissue caught an escaping tear.

"You can open your eyes."

Lindsay did and was amazed to find a beautiful bride staring back at her. "Mom."

"You're stunning, baby."

Lindsay nodded. She felt stunning and ready to begin her life with Zach.

"Let's go. Your man is waiting."

Rounding the corner of the chapel, she spied the replica of the fountain from the plaza and thought of the wish she'd made with Zach. The wish for true love had been meant for Antonio and Christina. Lindsay supposed she'd been pushing it to make a wish for another couple, but she couldn't be disappointed that fate had chosen to grant true love to her and Zach.

This time when she walked down the aisle her mother escorted her and Lindsay's heart swelled with joy as her gaze locked with Zach's. He'd changed into the suit he'd been wearing when they'd met and she loved the symbolism of the gesture. He knew her so well.

There was no shaking as she placed her hand in his,

just a surety of purpose, a promise to always be there for him. The warmth and steadiness of his grip was the same as it had been earlier and she recognized he'd always be her rock. She suddenly realized something she'd missed when taking in the surprise he'd given her.

"What about your parents?" she whispered.

"They couldn't make it."

"I'm sorry." And angry. His parents didn't deserve him.

"Pixie—" he cupped her cheek "—you're all the family I need."

Her throat closed on a swell of emotion. She swallowed and pledged. "I love you."

"I can't wait for you to be my wife."

"Ahem." Antonio placed his hand on Zach's shoulder. "The priest is waiting."

"Right." Love and anticipation bright in his gaze, he gave the nod. "We're ready, Father."

"We are gathered together on this glorious day which the Lord hath made, to witness the joining of Zachary Sullivan and Lindsay Reeves, who have been blessed with God's greatest of all gifts, the gift of abiding love and devotion between a man and woman..."

* * * * *

Join Britain's BIGGEST Romance Book Club

- EXCLUSIVE offers every month
- FREE delivery direct to your door
- NEVER MISS a title
- EARN Bonus Book points

Call Customer Services

0844 844 1358*

or visit

millsandboon.co.uk/subscription

* This call will cost you 7 pence per minute plus your phone company's price per minute access charge.

BKCB3

MILLS & BOON®

Why shop at millsandboon.co.uk?

Each year, thousands of romance readers find their perfect read at millsandboon.co.uk. That's because we're passionate about bringing you the very best romantic fiction. Here are some of the advantages of shopping at millsandboon.co.uk:

* **Get new books first**—you'll be able to buy your favourite books before they hit the shops
* **Get exclusive discounts**—you'll also be able to buy our specially created monthly collections, with up to 50% off the RRP
* **Find your favourite authors**—latest news, interviews and new releases for all your favourite authors and series on our website, plus ideas for what to try next
* **Join in**—once you've bought your favourite books, don't forget to register with us to rate, review and join in the discussions

Visit **www.millsandboon.co.uk**
for all this and more today!